CUTTING LOSSES

A REDEMPTION STORY...

Brooklyn Prairie Publishing

Copyright © 2024 Jodi Culliney

All rights reserved.
ISBN: 979-8-9908336-4-7 - ePub.
ISBN: 979-8-9908336-5-4 - Paperback

Book I: *Excess Baggage* - A Love Story

Book II: *Cutting Losses* - A Redemption Story

Book III: *Mixed Messages* - A Love Story

Book IV: *Second Chances* - A Later in Life Love Story

Map of Beverley

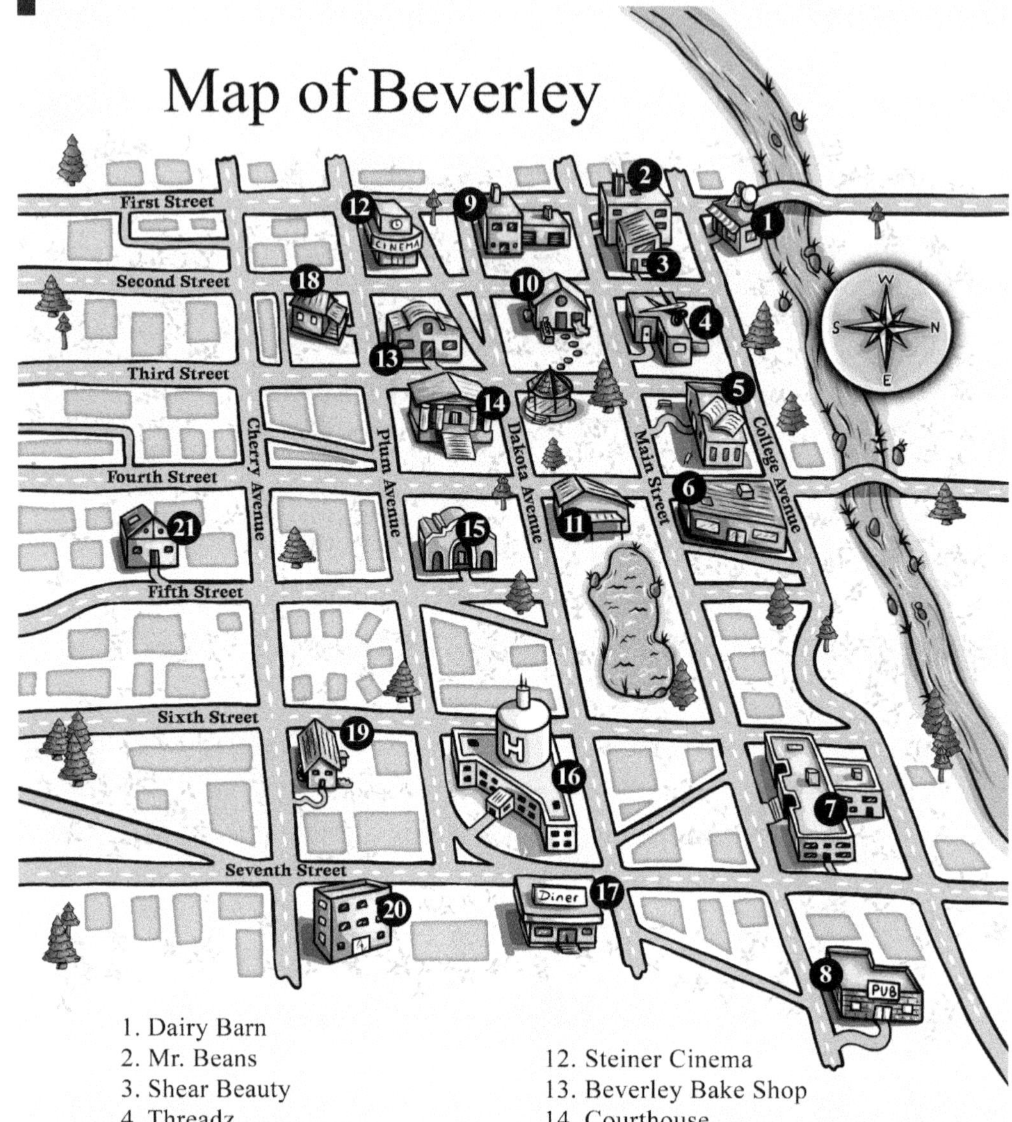

1. Dairy Barn
2. Mr. Beans
3. Shear Beauty
4. Threadz
5. Beverley Carnegie Library
6. Bits & Bobs Hardware
7. Beverley Community College
8. Shorty's
9. Check Care Auto
10. Flower Power
11. Cattleman's Club Steakhouse
12. Steiner Cinema
13. Beverley Bake Shop
14. Courthouse
15. La Hacienda
16. Beverley General Hospital
17. Betsy's Diner
18. Effie's House
19. Ruth & Sean's House
20. John and Ellen's Apartment
21. Henry's House

CUTTING LOSSES

A REDEMPTION STORY...

JODI CULLINEY

PROLOGUE

As he watched her walk down the aisle, his stomach was filled with knots. Tomorrow would be the culmination of all of their dreams and plans, and they would formally begin the life they have been building for eighteen years. Tessa always liked to round the number up to twenty, but Josh tried to remind her (gently) that it was just eighteen years—after all, why bother stating a fact unless you're going to be exact? When Tessa had suggested they not see each other before rehearsal, the notion had struck him as outdated and unnecessary, especially for the rehearsal. "What is the point?" he had asked her. Sure, he vaguely understood the reasoning behind the tradition for the day *of* the wedding, but the day before? After Tessa had let it slip that it was actually her sister's idea, well, that made more sense. Tessa's sister was always trying to get her to defy or irk him in some small way, it seemed, and more so every passing year. It harkened back to college, he supposed, when he and Tessa had split up, each needing their space after years together. Since they had begun dating as teens, their break-up had made perfect, and logical, sense.

Pulling himself back to the present, Josh smiled encouragingly at Tessa, who had surprisingly stopped halfway down the aisle. What in the world? Why wasn't she moving anymore? For the past two years, all she had done was harp at him about getting married, and now she was looking around her as if she was confused somehow as to how she had gotten here. He knew they should have just flown somewhere to a beach and had a small ceremony, but no: Tessa had insisted on having this lavish production, with more attendants than necessary in his estimation. Josh glanced at Tessa's dad, who could always be counted on for his encouragement; however, he seemed at a loss as well.

Looking to his right, his eyes skimmed the line of bridesmaids, all looking as perplexed as he felt, with one exception: Ruth, Tessa's sister and matron-of-honor. In place of the confusion on all the other faces, she bore a knowing smile and seemed to be bursting with a new energy. The three of them: Tessa, Ruth, and Josh, had been thick as thieves in high school, after Tessa and Josh had met in an after-school club. Josh had been the new kid in town and became entranced with Ruth as soon as Tessa had introduced her older sister to him, but it soon became clear that Ruth only saw Josh as a friend. After Ruth had started dating another boy, Josh had turned his sole attention to Tessa, who he had begun to suspect had feelings for him. Now here they were, eighteen years later, on the eve of their wedding. Only his bride-to-be was backing up, getting farther away. As Tessa neared the last row, she turned, forced open the large wooden doors, and fled out into the waning sunlight, leaving Josh awkwardly alone in front of their bridal party and family members. A slight movement to his left caught his attention, and his college best friend, Sam (or Fitz, to those from Alpha Delta Phi) took a few steps away from the rest of the groomsmen, only to stop suddenly and look back at Josh, which perplexed him even more.

What should he do? Race after Tessa? All eyes were on him, and Josh felt their measured judgments, the insinuations of expected failure. He loathed having to think on the fly, forced into making rash decisions. They had planned all of this so carefully—well, Tessa had. Too preoccupied with his surgical residency and impending fellowship, Josh could not be bothered with minor wedding details. The knot that had been forming in his stomach was growing, threatening to choke him. At this point, he needed air more than he needed answers, so he followed in Tessa's wake and charged out of the church.

CHAPTER
One

Josh

Two Months Later

Alone in his office, Josh raked a hand through his dark blond hair, already disheveled and sadly in need of a cut. Before his cancelled wedding, one of the highlights in Josh's day was poring over any case notes he had in preparation for the next day's surgery; yet in the days since he had been abandoned at the altar, there had been few of those. Since he was a child, problem solving had been his strongest skill, which is what had drawn him to surgery. He'd always known he wanted to be a doctor; unfortunately, although Josh had excelled in school, his communication skills were routinely found to be lacking. However, his finesse with precision had convinced him to concentrate on surgery. Therefore, instead of being a small-town family physician, where interpersonal relationships were not only common but expected, Josh had instead followed med school with an internship in one of the biggest hospitals in New York City, and he was flourishing. Career-wise, that is, not relationship-wise.

Try as he might, he could not stop dwelling on the loss of Tessa; she had been such an integral part of his life for so long that he honestly didn't know how he was going to move on from her. Although she certainly wasn't perfect, she had been perfect for him. Or so he thought. Since she had left him, he had been hoping every day that she would come to her senses and come back to him. She was still living in the cozy Brooklyn apartment they had shared, and today he had gotten a text from her asking to meet her there when he was done with work; after a glance at the clock, he realized he needed to start heading over there. Currently, he was staying with Cal, a pediatrics resident that he had gone to med school with, who was also recently divorced. The two of them often spent their free time together commiserating over their failed relationships, so when Josh needed more reliable, yet short-term, lodging, Cal had offered up his apartment's second bedroom. Josh thought longingly of the tree-lined street in Brooklyn where his neighbors greeted them with a wave and "hello", and he was anxious to be heading "home".

Perhaps this missive from Tessa was going to end up being good news, he thought hopefully. The fact that she hadn't demanded he move completely out of their apartment had given him an optimistic feeling. I mean, he thought, if she were truly done with him, wouldn't she have insisted on moving out all of his stuff? Maybe she was having second thoughts, he reassured himself. Tessa was a woman who needed a man to take care of her, after all. She had almost come undone the first time they had broken up, he often liked to point out to himself. "We couldn't get back together fast enough," he whispered to his science journals.

Suddenly, his office door flew open and Lana Miller, his office mate and fellow surgical resident, breezed in. Her honey-colored hair was in a low ponytail, her signature look for work. Lana was his complete opposite: easy-going, carefree, and low stress. She beamed a one-hundred-watt smile at him. "Hey, Josh, I thought I may have missed you." She paused and took a breath, and while looking down at her desk, she asked, "Do you have any plans for tonight?" And then her denim-blue eyes met his, and Josh became uncomfortable, thinking back to the intimate dinner the two of them had shared a few days ago.

When Lana had become his office mate two years ago, he had been relieved to find that the two of them had an exceptional amount in common, even though he was five years older than she was. She was fresh out of med school and ready to take on the world of surgical residency, while he was heading into his final two years of it. The two had clicked and became friends along with co-workers and office mates. It had been Lana who he had sought guidance from last year when trying to juggle wedding planning and applying for what would be his hard-earned fellowship. Now he wondered if seeking her help had been a mistake and had eventually prevented him from fixing his troubles while also causing even more. It had been Lana who had suggested to Josh that perhaps he and Tessa would be better off postponing their honeymoon (a honeymoon his bride-to-be had spent months perfecting).

Something had changed after their late-night dinner, though. Leading up to it, Lana had seemed a little too quiet all last week, which was completely unlike her, and then on Friday, while the two of them were sharing the pastries and coffee that Josh had brought in from their favorite coffee shop, Lana had looked at Josh from underneath her long eyelashes, and for the first time since meeting her, Josh became uneasy. "Josh, I've been thinking that it must have been a while since someone has made a home-cooked meal for you."

Well, he hadn't expected that turn of events. Since his wedding imploded, two nurses, a woman from admin, and even a patient seeking a consultation, had asked him out on a date. Usually, it was seemingly innocuous coffee or lunch (the patient had slipped him her room key card from the hotel across the street, though); he had been surprised to find how quickly his earth-shattering event had seemed to spur on countless women looking to pick up the pieces of his shattered heart. The attention flattered him, if he were being honest with himself, but no one could ever take the place of his Tessa. Except maybe Lana, who could truly be well-suited for him. He had tamped down his surprise at her suggestion and admitted that he actually couldn't recall when anyone had cooked a meal for him. The months before his doomed ceremony had all been chaotic, with Tessa obsessing over fine-tuning their big day and Josh spending more and more time in his office.

Lana had then taken the reins, and knowing they were both off the next day, she had invited him over for dinner the following night. Josh was aware enough to know that flowers would be expected upon his arrival, and had let the bouquet of wildflowers, hastily purchased from the deli across the street, lead the way into Lana's studio apartment on the Lower East Side, where the scents of garlic and basil permeated the narrow hallway leading to her door. Josh had never been to Lana's place until that evening, and he saw hints of her throughout the small space: pictures of her siblings and mom in frames on the wall, a small bookcase that held authors with names ranging from Jodi Picoult to Lisa Gardner, and Kate Atkinson to Tana French. In the tiny kitchen area, she had two pots simmering on the apartment-sized range, with bubbling tomato sauce in one and steam emanating from the other pot waiting to cook the pasta. Her meal had been decadent, and their conversation lively, but after a couple of hours spent in conversation, all they seemed to have in common was their love of surgery, and Josh felt the loss of Tessa that night more acutely than he had since she had fled from him.

In the days since that dinner, Josh had done his best to not be alone with Lana for too long, as her longing was almost tangible. All of the little things they had done for each other before now seemed too loaded with insinuations to even consider. Best to be completely honest with her now and answer her question directly.

"Yes, actually, Tessa texted me about coming over tonight—she said she needs to talk to me." Josh paused for a beat and then told Lana bluntly, "I'm thinking that maybe she is reconsidering our breakup."

Lana looked crestfallen as her shoulders drooped, and the smile left her face. "Oh, I had no idea you two were still in contact after what she did. How could she even face you after humiliating you so terribly?"

"Look, Lana, I know I have said a lot of things about what happened with Tessa and our break-up. I probably said too many things, but now that I'm able to be honest with myself, I have to acknowledge that many of her gripes about me were true, to some extent." Josh looked down at his phone, which had started ringing, and saw that Fitz was calling him. "Wow, my friend Sam is calling—I haven't talked to him since the rehearsal."

"Sam—isn't he your writer friend? You mentioned once that you wanted to introduce us. I'd love to get to know more of your friends, you know." And there it was—overwhelming expectation from her that it filled their small office. Yes, he wanted to introduce them, thinking the four of them could maybe all get together: he and Tessa, and then Sam and Lana.

Lana was just Sam's type, too: honey blonde hair, big blue eyes, and wicked smart. Serious Sam, lover of books, which is how he got the nickname of Fitz in college—he could always be seen with a copy of F. Scott Fitzgerald's *Tender Is the Night*. He knew from the past that no woman could resist Fitz: dark-haired, slightly brooding and intense.

"You know what, Lana? That is an excellent idea! I'll call him back later and bring it up. Right now, I need to head to Brooklyn to see Tessa, and it seems time has slipped away from me as usual—I'm going to be late. See you tomorrow," and he waved at Lana as he strode to the door, thinking only of Tessa and how much he was looking forward to their future together, once again.

CHAPTER
Two

Tess And Sam

As she watched Sam lift a particularly heavy box and carry it from their bedroom to the living room, Tess released a sigh filled with appreciation and anticipation, knowing that those very same strong, sexy-as-hell arms were going to be wrapped around her as soon as they were done packing for the day. Well, and as soon as they dealt with the very unappealing job of breaking the news to Josh (her former fiancé) that she and his college best friend were in a committed, sex-fueled, and love-drunk relationship. On second thought, she should definitely leave out the sex part, right? She asked herself.

Walking over to Sam, she stacked a smaller box on top of the one that he had just carried in, and as she turned to go into the almost-empty kitchen and retrieve another packed box, he grabbed her and spun her around in his arms. "What time is Josh due to arrive?" Sam asked, while kissing a line down her neck. "The sofa is right here, and extremely comfortable," he whispered, as he tried to coerce her onto said sofa.

Tess laughed, thrilled at how mad with lust Sam was for her, but also disappointed, knowing they did *not* have time for a romp in the living room. Or anywhere else. Desperate to divert his attention, she knew talk of Josh would do just that: "What exactly did he say when you talked to him?" she asked Sam as she stroked the back of his neck, unable to leave the circle of his arms just yet.

Refusing to be put off by talk of his college friend (and his girlfriend's ex), Sam leaned down into Tess, ran his hands from her back, and then gripped her soft, voluptuous tush at the same time his lips met hers. Knowing this was the only way he would keep her from asking twenty questions about his non-conversation with Josh, Sam was only too eager to distract her.

God, she loved this man and the way he made her feel. Never in her life had she felt as sexy or as adored as she did when she was in the presence of Sam: her only regret in life was not taking a chance on him as soon as she had met him over a decade ago. Her fingertips lightly fluttered across his chest in a way she knew from experience would drive him crazy, and she matched him in intensity now as their kiss deepened. It was then that she noticed he was slowly moving them back into the bedroom. His hands had also left her bottom to move up to her chest, where he was methodically unbuttoning the pink top she had only just redressed in an hour ago.

His lips moved from her plump lips and kissed his way to her left ear, into which he huskily asked, "Did I ever tell you that I have a thing for fluffy redheads?" He knew if he could just maneuver Tess within a foot of their bed, he could convince her to think about nothing but the two of them for the next twenty minutes. Sam most definitely DID NOT want to discuss Josh, and he had a feeling seeing him tonight was going to be gut-wrenching for all three of them, so the less gloom before the doom the better, and the best distraction was in his arms. The love of his life.

As she simultaneously shivered and laughed, she subsequently, very reluctantly, pulled out of his embrace before he got them through the bedroom door, but not before she pulled his face to hers for one last kiss. "Seriously now—how did Josh sound when you talked to him?" Out of the two of them, Tess believed Sam was more nervous: she had already broken Josh's heart when she walked away from their wedding rehearsal, but tonight Sam would be responsible for some heartbreak as well.

Sighing heavily, Sam responded, "I actually haven't spoken to him yet. Unless you count the multiple messages I've left on his voicemail. Do you think he knows about us, and that's why he hasn't answered any of my calls? Maybe I should have gone up to his hospital and made him talk to me, since I can't seem to get him on the phone." Sinking into a kitchen chair, Sam opened the beer he had just pulled from the fridge, hating the idea of potentially hurting one of his best friends. "I hate that he's coming here tonight and we're going to blindside him, for all intents and purposes."

Tess rubbed Sam's shoulders and then wrapped her arms around him from behind him. "I know, Babe. I want, more than anything, to *not* feel like we've betrayed him, but we have. Or I have, at least: you're completely blameless. The truth is, though, getting him on the phone is a moot point. You were never going to tell him over a phone call, anyway. I don't know how he could know about us, since our circles don't cross anymore. Unless he saw us somewhere?"

She walked around his chair to face him, and sat down in the chair opposite his, and took his hands in hers. "We've been so wrapped up in each other for the last two months, but it's time to face reality. At least he replied to my text about coming over."

Last summer, as Tess was planning her wedding to Josh, she and her sister, Ruth, had taken Amtrak across the country from New York City and Philadelphia, respectively, with their final destination being Tess's bachelorette party in Napa Valley. After meeting Sam by pure chance on the train, when he helped her with her luggage, she kept running into him, and as they began to spend more time together in the confined spaces, the pair quickly began to fall in love over the course of three days. Ironically, Sam had been on the train traveling to Lake Tahoe for Josh's bachelor party, a fact she had not discovered for months. Despite having met through Josh previously, and briefly, years ago in college, the two had not recognized each other.

Looking around the apartment Tess and Josh had shared up until their break-up, Sam found it difficult to even recognize his friend's footprint of having lived here for several years: no medical journals on the coffee table, no Stephen King novels on the built-in bookshelves, and none of the snacks in the cupboard that Sam recalled Josh munching on in the middle of the night, when Josh would be pulling an all-nighter before an exam. In fact, the bookshelf now held copies of all of Sam's books, from his wildly successful science fiction trilogy to poetry, the magazines on the coffee table were subscriptions to *Writer's Digest, Cuisine at Home, America's Test Kitchen,* and *bon appétit,* and the snacks? Most of them were made by Tess herself, since she had started to win Sam's heart over with her homemade snickerdoodles, monster cookies, and Chex Mix. Also included in their collection were the three kitties sleeping in the windows at the front of the apartment: Rapunzel, who Tess had rescued after she followed her from the cemetery that was just around the block, and Sawyer, one of Sam's cats, who had fallen for the long-haired princess upon being introduced two weeks ago; Huckleberry, Sam's other cat, lounged in the opposite window, thoroughly enjoying his space now that his brother had a girlfriend. Tess had loved cats since she was a little girl, but Josh had not wanted the mess of a pet; he had reluctantly agreed to foster the gorgeous Rapunzel when Tess had carried her home. She was thrilled now to have three cats in their home, and Sam had been talking about working with a local rescue group once they moved so they could foster even more felines.

Tess took a deep breath, knowing that the moment of truth with Josh was going to change all of their worlds forever. What would Josh think of her after this? Would he still call her "Tessa", his name for her since she was fifteen years old? Honestly, she had always thought the name was even more formal sounding than her given name of "Theresa", but she had loved it when Josh called her Tessa, taking it as a testament of his love for her. She had discovered eight months ago, however, that his love wasn't enough for her anymore: it hadn't been enough for longer than that, but she had denied it to herself, and the truth had become unavoidable after she had encountered Sam on that train, and felt the force of his love envelop her in a way she had never experienced with Josh, no special nickname required.

Looking into Sam's dark brown eyes, she told him: "Josh at least admitted that there were too many cracks in our relationship, and we could never have worked out as a couple. Or anyway, he inferred it when we broke up. You and I were not the cause of Josh and me ending—only a happy accident because of it," and she smiled a wicked smile at Sam, one that usually ended with both of them shedding their clothes.

Sam reached out and pulled Tess's chair closer to his, touching their knees together. Framing her gorgeous face with his hands, he confessed, "I keep putting myself in his shoes and asking myself how I would feel if the tables were turned, and **he** was the one who was madly in love with my ex? I would go nuts, and considering that you, Theresa, are his ex, and completely amazing, I can only imagine he will be distraught."

Tess rose and then straddled Sam's lap on the chair (she always did love an oversized chair), and after pressing her forehead against his, she used her sultriest voice to ask, "So you're madly in love, huh?" Her mouth found his with an urgent need, and she traced the line of his lips with her tongue; he then used his lips to chart a course down her cheek, over her exposed neck, until finally reaching the tops of her breasts pushing up out of her bra. Sam slowly unbuttoned the remaining buttons of her blouse until her pocket began vibrating, startling them both.

Reluctantly plucking her phone out of her pocket, she looked at the caller ID and it read "Big Larry's Coffee Shop", which she showed to Sam before answering. "Hi, this is Tess," she said, clearing her throat and trying to get blood flowing back into her head.

"Hi, Tess, Larry here, and we are all set for tomorrow! I have the keys ready to go, and both places are empty."

"Oh, my goodness, Larry, I can't believe it! I can't thank you enough for all of this. You are helping to make my dreams come true," Tess said sincerely, and suddenly overcome with emotion.

Larry answered earnestly, "Tess, you have been the best vendor for baked goods I've ever had in over forty years of running my coffee shop. I love you, the customers love you, and my whole family loves you. You taking over the coffee shop is truly the perfect ending for me and the perfect beginning for you."

After agreeing to meet with Larry in the morning for the keys, Tess hung up and tossed her phone on the back of the sofa, squealing and dancing in a tiny circle. "It's happening! I can't believe it, Sam—everything is coming together!"

Sam lifted her up in his sturdy arms and swung her around, nuzzling her neck in the process. "I'm beyond happy for you—for us! Starting this journey together. I can't wait to see you behind the counter or in the kitchen baking up your lemon-blueberry muffins, or your cinnamon roll babka.

No, wait—your chocolate cream pie and your red velvet cupcakes. When can I include those recipes in my next novel, by the way?"

Laughing, kissing and more squealing ensued, until Tess questioned hesitantly, "Is this all really happening? I'm taking over Big Larry's Coffee Shop? **And** we're going to live in the apartment above?" Taking a deep breath, Tess exclaimed, "God, I just wish Josh would get here; then we can clear the air about everything and really start our life with a clean slate."

Sam nodded his head, "I'm not looking forward to upsetting Josh, but I agree with you—we need to tell him about us before we officially move in together." Sam had never felt lower in his life than he did now, and the sense that he had betrayed his best friend from college and was going to flip his world upside down was looming large in his conscience.

Tess picked up her phone to check the time. "Ugh—this is so Josh, by the way. Never on time for anything that doesn't include a scalpel." Tess walked back to the sliding door opening up to the garden behind the bedroom. She had loved this apartment at first sight when she and Josh had moved in five years ago: the ground-floor apartment, known as the garden apartment, in a two-family house. She delighted in having her afternoon coffee out there, or a cup of tea on a chilly Sunday afternoon, curled up on the chaise with a book. Every time she pictured moments spent out there, though, they were always just of her—no Josh. She had envisioned the two of them having dinners out on the patio, or just tall glasses of iced tea on a hot summer night, listening to crickets chirping, or sipping cocktails with birds singing in the drizzle of a spring shower. Quickly, reality had taken over, and she realized Josh was spending all of his free time in his hospital. Recalling all of the cancelled dinners, his texts sent well after the time he was already supposed to be home, made Tess appreciate even more the last two months since she had walked out of her wedding rehearsal. She supposed things with Sam had progressed more quickly than some would deem appropriate (especially considering he had been one of Josh's groomsmen), but both of them wanted to waste no time being without each other anymore. Sam, fresh off his book tour for his third book in the popular series, had been staying with her for the last two weeks, after more than a month of them each trading off weekends to see each other: Tess going to Boston or Sam coming down to Brooklyn. All by train, of course, in their signature traveling style.

Sam was so attuned to Tess that he sensed her change of mood from excitement to one of contemplation as she stared out the glass doors. He wrapped his arms around her and put his chin on the top of her head, feeling her back sink into his chest. "You're sure about all this? You love this garden view, I know. We won't have backyard access above the coffee shop."

Turning around in Sam's embrace, Tess's green eyes glowed as she reached up and stroked his cheeks, relishing the feel of his beard under her hands. He had stopped shaving after his book tour ended a month ago, and she was surprised to find herself even more attracted to him. "I do love the view, but I also felt more alone here than ever before in my life. Until you, that is. Now I love this view," she whispered, gazing into his eyes, "and I never feel alone anymore." As the doorbell chimed, they turned in unison, looking toward the front of the apartment.

CHAPTER
Three

Effie

Euphemie Van Holland, age thirty-six, died peacefully in her sleep last night, while surrounded by her loving and supportive family.

Wait—what??? Loving and supportive may be taking things a bit too far. It was one thing to compose one's own obituary, but to add in complete fiction? Besides, this was a new low for her anyway, she thought to herself. She would never want to be called by her given name—only Effie was acceptable, under any and all circumstances. The truth was, she would never have needed to be mentally writing her own obituary if she hadn't so cleverly and thoroughly killed her entire existence, bringing her here: the place where all soon-to-be single, bordering-on-middle-aged women go to die. Her hometown, or more specifically, her childhood home, where her mom and stepdad oh so graciously (NOT) offered her a room at a very reduced rate, so she could crawl back and try to scrape together her shattered life. Who makes their only daughter pay rent on a room in a house that has been in the family for three generations? Well, time to face the music, she thought. What songs would be on this doomsday soundtrack? "(Don't Fear) The Reaper"? "Bad Moon Rising"? "My Heart Will Go On?" No—not Celine. Effie shook her head—too optimistic for her current situation.

As Effie was reaching for the door handle, a gust of wind flew up, courtesy of the never-ending winter that seemed to befall every February in South Dakota, and tangled her raven-colored hair across her face. Unfortunately, the queen of the house appeared at the door almost simultaneously, "Euphemie, for heaven's sake, when was the last time you cut your hair? No wonder you're concerned with having an issue finding another job. And my goodness, look how brown your face is. Darling, girl, haven't I reminded you repeatedly to stay out of the sun so much?" Diadema Van Holland was nothing if not practiced at reminding her daughter just how disappointed she was in her these last thirty-six years.

"Wow, Mom, nice to see you, too. Could we *at least* have a cup of tea before you start slinging the mud, or how about holding off until I actually get through the gateway to Windsor Palace first?" As Effie shrugged through the doorway, she put her bags against the entryway wall, grabbed her mom for a hug, and whispered, "And it's Effie, please, not Euphemie," and kissed her mom on the cheek, the gardenia scent of her mother's perfume rising up to greet her, and Effie breathed it in gratefully.

For all that her mom excelled at annoying her, Diadema also could be counted on as a soft place to fall (as long as Effie paid the fifty dollar-a-month in rent—alright, not a king's ransom, but just symbolic of her mom's economical reasoning). Diadema laughed, "Effie, right. I give you a regal name like Euphemie and you want to be called Effie. I shall do my best." With a flick of her manicured fingers, she motioned for Effie to follow her majesty into the sitting room.

Burnside Van Holland's blue eyes looked up from his copy of **The Wall Street Journal** (seriously—who reads **WSJ** in the middle of South Dakota?) and drawled, "Euphemie, dear, were we expecting you today?"

Staring blankly at her stepdad, Effie sometimes wondered how her mom could still be married to him after all these years. Aside from his money, of course, which her mom had taken an oath to love, honor, and obey. Diadema came from a long line of farming families, each generation having done exceedingly well, until the '80s, when they had started to sell off parcels of land. Effie often wondered if her mother's "nervous breakdown" thirty years ago hadn't been a little too convenient, since she had come back from Ohio with a clean mental state along with "a husband from the East". Her mom either added or subtracted "rich" from the proclamation, depending on who her audience was; she excelled in math that way.

"Why yes, dear father, I have arrived." Burnside was not what one would call warm and fuzzy, but he seemed to adore her mother in his own way—she would give him that, despite the internal dig about his wallet. Calling him "Dad" had taken her many years to master, and she only truly had become comfortable with it after she graduated from high school, a matter helped by the fact that he had handed her the keys to a brand-new Toyota truck as a graduation present, and the note of pride in his voice when he whispered, rather gruffly, how he knew she was destined for great things. Effie poured herself a cup of tea from the sideboard, first adding her sugar and milk, and did her best impression of flopping onto the settee, which was truly difficult since she did love a good cup of tea, and watched carefully as the liquid came close to spilling. It wasn't that she was without manners, just that being in this environment always brought out only her bad ones. Remembering her promise to herself to show her parents her mature side, she sipped her English Breakfast, and then began, "I want to thank you both for helping me out now. I truly appreciate being able to stay here and—"

"Hey, Sis—no one told me you were coming," a deep voice called from the hallway. Looking up, Effie saw the face of her younger brother peek into the sitting room, and she felt a smile spread across her face looking at him. Ten years older than Hamilton, she had adored him since his birth. However, where her parents held Effie up to meet the high expectations they had set, Hamilton was allowed to set his own course, often having his questionable behavior explained away with "high IQ", "he's never been challenged", or perhaps the best of the bunch "he's misunderstood". Truth was, he was brilliant and gorgeous, with golden hair and eyes the color of the Caribbean; he was also lazy and seemingly forever sixteen.

Effie rose from her perch and kissed her half-brother on the cheek, and he squeezed her in a bear hug, "Someone's been enjoying the good life, I see—huh, Effie?" and he squeezed the roll of her waist, which had risen above her pants.

Batting his hands away, she responded sharply, "And I see someone is home to mooch off Mom and Dad?"

Ham laughed out loud, "I guess Mom hasn't told you the good news—I moved in last year."

"Children, please, can we not stay civilized for more than five minutes?" begged their mother, having foregone the tea for—was that vodka or gin in her glass? Effie had never been able to tell the difference from afar until Diadema had at least two drinks in her.

The definition of irony was here in this room—Effie's biological father had died in a car accident when she was five. She had been too young to have genuine memories of him, and she only remembered how she had felt around him: safe, loved, and cherished. When he had died, and it was revealed what his blood alcohol level was, her mom had spiraled and was subsequently shipped away by Effie's grandparents to a distant relative in Ohio. While Diadema was living there for a year, her parents had taken care of Effie, and she had been subject to their racism and thinly veiled comments concerning her heritage, nothing she had been privy to before her beloved father was taken from her. When Diadema had been in college, she had fallen in love with Nathaniel LeBeau, a member of the Grass Valley Indian Reservation. The couple had moved quickly with their relationship, marrying just months after meeting, and Effie's birth less than a year later. After they both had graduated, they had moved into his family home and Diadema had taught grade school on the reservation and Nathaniel worked for the tribal police. Diadema's family had ostracized her from her family for having the audacity to marry a "no good Indian" (one of the more generous terms given by her grandparents). Having just been accepted into the University of South Dakota School of Law, Nathaniel was out with friends, celebrating when he'd gotten a call at the bar that Diadema, six months pregnant at the time, was having a miscarriage. In his haste to get to the hospital, he had misjudged a curve ahead on the dirt road he must have driven a thousand times and crashed his car into a tree. Diadema was left mourning the loss of her husband and her infant son on the same night. Her parents had swept in and rescued their daughter and granddaughter from the nasty clutches of the "Red Man", whisking them away and making it impossible for anyone in Nathaniel's family to have any contact with her during that time. The situation only worsened upon Diadema's return to South Dakota, already married to Burnside. Now here her mother was: day drinking hard alcohol, and never having once let Effie forget what it was that had killed her father.

Having become emotional thinking about her father, Effie cleared her throat. "No, Mom never said you had moved back home," she replied to Hamilton. It dawned on her then that there must have been a deliberate decision for this misdirection from her mother. "Mom, why didn't you mention Ham was living here again?"

Her mother waved her diamond encrusted hand. "Dear, it must have just slipped my mind; now that everyone is talking about it, I guess you should know that your brother is in your old room. Do you recall that I turned his room into my walk-in closet?" Effie closed her eyes and braced herself, dreading the words she knew were coming. "Unfortunately, Euphemie, you will have to sleep in Daddy's office on the pullout in there."

Effie cringed, for more than one reason. Reason number one: hearing her mother refer to her stepdad as "daddy" was a real stomach-turner, and reason number two: the pullout sofa had been devised as a medieval torture device, was a chiropractor's dream, and only manufactured to ensure job security. "I don't understand why Ham can't stay in there, then." Effie protested. "Or why can't I stay in the spare room?"

Diadema's brown eyes widened. "Sweetie, Daddy has moved his office to the spare room—the afternoon light is remarkably better there than in his old office. This way you'll be able to wake up with the sun and get a jump on your day. Besides, Hamilton's things are all stacked up in your room. Just think about how uncomfortable you'd be. Anyway—who is hungry for a late afternoon lunch? We can discuss your job prospects, Euphemie."

Great, she thought—fuck my life.

CHAPTER

Four

Josh

Staring at the gleaming wooden door of the apartment he used to share with Tessa, Josh felt electric with excitement. He also wondered why he was standing out here and shivering in the brisk February night, when he had a key to the place. Would it be inappropriate to use his key and let himself in? Now that he had given her two months to get her priorities straight, he had no doubt that she was ready for them to get back together. Having decided to take his cues from her, it had killed him to give her the space she had seemed to need, but in his world, you don't throw away almost twenty years of history. The two of them would reunite tonight, and then they could work on finding an apartment closer to his hospital—she could find work in a bakery on the Upper East Side, until they got pregnant, that is. First the wedding, of course, and then they would focus on starting the family that would inevitably follow a year or so after that. Tessa was still in her early thirties, so they had plenty of time to have the two (possibly three) kids they had always talked about.

As he rang the bell, he also pulled out his apartment key and slotted it into the lock, turning it just as the door opened. His beautiful Tessa, he thought while turning the corners of his mouth down in disapproval: she was wearing her glasses even though she knew he preferred seeing her radiant green eyes glass-free. "I guess the natural look is in?" he commented, his own eyes taking in her makeup-free face before him, with her glinting red hair pulled back haphazardly in a simple ponytail. "No matter what, you look beautiful, Tessa," and as he reached for her to grab her for an embrace, she sidestepped him to let him in to the apartment. As she did so, he saw the tails of three cats dashing for the bedroom at the back of the apartment. Three cats? Since when did Tessa get two more cats? He had begrudgingly agreed to the one when she had brought it home, soaking wet from the rain. But two? No, he would have to put his foot down about this predicament.

"Hi, Josh, it's good to see you too." Tessa held his front door open for him, while seemingly ushering him inside. "I'm glad you could make it tonight—I remember what a haul it is for you to come from your hospital," she said, as she closed the door.

What did she mean by that? Although it *was* almost an hour (and two different subway lines) from upper Manhattan to this part of Brooklyn, he didn't recall ever making a fuss over it. As he took off his coat, he hung it up on a hook just inside the entry and noticed an unfamiliar leather jacket also hanging there. Now that he was inside, Josh wasn't feeling as confident as he had been when standing on the doorstep, but that changed as soon as he noticed the boxes stacked up to one side of the living room. "What's all this?" he asked hopefully, remembering that after their failed wedding rehearsal, he had broached the subject of them moving. Was it possible she was one step ahead of him, despite being so against the idea of a move to Manhattan all those months ago?

"Why don't you come over here and sit down, Josh?" As if he were a guest in his own home, Tessa led him to the sofa and gestured to it. "Would you like something to drink?" she asked, and he noticed her twisting her hands together, a sure sign the woman he had known for eighteen years was feeling nervous. "We have beer, if you want one?" Beer? When had they ever kept beer in their fridge? Wine, yes, and maybe some harder spirits in the cabinet above the fridge, but never beer, which Josh had always considered too low-class once he was in med school.

Feeling some exasperation about what was taking her so long to address them getting back together, Josh sighed heavily. "No, I just want to clear the air between us." As he took a seat on the sofa, he turned to face the woman he still loved. "Look, Tessa, I know you were under an extreme amount of stress before our wedding, and I forgive you for walking out of the rehearsal," he began the speech he had prepared while on the D train. "Upon reflection, I can see how you maybe thought that I was too involved in my work, but now that my fellowship application is done, I can relax and refocus on us." Smiling at her, Josh tried to reach for her once again, but she had turned away from him.

Josh watched as Tessa took a seat in the plush armchair that backed up against the bay window. As the light played off the copper accents in her hair, his breath caught in his throat: she had never looked lovelier than she did now. Slightly more disheveled than he was used to seeing her, but she was radiant, with her cheeks blushing pink and her jewel-green eyes glowing, despite being hidden behind her glasses. Admitting to himself that even though he did prefer her to wear contacts, her glasses framed her heart-shaped face perfectly. Josh took a seat on the edge of the sofa and angled himself so he could look even more directly at the love of his life.

Tessa studied a spot on the ceiling as she said, "Josh, I hope you know that I will always care about you and want the best for you." Wait, Josh thought: this wasn't sounding like a preamble to a getting-back-together speech.

"I'm sorry—what? What is this, Tessa?" Josh demanded gruffly, and he conceded silently that it may have come out a little too forcefully. Tact had never been one of his strengths.

Tessa, now with her eyes focused beyond Josh's shoulder, began again, "Josh, some things have happened, and we need to just be honest with you right now." WE? What was she talking about: "we need to be honest"? Josh followed her eyes and turned his body, looking behind him to the kitchen where, to his amazement, his college friend Fitz was leaning, braced against the door frame.

Okay, this was getting weird now. What the hell was Fitz doing here, in Brooklyn, in his apartment? Furthermore, what had he *already* been doing here prior to Josh's arrival? Were they staging some kind of intervention, thinking Josh was a workaholic? "Umm, I'm not sure what is going on here," Josh admitted, looking from Sam to Tessa, suddenly feeling more uncomfortable than he ever recalled feeling before in his life, as he caught a glance between the two. He watched as Sam sauntered into the living room from the kitchen and handed him a beer. Handed *him* a beer in *his own house.* "What do you mean 'we need to be honest'?"

"Look, Doc, we never intended to hurt you. Please…if nothing else, please believe that." Josh held up a hand, wanting to keep from hearing any more that either one of them had to say, while also understanding that hearing it was inevitable. He still wasn't entirely certain he knew where this conversation was going, but he had a feeling he wasn't going to like it.

"Could one of you please explain to me what you both are doing here, when the last time I checked, neither one of you gave a damn about the other one? I mean—that's the truth, right? Neither one of you could even stand to be in the same city as the other one, let alone in the same room. And I don't get how you even know where I live, Sam," Josh asked, intentionally *not* using his nickname. Had Sam hoped that by using Josh's nickname, somehow he would look beyond the fact that two of the people most dear to him were here, for some reason, together, in the apartment he had shared with Tessa up until two months ago?

"You mean where you used to live," Tessa said so quietly that Josh strained to hear her. "You packed your bags two months ago and moved out, remember—after I cancelled our wedding," she reminded him (as if he needed it) and nodded over to the boxes stacked up in the corner. "I've packed the rest of your things up and have arranged a mover to come tomorrow and put them in a storage space I've rented for the next six months." Tessa pulled out a key and an envelope that had an address on it and slid it next to a magazine on the coffee table near Josh.

Josh was taken aback. "I guess I didn't know that me packing a couple of bags and staying at a friend's place meant I was moving out. I thought we were just on a break while you got your head together? I mean, I have still been paying the rent here, after all."

Tessa nodded and said, "I also included a check in that envelope to cover rent for the last two months." With her eyes, she seemed to be imploring Josh to understand what was happening without her having to explain it in finite detail. "Look, Josh, this isn't about rent, anyway. This is about us moving on with our lives." Suddenly, she dropped her head in her hands.

Moving on with our lives? What the hell did she mean? Without Tessa, he had no life. "What are you talking about, Tessa? You texted me, asking me to come over tonight, telling me you want to talk about the future, so forgive me if I am a bit confused right now. Can you please explain what Sam is doing here?" he demanded, pointing at Sam. "I'd like to know what he is doing here, with you, in my home."

With that, Sam, who had been sitting on the arm of the sofa, rose to his feet and walked two strides over to where Tess was sitting in the chair. Josh had never felt more like an idiot in his entire life, as lightbulbs exploded inside of his head. "What—are you telling me that you two are together or something?" He scoffed. "Is that your big news for our future?" Josh was shaking his head, trying in vain to compute how any of this was happening.

Tessa was reluctantly nodding her head. "Josh, I have been trying to figure out a way to tell you about us for weeks now." She raised her head, and he saw the tracks of her tears on her rosy cheeks. "I'm sorry, and this is all on me. The truth is that Sam and I met on the train last summer," and she paused as if considering her next words.

"What do you mean you 'met on the train'? You mean the train you took to your bachelorette weekend?" As Tessa grimly nodded her confirmation, he looked with overwhelming anguish to Sam, "But you never even came to my bachelor party—what were doing on the train?"

"No, I didn't end up arriving for your party, but I was on the same train as Theresa, unbeknownst to both of us. You know how I hate flying," Sam attempted to explain. "I wanted to work and travel in peace, so I was taking the train from Boston to Reno. Then I got the news about my mom and had to head back when the train got to Denver; I never made it to your party, but I was on the way." Sam glanced over at Tessa, and flashed her a secret smile, and seeing it was like a knife in Josh's chest. "While I was eating breakfast that first day on the train, I noticed Theresa on the platform in New York, struggling with her baggage, so I jumped out to help her, not even realizing she was your Tessa." Of course he did: Sam, ever the gentleman. Sam, always so irresistible to every woman he meets. Sam, the writer, gifted with his words, so sure of what to say. "During those few days while I was on the train, I fell in love. Hard." Josh found it impossible to meet Sam's eyes, yet he steeled himself to do so. "I'm sorry, Josh," whispered the man who had been the first friend he had met after joining the fraternity.

Perched on the edge of his seat, Josh sat listening to the two of them detail the timeline of their budding romance, all the while feelings of betrayal and loss threatened to choke him. Two of the people who he had trusted, trying to let him down gently: he knew he hadn't been the best of friends to Sam lately, especially considering that he knew what Sam's mom had been going through after a breast cancer scare, or the most perfect fiancé to Tessa, but did he deserve this sort of payment for his lack of attention and minor emotional involvement? All of his life Josh had struggled to channel his emotions correctly, often being mistaken for having cold feelings, or worse, none at all, when nothing could be further from the truth. At times, his breadth of emotion felt so massive that he could do nothing but compartmentalize or he would become quickly overwhelmed. His biggest mistake was in believing that Tessa had understood this, apparently. And what about all of those late-night conversations with Sam in college, where the two had bonded and become as close as brothers, or so he thought? Josh should be used to this intense feeling of loneliness, one that he had last felt so intensely after losing his mother when he was twelve: even that life-altering event had not prepared him for this catastrophic moment in his life.

Suddenly, he could not stand to be in this room with the two of them any longer, especially once he clearly saw the traces of Sam everywhere: the beer, the magazine, the jacket. Josh staggered to his feet, reaching for the beer that had been handed to him by his friend, and grabbed the envelope his fiancée had so graciously prepared for him. Much as Tessa had done at their wedding rehearsal, he fled towards the door. Ripping it open so quickly that it threatened to fly off the hinges, Josh lurched outside and stumbled down the block, until he finally collapsed and let the wealth of painful emotions overtake him; he was left sobbing against the brick wall of Big Larry's Coffee Shop, the now-empty bottle sliding from his hands and shattering to the sidewalk.

CHAPTER
Five

Effie

Finally collapsing onto the medieval torture device her mother insisted on calling the spare bed, Effie recounted all of the reasons she had thought staying at her parents' house would be a brilliant idea. She attempted to, at any rate, but nothing was coming to her. Who was it that had first uttered the phrase "absence makes the heart grow fonder"? She'd love to go back in time and slap them silly. Absence from Clover Lake, her hometown, made her consistently glad to not be there, and now that she was here, she wanted to slit her wrists. Okay, not really—the last thing she needed was for her mom to be calling for crisis intervention. Effie had an unfortunate penchant for the dramatic, made particularly morbid when bad mojo was following her, and she had had an excess of the bad mojo for *at least* the past year.

Knowing only Clint Black could soothe her wounded spirit right now, she began with "State of Mind", a song that always took her back to attending college in the Black Hills in Western South Dakota. Having been the only person with any noticeably Native blood in her high school, it had been refreshing to finally be somewhere surrounded on a daily basis with other people who looked like her. Not that she hadn't encountered Native kids from other schools during high school activities. She had, of course, but she couldn't escape the underlying message from her mother to always ACT WHITE. Whatever that meant. Having had no contact with anyone from her father's family since she was five had made it fairly easy for her to forget, sometimes, that she was of Dakota descent (Effie had a memory of her father teaching her to refer to her heritage as Dakota, not Sioux, since Sioux was the term given to them by French explorers). At first, she was too young to do anything about it on her own, and then, as a teenager, she was too wrapped up in herself. In college, though, curiosity had gotten the best of her, and she had become interested in locating her grandparents, but she had nothing to go on. It turned out LeBeau was a fairly common name on the Grass Valley Indian Reservation; her mother was of absolutely no help, and had done her best after marrying Burnside to eliminate all traces of her first husband from her past (except for Effie, although at times it seemed she had tried to do that, as well), and that included having Burnside adopt Effie when she was nine.

Looking hopefully at her phone, Effie was dismayed to see that no one had tried calling her since she had left Denver two days ago. She then glanced down at her hand, saddened to see that the only remnant left behind from her wedding ring was a white shadow. Hugging her knees to her chest helped keep her overwhelming pain from escaping. How was she going to start over when all she wanted to do was go back and rewind it all?

As her upbeat song ended, Adele came on over the speakers. As her luck had gone lately, of course it had to be from **21**, and "Take It All" began to play. "Didn't I give it all? Tried my best..." Effie sang along, and alone here in what used to be her playroom as a child, before it ever became Burnside's office, she finally let her guard down. All through their late lunch, Effie had done her best to needle her mom, knowing how easily she could push her buttons. Anything to assist her in *not* contemplating her failed marriage. You never fall in love and expect it to end. Who ponders the finality of a relationship, let alone one in which the vows you made were, to you at least, sacred? Everything she had, she had put on the line for Damon—her money, her time, her self-respect, and her dignity. And she had begged him—fucking ***begged*** him to give them another chance. God, she had been pathetic. After every second, third, fourth chance she had graciously and lovingly given him, his response had been to turn and walk out the door. Now she had no husband, no job, no money. Damon had made some "wise investments" that were "sure to pay off", and maybe they would—but not for Effie. All she was left with was humiliation.

She had played it safe for so long. Watching her mom collapse after her dad died had burned into Effie's brain to never let anyone hurt her like her mom had been emotionally crippled back then. All that followed had been so ugly, and Effie so terribly young, that she didn't want to have to survive something equal to it, so she'd only had brief romantic entanglements: shallow involvements that would not scar. Until her silver-tongued devil had strutted into Fort Collins, Colorado, where she had been slinging drinks part time in a popular bar, having just earned her master's degree in library science at the university. Damon was so assured and confident, with his blue eyes and light brown hair. Originally from California (should have been her first clue) he was a tour manager for a rock band out of Denver (umm…second clue, anyone?) and he only had eyes for her exotic beauty (his words, not hers); for someone who loved to read immensely, she had failed miserably to read him.

Looking up at the shelves in her current bedroom, she saw her high school yearbooks all lined up in chronological order. Well, at least her mom provided some light reading in here, Effie thought. Pulling her head out of her funk, Effie rose up on her long legs and reached for her freshman yearbook. Plucking it off the shelf, she sat back down and turned to the index of names at the back. Scrolling her finger down, she finally came to Van Holland, Euphemie, and located the first page in her listing. Track and field—graced with runner's legs, Effie had quickly found her place among the track team in middle school, and continued it in high school. Excelling in the fifty and one-hundred-yard dashes and any relay she could participate in, she had been the fastest girl in her class since kindergarten. More than just a runner, though, Effie had also eventually been a star of the stage, and after utilizing the index once again, she opened the yearbook up to the drama section. Since she had just been a freshman here, most roles had been small or supporting ones. She found her very first Three-Act Play: *Li'l Abner,* and when she squinted, she could mostly make out her face in a group photo taken on opening night. Effie rose up again and collected the rest of the yearbooks. Maybe her hometown hadn't been such a horror show after all, at least not her high school years. Using the same process for her sophomore yearbook, Effie again found herself poring over the theatre photos, and this time, another face caught her attention. Who was that boy standing behind her? Why couldn't she remember him? In the photo, she was turned to face him, and the expression on her young face was so filled with joy as she was clearly speaking to him. She'd always prided herself on being good with faces, and although there was something buzzing in her brain, she could not place him. Finding his name in the caption underneath made her pause. As a result, she flipped back to the index and found his other listings. Turning to his class photo, she nodded her head as she realized he had been a grade under her, which was why he hadn't shown up in her freshman yearbook. Okay, time to look in her junior yearbook. She went directly to his listing and then the drama section, where she saw a picture of the two of them together on stage. Since there had been fewer boys interested in theatre, males were able to get bigger parts sooner than females, so when she had been a junior and he was a sophomore, they had been cast as the leading roles in the year's musical: *Grease.* He'd been Danny to her Sandy, and her first kiss. God, now she remembered what a crush she had on him. He'd been taller than average, like her, unlike so many of the other boys even in her own year, so she had not towered over him. Blond, blue-eyed (not that she had a type or anything), super nice, and so smart. So why did she have trouble at first recalling him? Opening up her final yearbook, she went to stalk him again, and this time didn't see his name in the index. What? That can't be right, but there was no listing for him. She then opened the book to what should have been his class— the junior year class photos, and no photo or mention of him there either. What the hell? What had happened to Livingston, Joshua?

CHAPTER

Six

Lana

As she usually did whenever they either shared a shift or had an overlapping one, Lana placed the hot Americano, with an extra shot of espresso, on Josh's desk, along with one of the banana nut muffins she knew he liked. When she had come on staff at the hospital two years ago, Josh had been the first person she had met, and he had been gracious and welcoming to her, even though he was already three years into his residency. Now he was finishing up his last year, and Lana felt a pang of longing, knowing that she would be losing her office mate and close friend.

After putting her iced coffee and almond croissant on her own desk, she shrugged out of her heavy winter coat and crossed the room to hang it up behind the door. Well, this was weird, she thought to herself, as her coat was now the only one hanging up. Josh should be in by now—she could have sworn she had seen his name listed on the surgical board for a surgery at ten o'clock this morning, and he always arrived two hours prior to any of his surgeries. He was the most brilliant and driven man she had ever met; when he talked about a new procedure he was studying up on, or they discussed a particularly challenging case, Lana loved watching his blue eyes light up with excitement.

Finally, sitting down at her desk, she didn't know whether to be concerned about Josh or not. A glance at the wall clock told her it was a quarter after nine, and just as she was reaching for her phone to send him a text, the office door slowly opened, and Josh filled the doorway. His appearance shocked Lana—his sky-blue eyes were bloodshot, and a crease bisected his cheek, indicating his face had been on a pillow until not so long ago. And wasn't that the suit he was wearing yesterday? She questioned herself. Oh no, this was the day she had been dreading: he and Tessa must have gotten back together last night. Lana knew it was bound to happen, but she had, of course, been secretly hoping the break was permanent. Knowing it sounded like a cliché to even herself, Tessa did not "get" Josh the way that Lana did. For two years she had to sit in silence, holding her tongue and her own desires, while she listened to Josh unload about whatever grief Tessa was causing him at any particular moment. Once Josh had divulged to her about Tessa running from their wedding, Lana had seen a glimmer of hope for herself, but she had been patient. About a month after his negated nuptials, Lana had taken the plunge and invited Josh over for dinner, and it had been wonderful. Josh had brought her the most gorgeous bouquet of flowers, and the two of them had shared a bottle of Cabernet over the homemade spaghetti Bolognese Lana had spent the afternoon preparing. God, they had such a vast array of topics to talk about—so many interests in common, other than just the normal surgery talk that greatly consumed their work lives. And for a moment—one single, fleeting, anticipatory moment—as Lana walked Josh to her door, their eyes had locked, and she had felt that sexual pull between them. She had leaned forward, certain he was going to kiss her, but he had instead given her a one-armed hug and bade her a good night. Her disappointment had been almost overwhelming, but then she had rallied and reminded herself that *of course* he couldn't kiss her yet—it would not be appropriate, considering he *was* just out of a long-term relationship.

Unable to take any more of the dreaded silence, Lana finally forced herself to ask, "How was your night with Tessa, Josh?" She steeled herself for his celebratory news.

Josh let out a shaky sigh. "It wasn't, actually." He then slumped into his chair, still in the overcoat he had not taken off since leaving Brooklyn last night, and put his hands over his face. "There was no night with Tessa. Well, I guess there was, but she wasn't alone," he said through his splayed hands.

Lana waited for more explanation, but Josh was not forthcoming. What could he mean: Tessa wasn't alone? "Oh, I guess her sister must have been there?" she asked, knowing Tessa's sister had had a baby a few months ago. Just another example of how much she knew about and listened to Josh!

"No, Ruth wasn't there. I wish, actually, that she had been. No, it turns out my good old buddy Fitz was there, and it looked to me like he has been there for a while now." Josh let out what sounded to Lana like a laugh that was slightly maniacal. But as she surveyed him, she then understood that he was actually crying — his shoulders were shaking from his efforts to hide his pain. Unsure of whether to ask anything more, and not wanting to upset him further, she stayed silent.

Just as she was going to offer whatever support she could to Josh, he lowered his hands from his face, and she then she fully took in the evidence of his misery. "They've betrayed me, Lana. Two of the people who I trusted—who I believed to be honest and sincere—have been having an affair behind my back; while I was sitting here, day after day, planning our reunion, my fiancée was involved with one of my best friends."

His anguish was palpable, but in an effort to hopefully make him see things clearly, Lana couldn't help but point out, "But, Josh, she walked out on you at your wedding rehearsal. She called everything off. You weren't together anymore."

"You think any of that matters?" he lashed out. "What matters is that I still loved her! Oh, and if you want to hear something really rich, get this—turns out they started up *BEFORE* the wedding." At Lana's gasp, Josh proceeded to detail every bit from his meeting with Tessa last night.

"This is something I never believed she was capable of. Maybe I expected some jealousy from her about you and me working so closely together, being alone for such long hours, but never did I imagine *she* would cheat on *me*." Josh laughed again, "It's ironic, really, since I hurt her years ago when I broke up with her; I know that. And now she, I guess, has finally gotten back at me."

Lana's heart was breaking for him, because Josh didn't deserve to be hurting like he was now, no matter what had happened in the past between him and Tessa. She rose from her chair, walked over, and embraced him. Like a lightning bolt splitting the sky in a storm, she felt a change in Josh. He lifted from his chair, cupped the sides of her face, and suddenly his lips were on hers. God, she'd been dreaming about this moment for over a year now, and kissed him back fully. Until that said lightning brought the rain, and then doused her passion. This wasn't right—she didn't want to be someone's rebound, or worse, revenge, so she pulled back from Josh's embrace as gracefully as she could. Lana grasped his hands in hers and remorsefully said, "This isn't right, Josh. Not here and not now," and tried to capture his gaze with hers, but he quickly turned from her, roughly shoved his chair into his desk, and slammed out of their office. Lana rushed to the door that was still swinging on the hinges, and tried calling after him, but he had already turned around the corner to the surgical wing.

With tears in her eyes, Lana felt a terrible sense of loss, worried that the two of them had just crossed a fragile line in their friendship.

CHAPTER
Seven

Josh

What the hell had he been thinking? Everything he touched was turning to shit, and now Lana was his latest debacle. Turning the corner from his office corridor, he attempted to firmly stride down the hallway leading to the main office for surgery. Never before in his life had he felt like he was barely holding on, in desperate need of a life vest in his sea of misery. The human-sized ache in his heart left by Tessa and Fitz was growing, despite his attempts to staunch it with bourbon last night.

Once he had left his apartment (damn it—he needed to stop thinking of it like that; no matter: soon it will be someone else's den of misery) he had forlornly walked the few blocks to the subway and gotten on and headed back to Manhattan. What else was he going to do? During the excruciatingly long ride, memories of his life with Tessa and all of the dreams they had shared had consumed his thoughts. What had gone so miserably wrong for them? What had he done that had justified this emptiness? Josh had trudged up the stairs at his station, but could not face going back to his morose little room at Cal's. Cal had been very generous with Josh for the past two months that he had let Josh stay with him, but neither one of them had ever considered the cohabitation would have gone on for so long—Josh had thought he'd *maybe* be there for a couple of *weeks*, never mind *months*. He'd fucked up Cal's life, too, by now. Cal shared custody of his four-year-old daughter, and he had her every weekend. Or he tried to, anyway, but with Josh staying in her princess room, that meant little Taylor had to sleep in her sleeping bag on the floor of Cal's room, and no one was particularly thrilled about the arrangement. Josh had overheard Cal's ex-wife grilling him about it last weekend, and she had threatened Cal that if Josh weren't out by the end of the month, Taylor would no longer be allowed to stay unless she had her room back. Christ, Josh thought, how pathetic was he? Not only robbing a preschooler of her beloved room, but now possibly of her devoted daddy.

Unfortunately, instead of going to straight to Cal's, Josh had stopped in at the Pig 'n Whistle, the pub right outside the subway, and promptly upon bellying up to the bar, he had ordered two bourbons, straight, and like a man dying of thirst, he made quick work of them, and he then signaled the bartender for two more, and then two more after that. From that point, the burly man behind the beer-stained bar had cut Josh off and suggested he go home. Josh had then suggested the barkeep go to hell, and under the threat of physical removal, Josh had dragged his sorry ass out of the bar and finally to Cal's. By this point, it was almost three in the morning, and the knowledge that his alarm would sound in a little over two hours was almost a buzzkill. Almost. Fortunately, Josh remembered the bottle of vodka Cal stored in his freezer, and continued his pity party until he woke, lying on the bathroom floor beside the toilet, to his shrieking alarm. He had somehow managed to drag himself to his bed and then slept for two more hours, which had consequently made him late for work. Josh had *never* been late arriving at work. Ever.

Ducking into the men's room, Josh finally got a good look at himself in the mirror, and to say he had trouble recognizing the reflection of a stranger would be an understatement. He hadn't had a chance to shower or shave this morning, just a quick brushing of his teeth and then he was stumbling out the door. Jesus—he'd been in such a stupor that he only just realized he was still wearing yesterday's suit. Hanging his head down to the sink, he carelessly tossed water onto his face in a sad effort to erase the scum from the day before. Combing his damp fingers through his hair, he imagined what Tessa would have to say about this. She had loathed it if his hair was too long, or if he had any trace of stubble on his face. Yet, he noticed last night that Fitz had grown out a beard, so Josh wondered if it wasn't just his own face Tessa couldn't stand the sight of—stubbled or not.

Well, this would have to do, he thought to himself. Strangely, his own mother now entered into his mind, and Josh took a minute, trying to recall when he had last thought of her. After she was gone, when he'd been in school, every success he'd had he would compel him to think of his mom and wonder if she would've been proud to see her only son, her only child, excel at such a high level. Until the second she was gone from his life, all her words to him had been filled with love and praise. She had stopped working when he was born, and had been a stay-at-home mom, and when Josh had first walked at seven months of age, he imagined her cheering him on (she had loved to retell the story to one and all about her amazing Joshua, walking at such a young age—no, he never learned to crawl, she would recount, just took off walking), but he did have a vague memory of being three years old and learning to read, with the aid of his mom encouraging him, helping him to recognize the letters and sounding them out into their words. He'd begun kindergarten a week before turning five, and despite everyone trying to convince Melanie to wait another year, she persisted. Skinned knees, sprained ankles, fractured arm, cut fingers—all had been seen to and nursed by his devoted mother. Until that day. The dreaded day that changed his life. Josh had been lying to everyone for eighteen years. In actuality, Josh *and* his father had been lying. Unable to face the truth about Melanie Livingston, Henry Livingston had simply uprooted the two of them when Josh was sixteen, and moved them to a town forty miles away, far enough away where no one would know the truth, but close enough should Melanie ever change her mind. While Henry and Josh told their new friends and neighbors in their new home of Beverley, South Dakota, that devoted and beloved mother Melanie Livingston had tragically died of cancer, in actuality, everyone in their old town of Clover Hill knew that she had simply vanished from their lives of her own accord three years before that. Henry and Josh had each awoken the day after Christmas, when

Josh was twelve, to surprise gifts for each of them: "Dear John" letters, one to her husband, Henry, and one to her only child, Joshua, explaining how difficult she found it being a stay-at-home wife and mother, and how she simply could not cope anymore in her daily loneliness. So, in an effort to save herself, she had to walk away from both of them. So generous in her acknowledgment of the pain she knew she was causing, she granted them whatever time it took for them to heal, but then encouraged each of them to move on with their lives. They had been the talk of the town for weeks, months, years, until neither one could take it anymore and Henry moved them to Beverley. Henry had been fielding offers from all of the single, appropriately-aged females in Clover Lake, but he never did get over the loss of his wife, and to this day he was still single, and as far as Josh knew, still waiting for Melanie to find her way back to them. Josh, however, had accepted his harsh reality of abandonment, vowing never to be hurt like that again. Funny how life can continue to slice you into little pieces, leaving your shattered remains to the whims of the wind.

CHAPTER
Eight

Effie

Despite the chill in the air, Effie had decided to walk to the grocery store to pick up items she needed to make dinner for her family tonight. There had been a time, back when Effie was a teenager, that she had done most of the cooking for the family instead of her mom, anyway. Not that Diadema didn't have the time—no, time was always in great wealth for Diadema. She simply lacked the motivation, imagination, and dedication for coming up with dinner options that the entire family would enjoy. Grilled chicken breast, baked potato, and steamed broccoli were considered an acceptable meal for her mom, on repeat five days a week, but unacceptable to Effie to be eaten every single night. Luckily, the store was a five-block walk, which was also enough time for Effie to come up with a grocery list, but not too far to struggle with her items on the walk back home. Living in Denver had afforded Effie the opportunity to be able to live, work, and play all within walking distance, and she detested driving in the city unless absolutely necessary. Another upside to living in

Denver was her stamina for cold weather: Effie liked to challenge herself every year when the air first turned frosty by seeing how long she could go without wearing an actual coat outdoors. Current record: thirty minutes for thirty degrees. In short sleeves.

Pulling the door open to the grocery store, Effie made note of the announcement on the peg board just inside the vestibule, and then once fully inside the store, she smiled at the cashier who greeted her. Maybe small-town living would be bearable after all. "Euphemie, my goodness, is that you?" called a high-pitched voice from the end cap two aisles over. Maybe small-town living would NOT be bearable after all. Recognizing the owner of the voice as being Audrey, the woman who wrote the only gossip column (excuse me, 'personal informational news' column) in Clover Lake's only newspaper, Effie knew this meant she was going to be said news in next week's paper. Fuck my life, she thought, which was currently the most-played track in her head.

"Oh, hi, Mrs. Johnson," Effie responded, wondering at what age it was appropriate to begin addressing everyone by their first names. "Yep, it's me, but you can just call me Effie," which Audrey Johnson should have known, since not only was she a first-rate columnist, she had also given Effie clarinet lessons for two summers in a row, when she was ten and then eleven, and Effie had tried her damndest at that young age to convince everyone to call her by the shortened name.

"My goodness, some things never change—you look almost exactly the same as you did in high school. I always envy people who can gain a little weight and still look good. I see you still like your hair so long. Well, I suppose it looks better on some people rather than others, especially those with a certain heritage. Oh, I just talked to your dear mother last week, and she never mentioned anything about you coming for a visit. Was this last minute? I'm sure it must have been, or the news would be all over town by now." Audrey finally paused long enough to refill her lungs.

Effie gave Audrey a friendly grin in return, because, really, even though she badly wanted to reply to the little insults, what else could she do? "Oh, you know Mom—always likes to keep the good stuff to herself." Then, feeling particularly magnanimous, she added, "But, yes, it was kind of last minute. I'm actually going to be staying at Mom and Dad's for a while."

Audrey's ears perked up with this news. "Oh, really? Are you still living in Denver?" Effie noticed then that Audrey wasn't shopping—she was stocking. Wow, things must be tough all over if Audrey Johnson was working in the grocery store. Perhaps Effie wasn't the only one in financial straits.

Effie said noncommittally, "Not really. I'm experiencing some change," and wanting the questions to stop, she turned to go the produce aisle.

"How is that handsome husband of yours, by the way? My goodness, he is good looking, isn't he? Your mom does love to flash his photo around town. I guess I would, too, if my daughters had married someone who looked like that." Drawing in a deep breath, Effie was forming a response in her head, when Hamilton unexpectedly strutted to the front of the store, and Effie grabbed her brother as a lifeline.

"Hamilton, I have been looking for you—remember we told Mom that we would make dinner? Leave it to you to slink off and get your beer first," Effie said snidely, noting the six-pack in his hands. Typical Hamilton: going to the grocery store for the only item *he* needed: never mind that he would devour the dinner she was planning on preparing tonight. Grabbing his arm and steering him to the produce section then, he tried in vain to pull away from her grip.

"Okay, what the hell, Effie? What's your deal? You don't even have a cart," Hamilton complained.

"My deal is that Audrey Johnson was asking too many questions concerning things I don't want to talk about," replied Effie, as she picked some red and yellow peppers, a huge head of garlic, a yellow onion, and two bags of Caesar salad mix, tossing them into the hand basket she just picked up. "And what are you doing here? If you were coming to the grocery store, you could have asked if anyone needed anything, you know."

"Since when do I need to check in with anyone?" Hamilton furiously typed on his phone while following her around to the next aisle. "Just because I'm living with Mom and Dad doesn't mean I have to be at someone's beck and call." He put his phone back in his pocket as it dinged with an incoming message, which he looked at and then ignored. "You never did say what brought you back here—what's going on with you?"

Looking pointedly at her brother, she said, "I would rather not talk about it. Why don't we discuss why *you* are living back home again, or who you were texting just now?" Seeing his jaw tense, she knew she had made her point. "No, huh? Why don't we just stick to buying groceries," and she flashed their mom's credit card at him, and they proceeded down the aisle, making sure to get more of the ingredients she needed to make her famous Cajun pasta.

Shopping was really the mindless activity she needed right now, and making dinner gave her something to look forward to. Since she had arrived at her mom's house several days ago, she had refused to leave the property. Torn between shame and anger, with a side of hopelessness tossed in for fun, she had managed to dodge her mother's inquiries into her life. Diadema had never been this interested in her life before this, not wanting to get her hands dirty, but Effie supposed that with both of her children back at home, grilling Effie for answers was probably easier for her mother than asking herself why her golden child, her perfect son, heir to the throne, never seemed to truly leave the nest yet, at the ripe age of twenty-six.

"Hey," she said to Golden Boy, "can you take this basket up and start checking out? I just need to grab one more thing," and she forced the basket into his hands, and watched as he lazily sauntered the length of the aisle to the front. Only then did she turn around and go back to the manager's office. She had known Boyd Timmons since she was a child, even though he was a few years older than her—he'd been the hottest lifeguard at the city pool when she was in middle school, and every female from twelve to sixty had a crush on him. Shortly after graduating high school, he had begun working full time in his family's store and had never left Clover Lake.

Knocking on the door that read "Manager", she hesitantly opened it after hearing a voice calling, "Come in." Stepping in through the doorway, she smiled as she saw Boyd, who had retained most of his hair into adulthood, but none of the good looks that had made her swoon during puberty. However, he beamed when he saw her, and the smile transformed his face.

"As I live and breathe, is the famous Euphemie Van Holland standing before me? My god, you look even better now than you did twenty years ago."

"Oh, yeah, is that something you did? Check out freshman girls when you were a senior?" And then she smiled to let him know she was kidding. "And I just go by 'Effie' now, please. How have you been, Boyd?"

He got up from his desk and walked around to perch on the front of it. "I guess you heard that your stepdad tried to buy the building last year?"

Effie was startled to hear this bit of news, but her mom wasn't the sharing kind—at least not with her daughter. "No surprise, I guess. Burnie won't rest until he owns every single building in Clover Lake. Real titan of business, that guy."

Boyd threw his head back in a laugh. "Well, he tried and failed here. Thankfully, my dad turned him down. I guess if your goal is to conquer a village, set your sights low, right?"

"Yeah, it takes a lot of business prowess to take over a town the size of Clover Lake—population eight hundred and ninety-nine."

Boyd emphatically told her, "Hey—it's actually nine fifty as of the last census."

Effie put a hand to her chest and then bowed. "I stand corrected." Effie paused and looked around the room, hoping things wouldn't turn awkward now. "Actually, Boyd, I came to find you about that sign I saw in your entryway."

With a confused look on his face, Boyd asked, "I'm sorry—what sign?" And then a pop of recognition mixed with cautious optimism crossed his face. "You don't mean my 'Help Wanted' sign, do you?"

She nodded. "Exactly what I mean. Look, I'm in town for a while and I need to make some money. I'm not sure how permanent it will be, but I could really use the job." Did it sound like she was begging? Please don't let him think I'm begging, she thought. But she was desperate, no doubt.

Boyd looked slightly taken aback, but smiled at her, and then he paused. No Boyd, she thought, no pausing, just nodding and agreeing. Then, "But don't you have a fancy degree, Effie? Why would you want to run a register and stock canned goods if you have a degree?"

"Yes, I have a Master's Degree in Library Science, but it's not fancy—I'm just a librarian, Boyd. Picture all this," she said, pointing her fingers at herself, "but with my hair in a bun and me wearing a cardigan. Both of which I could totally rock while stocking canned goods and running a register."

Finally, she got the nodding she had been hoping for, along with a slightly leering look as he appraised her from head to toe; he followed it all by saying, "When can you start?"

Leaving Boyd's office on a high might be pushing it, but she was feeling moderately more optimistic about her life right now. This was good, she told herself. She could make some money and think about her next step. Hamilton was looking impatiently down the aisles for her, it seemed, and as she got closer to him, he gave her a look of exasperation.

"What took you so long? I've got places to be this afternoon," her brother chastised her.

Effie snorted at that. "Good one, Ham. How does someone with no job and no place of his own have such a demanding schedule?"

"I don't know, Effie—you tell me?" Hamilton glared at her, and added, "Not only that, but you didn't leave me Mom's credit card—you don't expect me to pay for all of this, do you?" With his parting shot, he handed her the grocery bags and said, "Peace out." Leaving her to carry them home, along with his six-pack of beer. First, she had to pay for everything, of course. Another one bites the dust.

"Little shit," she muttered. Her phone buzzed in her pocket, so she put the bags on the sidewalk to free her hands. Reaching into her jeans, she swiped to answer the phone.

"What the hell have you done, Effie?" A voice yelled at her on the other end.

CHAPTER
Nine

Josh

Tearing off his scrubs, Josh closed his eyes and desperately wished he could shed his own skin as easily. Just rip at it and become someone new, someone else, and then maybe begin his life over. Because right now, he had completely and utterly messed up the life he had. Becoming a doctor, a surgeon, had been his dream longer than anything else, and not only was it the only thing he had ever really been any good at, but this was also the only profession he could ever see himself doing. In college, when his fraternity brothers were out partying, Josh was studying. In med school, his friends had been hooking up and having mindless sex, but not Josh—he had attended advanced lectures, or pored over science journals. Medicine had been a beacon every time he had found himself aching for his mother. Not only did he possess true talent with his precision, but he was utterly dedicated to it. After last night, it seemed he had even forsaken his relationship for it.

Turning toward the swinging doors, he looked at Dr. Scanlon, the head of the surgical department, as she came through. "My office—five minutes." And then she was gone.

Entering the locker rooms, Josh collapsed on a bench, wanting nothing more than to go to sleep. He was just *so tired*. Perhaps Dr. Scanlon would give him a chance to explain about everything: about his failed wedding, his runaway fiancée, his former friend, and now being officially homeless. Oh, wait—he forgot to add his poorly timed seduction of his office mate. None of that mattered, though, and absolutely nothing could begin to excuse what had just taken place in the operating room.

He had performed surgeries before that were so complicated, his attending surgeon had to take over, but this surgery was first-year residency stuff—gall bladder removal. A procedure that Josh should have been able to do in his sleep. Evidently not, ironically, as he had miserably screwed up, despite feeling like he had been sleepwalking all day. He stood up and ran a hand through his hair. Nerves were getting the best of him now. He had never made a mistake. Never. Until today, when mistakes were all he seemed to be able to get right.

Reaching into his pocket, he grabbed a mint and popped it into his mouth in a desperate attempt to keep his nausea at bay. Sliding his phone out of his pocket now, he looked at the screen, searching for at least one person who was thinking of him today, and he came up wanting once more. Slowly he walked down the hall to Dr. Scanlon's office, which he knew from experience had an amazing view of Central Park, and one which could usually soothe him. Forcing himself to knock, he waited for her reply and then opened her door with trepidation.

"Come in, Dr. Livingston. Please have a seat," and she motioned to the only empty chair in front of her mahogany desk. The other chair held his attending surgeon, Dr. Gilmore, someone who Josh held in such high esteem that to be dressed down in front of him made him sick to his stomach.

Dr. Scanlon began, "What happened in the operating room today—"

Josh interjected, "I know I messed up. I made a monumental error, and I am extremely sorry. Please rest assured that it will absolutely never happen again."

Dr. Gilmore turned to Josh and said, "Dr. Livingston…Josh…you are one of the finest surgeons I have ever had the privilege of overseeing. Your professionalism has been impeccable, and your focus has never been in doubt."

Josh nodded and said, "Thank you, sir."

Dr. Gilmore held up a hand. "However, things have been different for the past two months. You have been distracted, and a few times even somewhat tardy. I let it go, because that was not the behavior I have come to expect from you, and also because I knew what happened with your wedding. I cannot, however, overlook what happened today: this should have been a basic, run-of-the-mill surgery and if I hadn't been there, the outcome could have been fatal. As it is, we will be lucky to avoid a lawsuit, but at least the patient survived."

Josh choked back his emotions—he knew he had made a grievous error, but possibly fatal? Never before had he gotten things so terribly wrong. He pleaded, "Tell me what I can do—how I can make things better?"

Dr. Gilmore appeared sympathetic. "It's not just my call to make anymore, Josh. Do you remember last month when I gave you your second warning?"

"You told me that was just a formality. I made one misdiagnosis!" He sputtered indignantly.

Shaking his head, Dr. Gilmore corrected him, "And the week before that, you made those sutures that became extremely infected and almost caused sepsis."

"To which I was told there were mitigating circumstances." Josh took a minute to tamp down his outrage. "I guess I'm not following what exactly is happening here. Am I getting a dressing down, or is this something more serious?" How dare they? Josh fumed again. After all of the hours he has put in, so many of which have been unofficially on his own time? How many lectures he has attended at other hospitals? The number of procedures he has observed and then been the first resident to attempt, and succeed at, on his own?

Dr. Scanlon finally spoke again. "At this time, we are advising you to take a leave of absence. For three months, at least, and then we will re-evaluate. This is not a punishment, but a time to reflect and get centered again." Looking directly into Josh's eyes, she said, "You are one of the brightest and most talented surgeons ever to be in our program. And you can be again. Right now, however, you need a break. It's nothing to be ashamed of, and it often happens in these high-pressure environments."

Josh felt his eyes start to water. "But I'm so close to being done with my residency. And then there's my fellowship—"

Dr. Scanlon broke him off. "I'm sorry, Dr. Livingston. We never intended to tell you this way, but you didn't get the fellowship."

"But I'm the only one who —" and suddenly it dawned on Josh what should have been crystal clear from the beginning. All of her knowledge about the application process, her "helping" him with his paperwork. God, he was even blinder than he had previously surmised. "Lana applied, too. Am I right?" At their nods, he continued, "But she's years behind me—I don't understand."

"As you know," Dr. Scanlon began, "there's no timeline set in stone for finishing a residency, and the fact *is* that Dr. Miller is on the fast track. Her fellowship application was a surprise to all of us, and I'm not sure she was completely serious when she submitted it. Once we took everything into consideration, though, we had no doubt about offering it to her."

Dr. Gilmore added, "Please be assured that the decision was made before I issued you that warning last month."

"Last month? So Lana has known the truth about the fellowship since then?" It couldn't be, though. She would never have shared an office with him for four weeks, and not said anything, as day after day he spoke about how much getting the fellowship would mean to him.

"We asked her to not say anything until we spoke with you," explained Dr. Scanlon.

Feeling utterly defeated, Josh asked, "So what happens now? I finish out the week, or the month, or what?"

Clearing his throat, Dr. Gilmore said, "Your leave starts now. All of your surgeries have already been, or are in the process of being, reassigned. Please make sure all of your personal information is up to date in your personnel file, so we can be in touch in the future. After your leave, you will be free to come back here to finish up your residency, or you can be transferred to any other accepting hospitals, if that is what you wish."

Dr. Scanlon nodded, adding, "It is our hope that when you have finished your leave, that you will continue on here."

Josh stood up as both of the other doctors did, and he shook their hands as a sign of respect to them, and a last-ditch effort to not look like an utter failure. His mistakes weren't their faults, and the least he could do was walk out of the office with his head held high, holding on to whatever dignity remained for him. Despondently he walked to his office, and upon opening the door, he found Lana gone, leaving it empty, for which he was extremely grateful, for the first time today. He took the muffin that still sat by his computer and threw it in the trash. No wonder Tessa left him. She had probably seen this coming for years—the dressing down he direly needed. And Lana's secret stung, too—how could she not have told him that she had also applied? He wouldn't have held it against her: she was a brilliant surgeon, as well. But today, after hearing about his multiple rejections and betrayals, for her to share this space with him and act like his friend, as if nothing else was going on? Josh collapsed on the desktop, having no energy to take his grief outside, in the dark, where it belonged. What was one more humiliation if someone discovered him sobbing in his office?

CHAPTER
Ten

Effie

Effie shrugged off her work smock as soon as she entered her parents' house. She had been working full time at Fresh Mart Grocery for a little over a month now and had surprised herself at how much she enjoyed it. She had the opportunity to connect with people she hadn't seen, really, since she was about twenty years old. When Effie had gone to college, she had chosen a state school in the western part of South Dakota, not wanting to stay too close to home and still be surrounded by all of her classmates at colleges whose locations were nearer to her hometown. She had longed for a change, and fortunately, she hadn't needed to go out of state. South Dakota could seem like two different states at times: the Missouri River split the state almost exactly in half.

East River (as it was affectionately known by Dakotans) was much wetter, with more lakes and rivers, and it was fairly flat, although there were nice rolling hills, especially around Clover Lake. Dotting the landscape were farms, many of which still held neglected and unused farmhouses and barns, chicken coops and outhouses. On the gravel roads found out in the countryside, rusting, decades-old farm equipment often stood in the backyards, telling tales of having worked the land, sowing crops and harvesting them either in late summer or early fall. Plenty of farms were still actively in use, and more than once, a driver would need to pass a tractor traveling on the highways in the area.

West River was drier, with the Black Hills rising up as soon as you got to Rapid City, pine trees making up the majority of the national forest and providing a scent that perfumed the air perfectly. As often as she could, Effie would drive through the Badlands, the closest thing to a moonscape she could imagine. Ranching was more common out west, cattle, sheep, and even buffalo, but there was the timber industry and even active gold mining. During college, she had waitressing jobs up in Deadwood, walking the same wooden floors (littered with peanut shells) that Seth Bullock, Calamity Jane, and Wild Bill Hickok had over a century ago. Reservations like the one her father's family came from were scattered over the state, sometimes in places that her mother's family would have never wanted to settle.

Although she had come home for the first two summers of her college years, once she was entering her third year, Effie had gotten an apartment with two friends and made Spearfish her home. During her freshman year, she had gotten a job at the university's library, falling in love with the order and steadiness of the work there. Students and faculty streamed in with all sorts of interesting questions and requests, and to her, helping them find exactly what was needed was exhilarating. After graduating with a degree in English, she had then followed her studies to Colorado and enrolled in grad school there to earn her master's so she could be a librarian. Effie had been grateful to her parents for paying for her bachelor's education, but wanted to pay her own way for her master's degree, so she had worked as a bartender at night and cleaned hotel rooms during the morning and early afternoons for two years prior to her enrollment for her advanced degree. Once she was in school again, she had only kept the bartending gig, because the tips were insane—drinkers love a female bartender, it turned out.

And then Damon had walked in. Hair the color of ripened wheat and eyes the color of the sky—damn, he was sexy. She had been in her last year of her master's program, and he had been the tour manager of the group playing at her bar that night. She never could remember the name of the band—they'd been terrible, only playing cover songs from hair metal bands of the '80s, and he hadn't been their tour manager for that long. Longevity not being Damon's forte, he had gotten a new band to manage shortly after they met. And then a new band the following year. Wash. Rinse. Repeat.

Thinking about Damon, she recalled the furious phone call she had received from him last month. "What the hell have you done, Effie?" he had yelled at her over the phone.

What the hell had she done? She had left him. After years of never being quite sure what Damon was up to when he was on the road with whatever band he was promoting, after years of him denying any wrong-doing whatsoever, claiming that taking suggestive photos with various women was part of the job, she had had enough. Enough of burying her head in the sand, enough of being lied to, enough of feeling like *she* was never quite enough. Every accusation of hers came with a fresh denial from him, and he was clever and cunning. He had a way of turning every-thing around and making it her fault, so she would be the one to apologize. During her last accusation of infidelity, he had packed a bag and said he was leaving her this time, until she had dissolved into hysterics, begging him to not leave her. He had held her at bay with the promise of starting a family "When this tour is done, Babe, we will have a baby then". Knowing she had so desperately held on to him made her self-loathing even keener.

What the hell had she done? She had closed out their joint bank ac-count, leaving Damon one dollar to enjoy his new life, after finding the hidden credit card bills he had procured in secret, putting both of their names on them. That was six months ago, and she had crumpled with astonishment. Being unfaithful was one thing, she told herself. Damaging any future she had, any chance she had of rebuilding her life after Hurri-cane Damon, that was a step too far. She had worked so hard to be debt-free after grad school; she had been one of the lucky ones to have no school loans from earning her bachelor's degree. "Just get your parents to pay for them," was his response.

What the hell had she done? Filed divorce papers before she left Den-ver, ensuring she would never have to deal with him again. She had packed up her things in her car, not minding that packing light then meant she would have to start over with almost nothing—it would be worth it. And then she had turned over the keys to the friends of hers who would sublet the fully furnished apartment until the lease was up in two more months. Damon had sold her out, and she was laying his shit bare, to quote Adele. "Just keep the lease in your name, Babe, since I'm gone for weeks at a time," he had encouraged her to do after he had moved in with her, and so she had.

"What the hell have *I* done? Why don't we start with what the hell *you* have done?" she countered angrily to him on the phone a month ago. "Or maybe I should put it this way—what *haven't* you done?"

He sputtered, "I want my shit back now! Those fucking friends of yours won't let me into our apartment."

"I'm pretty sure you mean *my* apartment, don't you? After all, your name isn't on the lease. And this is where it gets sticky—since the apartment was rented before we were married, and I never changed my last name, you don't really have any rights. You were okay sticking me with the bills for everything else, but now when it suits you, you want ownership over your shitty concert tees and sleazy leather pants?"

"I will take you to court over this!" He declared, his voice sounding unhinged.

"Try it, Damon, and you will find yourself on the hook for those credit card bills you racked up in my name. Oh, and I know you have been jobless for the better part of the year, so why don't you just come clean, for once in your life, about where you have been going every time 'the band' has been 'on tour'?" Sure, he couldn't see her do it, but putting air quotes around his bullshit phrases gave her a modicum of satisfaction.

"I meant to tell you—I wanted to explain, but you don't know how hard it is for me. Having to compare everything I can give to what your family can. Do you know how inadequate your dad makes me feel whenever they visit? No one is good enough for his stepdaughter. Like just because I didn't go to college means I am garbage, or what about all his digs at me for being from California? They make me feel like I'm worthless."

"Give me a break, Damon—you were almost never around when my parents visited, and only once did you come back with me to Clover Lake. None of this explains what you were spending all of my money on." And then he was silent, as she knew he would be. One thing about Damon, he knew when to shut up. "You see, being a librarian means I am pretty good at looking things up. And I followed all of those credit card statements back to California. Back to a certain woman living in La Jolla. Funny thing—airplane tickets correspond with all of the times you were supposed to have been on tour with the band for the last year. No hotels, though, so at least we saved money on that, huh?"

"I tried telling you how unhappy I was—how unfulfilled. But you never listened. You just kept at me about wanting to have a baby, wanting to start a family. What about what I wanted?" Damon protested.

"And I have never been more grateful in my life to be denied something. God, the thought of being tied to you now, knowing what a spineless, lying—" Effie took a deep breath, not wanting to demean herself anymore by engaging her ex. Wanting to sever all communication with him at this moment, she told him, "I will call Kristy and ask her to work with you to retrieve your stuff. It's all boxed up, anyway, so she can just put it on the landing. But from this moment, I don't want you to call me. Ever."

And she had heard only silence from him since. What she hadn't admitted to him was that she had also learned another truth—the woman she knew about in California, who she had found on Facebook, also seemed to have had a baby in the time Damon had been catting around there. She shuddered, knowing how close she had come to being tied to him long term.

CHAPTER
Eleven

Josh

Who knew Tessa moving them out of their apartment would be so helpful, especially to him? Thought Josh sarcastically. Last month when *she* had shattered his life (part one) and had his belongings moved into storage, he had at first been furious at her presumptuousness, but when he was officially put on his leave of absence due to his *career* shattering his life (part two), having everything taken care of had made it that much simpler to leave New York City, the place that he had grown to love over the past sixteen years, since first arriving there for college. He had no car, having given it up when he moved to the Big Apple, so he had gotten a one-way airplane ticket back to South Dakota, packed his two suitcases at Cal's and taken a flight out the next day after his meeting at the hospital—no sense in putting off the inevitable, he told himself. If he were truly going to get his head together, the last place he needed to be was in the place everything had gone so wrong for him. His most difficult task was calling his dad, who at first had been thrilled when Josh had told him he was coming home, thinking it was for a short visit, but Josh couldn't stop the tears from clogging his throat, and in bits and pieces he had told his father everything: from Tessa and Fitz, to Lana and the hospital. When his dad realized that Josh would be home for a much longer stay, his voice became tinged with pity, and that emotion from the most stoic person Josh knew was almost his undoing.

Henry Livingston was the most quietly empathetic person Josh had ever known, and it killed him to have to disappoint his dad in any way. All Henry had ever wanted was for Josh to be content: "Do whatever makes you happy, son" Henry would tell Josh. His dad had always been the one there for him: at his eighth-grade graduation, when his classmates had two parents beside them for pictures; at his senior prom, pinning on his boutonnière in preparation for the big nights, a job normally done by the mother of the teenager; and then at his high school graduation when Josh had been valedictorian—two parents could not have made as much noise as his lone, single father. Although Josh had been blessed to also have aunts and uncles, and grandparents supporting him, too, nothing could take away the yearning for his mother at certain times, yet his dad had ensured that Josh would always know he was loved.

On the dreadful day of the wedding rehearsal, when Tessa had walked out on him, one of the hardest things was having to see the confused look in his father's eyes, who had been completely dumbfounded that she would be walking away from his son. All Henry had ever heard from Josh was how happy they were together, how perfectly they complemented each other, and since Henry had been a witness to their timeline of love, he could not argue with Josh's assurances. But his dad also knew how deeply love could hurt, had been on the unfortunate receiving end of being badly burned by love, so Tessa leaving Josh at the altar had come as less of a shock to Henry than to his son.

Josh's career interruption, however, had been a devastating blow to both father and son. Henry was a mechanic, and he prided himself that Josh had inherited from him his ability to diagnose the problem and the precision to then fix the problem. "Just come home, son," he had said to Josh on the phone that day when he had called him; his dad took the day off from working at his auto shop to pick him up at the Sioux Falls airport. Josh had been a river of emotion since his near-fatal mistake with his surgery, unable to forgive himself for almost being responsible for mortally wounding a patient, so he had cried on the shoulders of his father, his idol, and Henry had done his best to comfort him.

Now he had been back for a month at the home his dad had owned since Josh was sixteen, back in Beverley, and he and his dad had taken to sipping iced tea on the wraparound porch in the evenings, after his dad finished with work. The weather was finally feeling more spring-like, and they watched the younger kids ride around on their bikes, and teenagers learning to rollerblade or skateboard.

As he shook the ice cubes around in his now-empty glass, Henry said, "I was thinking, Josh, about this car I'm having a situation with. The owner keeps bringing it in for a diagnostic, but every time she comes back with it, I can't find anything wrong with it. I run all these tests on the computer, I get nothing. Of course, in typical car fashion—"

"It doesn't happen when the car is actually there?" Josh finished for his dad.

Henry chuckled, "Too many years of me talking about cars, huh? Anyway, I could use an extra pair of hands down at the shop. You've been here for a month now, and as far as I can tell, you must be all caught up on *The Young and the Restless*—why don't you come down tomorrow? After *Judge Judy*, of course."

Josh pretended to be defensive. "Hey—you know it's *Hot Bench*, if we're talking about going to the shop in the morning!" Josh then let out a burst of laughter, as he had been doing a bit more since being back home. After some consideration, Josh heartily agreed, "What the hell? I always did love to diagnose a car issue. Sure, I'd love to help out." Then he glanced down at his watch and saw that the timer for their dinner was going to go off in two minutes. "I'll be right back, Dad. I need to take the spaghetti pie out of the oven and let it rest for fifteen minutes. Do you want more tea?"

"Nah, I'm good until supper," his dad declined. "Spaghetti pie, huh? When did you learn to cook? We've been eating like kings since you've been back!" After his mom had deserted them, he and his dad had struggled with the culinary arts, and mealtimes had been very basic boxed/canned/frozen types of meals, and when he and Tessa were together, she had done all of their cooking; since Josh had been back home, however, he had cracked open Betty Crocker and Better Homes and Gardens cookbooks for recipe ideas, and even taken to searching for ideas online. Spaghetti pie, however, was a dish his grandmother had taught his mom how to make, and he had found the recipe card stuffed into an overloaded recipe box in the bottom of a kitchen cabinet.

Josh sighed as he opened the screen door, feeling thankful the temperature had been above average for March in South Dakota, with highs in the fifties. He heard his phone ping, and when he pulled it out of his pocket, he saw he had a new message. Opening his email, he saw it was from Lana. He hadn't spoken to her since before he had completely unraveled at the hospital that day, having at least been spared from her witnessing his final humiliation. She had tried to call him more than once, and had left a couple of voicemails, but Josh had not picked up any of her calls or returned them. Not out of anger, but shame. His own behavior, and his shortcomings overall, mortified him that day. He could not fault Lana with applying for the fellowship—she lived for her career as much as he did, and was a brilliant surgeon, perhaps even better than he was. What he did fault her for was not being honest with him, he mused, and took a seat in the recliner to read her message.

"Dear Josh," the email read,

"I have tried to reach you so many times by phone, but I understand why you never pick up. I can never apologize enough for what you must see as a betrayal. The fact that I got the fellowship must have been such a shock to you, especially since I never told you that I had even submitted an application. The truth is, I only did it as "practice" because in two years I had planned on applying for it seriously. You had said such great things in your application, and all I was looking for was feedback from the committee on mine. Therefore, needless to say, I was floored when they contacted me saying that I had gotten it. From that first moment, I felt guilty. It was all you had talked about since last year. You even gave up your honeymoon to show how dedicated you were, and I ruined it for you. If you never speak to me again, I understand, but I want you to know that I believe you to be the single best, most determined, truly talented surgeon. Your professionalism has never been in question for me, and I have been honored to work by your side these past two years. You have taught me so much in that time—from simple procedures to understanding the complexities of more involved ones. And all of the knowledge you have gleaned, on your own, from science journals I never subscribed to, and lectures, that I, for personal reasons, could not attend, but that you generously shared with me. I am truly grateful for it all. I want you to know that I did not keep my receiving the fellowship a secret from you out of spite or fear, but because the committee told me to do so. I did not even tell my own family about it and had to sign a non-disclosure form upon receipt of it. I had no idea they would take so long to announce it, though, and for that I also apologize.

On a more personal level, I want you to know that on any other day, that kiss in your office would not only have been welcomed, but also heartily reciprocated. I have had feelings for you since I opened the door to the office we share and saw you reading one of your journals. I hid what I felt for you out of respect for your relationship, but I am in love with you, Josh, and when the time is right, whether it is when you are back at work or before, I would love to start over again on a personal level, if that is something you would be interested in.

Please keep in touch and let me know how you are, regardless of how you feel about me personally. I wish you all the best and hope that you are using this leave of absence to find peace within yourself. You deserve it.

All My Best,

Lana".

CHAPTER
Twelve

Effie

“Mom, I just don’t understand why you can’t take your car to a mechanic here in Clover Lake. Wouldn’t it be decidedly simpler than driving forty miles over to Beverley? I mean, isn’t the whole purpose of keeping your car maintained so it lasts longer? And doesn’t *driving it* wear it down? Therefore, taking it to one of the mechanics here seems to make more sense,” and then upon seeing the look of consternation on her mother’s face, Effie muttered to herself, “to me anyway.”

Diadema smiled at her daughter, knowing that since Effie hadn’t outright refused to do her the favor of helping her with her car meant that she would, indeed, drive her car over to the “big city” of Beverley. “Sweetie, you know Burnside only wants the best, and he considers the best to be this particular auto shop in Beverley. Besides, you said just this morning how you wanted to do something fun on your day off. Since the auto shop is on Main Street, you can take the car in, go have lunch downtown somewhere, maybe do a little shopping. Oh, you should check out the city library—they renovated it about four years ago and it is absolutely stunning now." Man, her mom was really working all the angles in order to avoid taking her own car to the auto shop in Beverley—the question was *why?*

Effie and her mom had been getting along surprisingly well for the past month: the two had developed a routine of having breakfast together in the sunroom on the days that Effie did not have to work an early shift at the grocery store. Rising much earlier than either woman, Burnside was usually in his office already by the time Diadema came downstairs for the day. She would brew a large pot of flavored coffee (Diadema favored the Southern toasted pecan flavor, but Effie had a soft spot for the dark chocolate mocha blend), and then Effie would make some omelets with mushrooms, spinach and Swiss cheese for her and her mom, and the two would watch the morning show, or scroll through their Facebook accounts. Effie loved to indulge her mom, often sharing information she obtained from working the register at the store: it was surprising how much you could learn from a customer while scanning a can of green beans, and Effie was all caught up on the town's gossip since her first day.

The newly found tranquility between mother and daughter made Effie consider that perhaps she had been selling her mom short all these years. She had always considered Diadema to be fairly shallow, and maybe even weak, especially after she was old enough to understand just how racist her grandparents were. Diadema would often excuse the words of her parents by pointing out their age and the attitude of the times they had grown up in, but she had never bought that crap. More than once, Effie had come to the defense of her mom, who never seemed to stand up to her parents, and just took whatever abuse they would fling her way. She studied her mom now and decided to take the plunge.

"Mom," Effie began as she poured them each a cup of coffee, "can I ask you something maybe a bit personal?" At her mother's distracted nod, she continued, "Were you aware of how Grandma and Grandpa felt about my dad when he was alive? I mean, it just seemed like if you knew how they had felt, how did you take the risk and love him anyway?" Effie could never reconcile the person who had, seemingly, rebelled against her parents by loving Nathaniel LeBeau, when after his death, she had gone straight to what had been expected of her all along—Burnside Van Holland.

At this question, Diadema did not get the look on her face that Effie feared she would, which had been one of annoyance or shame. No, instead, her mom had a look of wistfulness with a dash of longing come over her freckled features. "Oh, Euphemie, when I met your father in that university movie theatre all those years ago, I knew he was the one." Placing her phone beside her breakfast plate, her mom said, "Did I ever tell you that we were both there separately, each of us was waiting for our friends?" Effie shook her head, stunned that her mom was opening up to her about her dad. Diadema continued, "I was waiting for my girlfriends to finish up in the restroom, and he was waiting for his friends to even arrive. Well, he had just gotten one of those huge buckets of popcorn, and I tripped over my sandal—it had gotten caught on the rug by the snack bar. Anyway, I tripped and flew right into him." Her mom laughed, the sound filled with such joy that Effie got tears in her eyes. "Popcorn went all over—I was still picking it out of my hair the next day! I was sure he was going to be furious, but I looked up into the most breathtaking, kind face I had ever seen. His eyes were so like yours are—that golden brown color. The color of a fawn, he said, when you were born. We started talking, then, and he was more concerned over my trip than he was about his spilled popcorn. The manager of the snack bar had seen what happened and assumed we were on a date, so offered to refill the bucket. Then your father turned to me and asked me if I wanted to go across the street instead, because the theatre was right across the street from the city park. I looked into those eyes, into his face that was so earnest and serious, and knew this man would never let me down. We walked across the street without telling any of our friends, and it was the beginning of everything." Diadema drew in a deep breath. With tears in her eyes, she continued, "Six months later we were married, and everyone told us it would never last—we were too young, too different…we needed to finish college. But I knew Nathaniel was the smartest man I had ever met; more than that was his sincerity, and his love of life. Even though he had grown up around poverty, and had seen some pretty dismal conditions, he always saw the beauty in the world, and because he did, so did I. For those reasons, when my parents said anything against him, all it did was remind me of how much I loved him and how complete he made me. They thought I was rebelling against their ways, but in the end, all I was doing was choosing love. I'd like to think they both realized that in the years before they passed—recognized how wrong they were." Diadema paused to take a sip of coffee. "The thing is, you can't change anyone else's mind unless they are open to change."

Effie had never heard her mom speak so openly about her love for her dad. "Is that why you never talked about him when I was growing up? It hurt too much?" She knew her parents had been deeply devoted and in love, but after her dad died, Diadema had been so consumed by her own grief that was all she saw. Effie would hang on every crumb her mom fed her about her dad, afraid that asking for more would silence her mom completely.

"Partly. I missed him profoundly, and it burned to even think of him, and then losing our baby on the same night? Unbearable—then I sunk into depression and went to Ohio to 'get better' according to my parents. I did, I suppose, but I was also filled with an enormous amount of guilt for having left you with them." Her mom reached across the breakfast table and took Effie's hand in hers, and she looked at her daughter's hand, with her close-cut nails polished a bright blue. "I've always been so consumed with how much you look like your dad; I never realized how much your hands are like mine." She reached out and tucked a strand of hair behind Effie's ear, and said, "My beautiful daughter. No amount of remorse can make up for failing you back then. I never should have left you with them—I never should have left, period, but I didn't know what else to do. I had to get help, and my father's cousin had done some in-patient therapy at a hospital there, after she had suffered from postpartum depression. Meeting Burnside in Ohio was such a blessing, but I can acknowledge now that maybe it was too soon. I know he can come across as stuffy or pompous, even, but he has such tenderness and patience. On the outside, he was the complete opposite of Nathaniel, because he came from wealth, but inside, he tremendously reminded me of him. Neither man was anything like my father, who was always too quick to anger, so kindness was important to me. I did feel at first like I was betraying your father by falling in love again, but Burnie helped me to heal."

Effie reached out to her mom and pulled her close, tighter than she had held her in at least a decade and let all of the frustration and despair out that she had been holding in: the ending of her shitty marriage, quitting her beloved job at the library back in Denver, missing the father she hadn't been old enough to make any memories with. As the tears flowed, the more she kept holding on to her mom. Now, more than ever, Effie knew she was finally at home.

"Now," said her mom as she pulled back to look in Effie's face, "when are you going to get these split-ends taken care of?" And brushed her hands through Effie's hair.

CHAPTER
Thirteen

Josh

Josh wiped his brow with a rag he had taken to carrying in his back pocket, much as he had grown up watching his dad do. The past several weeks that he had spent helping his dad at Check Care Auto had been as fulfilling as they were therapeutic. Working side by side with his dad, diagnosing and then fixing car problems as his dad had done with his grandfather, brought to Josh a sense of peace he had been missing for so long.

Josh took a deep sniff of the air, and recognized the special coffee blend that Henry ordered on the internet. "I hope you brought some real sugar to the shop, and not that artificial sweetener," he teased his dad. Josh had been heavy as a child, always being reassured that he would grow up and out of it, and he had, eventually, in college. However, the time he had been overweight had left an indelible mark on him, and he had adopted a healthier lifestyle that, admittedly, he had occasionally taken to extremes. He was striving to be a better person on the inside these days, and his dad had given him endless hell when Josh had come back home about the artificial sweetener.

"Son, I'm no doctor, but even I know that stuff is full of chemicals." His dad had taken to using the phrase "I'm no doctor" whenever he wanted to make a point to Josh about anything, regardless of whether it was medically related or not.

Thinking about the sweetener made him think of Tessa, or "Tess" as he was trying to re-teach himself to call her. His attitude toward her last year leading up to the wedding had been abhorrent, he reluctantly admitted now in retrospect, and he was sure it had more than likely aided in the demise of their relationship. He also could see how Sam (not Fitz) could be exceedingly better for her than he, Josh, ever was. She had been correct the night when she had broken it off with him, telling him they had been what each needed as teenagers, but not as adults. Years ago, when he had graduated from college, Josh had actually broken up with her, probably sensing the truth of their relationship: that they both needed to grow. It had been too easy, upon seeing her four years after their break-up, though, to get back together. As much as Josh loved a puzzle to solve, he also craved familiarity, which undoubtedly stemmed from the abandonment of his mother.

Looking up to the garage doors, Josh saw a vintage Ford Mustang pull up to the shop, and a woman stepped out of the car, leading with the longest pair of legs Josh had seen in a lifetime, encased in tights and leather boots that went over her knees. The bit of thigh he glimpsed between the boots and her mini-skirt made his mouth water. With a pair of large-framed sunglasses adorning her face, her features were hidden, but her glossy midnight-dark hair hung straight over her shoulders and down her back, and his fingers itched to touch the strands and see if it was as soft as it looked. Josh exited the shop through the large bay doors and squinted at the sun that nearly blinded him—he could use a pair of those sunglasses, he mused silently.

Josh smiled at the customer, greeting her, "Good morning, Ma'am. How can I help you today?"

The woman put a hand to her chest and laughed, "Good lord— 'ma'am'? Really? My mom has been suggesting to me for the past two months that I need a makeover, but I thought that was just her way of expressing her version of love." Josh joined her with a robust laugh, and he saw the dimple her chin made when she smiled. His day was getting better by the second, he thought to himself.

He bowed. "Please accept my sincere apologies. I never know what form of address is correct: ma'am, miss, m'lady?" Much to Josh's chagrin, his dad refused to do vehicle intakes or check-ins on the computer: he only added in the details when finally doing the diagnostics, or, in simple cases, when a customer was picking up their car. Looking down at the clipboard he held in his hands, the preferred method his dad used for any vehicle appointments or intake, Josh was overcome with a lightheartedness he had not experienced in years—was he merely joking around with this customer, or was it something else entirely? To his disbelief, it reminded him of...*flirting*? Scanning the list for today, Josh confirmed, "Van Holland Mustang?"

His mystery woman nodded her head and then turned to look back at the car as a younger man popped out of the passenger side. The two couldn't appear more different, as the man was so fair-haired, compared to the shiny raven-black hair of the woman in front of him, so Josh wondered what their relationship was. The man walked toward Josh, sticking out his hand, and introduced himself. "Hamilton Van Holland—this is my mother's car."

Josh shook his head, amazed at how young the woman appeared, and wondered what she had hidden behind those sunglasses. "Wow—I apologize, Mrs. Van Holland. I should have been expecting you and the Mustang—" but a boisterous outburst of laughter cut him off.

Then his mystery woman, who he guessed wasn't really a mystery anymore, lifted her sunglasses to wipe the tears of laughter from her eyes. "Oh, my god—first I'm a ma'am and now I'm my mother? Could someone please kill me now and get it over with?" She then opened her eyes and looked at Josh, and the most mesmerizing pair of eyes he'd ever seen struck him: tawny-colored; they weren't brown, but they weren't hazel or gold, either. Josh felt something like a flicker of remembrance, looking at her; then it was gone. "No, I am not this fella's mother, thank god. He'd be in for a rude awakening if that were the case. He has, however, driven me completely nuts on the ride over, so if you have an area where I could put him for timeout, that would be much appreciated," and then she winked at

Josh. When was the last time any woman had winked at him, never mind a woman who he was feeling such a magnetic connection with?

"Hey, Sis, are we good here? I need to get some caffeine," Hamilton pointed to a coffee shop located diagonally across the street. Without waiting for her reply, he then ambled to the end of the block, stopping to talk to a long-haired blonde who had just come out of Threadz, the neighboring clothing boutique.

Josh brought his gaze back to his mystery woman, thankful that he had just happened to be here when she had brought the car in. "So we have two cars in the bays now, and I see that Mr. Van Holland scheduled an appointment for eleven this morning," Josh brought his arm up to check his watch, "which is in twenty minutes. We should be finished with one of those cars by then and ready to start on yours."

Mystery woman nodded and said, "Okay, that sounds great. I am going to take a walk around, if that's cool? I haven't been to Beverley in years."

"Me neither, until a couple of months ago. Are you from around here?" he asked casually. Or he hoped that's how it sounded, and not weird or stalker-like.

She shook her head, "No, I'm not. Or I guess I was. I actually grew up in—"

A booming voice interrupted them, "Josh, can you grab that phone? It's been ringing off the hook and I can't get to it." Suddenly he became attuned to the shrill sound coming from his dad's office.

"Sure, Dad," and Josh threw the woman an apologetic smile and made a dash for the landline in the office located to the side of the garage bays. He had been trying to convince his dad to just switch his business phone to his cell phone, but his dad said that his long-standing customers preferred calling to a physical location rather than a cell phone. "I want people to be able to open up the phone book and know they're calling my actual business." Despite Josh's attempts to rationalize that any phone should be able to be used, and would not only be more convenient but also timesaving, he could not sway Henry. When Josh argued for keeping the shop's phone, but getting some cordless phones, his dad's response to that had been: you'll see.

After Josh's mom had performed her disappearing act, Henry had thrown himself into his job, often working on cars until late into the evening. Josh had gotten tired of spending every night alone in their empty house, so that's when he had begun to hang around the shop back in Clover Lake. Josh had never taken an interest in the family business before, but once he realized spending time with his dad and helping out at the shop help eased the sharp pang of abandonment, he learned everything he could. The shop in Clover Lake had been owned by his grandfather, and both Josh's dad, Henry, and Henry's brother, William, had worked there, until Henry found Clover Lake too stifling. Filled with an excess of reminders of his life before Melanie had left them, the town had become too small, so he then scouted out other neighboring towns, eventually going as far as Beverley, and felt that the buffer of forty miles from their memories would be beneficial to both father and son. Henry had bought the garage in Beverley, leaving his dad and brother to run the original Check Care Auto. Although his business had been new in town, it hadn't taken long before his auto shop was a success, due to the larger population of Beverley and Henry's fair pricing and honest assessments.

Josh finished taking down the information from the customer, whose call he had answered in the nick of time, right before the answering machine could pick up (yes, his dad still believed in an old school, "leave your message at the beep", answering machine). Hoping his mystery woman had not yet left to go explore Main Street, he jogged back to the front of the garage and then out the bay door. Looking around, he felt a sinking sensation when he didn't see her.

"You looking for the hot babe who just dropped off the Mustang?" asked Chuck, one of his father's first employees at the shop, who seemed to set out to prove daily that he was at least one generation behind in the crusade for women's rights, but who his dad also swore was an incomparable mechanic.

"I believe you just mean 'woman who dropped off the Mustang'? You really need to watch it, Chuck. I am sure that none of the women I know would be pleased to be referred to as a 'babe'." He sighed, and realized Chuck was waiting for him to confirm that yes, indeed, he had been looking for the mystery woman, which he reluctantly confirmed by saying, "I didn't get her contact information."

"Well, lucky for you, my young protégé, she told me to give this to you," and he handed Josh a slip of paper with a phone number written on it. "You're welcome," said Chuck, as he sauntered back to the garage bay.

78

CHAPTER
Fourteen

Effie

E ven though it was sunny, it was still the end of April in South Dakota, and Effie shivered in the thin jacket and short skirt she had mistakenly worn this morning. When had mechanics gotten so elegant? She wondered. Effie was not a woman easily stunned, yet the mechanic who had mistaken her for her own mother had accomplished just that. Because of her exotic looks (some would say in spite of, maybe) Effie had always been able to attract the attention of men; unfortunately, she also tended to get swept away very quickly, which led to her thinking with her heart and not her mind. Too often, she would convince herself she had met Mr. Right, only to find out eventually that she was wrong, yet again. Her longest relationship had been with Damon, but not because he differed from the rest of the men she had chosen previously. No, she had only ignored the signs she had seen and misgivings she had felt, convincing herself that he was **THE ONE.**

The mechanic, though, there was something about his demeanor, some fragility she could sense. Behind his sky-blue eyes, a heartbreak was lurking, but not one intended for her; no, it was one he had experienced, and pretty recently, she was guessing. Thinking of the attractive mechanic made a surge of attraction course through her veins, despite the case of mistaken identity.

Effie popped into Mr. Beans, the coffee shop, for a hot beverage, but having had her fill of coffee at breakfast, she decided quickly against that. Ooh, she thought as she perused the menu behind the counter: the hot cocoa sounded luscious: a blend of sweetened cocoa powder and melted chocolate, with warm milk, a splash of vanilla extract, then topped with whipped cream and chocolate sprinkles. Yes, please! Effie was finally the next person to order, and she ordered the Supreme Hot Cocoa, and in order to fully fuel her touring downtown Beverley, she also ordered a hot chicken salad sandwich on a croissant.

After informing her that someone would bring her food and drink out to her when it was ready, Sadie, the cashier, pointed to the near-empty dining room, suggesting she find a table. Effie scanned the room for her brother, but there was no sign of Hamilton. However, she saw a blonde woman sitting alone, with her back to the room, and she looked like the woman she had seen her brother talking to earlier. Effie crossed the room and said to the woman, "Excuse me, do you know —"

Instantly Effie knew she had made a mistake, as the woman turned to face Effie: this was not the same blonde she had seen her brother with earlier. No, this woman was around Effie's age, way too intelligent looking for Hamilton, not to mention she had been reaching for a baby wrapped up in a pink sleeper in the stroller tucked up against the window when Effie had approached her.

The woman smiled up at Effie. "Yes?"

Effie blushed, "Oh, I'm sorry—I thought you were someone I had seen my brother talking to earlier, so I was going to ask you if you knew where he went. He is completely unreliable and always has his phone on silent." Effie stopped and took a breath. "I'm sorry, TMI, right? Anyway, sorry for bothering you."

As she turned to look for a table where she could call her friend Kristi (nothing like the "waiting for my car" phone call, she thought, but it was far better than her previous call to her friend, the "put my shitty ex's crap out on the landing" call) the woman called out, "Wait." Effie pivoted on her heel and faced the woman again, who was still smiling at her. "Are you waiting for your order?" Effie nodded an affirmation, and the woman said, "You're welcome to sit with me."

"Are you sure? It's pretty empty in here; I don't think I'll have a problem finding somewhere else to sit," she laughed, and at that moment a dark-haired, multi-pierced young person, whose name tag read Colt, brought her order over on a small tray, placing it on the table across from the blonde woman.

"There," the woman said, "it's been decided. Sit, sit," she gestured with her one free hand, while the other lifted her shirt up so she could feed the baby fussily squirming in her arms. "My name is Ruth, by the way. And I am in desperate need of some adult company, so please don't make me beg!"

"Hi, Ruth—I'm Effie. Thanks for the invitation to join you—this place is really filling up now," Effie remarked surprisedly, as she watched at least ten people stream in from the street looking for their java hit.

"Yeah, it did yesterday this time, as well." Ruth took a sip of her drink, flinching as she hastily pulled back from the steaming liquid. "Damn—I always forget how hot my coffee is, despite having burned my tongue twice now," and she laughed.

Effie was charmed by Ruth and grinned at her. "Are you a regular here?" Effie smiled at Sadie, who was wiping off the table next to theirs.

Ruth shook her head, "No, actually, although I did go to school in Beverley, we lived in the country; I don't recall this coffee shop being here back in my teenage years. My husband and I are just in town for a few days." She tilted her head to the side and switched her baby around. "Maybe I should have said I don't come here often *yet*. Sean, my husband, is at an interview at the hospital. He's a pediatrician, and we are looking to relocate here, well he is; I would, obviously, be moving back. He got a tour of the hospital yesterday and today is meeting with all of the bigwigs."

"Oh, really? Wow—where are you moving from?" she asked, before taking a bite of her sandwich, which was filled with juicy chunks of chicken and crunchy almonds, all folded together with a blend of mayo, cream cheese, and sharp cheddar. Served warm on a flaky, buttery croissant, it was hitting all the spots Effie needed it to hit.

Ruth answered, "Philadelphia." Lifting up her cup, Ruth more carefully registered its temperature by taking a tiny sip this time. "MMM, much better. Vanilla latte with an extra shot of espresso always keeps mama happy, doesn't it, Eloisa," she cooed to the baby. Then she raised her emerald eyes to Effie's and said conspiratorially, "Don't tell my husband, though. I kind of promised him I would be caffeine-free while I am still nursing," and both women laughed.

"Your secret is safe with me. I love the name Eloisa: so classic and beautiful," Effie told her.

"Thanks," Ruth replied. "We named her after my grandma Bergen. Your name is interesting: Effie. Is that short for anything?"

Effie nodded, "Euphemie, actually. I've found that Effie suits me better, much to my mother's consternation."

Ruth's eyes grew large. "Wait—are you Euphemie Van Holland?" At her nod, Ruth continued, "I'm Ruth Lefferts. Well, I *was* Ruth Lefferts; now I'm Ruth Mills. You're from Clover Lake, right?"

At her nod, Ruth continued, "Sorry, my boyfriend in high school ran track, which meant I went to all of his meets, and I remember you. You were like lightning out there. I loved to watch you—you made it seem so effortless." Ruth looked appreciatively at Effie, saying, "I always wished I had legs like yours."

Effie laughed, "I can't believe you remembered me. A couple of months ago, when I first got back home, I spent an entire night reliving my glory days, and I could not remember half of the people I saw."

"Let me guess—you were going through your high school yearbooks?" Ruth gave a giggle. "I just did the same thing yesterday! My parents are downsizing and have ordered my sister and I to go through all of our precious girlhood memorabilia. At least once we move here, I can bring all of my stuff directly to our new place."

Effie groaned, "Ugh—moving is the worst. I'm kind of in-between places right now, too. I lived in Denver until a couple of months ago, and I kind of feel like I'm having maybe a mid-life crisis," she confided in Ruth. "My marriage ended, so I just blew up the rest of my life—figured why the hell not? Truthfully, I never really enjoyed living in Denver, it's just kind of where I ended up. Consequently, I quit my job, moved out of my apartment, and now I'm living with my parents and am working part-time at a grocery store over in Clover Lake."

Recognition flared in Ruth's green eyes. "Blowing up your life seems to be a hot trend these days. My sister blew up her life and called off her wedding the day of the rehearsal, but now she is deliriously happy with the man of her dreams, and they just got engaged." Ruth's eyes darkened as they got a bit misty, and she wiped them. "So, Effie, what kind of job did you quit in Denver?"

"I was a librarian for the Denver Public Library system—my dream job, really, since I have loved to read for as long as I can remember."

Ruth smiled, "Same here." Ruth then snapped her fingers, "Eloisa and I went to the library yesterday afternoon, and I think I saw a 'Librarian Wanted' sign on the front desk."

"Really?" Effie asked tentatively. "The thing is, I don't know where I go from here and wasn't necessarily planning on a permanent move back. I feel like I'm stuck, and I know that living with my parents isn't helping me move forward. Beverley is probably *just* far enough from Clover Lake, though, to give me some breathing room." Effie paused momentarily to sip her cocoa, and then admitted, "My marriage was a complete shit show, and I have just been spinning my wheels for so many years. It's hard to get back on track." Effie laughed disparagingly at herself. "If I'm honest, other than becoming a librarian, I have never really been ON track, I guess."

Ruth put a now-sleeping Eloisa back in her carriage and then gave Effie an earnest look. "I realize we have just met, but in my opinion, it wouldn't hurt to go and check out the job posting at the library, right? Besides, I'm moving back here in a few months, and I would love to already have a friend in town—I'm pretty self-absorbed like that. Even though I grew up here in Beverley, I haven't seriously reconnected with old classmates yet. You know how social media is—it keeps everyone in the loop, but only on the surface."

Effie agreed, and having finished her sandwich and beverage, stood up and took both of their mugs to the bin by the garbage. Suddenly she found herself grinning and saying, "What the hell? I've got nothing to lose." She looked at Ruth and asked, "Want to take a walk with me to the library?"

CHAPTER
Fifteen

Ruth

After depositing her new friend at the library, where, luck would have it, they had two librarian positions available, Ruth entered Effie's information into her own cell phone. Shaking her head at the way fate sometimes intervened, Ruth marveled at the chance meeting with Effie in the coffee shop. The instant she had turned to the voice speaking to her, Ruth had felt a sense of recognition, but had not been able to place her right away. It had been seventeen years, after all, since Ruth had been in high school, and people do tend to change over time; however, Euphemie Van Holland had remained as attractive as she was back then: perfectly straight, gleaming dark hair and sparkling tawny eyes. Ruth had always been awestruck watching her race in high school: Effie had more of a lean runner's body back then, and she had filled out very nicely in adulthood, Ruth thought, with a touch of envy. In fact, Effie's body had been one that Ruth, who had been plump growing up (and still was, pleasantly so, and growing more so every day), had envied, in the way all teenage girls were predisposed to doing. Effie had been taller than the average girl, with those sinfully long legs, and possessed the most gorgeous light brown skin that always seemed to be glowing. Ruth was sure her high school boyfriend, Chase Withers, had held a bit of a crush on Effie, who had only been known as Euphemie in high school. Though their schools of Clover Lake and Beverley were in different classes because of their sizes, track and field athletes would get the chance to see their best athletes compete every year in invitational events, bringing everyone together.

After many years of living in Philadelphia, Ruth was looking forward to moving back to her hometown—hopefully, anyway. Her husband, Sean, a Philly native, was also interviewing at two hospitals in Sioux Falls, the largest city in South Dakota. Secretly, Ruth hoped he would get the job here in Beverley, her hometown, and where her parents had just downsized from a large farmhouse ten miles in the country to an apartment in the "city".

Ruth was looking forward to living closer to her parents and having them be vital in the lives of her children. Yes, children, because even though Ruth and Sean had a five-month-old daughter, they had confirmed last week that Ruth was expecting again, and due in November. Ruth and Sean had exploded in laughter when they found out, because their children would be twelve months apart. The two of them wanted to have them close together, but this had been a *bit* unexpected. Having another baby so soon also meant that Ruth, who, although currently out on maternity leave, was employed as a speech pathologist by the Philadelphia School District, would not have to even consider looking for a new position immediately after moving to South Dakota.

Ruth's cell phone rang, and seeing it was her mother, she answered immediately, "Hey, Mom, what's up?"

"Ruthie, dear, your father was just wondering if you and Sean wanted to go and have supper tonight at that new steakhouse that opened up last year over by the lake? There is the most magnificent view of Lake Shelley from the dining room. Do you think Sean will be done in time?" Lake Shelley was a small lake at the east end of Main Street, and just across the street from the city park.

Ruth's stomach began growling at the mention of food. Maybe she should go back to the coffee shop and have that hot chicken salad sandwich that Effie had eaten earlier—it had smelled divine! "Yeah, Mom, that sounds great. Sean texted me a few minutes ago and said he should be finished in about an hour." Ruth paused then, having second thoughts, "I don't know about taking Eloisa, though. I hate to be one of those parents with a crying baby in a restaurant."

"Oh, don't worry, Maggie from next door said she would be delighted to watch her," her mother, Ellen, proclaimed. Maggie was a high school English teacher, recently transplanted to Beverley, and the new neighbor of her parents, Ellen and John Lefferts. Maggie had watched Eloisa the other afternoon while Ruth and her mom had made a trip out to the farm-house to collect a few boxes of home goods that her parents were ready to unpack and put away in the new apartment.

"Okay, Mom, I'm going to pop in at the coffee shop and then head back to the apartment." Hanging up with her mom, Ruth began to cross the street to walk through the city park, when something caught her eye on down the street. Normally an auto shop would never draw Ruth's atten-tion—cars were Sean's territory, not hers, but standing in one of the open bays was a man whose profile seemed so familiar to her. What was it about him? Unable to figure it out from that far away, Ruth began walking closer to the shop. Ruth had never been one to leave any stone unturned, and if there was a quagmire to be had, she jumped in headfirst, and considered it one of her more charming qualities.

Suddenly Ruth gasped: no, she thought. Her mind was playing tricks on her—part of her pregnancy brain she was experiencing with her sec-ond child. When she had been pregnant with Eloisa, her morning sickness had been off the charts, but it seemed that pregnancy brain was going to plague her with this one. Closer and closer, she neared the auto shop, but she must have blinked because the man wasn't there anymore. Oh, well, she thought, it must have been a trick of the afternoon sunlight. Attempt-ing to turn her stroller around to head to the coffee shop, it was then that the man stepped out of the opened garage door once again. Up close and personal this time, there was no denying the truth.

"JOSH?!" What the hell was Josh doing in Beverley? I mean, Ruth thought, she knew relatively why Josh would be in Beverley: his dad lived here, but in all the time he had been engaged to her sister and living in Brooklyn, she was certain he had not visited, because every time Tess made her annual visit back, always in the summer, Josh never came back with her, even though their families lived in the same county. It used to kill Tess that Josh wouldn't visit his dad more often, and she would warn him that he would regret it one day, but her words had never held any sway with him. Even though Sean was also a doctor, a pediatrician, he didn't value his career over his relationship with Ruth or with his own mother, who had been recently widowed last year, or his sisters. No, only Josh had seemed to care more about his stethoscope than his fiancée.

Josh seemed to blanch. "Oh my god—Ruth?!" He looked around, as if searching for someone to save him. "What-what are you doing here?"

"You mean here at this garage specifically, or here in Beverley generally?" Ruth laughed then, considering it her gift to him to let him off the hook. That last time she had spoken with Josh had been after her sister had walked out on him at their wedding rehearsal, and he had accused Ruth of somehow scheming to come between him and Tess. Little did he know, she thought now…

Josh was shaking his head. "Of course, of course. Until a few months ago, I hadn't been back here in years. I forget that others are better than I was about visiting home. Obviously, you must be here to see your parents—are John and Ellen with you?" he inquired, once again casting his glance around the area. Ruth was certain he was trying to see if her dad was nearby, as her father had always been a staunch Josh-supporter.

"No, they're at their new apartment, which they've slowly been moving into over the past few months." Well, thought Ruth, Josh was acting slightly stranger than normal, and the fact did not go unnoticed by her that he hadn't exactly answered what he was doing at his dad's auto shop. And what was he doing wearing coveralls? With stains on them?

An expression of awareness came over Josh's face. "Oh, right, Tessa-I mean, Tess-told me they were making the move to the city. Does this mean your dad is fully retired from his veterinarian business?"

"Well, kind of, and kind of not. You know my mom, though, she is trying to prod him into retirement, but he still has a few long-term clients he sees; I guess the new vet he sold his practice to is thankful to have him as a backup." Ruth paused, unable to believe that Josh, who, all the while in college, had seemed so disdainful of his dad and the garage, was now here, seemingly *working* at the garage. Could that be right? "I don't know if Tess also told you that Sean and I are moving here, also?"

Josh gestured toward the side of the building, which had a bench for customers to sit on and enjoy the sights of Main Street while they were waiting for their cars. They each took a seat, and while Ruth filled him in on the news of her life, it dawned on her that he was still remaining disturbingly quiet about his own. Josh had never been what one would call an over-sharer, but he was not normally silent, either.

Because they had known each other for almost twenty years, Ruth reached over and took his hand and squeezed it. "So, Josh," she began tentatively, "how are you? What are you doing here, if I may ask?" May as well help her old friend to start giving her information.

"You know how it is—you get girl, you lose girl; you get job, you lose job. And the world keeps spinning 'round." Okay, Ruth thought, something was really wrong if Josh was being flippant. Josh could be many things: serious, dedicated, clueless (at times), careful, and cautious, but never flippant or glib.

"Oh, Josh, what happened? What do you mean 'you lose the job'?" Ruth inquired softly.

Josh brought both hands up to his face and rubbed his cheeks. "I fucked up, Ruth." His words stunned her—Josh almost never used profanity. "What more can I say? I was too laser-focused on work, and that blew up my relationship with your sister; then when she left me, I was so distracted that I lost my focus and began to make mistakes. Ironic, huh? Then after I found out about her and Sam—kudos to them, by the way—I almost killed someone." At Ruth's gasp, he quickly followed up, "I didn't, really, but I did make an egregious error that could have been fatal. The hospital put me on a leave of absence, and essentially my residency is on hold. All that time I spent trying to get the surgical fellowship was a waste, because I failed at that, too." Suddenly, grief took over Josh's body, and he began sobbing in earnest. At a loss for words, for once in her life, Ruth could do nothing more than wrap her arms around Josh's shoulders and absorb his pain.

As she sat on the bench, she rocked with her friend in her arms, much as she did when trying to calm and comfort her daughter. Finally, as his breath became steadier, she whispered to him, "Josh, I'm incredibly sorry to hear all of this. I know you, and you did not deserve this. You are beyond brilliant; maybe you could somehow see this as a chance to hit the reset button?" She gently pulled away from him and studied his bleak expression. "What is your plan? You must be going back?"

"Ah hell, I don't know, Ruth. Honestly, I don't know what is back in New York for me." At her look of horror, he added, "No, don't worry, I'm not making any rash decisions." Josh gestured to the auto shop, saying, "I had no idea how much being here would help. When I first got back to Beverley, all I did was mope around the house, feeling sorry for myself. Thankfully, my dad saved me, once again, and got me working here with him."

Ruth reached down into the stroller and brought out two bottles of water and handed one to Josh. "Here, my friend, you need this as much as I do. How is your dad, by the way? I didn't get a chance to talk to him at the rehearsal." Ruth flinched, cursing her mindless chatter. "Sorry— maybe we shouldn't talk about that night?"

Josh laughed, in a humble kind of way. "I can't hide from the truth any longer, Ruthie. I hold no bitterness toward Tessa—sorry, I mean Tess; I don't know if I'll ever get that right." After Josh drank a few gulps of water, he continued, "Anyway, I have fully accepted most of the blame for us ending. I didn't cherish her like I should have; I took her for granted, and she deserved more than that. As for Fitz, I can't blame him for falling in love with her. I know he says he didn't recognize her on the train, and I believe him, but I wonder if deep down, a part of him maybe did? When I think back on things, I realize that he was always asking after her, and genuinely seemed upset that she deeply disliked him."

Ruth nodded, because she agreed with Josh that there had been a deeper previous connection between Tess and Sam, but also because there had been no shortage of underlying factors to their break-up. "If you had seen them together on that train, Josh, it was as if there were other forces at work. They could not stay away from each other, almost as if they were being drawn together despite common sense and logic. And you were right—there were cracks already in your relationship with Tess, because if there hadn't been, and you both had been fully committed to each other, nothing could have broken the two of you."

Josh looked down at his water bottle, almost as if he hated to ask the next question, "So…how are they? Sam and Tess?"

And here Ruth had a glimmer of hope for her longtime friend and almost-brother-in-law, with the fact that he used both of their "real" names: "Tess", what she had always preferred over the "Tessa" Josh had insisted on calling her, and "Sam", not the nickname of "Fitz" Josh had bestowed upon him in college. Because of this, Ruth wanted to be honest with him about one more truth that he deserved to know. "Well, Sam and Tess are very well. You should know that he proposed to her a couple of weeks ago, and they are getting married this summer. June, actually," she told him, ripping the Band-Aid off entirely.

Josh's eyes widened in surprise. "Wow—that's…that's soon. And summer, huh? Tess always said she didn't want a summer wedding. I guess that just meant our wedding." Josh shook his head. "Sorry, one last bout of me feeling sorry for myself." He took a long drink of water and said, "You know, I am happy for both of them." Josh looked over at a voice calling his name from inside the garage. "Wow, I can't believe I've been sitting here with you for so long. I need to get back to work, I guess." They both stood up, and she grabbed him for an enormous hug, happy that Josh was possibly beginning to heal from all that had cut him down.

CHAPTER
Sixteen

Effie

F labbergasted—that was the only word to describe how Effie was feeling right now. In all the places in South Dakota, her chance meeting with her new friend Ruth at the coffee shop had been an unbelievable gift that she hoped was going to keep on giving. Thanks to the heads-up from Ruth, Effie was now having an impromptu interview with the head librarian at the Beverley Carnegie Library! It was Effie's great fortune that afternoon that Liza Bloomingdale had been manning (womanning?) the front desk when Effie inquired as to the status of the "Librarian Wanted" sign. After listing her qualifications and job history, Ms. Bloomingdale asked a clerk, who was nearby shelving a cart filled with new-release fiction books at the time, to cover for her so she could have an informal interview with Effie.

"I've got a good feeling about you," Ms. Bloomingdale had told her. "And I'm almost never wrong." The two women had discussed the rise in young adult literature, and how it had taken over the fiction world in the past decade. Over the past couple of years, the library had been increasing its selection; due to this, the head children's librarian was finding it difficult to maintain both children's and young adult literature, while also providing activities and story times for younger children.

Effie would have to fill out the application online, but the job had been posted for a month now, with no one truly qualified having already applied. An added bonus for the library was Effie's young adult lit knowledge, and having worked in an urban library, being able to share her thoughts and ideas on drawing younger people to the library.

Well, spring was the perfect season for change, and Effie figured no time like the present for another change as well, and she ducked into Shear Beauty, a salon she and Ruth had passed on their way to the library. Could this day get any better? A stylist was immediately available! Sliding into the chair, Effie described the cut she was looking for, and twenty minutes later, she was a new woman: shoulder-length hair, with long layers for an extra bounce. Effie's hair was thin, but she had a lot of it and with the weight of it gone felt like she was ten pounds lighter, especially emotionally. Damon had loved running his hands through her waist-length hair and would frown whenever she would deign to cut even an inch from it, so in a feeble attempt to try to make her marriage a happy one, she had not had it truly cut in over three years: cutting it now seemed like a perfect kiss off to her soon-to-be ex-husband.

On her way back to the auto shop, Effie ducked into Mr. Beans and ordered an iced tea to go, and also grabbed a copy of the town's newspaper, thinking a change in her living situation would be preferable for a variety of reasons, one of which was she could avoid driving forty miles to work every day from Clover Lake. Heading out into the late afternoon sun, Effie squinted at her buzzing phone. Golden Boy was calling. She really should be more mature about her childish brother and reprogram his actual name to his number, but she couldn't get over the way he continued to be doted upon by their mother. Growing up had been difficult enough after her father had died, especially after having her sense of self be pulverized by her grandparents while she lived with them; it had taken some time for Effie and her mother to make their way back to each other after Diadema returned from Ohio, and the journey had been made more difficult after Diadema had announced that she was having another baby when Effie was ten years old. Although Burnside was a decent enough stepfather, he had never truly felt like her "dad", despite formally adopting her at the age of nine. At the time, Effie had felt she had no choice when the judge had asked her if she wanted Burnside to adopt her—what would her mother have said if Effie had said no? It was inconceivable as an option. Her mom had been so consumed with making her marriage to Burnie a good one, Effie had been essentially pushed aside; when Hamilton came along, putting Effie on the back burner had been a done deal. Ham's blonde hair and lighter skin made the difference in their colorings, and therefore their lineage, unmistakable. Her grandparents had doted on Ham, often criticizing Effie for the way she played with him or talked to him. Effie could do no right in their eyes, and Ham no wrong.

"Yes, baby brother?" she answered her phone just as he drove up to the curb. Hanging up, she reached for the door handle. "Curbside pickup: I like this side of you."

He retorted, "I tried calling you like five times—don't you ever pick up your phone? The shop called me when they couldn't reach you. As if I don't have anything else to do today but run your errands?"

"What crawled up your butt and died?" she quizzed him as she got into the car. "Need I remind you: you were never invited along today. You hopped into the car as I was getting ready to leave," she pointed out, and then decided to defuse the situation with her brother, who must really have a bee in his bonnet, because normally he was quite easygoing. "Sorry if I missed your calls—my ringer must have been turned down. What's with all the mystery, anyway?" As they turned the corner from Main Street, Effie looked and saw the man from the auto shop staring after them. She lifted a hand to bid him farewell, and, with a slight frown on his face, he slowly returned her wave. Wondering at his melancholy made her regret not answering the shop's call, which, according to her call history had evidently come in as she was at the salon. "Well?" she prodded her brother. "What's up with you? Why are you so secretive? And now that I'm thinking about it, why are you spending all day in your bedroom all the time? Shouldn't you have outgrown all-day self-satisfaction at your age?"

At her pointed stare, Hamilton refuted, "God, you're sick. Like seriously, there's something wrong with you," and then both siblings burst out laughing. "Okay, if you must know, and please don't say anything to Mom or Dad yet, but I have been taking online classes at the community college here, and there was a guest lecturer today that I wanted to attend."

Holy hell, could there be any more surprises today? "Ham, that is incredible! But Mom and Dad don't know?" As he shook his head, she asked, "Why? They would be thrilled." And then she wondered if she had just answered her own questions. Having been adored since birth, Ham had never had anything expected of him in his life. He had gone to a state university directly after high school, but had failed and bailed after one semester, and then worked dead-end jobs while couch surfing with friends, in between mooching off of their parents.

"Yeah, I know. I just didn't want to get their expectations up, so I never said anything. And now that I only have one semester left until I graduate, I feel it will be awkward to tell them."

"Oh, Ham. I know what you mean." She was so proud of her brother for doing this, on his own, and she told him so. "What are you studying?"

"Working on an associate's degree in human services, which I then hope to transfer to a university, preferably one far away from here, and study social work," her brother informed her.

Amazed could not even begin to describe her reaction to Hamilton's proclamation. No doubt her brother could be a very caring and empathetic person, once you got past his frivolous façade, but follow-through had never been his strong suit. He did seem to be quite earnest now, though, as she agreed with him that going to a university somewhere more than a two-hour drive away would be most beneficial for him, and she told him just that.

"I know, better than most, how being away from Mom and Dad can certainly make breathing easier. I'm proud of you, you know," she reiterated. "You really have matured, Hamilton, despite the lack of encouragement you've gotten from Mom and Dad to do so." After Effie was adopted by Burnside, it had taken her several years to be comfortable with calling him her dad, and to this day the word still occasionally had a tendency to sit at the back of her throat, not wanting to make its way out.

After Hamilton cast her a sidelong glance, he asked her, "Now, can we talk about your new haircut? I should have let you pick up the car after all—that dude was disappointed to see my ugly ass instead of yours there. He would have been blown away." As Hamilton approached the state road to take them back to Clover Lake, he told her, "You're way too good for a mechanic, though. Hell, you're too good for any of the losers you've been with. Can I just say, right now, how happy I am that you left that douche-bag husband of yours? That guy was such a dick, Effie," Hamilton stated as they roared out of town.

"What? You barely even knew him!" She sputtered.

"Bullshit! I came down at least five times to Denver to visit you!" Ham protested.

"Exactly! And I think he was only there once," Effie argued, intent on proving her point.

Ham glanced at her out of the corner of his eye. "And? Didn't that say anything to you then? He didn't give a damn about hanging out with your brother. I made sure to go down there when he was not on a tour, because I was in awe that you had married such a cool guy—tour manager for rock bands? Even the guy who I buy pot from was impressed—gave me a huge discount when I told him." Effie playfully slapped her brother's shoulder. "Look, all I'm saying is that I have heard from you for the majority of my life about how I sell myself short, and I don't challenge myself—but what about you? You are my kick ass big sis, who always listened to the coolest music, who fucking put all of these pale-ass bitches to shame around here, and was the fastest, smartest chick in the state. But your taste in men sucks, Sis. You need, like, a dude makeover."

Effie laughed, "Well, I do not dispute you there. How about we wait until my divorce is final, though, before you have me walking down the aisle with anyone, though, huh?"

"No, no walk down the aisle. Baby steps, Eff, baby steps. And maybe the next time you take Mom's car to the shop, you'll be ready to practice on Josh."

"Josh? Who's Josh?"

CHAPTER
Seventeen

Josh

Seeing Ruth last month had been a touchstone that he had needed desperately. For the past eighteen—no, almost nineteen now—years, Ruth and Tess had been so significant in his life. It had been Tess he had met first, when he was new in Beverley, and she had sat at his table waiting for an extracurricular activity to start. Tess was a couple of years younger than he was, but Ruth was in his grade. The three of them had become a tight circle of friends. Josh had begun to develop a crush on the older sister when he then befriended Chase Withers, his partner in chemistry. Josh's first experience in heartbreak had been watching Chase and Ruth become close and start dating. It had only seemed natural that Josh and Tess pair off and begin a relationship as well. Ruth and Chase had not lasted after high school, but Tess and Josh had, and they had stayed together until Josh was ready to graduate from college. Josh's friendship with Chase had also lasted, and he had even been in his wedding to Tess—well, he would have been, in any case.

Josh was now ready to be completely honest with himself and admit that he and Tess should never have gotten back together all of those years ago. Although he realized he'd made a mistake the minute he had broken it off with her back then, in reality, they had already grown and begun to develop emotionally apart from each other. The reason they had reconnected had been due more to familiarity than long-lasting love.

Picking up his phone, he texted Sam, who he had not spoken with since that dreadful day in his old apartment. Noting the time, he realized he was due to meet his cousin Liam for dinner in less than an hour. One advantage of being back home was his ability to spend more time with his cousins, since there were several who lived within an hour's drive of Beverley, and he and Liam were particularly close, having grown up more like brothers than cousins due to their proximity in age.

His phone rang almost immediately, and he answered without looking at the caller ID, "I hope you're not canceling on me for some hot date, are you?"

A lengthy pause occurred on the other end. "…Umm, well, this is awkward."

"Sam! God, I'm sorry, I thought it was Liam calling—we're meeting for dinner later, and he has canceled twice with me in favor of last-minute dates." Josh laughed, with the hope that Sam would know all he wanted now was their friendship to be righted.

Sam joked, "That sounds like the Liam I've come to know and love. Is it any wonder that he's still single?" Well, Josh wasn't sure what to say to that, considering HE was still single, and now Sam was engaged to his former fiancée.

"Damn, Josh, I'm sorry. Lame joke, and thoughtless comment." He heard Sam take a deep breath on the other end of the line. "I have wanted to reach out to you so many times over the last few months, but anything I thought of saying just sounded so trite and inconsiderate. Thank you for your text. I know nothing I can say will ever make up for me hurting you. I'm not proud of how everything went down that night, or especially in the time leading up to it, either."

"You mean the night you and Tess finally decided to be honest? Or the night she left me at the altar?" Okay, so it appeared that Josh still had some anger left inside. "Sorry. I thought I was above this. I hadn't planned to rehash anything on our call."

"No, no, please, you're right—I should have come to you the night after Tess left the church, and told you I was in love with her, and explained everything then. Or if I am completely honest, I could have reached out after I found out who she was, but I did not want to be a factor in you guys breaking up. I'm sorry." Sam was silent for a moment, allowing both men to process all of the pain caused and received. Then he continued, "I know it seems like we were keeping it from you intentionally, but we weren't. I guess even though we both knew this was it for us, we kept telling ourselves we wanted to wait and see where it went before we had to hurt you. All we could see was our love, and I'm sorry if that hurts hearing it, but that is the truth. The moment I met her on the train platform, my life began in a new way. I honestly didn't recognize her in any way, but if I had? I can't say it would have ended any differently. If I'm brutally honest."

"I know, I know. It's difficult to hear, but I have done a lot of personal reflection these last few months, Sam, and I am owning my part in this. I have been so selfish in my professional life, and the last thing I can do is begrudge two people I care deeply about to not be selfish in their personal lives. Tess and I never had the kind of passion or connection you seem to have for each other, and in the end, that is what hurt the most." Josh took a minute to bring his emotions level again.

He heard a whistle on Sam's end. "It takes a lot to be that self-aware, Josh. In the name of full transparency, I want you to know that Tess and I are engaged. It only just happened last month, and you have been on my mind so often since."

"Actually, I happened to run into Ruth a few weeks ago here and she told me the news, so I have been processing it since then. Congratulations—I wish you both the best, sincerely." Josh looked at the time and knew he needed to wrap up the call in order to meet Liam on time. "Listen, I need to cut this short because I am still meeting up with Liam, apparently. Thanks for calling, Fitz; I'm sure it wasn't easy."

"It was what it needed to be, Doc. Let me know where to send the invitation, okay?" And they both laughed.

Knowing Sam was kidding on the square, Josh replied, "Yeah, not sure we're there yet, but please give Tess my best. Take care, Sam."

"You, too, Josh." And with that, the line went dead. Josh felt finally and completely liberated from the hurt and anger he had felt following the tragic night all those months ago when he had met with Tess and Sam. If forgiving them and understanding how his own actions played such a tremendous part in his heartbreak meant that he was at last able to move on with this part of his life, then he was ready to do all of that and more. Beginning, he supposed, with being on time to meet his cousin for dinner. During the years of his residency, Josh was habitually late for nearly every engagement he had outside the hospital.

Josh grabbed his keys from the hall table, said goodbye to his dad, who was hosting a poker game with some of his old friends tonight, and then was in the driver's seat in his "new" car, a 1972 Dodge Dart that had been collecting dust in the lot behind the garage until Josh, his dad, and his uncle, who drove over from Clover Lake on the weekends, had begun working on it last month. Although it still needed a bit more work, Henry had deemed it safe to drive the streets of Beverley—Henry had also suggested perhaps father and son could fully restore the car together while Josh was home.

Reflecting on this new, forgiving nature of his, Josh wondered if this was how his dad had felt in the years since his mom had left them. Henry never talked much about his mom or his feelings toward her; despite a common misconception about him, Josh had been sensitive and empathetic enough to never press his dad on anything concerning his mother, Melanie. Did Josh have questions? Yes, too many, as a matter of fact, but the last thing he had ever felt the need to do was drill the parent who had *stayed*. While Henry had no lack of women who were willing to be the second Mrs. Livingston, or at the very least willing to make Henry forget there had ever been a first Mrs. Livingston. As far as Josh knew, his dad had not dated anyone, or even been interested in anyone, in the twenty-plus years since Melanie had left. Was that odd or normal? When he and Tess had originally broken up after college, Josh had started dating another woman only about a month later, and in the entire four years in which he and Tess had been apart, he had dated a number of women, both casually and semi-seriously.

One of the things Josh had brought back to South Dakota was one of those DNA tests you took and sent in through an ancestry research site.

Tess had gotten it for him for his birthday last year, and he had immediately put it in his briefcase, thinking he would take it at work one day, only he had actually forgotten all about it until a few weeks ago, when he was emptying out the briefcase looking for some pre-operation notes he had taken on the surgical case that almost cost him his career. Josh had needed to go back over everything as part of his journey to be new and improved. He had pulled the notes out of the front pocket, and a small box came flying out at the same time. He remembered he and Tess were going to take their tests and submit them at the same time, and then compare their ancestries. He had failed to fulfill that duty of his as well. The more he considered his missteps and failings from the past, the more he knew he must strive to do better in the future.

Pulling up to the restaurant, Josh scanned the parking lot and noticed his cousin's car. Josh parked his car next to Liam's shiny blue Corvette, exited and locked the doors, and strode to The Cattlemen's Club Steakhouse. He immediately picked out the top of Liam's head, where he sat alone at a booth on the side. Josh made his way through the teeming restaurant, and as he did so, a movement across the dining room caught his eye. Two people were just being seated, a man and a woman, and the woman had the shiniest, darkest hair Josh had ever seen, so sleek that it mirrored the lights shining from above, with the ends just skimming her shoulders. The tilt to her head made him pause, but he couldn't see her face yet. At that moment, out of the corner of his eye, he noticed Liam waving to him from the booth, and it broke his spell of reverie.

CHAPTER
Eighteen

Effie

What had been posed to her as a "farewell" dinner was turning out to be much different than anticipated. In fact, it was all that she dreaded when going out for a casual meal with the opposite sex: your dinner "date" mistakenly believed it to be, in actuality, a DATE. Which this was not supposed to be—for Effie, anyway.

After her impromptu interview with the library last month, Effie had immediately, upon returning home, filled out the online application, and enclosed her resume and letters of reference. While she was at work at the grocery store the following day, she had received a call from Ms. Blooming-dale saying that the city council was meeting at the beginning of the month, and a couple of members wanted to interview her for the position. Ms. Bloomingdale assured Effie that it was only a formality, however, and the job was to be hers! Luckily, Effie was working back in the stockroom when her phone rang, so she was able to get her fantastic news immediately. Effie had been on cloud nine ever since. The hardest part had been after her "official" interview" with the city council, having to tell Boyd she needed to submit her two-week notice. She had genuinely enjoyed worked at the store, especially when Boyd was there. He had a fantastic, laidback attitude, and he had been integral in reintroducing her to some people who had gone to their high school and still lived in the area.

To Boyd's credit, he had taken her news really well, and a certain glint had come into his eyes when he suggested that they go out for dinner as "congratulations" and "farewell". Seeing as how he was currently her closest friend in Clover Lake, she readily accepted.

"Here I go again on my own, going down the only road I've ever known," she sang bleakly to herself now; she was living the Whitesnake dream here, people, she thought to herself. Why must she *always* fail to read the signs of men? What she had mistakenly (presumptuously) believed to be a friendly dinner outing was clearly more than that to Boyd. Her first clue should have been when he said, "I'll pick you up at seven". No, back up. Her first clue *actually* should have been when he suggested the Beverley Cattlemen's Club for their dinner destination.

"Umm, okay, but wouldn't it be easier to just go someplace here in Clover Lake? We wouldn't have to drive so far," she countered. She enjoyed Boyd's company, but the thought of driving almost an hour each way *and* having a possibly long dinner seemed a bit too much. He insisted, though, and she had given in. What could it hurt? Besides, she planned to look for a new place to live, in Beverley, so she could be closer to her new job; she may as well get used to big city dining, she had laughed to herself.

Thankfully, fate intervened on the day of their dinner, as two calls she had made about prospective housing had been returned to her, and she scheduled appointments to see each place that day. Effie texted Boyd her news and informed him that she would just meet him at the restaurant later that evening. He had replied with a frown-faced emoji, but had followed it with a selfie of a shirtless Boyd. WHAT?!?!?! How did a friendly dinner date go to a creepy dating app hookup? "Boyd," she scolded the photo, "no…just no." Hence the song reference, because once again, she had either given off the wrong vibes or misread his signs. And yes, she had previously had a childhood crush on him, but that was twenty years ago!

Thinking of past crushes cast her memory back to the afternoon she and her brother had taken the car to Beverley, when Hamilton mentioned

Josh's name. Her brother had failed to give her any more information, but it had gotten her curiosity bubbling. Something about those sincere blue eyes the mechanic had flashed her way seemed familiar to her, as if she had gazed into those same eyes for long periods of time, but she could not place them. Probably for the best, though, as he didn't need her train wreck of a life to crash into his. The mechanic had given off some nice-guy vibes, and appeared to have a funny and quirky sense of humor, which she always found so attractive. She asked herself why, if these were qualities she valued and found attractive in a partner, did she never pursue that kind of man? Well, maybe because she had never really had to pursue anyone— no, unfortunately for her, she attracted a little *too* much attention from the opposite sex: that's why she continuously ended up with the wrong man. Case in point tonight: Boyd.

Boyd had mentioned on more than one occasion that he was fresh off of a divorce, as well, but unlike Effie, he and his wife had three young children that were also in the mix. Effie had kind of always been on the fence as far as having kids went, and she had never been happier with her indecision than now: it was difficult enough getting her own life sorted, how would she have coped with a child who depended on her, let alone having to remain tied to Damon for the rest of her life? Now he could be someone else's lifelong problem, and this knowledge brought her an inordinate amount of comfort.

Well, she told herself, you may as well just get it over with, and she opened the doors to the restaurant and dragged herself through them. Was there any chance that she had misinterpreted Boyd's intentions tonight? Maybe he *was* only wanting to wish her well. The entrance just inside the doors was packed with people, the floor littered with peanut shells, and in the corner stood a gigantic barrel of peanuts with diners snacking on them and discarding their shells simultaneously. Stepping around the crowd, Effie was intent on locating the hostess among the throng. Relieved because Boyd had told her he had made a reservation, just as she reached the podium, a bouquet of flowers greeted her, with Boyd's face behind them.

"Wow, Effie, you look gorgeous," and he leaned forward and kissed her on the cheek, his eyes tracking down her form, currently encased in a pair of black jeans below a cream-colored Aran sweater that had been brought home from Ireland by her mom. "These are for you," and he thrust the flowers at her, leaving her no choice but to take them while also juggling her purse awkwardly. What was she supposed to do with these during dinner? Put them on the floor or on the table? Feeling annoyed, followed quickly by a large dose of guilt, she shook her head and pasted on a smile while the hostess escorted them to a table set back from the main dining room. Deciding to put her flowers and purse in the empty chair next to hers, as she bent over, a movement across the dining room caught her eye.

Among all of the other diners in the packed steakhouse, only one happened to call to her. Tall and blond, with a graceful ease to his movements, was mechanic Josh. And he looked yummy enough to eat as an appetizer—hell, she'd enjoy at least three courses of him. Wearing a pair of Wranglers that fit in well with this crowd, a dark green Henley sweater adorned his top half, and the cut across the shoulders implied that it was either borrowed or from a time he hadn't been so broad. She looked away hurriedly. No…why did he have to be here? She agonized. Out of all the people to see her here on this "date" with Boyd, why must it be the *one* decent man she had been attracted to in forever? Okay, she was only *assuming* he was decent, and the only basis for that, really, was the fact that she had given his co-worker her phone number to give to him (sure, it was on the premise of calling her when the car was done at the shop) and nada. Zip. Nothing. No call or text or anything. Clearly, if he was a creep, he would have called her by now. So now she was *bothered* he didn't call her out of the blue? Boyd, here, would have not hesitated to use that phone number. After dating so many losers, she truly had no idea how a decent man comported himself.

"Effie? Effie?" Oh hell, what had she missed? Boyd was insistently saying her name, with a touch of annoyance lacing his voice.

Deciding to tell him a white lie, Effie answered, "Sorry, Boyd, I was just thinking how nice it will be to live in Beverley when I finally move." Real nice, if Josh was what she had to look forward to, and as she glanced around the dining room, trying to steal a peek at the mechanic, she found Boyd watching her closely, so she said, "This is a nice restaurant—have you been here before?" Nice Beverley, nice restaurant, nice, nice, nice. She should take a hint from her own words and start acting a bit nicer to Boyd, or this would be the longest night in history, she thought.

Boyd acknowledged stiffly, "No, it just opened up late last year, but with my schedule at the store and then my marriage ending, it hasn't left me a lot of free time." He flashed puppy dog eyes at her. What was she supposed to do with this routine? Jump his bones right now, make him feel okay about his failed marriage? Okay, seriously, she needed to stop with her inner sarcasm and give Boyd a chance to prove they were just friends. Nothing more.

The two pals took a few minutes to peruse the menus Molly, the hostess, had given them, and Effie used this as a chance to look over the top and study mechanic Josh from across the room. Her heart skipped a beat as a smile broke out on his face, and he laughed at whatever his dinner companion had just said. She watched as he slanted back in his chair, his solid torso stretched out, and his hand rubbed over his stomach. She imagined he was talking about how hungry he was, and then she noticed his long, slender fingers stroking the sides of his water glass. Suddenly Effie felt parched, and she also reached for her water glass, and in one gulp she swallowed half the contents.

A waiter had appeared to take their drink order, and Effie recognized him as Colt from Mr. Beans, so she smiled warmly up at him. Evidently, she hadn't made the same impression on him, because he glanced away from her to Boyd, who started to order a bottle of wine. Effie cut him off. "Sorry, Boyd, I'm more in a cosmopolitan mood tonight. Feel free to order a glass of wine for yourself, though."

Boyd smiled at her, assuring her, "Anything you want tonight, Effie, I am here to provide." Kill me now, her inner bitch told her. He then ordered a half carafe of red for himself. "I think I'm also ready to order—Effie?"

Pulling her gaze from Josh, she realized she hadn't actually read her menu, being too busy lusting after mechanic Josh while out to dinner with her friend and boss, Boyd. "You go first—I'm deciding between two things yet." Lies. All lies.

While Boyd was ordering a well-done ribeye (well done? who orders a steak well done? this whole dinner date was cooked to within an inch of its life) with a side of garlic mashed potatoes, Effie looked at the first item that she saw, which also, thank god, happened also to be a favorite. "I'll have the filet Oscar, please, medium rare. No potato, but could I get extra bread?" As she handed her menu to the waiter, she panicked when she didn't see mechanic Josh at his table anymore. Where had he gone?

CHAPTER
Nineteen

Josh

Josh returned from the men's room, only having used it as an excuse to walk past the table where his mystery woman was sitting. Her hair was shorter than when she had brought the car into the shop, and it suited her. He had hoped to make eye contact with her, maybe ask how the car had driven since he had last seen it. Any excuse for talking to her, really. As he neared the table, though, he saw the flowers in the chair next to her, and that only meant one thing to Josh: she was already on a date, with someone he thought he recognized from his early teen years. His stomach dropped as he identified the date: Boyd Timmons. When Josh was a pre-teen, Boyd, who was a few years older, had been the head lifeguard at the city pool in Clover Lake, and worshipped by everyone. Growing up, Josh had loved going to the pool during the summers and had been an excellent swimmer. After his mom had left, he had taken solace in food, and since his dad had not been the best cook, their dinners consisted of frozen meals like TV dinners and pizza, with an occasional box of Banquet fried chicken served to make their dinner seem extra special. The fatty, processed foods had taken their toll on Josh's weight, and by the time he was fourteen, his height not yet caught up to his weight, contributed to him being one of the heavier boys in his class. Although he had still enjoyed swimming, some of the older kids, led by lifeguard Boyd, had begun to torment him when he was at the pool. Feeling self-conscious, Josh had started to wear a shirt over his bare upper half, but that meant getting out of the pool in a soaking wet t-shirt that then accentuated his larger belly—it was mortifying, and not exactly the type of wet t-shirt contest anyone was going for. In the end, Josh stopped going to the pool altogether, and by the time he was sixteen, he and his dad had moved to Beverley, and all motivation to swim gone.

Wanting to avoid seeing Boyd right now, Josh took the longer way around back to his table. He guessed maybe he was destined to be unlucky in love. Things with Tess had gone so incredibly wrong, and then the disaster with Lana. He still hadn't responded to her email: not out of resentment or any ill will, just dumbfounded as to what to say. If he were a bigger person, a more generous man, he would simply write her back and congratulate her, but after all this time, a response just felt awkward: he would have to apologize for his poor reaction to her earning the fellowship and trying to kiss her, and then apologize for waiting so long to apologize. Perhaps his hesitancy toward the email had more to do with her personal confession, and he did not want to make the mistake of leading her on, in any way. He had only ever considered her a friend, a co-worker, and nothing more, despite his fumbling attempt to kiss her that dreadful day. When his mystery woman had come to the shop, she was the first woman he had felt an attraction to since Tess, and he had bungled that as well. Her phone number was still in his wallet, winking at him every time he opened it to use a credit card. What was he supposed to do with it? Had she only given it to him so he could call her that day about her car? He hadn't even gotten the chance to do that, since her brother had picked it up instead. Surely, she did not intend for him to call out of the blue. Right? Something in him could not put the folded piece of paper in the trash, though.

Sitting back down again across from Liam, he smiled at his cousin, who had taken it upon himself to devour most of the appetizer which had been delivered in Josh's brief absence. "Wow, Liam, you could not save me two of the scallops instead of just one? That's low, cousin, very low."

Liam grinned up at Josh as he sat back down at the table. "You know what they say: 'whoever leaves the table before the food arrives and is still gone when it gets delivered loses out?'," and then Liam laughed, almost maniacally.

"Yikes, that is harsh. And no, I have never heard that saying before." Josh took a drink of his cold beer, having gotten used to the taste since living back at home with his dad, and he had to admit to himself that sometimes it definitely hit the spot. "Sorry, but I had to go check something out," Josh began to explain.

Liam smirked, "I'm sure you did, and I saw you checking her out the entire way over there. She is still as fine as she was in high school." Liam rubbed his chin. "Actually, no, scratch that. She is *finer* than she was back then—used to be a little too skinny. All that running." Ironic, really, thought Josh, since Liam had also been a sprinter in track. "She has filled out in all the right places."

"You know, it's no wonder you have never had a serious relationship— wasn't your longest one with Penelope, like back in eighth grade? Until she dumped your sorry ass," teased Josh.

Looking point blank at Josh, Liam asked, "Really? Are we really going there? Unless I am completely crazy, YOUR fiancée ran out on you at your wedding rehearsal." As Josh covered his face with his hands and groaned, Liam continued, "How is the delectable Tess, by the way?"

"Oh, you know, happily ever after, it seems. Or at least she will be when she and Sam get married this summer," Josh informed his cousin.

"Oh, my god—mic drop. Damn, I have to hand it to Sam; I never would have pegged him as the dark horse, but look at him taking care of business." Liam was a little too appreciative of Sam for Josh's comfort right now.

Wanting to find out who the mystery woman was, but also still trying not to pique his cousin's interest, Josh asked casually, "Anyway, do you happen to know that woman sitting over there?" Josh brought Liam's focus back to his mystery woman.

Liam gave Josh a look like he had lost his mind. "Yeah, Dude, and so do you."

Josh shook his head, because there was no way he could have forgotten someone like her. "No—I mean, I did meet her last month at the shop, but I never actually got her name, only her number."

Liam hissed across the table, "Let me get this straight: you have Euphemie Van Holland's digits, and I am just now learning about this? Not even that, but you have had them for *a month*? And you haven't called her?"

Josh held up his hand. "Wait—that's Euphemie Van Holland?"

"Well, I guess not anymore—she wants to be called Effie, according to my mom. But, yeah, that's her. Looking good, no matter what she wants to be called." And then Liam let out a low wolf whistle, at the same time as their waiter passed by their table, and it earned his cousin a look of interest from Colt.

"Wow. I can't believe I didn't recognize her last month. Why didn't she say anything? I'm so stupid—I should have known when they said the last name Van Holland, but it was completely out of context, and it's been so long since I've seen her. Still—Van Holland. I should have made the connection." No longer caring if his cousin knew he was interested in Euphemie, Effie (why were women always changing their names on him?), Josh questioned him, "Does she live around here or something? Do her folks still live in Clover Lake?"

"Okay, take a breath. She probably didn't recognize you either, same as you." Liam looked at Josh pointedly. "You have changed a lot since you moved away from Clover Lake, you know. As far as I am aware, she moved back from Denver a couple of months ago, and the circumstances seem questionable. I don't even know how long she's staying or what her deal is, but for now, she's living in Clover Lake with her parents." Liam gave Josh a knowing look. "You had it so bad for her in school."

Josh nodded, unable to deny it. "I did. That was one of the things that sucked when Dad and I moved here, but we both wanted a fresh start, so I moved on, where no one knew about Mom. And then I met Tessa and Ruth, and I guess forgot all about Effie."

Liam nodded his head, then said somewhat conspiratorially, "Word on the street is that she is just out of a bad marriage. Some musician or something, or he works with musicians. You know my mom is friends with her mom, so she got all the backstory. I wonder what she's doing with Boyd—I would think she has better taste in men than that. But, the last I heard, she was working at his dad's grocery store, so he must have somehow convinced her to go out with him. Man, do you remember how big of a dick Boyd was when he was a hotshot lifeguard?"

Josh finished his first drink and put it near the edge of the table. "I'm pretty sure that the kind of crap he pulled back then no one could get away with now. I always felt I had a target on my back every time we went swimming. What makes a guy so nasty to kids who are really younger? All we wanted to do was have fun at the pool. Remember that time I went to cannonball in and he made everyone clear out, saying typhoon Josh was going to flood the place?" Josh winced at the childhood trauma he had endured his last summer in Clover Lake. His mom leaving had been enough to weigh on his emotional development, but the torment and ridicule he had experienced, both from older teens and kids his own age, had made him question his worth as a human being. Luckily, he had Liam and several other cousins who lived close enough to visit every weekend, plus some friends, particularly those who were in the drama club. That's how he remembered Effie—she had been a year older, but they had grown close during rehearsals for the school plays. Josh had often gotten the feeling that she, also, felt like an outcast sometimes, and recalled some students bullying her for being Native, for being mixed race, for having a stepdad. Whatever made someone different would eventually make you a target, a lesson he had learned well.

Josh and Liam tucked into their entrees, and each one ordered a second drink—this time a bourbon and Diet Pepsi for Josh and a rum and Coke for Liam. Normally Josh would never have a second drink, but he and Liam were planning on walking over to the pool hall two blocks away after their dinner, so he intended to enjoy his night out.

"Listen, when we go to Shorty's after supper, I have a surprise for you, cousin," declared Liam.

"Ugh," Josh groaned. Liam's surprises were frequently of the kind that Josh could live without. "Liam, I just wanted to have a good meal with my cousin, and then shoot some pool. Don't even tell me we are pivoting from this plan."

"No, no, I would definitely say we are not pivoting, more like enhancing. You know how when a woman has a great face, but then she puts on makeup? It's like that," Liam said with a flourish.

Josh laughed, "Are you intending to stay single for the rest of your life? I will let you in on a secret—Tess hated it when I encouraged her to wear makeup; she always said that it was like I was implying she wasn't attractive enough without it. I learned too late from that, but I am determined to not mess up my future relationships." Josh inhaled deeply, slowly expelling his breath then. "I got so many things wrong with Tess, things I should have worked harder on after we got back together. I never should have taken so long to propose, and then I kept wanting us to wait to get married: those were huge mistakes, and I supremely regret not making her a priority. I felt so betrayed by both her and Sam, but in the end, it was only my fault."

"And that, my man, is why I have added something extra to our evening. See, I met this woman the other day when I was getting coffee, and she has this friend…"

CHAPTER
Twenty

Effie And Josh

Why in the world had she ever agreed to this, Effie wondered? First the dinner, which had been delicious but a bit of a bore (present company included), and now she and Boyd were squeezing their way into a bar a couple of blocks away from the restaurant. After they had finished their dinner, at which Boyd had, in the end, probably drunk an entire bottle of wine (but Effie had consumed only the one cosmo), Boyd had suggested they take a walk around the brightly lit section of town. Effie had agreed, because she wanted to become familiar with this part of Beverley. Located on the other side of the small Lake Shelley, the steakhouse was situated across the street from the city park, but at the west end entrance to the park was a sort of town square, the type more commonly found in New England towns, but seemed to perfectly fit Beverley. She could see the glow of the library's outside lights from across the park.

Thinking about her new hometown of Beverley, Effie cast her memory back to the year she had graduated from high school and her parents had taken the family on a celebratory month-long trip overseas, much of which was spent in England. The medieval buildings, the castles, stately homes, and absolutely gorgeous English gardens had entranced Effie. They had spent a week sightseeing in Yorkshire, where they had happened upon the magical market town of Beverley. Filled with unique shops and delicious restaurants, Beverley had been a surprise find for them all, and when they were due to return to London, they had decided to extend their stay up there for a few days to take it all in. Effie was in love with it all, especially the breathtaking gothic cathedral: Beverley Minster. When you come from a place where the oldest building in town was *maybe* one hundred years old, being able to stand inside a building that was built in the thirteenth century was beyond captivating.

Effie now shuddered as she considered the atmosphere of Shorty's, which was completely the opposite of captivating. She couldn't decide which was worse: the stickiness of the floor, or the lingering smell of stale cigarette smoke. After they had shouldered their way in, Boyd had waved at some goofball in the corner who wore a trucking cap pulled low over his forehead. Kill me now, she thought, as she watched Boyd head her way with a pitcher of beer in one hand and two frosty glasses in the other. Goddamn Boyd, she thought, you were supposed to be working off the wine you had with dinner, not get even more wasted. Trailing behind Boyd was the creep in the trucker hat, who happened to be leering at her as he ambled her way. "I've got to use the ladies' room, Boyd," she hastily announced, and then burned a trail from her "date" and his Neanderthal friend. Why, oh why, does this always happen to her? She had thought Boyd wanting to take her out for dinner was just going to be a nice meal and some light conversation. Quickly it had turned into one filled with way too many rage-tinged anecdotes about Boyd's ex-wife, and what a drag he found child support to be. Luckily, she had been able to keep her eye candy in view after mechanic Josh had returned to his table. As other diners blocked him from her view, she had been unable to discern who his dinner companion was, other than being male. Something about mechanic Josh was so familiar to her, but just as a fleeting memory would enter her mind, he would have a look or a mannerism that she didn't recognize. She thought they were around the same age, so maybe she just recognized him from high school activities or teenage nightlife almost two decades ago.

Dutifully trying to avoid the gaze of every other patron in this place as she made her way to the dimly lit restroom corridor, it occurred to Effie that maybe she should change her tactic—after all, she was going to be living here, so some of these people could be potential new friends. Not those people, though, as she walked past an older couple too intoxicated by either alcohol or lust to keep their hands off of each other. She shuddered, yet also oddly enough found she couldn't quite look away. As far as floor shows went, these two beat out drunken Boyd and his hipster friend. Sidestepping the couple, who by now had their hands inside each other's clothing, she tripped over a cowboy boot she hadn't seen due to her rubbernecking and went flying. Knowing she was possibly about to die while in the seediest possible place in the entire state made Effie blindly reach out and desperately grab the arm closest to her. Fortunately for her, the arm was attached to a solid body who must have foreseen her imminent demise, because she was suddenly but firmly braced by her guardian angel. Once she had steadied herself, she began laughing, and looking up, she saw a pair of bright blue eyes shimmering with laughter. Her eyes traveled down to his mouth, and all thought escaped her.

Josh could not believe his good fortune—when he and Liam had gotten to Shorty's, meeting up with Liam's lady friends, he had expected the night to go downhill fast. Much to his surprise, the women had turned out to be highly entertaining, though. Both were intelligent and easy on the eyes, and even though Josh had not felt an attraction to either woman, it had been nice just to be out, interacting with the opposite sex. Awkward on the best of days, Josh had never considered himself much of a lady's man, so either he was killing it with his witty repartee, or Sabrina and Kelly were genuinely out to just have a good time, even if it meant putting up with him and his cousin. Josh had gone to the bar to get his drinking partners another round, when suddenly a body came flying toward him, almost a human projectile. Luckily, the massive crowd inside the pool hall, which had yet so far prevented him from reaching the bar to fulfill the drink orders, provided him with additional stability to prevent both him and the human missile from falling down. Almost without thought, his hands gripped the arms pressed against his chest, and as he righted the woman in front of him, he noticed that the sweater she was wearing was of the same ivory color he had been staring at the entire time he was also attempting to eat his steak dinner. Until that moment in the restaurant earlier, he had not realized how difficult it was to consume a meal while also feasting on the sight of someone across a dining room, imagining how soft her sweater would be under his touch.

Effie had lost her breath in the fall, and now that she was in the arms of mechanic Josh, she had no hope of getting it back. Perhaps it was due to the lack of oxygen reaching her brain, or the fact she was so close to him, but recognition began to kick in for her. "Oh my god—is it…are you… Joshua Livingston?"

Never in his life had Josh been dumbfounded. No, he had always prided himself on being prepared and doing his best to anticipate any moments that could possibly throw him for a loop, but not this time. He had been loop-thrown and now was flailing in the wind. The object of his first teenage crush, way before he had ever had feelings for Tess, and before that her sister, Ruth: the willowy and winsome Euphemie Van Holland. He found he could utter no words in this situation, as completely overwhelmed as he was by the sight and feel of her. Breathing in the scent of vanilla and jasmine she seemed to be emanating made him feel intoxicated.

Effie laughed at herself, not entirely surprised that he wouldn't remember her. Although they had performed together in the school plays, other than that they hadn't run in the same circles, as she spent the rest of her free time either reading or running, while she had known Josh to be studious and dedicated to learning, and somewhat of a loner unless surrounded by extended family. Plus, it had been *so long ago,* and wherever he had gone after his sophomore year must have been so far away, since she had never heard about him again. Effie supplied, "It's me—Effie Van Holland. We were in school back in Clover Lake."

Josh shook his head, then promptly nodded, in case she mistakenly assumed that he didn't remember her. No one forgets Euphemie, of that he had no doubt, but it was no wonder that he hadn't instantly known her when she had been at the shop. No, this version of her was more of everything she had been back when they were kids—the mature markings of her face, like the laugh lines that told of someone who enjoyed life, the glints of silver running through her hair that only seemed to make it appear even darker, or the lushness in her frame that signified she did not deny herself a sweet treat. "Sorry—I am just in a state of shock that I didn't know you back at the shop, especially since I addressed you as Mrs. Van Holland." Josh chuckled at his memory. "I feel like such an idiot for not realizing it was you, which my cousin Liam pointed out when we were at dinner tonight."

Effie grinned, "I can relate—the minute I saw you at the shop, there was something about you that was triggering such a memory, but anytime I tried to capture it, it was gone. Have you ever had that happen?"

Before Josh could answer, he felt a slap on the back of his shoulders, and suddenly Liam was in his face, admonishing him, "Hey, Cuz, the ladies are waiting for us. What is taking so long with those drinks, anyway?" With a knowing glance in Effie's direction, followed by a slight smirk, Liam steered Josh to a table in the far corner of the room, where Effie could see two attractive women, one brunette and one blonde, waving to the cousins. Effie looked down at the demure clothing she had intentionally chosen for her night out with Boyd, now wishing she had worn something a little more alluring. To Josh's credit, he glanced back at her twice on the way to his table, and she swore she could feel a sense of longing in his looks, but maybe it was simply her own gaze being reflected back at her.

CHAPTER
Twenty-One

Effie

Groaning as she pulled herself out of bed, Effie wondered why her head felt as if it were being split open with a hammer. She had only had the one Cosmopolitan to drink at dinner last night, and the rest of the evening she had drunk either iced tea at the restaurant or cranberry juice at the bar. Her hangover-like symptoms probably had more to do with the company she had kept at Shorty's for the hour she had stayed than anything else. Boyd on his own when they were at dinner had been taxing enough on her nervous system, but Boyd plus sleazy friend had been overstimulating in overdrive—and not for the right reasons. Effie had been able, or so she had thought, to redirect his blatant interest in her when it had been just the two of them, but when he had a partner in his pursuit of her, Boyd had become insufferable. It was clear he had invited his friend (whose name she had trouble recalling this morning) to marvel at his ability in being a sex god, and Effie had not cared enough, frankly, to correct him—she hadn't cared enough to leave as soon as they got to

Shorty's, and then after encountering Josh, she hadn't cared enough to stop torturing herself by watching his double date with his cousin proceed in the shadowy corner of the bar. She had, at least, roused herself enough to challenge Boyd and his plus-one to a game of pool, where she soundly beat their asses in back-to-back games. It had kept her mind occupied enough to kill an hour, but then instead of feeling victorious over her wins, she had just felt miserable as she watched Josh and the blonde get closer and closer with every shot she made.

Unable to leave Boyd to fend for himself driving back to Clover Lake from Beverley, Effie had used her feminine wiles to get him in her car. Her absolute biggest seethe was drunk driving, and she would rather Boyd make a feeble pass at her at the end of their night than anything happening to him, or worse yet, someone else. He had, however, drunkenly insisted that she drop him off at his ex-wife's house, and no way in hell was she going to be held responsible for his murder, because really drunk Boyd combined with late-night Boyd had proved to be probably the most annoying combination of man. He had been at his worst when she had finally reached his place, and the ass had actually thought he still had a shot with her and began to paw at her as she was trying to keep him upright as he got out of her car. When he had tried pinning her up against the closed door, her threat of mutilation worked, and he quickly released her.

All of that, though, had been a side note of annoyance. Her true disappointment had been seeing Josh. Her interactions with him at his shop last week had seemed funny and kind and sweet, and once she knew that he was her old friend Joshua Livingston, it had all made sense; none of those qualities were evident when she was watching him at Shorty's, though. Gone had been the excited Josh when they had reconnected by chance up at the bar. Instead, he had never glanced her way once his cousin had retrieved him. He had clearly been on a date, and the disappointment had formed a rock in her stomach. She had heard him laugh a bit too loudly, and a couple of times Effie glimpsed what appeared to be a romantic entanglement between him and his date.

A knock on her bedroom door prompted Effie to fully open up her eyes, which she had only managed to squint so far. "Yes?" she croaked. Good lord, she hadn't felt like this since the morning after she had discovered the extent to which her ex, Damon, had been cheating on her. With credit cards in her name, Effie had discovered he was financing the lifestyle of his current, and pregnant, girlfriend. At the time she had phoned him, screaming at him, and then received another shocking blow: he wasn't "on tour with the band" as he had told her for the past three months but living with his new family. Her disillusionment with all of her life choices had been like daggers to her heart. How had she gotten everything so incredibly wrong? Part of her, she reckoned, had just wanted to prove to everyone that THEY had been the ones who were wrong, but she could only tell that lie to herself for so long. Unable to live one more minute in Denver, she had done justice to the library and stuck it out for two more weeks, while the library sorted out positions and hired someone new. She had been terrified that Damon would come back to their apartment before she could move out properly, but like the spineless rodent he was (was there such a thing?) he had stayed away until she had, conveniently, left town.

Her mom's head poked into the room then. "Boyd called here looking for you—he said you weren't answering your phone. He said he also need-ed a ride back to Beverley at some point to pick up his truck?" Diadema asked, with a confused expression on her face. "What in the world hap-pened last night? You didn't go home with Boyd, did you?" she followed up apprehensively.

"Good god, no," Effie vehemently replied. "I want to assure you that the LAST thing I would ever do is go home with Boyd," and she flopped back to lie on her bed, covering her head with a pillow. "Last night was a complete and utter mistake," and this time Effie was not talking about Boyd, but having to watch Josh on his double-date.

Her mom sat down on the edge of the bed. "It seems like you are learning from past mistakes? I know there was a time when you would have been inclined to pursue the attentions of the newly single Boyd—I know he can be quite the charmer when he wants to. He has never grown up though: he's a man-child, and an abhorrent one at that."

"Gee, Mom, that insight could have proved useful when I told you I was going to dinner with him—a dinner in which, he, by the way, got loaded on a bottle of wine, and then proceeded to get even more ham-mered after we stopped into a pool hall. I just thought he wanted to work off the booze, but I ended up having to drag his sorry ass out of there and drive him home." Effie rose into a seating position once again. "Ugh—he seemed so harmless when I was working at the store. Why couldn't he have just stayed being nice like that?" She studied her mom and found it ironic that now that she was moving out and into her own place in Beverley that she and Diadema had been forming such a tight bond over the past few weeks.

Diadema shook her head. "I am sure he is confused—one of those who made it big when in high school, but never moved beyond that. While you, my dear, are only beginning to shine." She took her daughter's hand and squeezed it. "I am so proud of you. I always have been, but I can see now that I should have told you more often. As you already figured out, years ago, my parents were not demonstrative or effusive with their love and praise, and I had always meant to do better with my kids. I'm sorry if I failed you," she told Effie, with tears trickling down her carefully made-up face.

Effie began crying in unison with her mom, and the two of them locked each other in a tight embrace. "I love you, Mom. I just always felt that I was the one failing you."

Diadema pulled away. "Never, and I regret I ever made you feel that way. I think I also need to explain more about your father's family, and why you lost contact with them." Her mom drew in a shaky breath. "I tried to shut down any questions you had, because I thought I was saving you, but I should have been more honest with you. Your dad and I faced criticism from not just my family, but his as well. He had been seriously dating another woman, one he had grown up with on the reservation, when he met me. His parents were furious with him when he broke it off with her—they never wanted him to leave Grass Valley in the first place, and both families thought their kids would get married and then settle back there. He tried to appease them by moving us back there after we graduated, but I never fit in through their eyes, despite doing everything I could. After Nathaniel died, they blamed me for being the reason he left the bar that night. Every time I would call them after we left to live with my parents, it devolved into some version of me causing his death." Diadema clutched both hands to her heart. "All we wanted was to live happily ever after, yet they would not let my memory of him rest," she sobbed.

Suddenly Effie was overcome with an intense memory from her past, when she was a child. It couldn't have been long after her dad died, because she got the feeling she was still five, maybe six, years old. "Was there a time we were, like, in the mall, and you called Grandma and Grandpa LeBeau on a pay phone? Why does this seem like something? And you were so upset—I remember you crying as you hung up the phone."

She watched as her mom blanched and then nodded reluctantly. "You remember that? Yes, it was the Christmas after your dad died. We had been over in Pierre on a trip to see the Christmas trees at the capitol. Since we were so close to Grass Valley, I thought I would call them to see about meeting up with them and let them see you before the holidays. We hadn't seen them since the funeral. Instead, I listened to a tirade about how if Nathaniel had never married me, he would still be alive." Diadema inhaled slowly, and then reluctantly admitted, "They also informed me that they were seeking legal counsel and would take you from me, bring you back to the reservation to be raised. I was terrified—your grandfather was an elder in the tribe, and highly respected. That's why we went and lived with my parents—I figured we would be protected by their money. But it was too much: the guilt that Nathaniel's parents were right, and it was my fault, and then the intense pain from losing the baby and my husband on the same day. I just broke from the weight of everything, and my parents sent me to Ohio."

Effie was taken aback. She had never experienced her mom being so fraught with emotion, but she now held the missing pieces of the puzzle to her own life. "Do you think that's why Grandma and Grandpa Sommer acted the way they did? They were trying to protect you? In their way?" All these years, she had considered each set of grandparents wanted nothing to do with her, when it turned out they were all damaged in their own ways.

Her mom shrugged, "Maybe. I would love to believe that, but I was always afraid that what happened with Nathaniel's parents just heightened their own misgivings and prejudices. Now it's too late to ask them." Stephen Sommer had passed away when Effie was twenty from lung cancer, due to his decades-long love of tobacco pipes, and Charlotte Sommer had passed away three years ago from dementia. "I never want that kind of divide between us," she told her daughter.

Something her mother had said a few minutes ago was eating at her, and it threatened to dampen the closeness they were sharing the more she pondered it. "Wait—you said we would be protected by their money. What did you mean by that?" Her mother looked away and Effie noticed that her hands were starting to shake. What the hell was going on? "Mom—what did you mean by that? Is there something you're not telling me?"

Diadema threw her an anguished look, pleading with her eyes, but Effie was not going to let this matter drop, as she had for so many years already. Insistently, she repeated herself, "What are you not telling me?"

"We took out a restraining order on them. On your grandparents—Nathaniel's parents." Her mom clutched Effie's fingers as she continued, with desperation in her tone. "They had threatened me, Effie. They threatened to take you away from me, so my parents hired a lawyer, and we won a restraining order. I had messages on my answering machine from them, letters, all telling me that you deserved to be raised among the tribe with your dad's family."

Mouth agape, Effie struggled for the ability to process what she was hearing. "So instead of working something out with them, you, what? Stood behind your rich white parents and cut off all of my ties to my Native heritage? God, Mom, that's fucked up. You do realize that? I understand that you were scared and grieving, but to cut off the other part of me? When your own parents could barely tolerate me? I can't believe a few minutes ago I was feeling empathetic toward them!"

"Effie, please, just try and understand—" her mom begged.

"Mom, I'm sorry. I need to get out of here." Effie pulled her hand from her mom's and rose from the bed. "I need to take Boyd back to his truck. I also need to take care of some stuff in Beverley, but first I have to shower and get dressed." Effie held open her bedroom door, indicating to her mom the time had come to leave. As she passed by Effie, Diadema tried to reach for her, but Effie shrunk back, not wanting to make her mom feel better about any of this. It seemed they were back where they always ended up: Effie unable to trust in her mom, and her mom always disappointing her.

CHAPTER
Twenty-Two

Josh

After booking a customer's oil change appointment for later in the afternoon, Josh hung up the phone. His body had refused to answer the call of his alarm just as dawn was breaking this morning. He had imbibed a bit too much last night (thank you, Liam) and had made a resounding vow to himself to avoid Shorty's for at least the next decade. Should be easy to do, considering he did not plan on staying in Beverley for much longer, though. When he had taken his leave from the hospital, he had reluctantly agreed with Dr. Gilmore that it would be taken in three-month intervals, and as such, could be reassessed at the end of every period. His three months were up next week, and before coming to the shop, he had a video call with Dr. Gilmore, during which he reluctantly agreed to extend it for another three months. Finally, he was able to see the light at the end of his potential career-suicide tunnel, and he was fairly certain that it all would be completely fixed after another term. He'd be able to be back in Manhattan by the time summer was winding down.

His attending surgeon had advised him to not be in a rush to bring his leave to an end and encouraged him to take this time and heal as fully as he could mentally.

"Hey, Dad, I'm going to run over to Mr. Beans and get us some lunch, okay?" he called to the back of the shop.

"Sounds great. Oh, Josh, get me one of those berry smoothies, too, will ya?" Josh smiled, as this had become the standard request from his dad whenever he got lunch from the coffee shop. Never in a million years would Josh have guessed his dad would become a smoothie drinker, but here they were. As he walked to the end of the block, he saw a Honda CRV pull around the corner. The windows in the car were rolled down, and Josh could see the driver was Effie Van Holland. Oh, he thought to himself, maybe his day was going to pick up, but then he could see that in the passenger seat sat Boyd Timmons, and he was instantly deflated. He had hoped that seeing her out with him at the steakhouse last night had been a fluke, but then to see them again at Shorty's and then now made him realize he had to face the music of them being an item. His instincts had been right last night, then, as Liam had commandeered him back to their table, without a chance to say anything else to Effie. As he had watched her across the bar the rest of the evening, so many times he had felt drawn to her, and he had tried to catch her eye, wanting to make a connection. She had been so funny and talented in school, and although he had felt she was out of his league at every turn, she captivated him completely when they would be running lines together during every play practice.

He recalled quite clearly the first play they had been in together, *Lil' Abner.* He had been astounded when he had won a minor role in it, and quickly during practice, it had become clear that most of the other actors had already established connections with other cast mates. Since he was a freshman, he had looked forlornly around the auditorium and had locked eyes with Effie. Since Clover Lake was a small town, they had occasionally been in the same extra-curricular groups as each other, like 4-H, band, and choir, but he wouldn't say they had been "friends". Effie had been very quiet, always seeming to be on the outside looking in, unless she was running in her track events, and Josh preferred to be NOT running track events. As puberty came along almost immediately following his mom's abandonment, he had gotten heavier. His self-esteem had taken a beating, then, and a short stint of acne hadn't helped. Effie, though, always seemed to shine. When their eyes had met that first day of play practice, Josh had looked away in a hurry, certain that she would probably prefer to pair up with an older boy (reference her date with Boyd last night). However, when he had looked up from his script, Effie was making a beeline for him.

"Hey, Joshua, can I sit there?" she had asked, indicating the desk next to his. "I feel like I'll only be comfortable with someone I already know. Since this is my first time in a play, some of these older kids are so intimidating."

Through his astonishment, Josh had managed to squeak out a response, "Sure—and call me Josh." Joshua was too painful to hear, since his mom had been the one to call him that. And that was it for Josh. For the next two years, he looked forward to performing in a play twice a year, and he and Effie had been side by side for all of them for two years. He still felt like an idiot that he hadn't recognized either her or her name at the shop. After he and his dad had abruptly left Clover Lake all of those years ago, he wondered if she had thought about him at all. He had missed the cousins who lived nearby and friends, along with the close-knit community of a small town. Not that Beverley was a huge city, but its high school was almost ten times the size of tiny Clover Lake. Josh had gone from knowing everyone to knowing no one, and the drama department at Beverley High School had already been full of kids who, like him, had been acting since freshman year, so he didn't even try to get in with them. Most of all, he had missed the fleeting moments of tenderness he shared with Effie, even if nothing had ever been reciprocated.

He guessed her taste in the "bad boy" hadn't changed, if her date with Boyd last night was any indication. What could she see in that mouth-breather, anyway? Unless, by some miracle, he had changed, but according to Liam, he was the same. And Liam would know, since his mother took it upon herself to know everything going on in the town. Before he left for New York City, he really should make it a point to get over to Clover Lake, but the town remained a painful part of Josh's past. He supposed it was difficult to lose your mother at any age, but to just have her walk out of your life, especially at the age of twelve? The world was confusing enough when you are not a child, yet not a teenager, without having to wonder what it was you had done to make your own mom stop loving you, and he thought about the letter she had left him.

"Dear Joshua," it began,

"By the time you read this, I will be gone. It has been a struggle for me every day to try and be happy in this life I created with your dad, but I can't keep my pain inside anymore. The truth is, I never should have been a mother. I never wanted kids—did Henry ever tell you that? If not, I am sorry you are learning it now. I may not have intended on being a mother, but being your mom, my beautiful boy, has been my only saving grace in this world. Unfortunately for both of us, I need bigger things out of life, things I have pushed aside to be a wife and mom. I have begged your father for years to go back to school, get a degree, but he only wanted to work in that auto shop, surrounded by his family. What about what I wanted? It was all swept away when I met Henry Livingston that day on the lake. Three months later, I was disowned by my family for not going to college, and then for marrying your father without their blessing. I was all alone. Your father tried, I will give him credit, but we had nothing to build a marriage on other than a summer of one-night stands. Whatever you do, Joshua, make sure you marry someone you have known and built a relationship with. Someone who suits you and fits your life. Take care of your father, please. I am sorry to put this on you, but he will need you when I am gone. Most importantly, get an education. Get a degree. You are spectacular, my son. Brilliant in ways I have been in awe of since you were a baby. Don't grieve for me when I am gone. Maybe we will find each other again one day, but know you will be in my heart no matter where I am.

Love,

Mom".

He had been shattered upon reading his mother's goodbye letter, whose contents had ranged from too explicit to too vague. She had left one for her husband, too, and to this day Josh had never asked his dad what she had written to him. Then again, Henry hadn't inquired too much about his son's letter. Her timing could not have been crueler, in Josh's eyes, as he had still needed her, just going into middle school, and then later high school. She had been his greatest cheerleader, always there for parent-teacher conferences, school recitals, tears when his father didn't understand him. It had always been his mother he had been closest to, not fitting in with his dad; that was, until his mom had walked out, leaving the two men in her life to forge a path toward a new life on their own, but together.

CHAPTER
Twenty-Three

Effie

"Effie, please, I'm sorry. Please let me make it up to you—let's go for dinner again tonight." Boyd snapped his fingers, "We can have a do-over! We can stay in Clover Lake this time, or, hey! I know! Let's spend the day together in Beverley! We can walk the riverfront, then follow it down by the lake, and have lunch in that cute little gazebo you pointed out to me last night. You'd like that, right?" he asked, but then made the unfortunate move of reaching over to rub her shoulders.

In complete exasperation, she swatted away his hand. The entire trip from Clover Lake to Beverley, which took about forty minutes, felt instead like two hours, with Boyd yammering on incessantly. All about himself, of course, and based on his stories, he was indeed proving himself to have peaked in high school. At least her mother had been honest about something this morning—no, no, she broke herself off. Not going there now. She had enough dealing with Boyd.

"Boyd, do you actually think, in a million years, I would *ever* go out with you? No do-over, no dinner, no lunch, no walk. In fact, I would like to erase last night from ever happening. And who was that sleazy friend of yours?"

"Oh, that—"

"Christ, Boyd," she interrupted him, "I don't really want to know. But what the hell? What—did you think you were getting lucky last night, maybe get a threesome going on? Or were you attempting to show me how great you are by having your gross friend as an alternative? You need to get your act together, concentrate on being a good dad to your kids, and maybe a decent man to your wife." Effie paused to take a breath and get her temper under control, which was much harder to do when dealing with a complete jackass. "I thought we were friends, and I immensely appreciated that after I moved back. But if you misinterpreted any of my kindness or gratitude as anything more, that is on you. Do you think I got out of one shitty relationship so I could immediately start one with you?"

"What about those clothes you wear to work? You're telling me you weren't trying to get my attention? And that haircut you got? Where it brushes against your shoulders? Effie, you know you drive me crazy. I remember when I was head lifeguard, and you would come to the pool in that bikini—" Effie held up her hand to cut him off before his reminiscing could begin.

"Seriously, Boyd? It's not enough that you are already coming across as some kind of obsessed stalker, but now kind of a pervert? For one thing, those 'clothes'," Effie provided air quotes, "that you mentioned? It was jeans and a t-shirt, which almost everyone else who works at the grocery store wears to work. And my bikini? I was fifteen, and you were eighteen! I may have had a crush on you back then, but I was clearly an idiot."

Boyd grinned, "See? You had feelings for me—who's to say you couldn't have them again?"

"OH MY GOD! You are deranged, and I can't deal with you anymore." Effie slammed on the brakes and pulled over to the curb. "GET OUT," she screamed, pointing to the passenger door. "NOW! Get out of my car."

"But," he sputtered, "we're not at my car yet."

"You can walk from here; it's only a couple of blocks. I want you out. You refuse to listen to me. Get out, now. And consider this my new resignation day. I'm done—with you, with Clover Lake, with everything."

With that, she pulled a U-turn and drove away from Boyd, who did her the courtesy of holding up his middle finger. Not to be outdone, she matched him and waved a one-fingered goodbye. Good, she thought, this saved her the trouble of spending any more time with him. Effie turned down a side street and then pulled up to the curb in order to get her bearings. Her day had been too emotional already, and it wasn't even noon. She knew one of the reasons she also felt frayed was because she could not get Josh out of her mind, and imagining him with that unknown woman from last night was making her crazy. She put her head on the steering wheel and cursed herself for becoming as obsessed as she had just accused Boyd of being. Closing her eyes, she let herself ruminate on Mr. Josh Livingston, and how excited she had been to recognize him after literally running into him at Shorty's. He was just as she remembered him back in school, at least personality-wise. He had changed, though, physically. He'd been much taller than she remembered, but that made sense since she had last seen him when he was sixteen. His hair was a bit darker blond now than it had been back then, and it suited his eyes so well. His face was leaner, and clear of any of the teenage acne that had tended to plague all of them in high school. His smile, though…his smile was the absolute replica of the one that the Josh she remembered fondly would flash her way when he was nervous, and it was that endearing smile that had drawn her in, and finally made her feel seen. She had always been somewhat of a loner, preferring her own company to others. Maybe it was being an only child for so long until her brother came along, or simply a product of her upbringing, but she had only ever felt truly comfortable in her bedroom with a book in her hand, immersing herself in a role on the stage, or running a race in track.

Teenage Josh had been the most sincere person she had ever met in her life, and it wasn't until she was in her twenties that she appreciated such sincerity. The ability to not just be honest, but also genuine and real— so few people had that. Watching Josh last night, it had been difficult to spot any of that precious commodity. From across the dimly lit bar, she could see the act he was putting on for the women and his cousin. She had known plenty of good-looking guys, even in high school, but what did she need to look at a pretty face for? It was grace and dignity, humanity and humility, that she found attractive. Well, that she wanted to, anyway. Damon proved her wrong on that—she had been at a vulnerable point in her life and had too slowly admitted to herself how much he was lacking, except for his pretty face.

Lifting her head from the steering wheel, she crossed her arms over her chest and let sorrow overtake her. She regretted walking out on her mom this morning. Effie could understand that Diadema had only done her best, given the tools she had at her disposal, and she was also cognizant of how scared and intimidated her mother must have been by both sets of parents, her own and Nathaniel's. Her phone rang from inside her bag, and she saw that her best friend from Denver, Alice, was calling her. She had not spoken to her in a few weeks, and in fact had avoided Alice's last couple of attempts at reaching out—it had been difficult for Effie to face the friend who had been a front-row seat holder for the mistakes she had made in Denver. Effie had never confided in her suspicions about Damon to anyone, and that made it worse. It looked, to all of her friends, as if she had been clueless and blind to it all, when in reality she just hadn't wanted the humiliation to be known by one and all. When the truth had become undeniable, the pity in the eyes of her friends had been overwhelming, which was one of the reasons she had made the decision to quit the library there, pull up stakes, and move back home. Alice had pleaded with her, trying to reason that taking a couple of weeks off was better than giving a two weeks' notice, but Effie had to leave for her own best interests.

"Effie, how are you?" Alice asked once Effie had answered her phone. "I haven't heard from you in a while and wanted to know if he got there."

"What are you talking about, Alice?" Effie was perplexed, but also dreading whatever her friend's next words were going to be.

"Damon—did he make it there? I tried calling you but never got you." Oh shit, oh shit, oh shit, Effie thought to herself.

"I don't have a clue what you're talking about—what do you mean, did Damon make it here? He doesn't even know where I am. I talked to him like a month ago and he was raging about wanting his stuff back. Ratty concert tees and unwashed underwear are not something I was holding onto, so I told Kristy to let him in so he could pack his crap up."

"I don't know about any of that, but he came around to the library, all pathetic like, and gave some sob story about you leaving him, and taking all the money, and wanting a divorce. Well, nobody was buying it, but he said he was desperate to talk to you, but couldn't reach you, and he wanted to know where you had gone."

Effie felt herself flush with humiliation, both because Damon had done this and because her friend was involved. What was wrong with him? Why wasn't he happy just moving on with his life? Instead, he had to plague her with demands for shit she knew he didn't care about. Maybe the better question would be: what was wrong with her?

Effie exhaled a shaky breath, "I'm so sorry this happened, Alice. The last thing I wanted was to bring any more friends into this situation—Kristy was unavoidable because she took over my rental, but I really thought I could make a clean break."

"It's not your fault, Babe. I'm the one who should be sorry. I should have tried harder to reach you. No one told him anything about you, so if he does show up, he didn't get the info from us. But as my grandma used to say, 'he may be dumb, but he's not stupid'. It won't take him long to try to find you in your hometown, I'm sure." Effie then heard someone talking to Alice in the background, and she thought the voice sounded like her wife. "Sorry about that—Carmen and I are taking the kids to the zoo today. Look, I know you don't like to talk about your problems, but you need to let people in, Effie. Your friends want to help you, no matter what. We have all been in shitty relationships and it's nothing to be ashamed of. You are so amazing and greatly deserve more than whatever kind of crumbs Damon or any of your exes were throwing to you."

The two friends said their goodbyes, and Effie dropped her phone. Why, every time she thought she was getting her life together, did it have to throw her a curveball? Although she was grateful to have reconnected with her friend, now was she supposed to be paranoid about Damon showing up in Clover Lake? No, no way would he: he was too lazy and self-involved to do something like that. He had enough on his plate with his other woman and their baby. Now she was even more so looking to start her life over in Beverley, where Damon could never find her.

Glancing into her rear-view mirror, Effie pulled away from the curb and made the turn around the block, and as she turned onto Main Street again, she saw Josh crossing the street back to the auto shop, carrying a flat of drinks. She was wrong to feel so alone—she had Josh here, and they could be just friends. Whatever spark she had thought she felt last night or last week, she was going to file away as "unneeded": if there was one thing Effie excelled at, it was cutting off emotions and moving on. She shouldn't care if Josh was seeing someone, because she was hardly in a place mentally for a relationship, anyway—hell, she wasn't even divorced yet. What mattered was having a friend here, in her new town, and she and Josh had known each other since grade school. Now seemed like a good time to pop in and say "hi" to a friend, she reflected, and she parked her car on the street and headed down to the shop.

CHAPTER
Twenty-Four

Effie And Josh

Finally, taking a sip of his steaming hot mocha, Josh walked over to the office to answer the ringing phone. As much as he enjoyed working in the shop, the truth was that most of his day was spent answering the business's phone, because it seemed that everyone else had selective hearing, or perhaps they just liked having someone else to run to the office, so they didn't have to stop their work. The question of why his dad didn't have cordless phones had been answered when he saw how careless the employees could be with their own phones, and he imagined, based on the evidence, that a phone would end up going home with customers, falling into an oil changing pit, or being crushed by an outgoing or incoming car.

After scheduling the phoning customer in for a tire rotation tomorrow, Josh walked out of the office and, much to his delight, he saw Effie talking to Phil, his father's longest-serving employee. She looked extremely delectable, in a fluffy pink sweater and black jeans. When Effie looked over Phil's shoulder, she broke into a smile after noticing Josh.

"Effie, hi, what brings you here this morning?" Josh greeted her.

Effie smiled, but Josh felt like she wasn't feeling as sunny as she was trying to portray. "Oh, I had to come to town to take care of some stuff, so I thought I would pop in and say 'hi', after we ran into each other last night," she said, somewhat stiltedly.

"Do you…do you want a coffee?" Josh stuttered. Or had he? It felt like he had stuttered, which was something he used to do YEARS ago when he got nervous. "I brought back one for my dad, but he took a car out on a test run, and he has a smoothie." When she tried to refuse, Josh said, "Please—he probably won't drink it, anyway. He prefers his own brew, and I have to admit that most of the time, so do I. It's a caramel latte," Josh said, in a voice he hoped sounded so enticing she would overlook his babbling.

This time Josh got what he felt was a genuine smile from her, and after calling to Phil that he was stepping out for a few minutes, he guided her to the side of the building to the bench where he and Ruth had sat just a week ago for their surprise catch-up. He caught the wink Phil sent in his direction just before they exited the shop, and felt himself flush, knowing he was not going to hear the end of this from the guys who worked there.

Effie took a sip of the latte and sighed in response. The drink was delicious, and just the bolt she needed. So was Josh's warmness, and his ability to put her at ease. Watching him in his coveralls when he walked over to her had left her slightly parched, as she admired the way the fabric stretched tightly across his shoulders. Up close, she now noticed that the top two buttons of his uniform were not snapped, and she glimpsed some chest hair peeking out from the V-neck, causing her to be breathless and slightly dizzy. Friends, she reminded herself—just friends. She cleared her throat and said, "Thank you for the drink—I needed this. I just wanted to stop by and say it was so great seeing you last night, even if all I did was crash into you." Effie gazed into his eyes, mesmerized by the blue pools of sincerity. These were the eyes she recalled from years ago. Eyes that she trusted and eyes that made her feel safe, and she was drifting back to that time, to that feeling of security. Suddenly, she scolded herself—she was here to see her friend, not get caught up in an old attraction. Perhaps if she had stayed focused on guys like Josh in the first place, she chided herself, she wouldn't have been so terrible at love.

Josh laughed, "I'm so glad that you did come by—I wanted to apologize for how rude I must have been when I left you so abruptly. You remember my cousin Liam, right?" At her nod, he continued, "Yeah, that's what I thought. Liam is very memorable. Me, on the other hand, not so much," Josh said, trying to make light of himself and hoping he had pulled it off. He was truly kidding on the square, though. Josh was used to weaving through life in the shadows, only really standing out in the medical field—or he used to, before going down in flames. "Liam is definitely a force, you know? I just wanted you to know that when he came up and interrupted us, I thought I was just going to take the drinks to our table and come back to you, but when I turned around, I saw you were with Boyd and didn't want to interrupt." Josh took another sip of his coffee, not really out of thirst, but as an excuse to study her face for a reaction about Boyd.

Effie rolled her eyes, "God, I wish you had interrupted! Seriously, my evening was pretty insufferable with him," she confessed.

Josh widened his eyes in genuine surprise. "Wow! Really? It looked like you were having a nice date in the restaurant and then later at the bar."

Effie gave a quick shake of her head, "Wait—what? I can assure you, whole-heartedly, that Boyd and I were most definitely NOT on a date. It was, at best, a casual dinner." She grimaced and then continued, "Well, for me, at least. I guess for Boyd it was something else," she admitted reluctantly, then followed up, "but that had nothing to do with me! And then he did me the favor of getting too drunk to drive his car back to Clover Lake last night, so I had to put up with him on the ride home, and then again this morning, when I graciously gave him a ride back here to retrieve his car."

Josh laughed and tilted his head to the side. "Oh no, that sounds horrendous. You went from just going out to dinner, to finding yourself suddenly on a date with Boyd, completely out of your control? I can relate—that's what happened to me last night, courtesy of my cousin." Josh scratched his chin, remembering that he had not taken the time to shave that morning. Tess had hated when he wasn't clean-shaven, so he used to be meticulous about it. "Not that I was on a date last night, but when we got to Shorty's, Liam had arranged some woman and her friend to meet us there for drinks. That's who he was dragging me back to at the table."

Effie nodded in understanding, "You seemed like you were having a good time, though, so Liam must have been right."

Josh shrugged his shoulders, "It was alright. I doubt I will be seeing either of those women again, at least in any sort of 'dating' capacity. One of them was pretty focused on Liam, but her friend was definitely not into me. I'm not always great in social situations—I never know if I'm saying the right things, you know? Anyway, it's for the best: I'm not interested in starting a relationship, casual or otherwise." Josh watched as his dad pulled up in his test car and parked it with a frown marring his features. Josh was aware he needed to get back to work, and could hear the phone ringing occasionally, but also being answered more promptly than when he was in the shop—it just felt too peaceful sitting here with Effie.

"I get it—I am fresh off the divorce boat myself. Or I will be in a few months, anyway," Effie confessed, looking down at her coffee. "None of my wedding guides or magazines told me that I would feel like such a failure going through this—how overwhelming the humiliation would be." Why was she baring her soul to him? She had not truly spoken to him in almost twenty years, and even at that, it wasn't like they had been particularly close. But she had wanted to be, and badly. And then he had left, but now she guessed she at least knew where he had gone—Beverley.

Josh wrinkled his brows. "Oh, no, I am so sorry. I know the feeling, though. Not that I am recently divorced," he hurriedly corrected himself. "But I had a broken engagement a few months ago." Josh pushed his ball cap off his head, so it sat slightly askew, and heaved a great sigh. "Who am I kidding? I was left at the altar, believe it or not." He cast a glance at Effie, saying, "We're quite a pair, I guess."

"You're actually the second person I have heard about in the past month who was left at the altar, so don't feel too bad about it. Broken hearts club, reunited friends," and she lifted her coffee to toast with Josh's. "To be honest, I am still having a hard time believing that I ran into you here, after not seeing you for so many years. I hadn't been here in Beverley since I went away to college. I moved back to Clover Lake from Denver a couple of months ago, and until then I had not been back there for any length of time in at least ten years, only for a weekend every six months or so. I didn't know what to expect after moving back, you know? I just wanted a fresh start, and I guess Beverley will now be that after being in Clover Lake."

Josh looked at her in surprise. "Oh, really? You're moving over here now?"

Effie laughed, "Yeah, I guess I buried the lede there, huh? You are looking at the newest librarian at the Beverley Carnegie Library," she proudly announced, "so you will probably be seeing more of me around here starting in the next week or so."

"Wow—that's fantastic, Effie." Josh congratulated her.

She poked him in the arm, "Yeah, so you better get that library card renewed."

Josh coughed and began, "Actually, I—" until he was interrupted by his dad shouting for him from the garage.

"Josh, you about done with that hour-long break?" He could hear the teasing in his dad's tone. He looked down at his watch, and although an hour was slightly exaggerating the length of time he had been sitting here with Effie, he knew it had been long enough, yet he wanted even more time. He looked into her golden eyes, and watched the way her pupils dilated, and then cast his eyes to her shoulders, where the ends of her midnight-dark hair brushed her shoulders.

"Josh? Josh?" Effie's voice broke him out of his reverie.

"Sorry, I need to get back to work," he said, rather stiffly, and then with a half-hearted wave, he ducked back into the shop.

"Was it something I said?" Effie questioned silently to his retreating back, wondering how he could go from warm and friendly to cold and distant so quickly.

Twenty-Five

Josh

It had been almost two weeks since they had shared a coffee break on the bench outside of Check Care Auto, and in that time, Josh had grown used to spotting Effie around Beverley. He supposed it was inevitable, considering the fact that the auto shop was only two blocks from the library, yet this was what made it even that more frustrating for him: all he did was get glimpses of her. Through her frequent trips to the coffee shop from the library, or walking back down Main Street on the way to the town square (if he stood at the exact spot around the back corner of the shop, he had a clear view of her sitting in the gazebo, where it appeared she liked to eat her lunch), he had seen her almost every day. Never once did she pop in to say 'hi' to him, or maybe bring him a coffee, as Lana used to do at the hospital. He wasn't comparing the two, but he had thought he and Effie had gotten off to a great start with their conversation, and he had been under the impression that maybe a friendship was growing. He hadn't even known for sure when she had started at the library, and it would be nice to confirm if she was now living in Beverley as well, he mused.

His disappearing act from her that day was strange, even to himself. They had been getting along so well, and then he could feel stirrings welling up inside him that he recognized as attraction. Not in the physical way (although he couldn't deny that), but in the actual way you connect deeply with someone else, and he hadn't had that with anyone since Tess; considering how that had ended, he was not eager to begin something new anytime soon. Especially since he was not staying here in Beverley. Was he happy here for the moment? Yes, but that had more to do with spending time with his dad and the workers at the shop and seeing his extended family frequently. Just because he was currently content didn't mean he wasn't eager to get back to New York City to finish his residency, though, despite his dad's many comments otherwise. Increasingly often, Henry had taken to pointing out how peaceful and stress-free Josh had seemed since arriving home, and Josh had to admit that it was true; however, he was born to be a surgeon, and the ache to operate was getting stronger.

Josh stretched and took off his coveralls—after staining a few too many of his favorite t-shirts, he had taken his dad's advice and begun wearing them, despite the fact he felt at least two decades older as soon as he donned the outerwear. On his first day at the shop, he had prided himself on not getting anything on his clothes, but he had been unable to maintain an uninterrupted length of cleanliness working on cars. He especially wanted to look decent today, since he was meeting with Ruth and her husband, Sean, at Betsy's Diner, located a few blocks off of Main Street. Ruth had called him yesterday, telling him she and Sean would be in town again to finalize details on their move back to South Dakota and had proposed the idea of the three of them having an early dinner, since they would be just arriving from the airport in Sioux Falls.

As he washed up in the shop's surprisingly pristine bathroom, he studied his face in the mirror and marveled at the change in it from those months ago on the worst day of his life. Or one of them, at the very least. Was it common to have more than one "worst day in your life" day, he wondered? Or does everyone have multiples? His eyes no longer were bloodshot, the lines on his face were due to laughing, not worrying, and he had to squint to really be able to detect the frown line that had just started to appear between his eyebrows. His face was no longer gaunt, having filled out, along with the rest of his body, since he had gained a few pounds thanks to his newly discovered culinary skills.

Josh took off the t-shirt he had sweat through during his workday and put on the button-down Oxford shirt he had carried with him this morning, recalling that Tess had always been particularly fond of the moss-green color, saying it accentuated the blue of his eyes. He closed those blue eyes now, and suddenly it dawned on him that the last time he had worn this exact shirt was at his rehearsal dinner—another of his worst days. Wiping at the tears creeping into his eyes, Josh was dismayed to discover that he still felt such a loss from that day. It was one thing to lose your fiancée, he supposed, but that day he had also lost the person who had been his best friend for so many years. Maybe this dinner was a mistake—he wasn't ready to sit down with a couple he knew were painfully, blissfully, happy. A couple who had almost been his family. What were they now to him? He figured Ruth would always be his first (unrequited) love, and one of his oldest friends, but what about Sean? During the seven years Sean since had been part of Ruth's life, the two couples had seen each other on a fairly regular basis, considering the two sisters lived two hours away from each other.

Making a flash decision, Josh took his phone out of his pocket to text Ruth that he couldn't make it. What would be plausible? Josh had never been comfortable with lying or half-truths, although he was sure Tess would disagree with that. One of her major complaints against him had been that he would go behind her back in favor of his career over their relationship. Maybe he could say that his dad needed him to work to-night—that an emergency had arisen at the shop and—. He had gotten no further than trying to figure it out in his head when a text popped up from none other than Ruth herself. Always the queen of directness, the message read, "At diner. Get your butt here. Don't even think of canceling." Well, there went that brilliant idea. How did Ruth always know how to suss out the truth? Tess had told him more than once that she could never hide anything from her older sister, because Ruth somehow got there in the end.

Well, no use in avoiding it any longer, he supposed. Part of him was looking forward to seeing his old friends, he admitted to himself, as he walked the short blocks to the diner. He loved Betsy's Diner, had since he and his dad had moved here almost twenty years ago—it was an old school, East Coast-style diner, and was in an actual renovated dining car located on what had been the location of the train depot when the rail line had made regular and frequent stops in Beverley, over a century ago. As he crossed to the other side of the street, his path took him past the library, and he looked around for Effie's car, in the hopes that he would see her.

Nearing Betsy's, he spied a rental car in the lot and assumed that was Ruth and Sean's car for this trip. How was Sean going to adjust from being a pediatrician in Philadelphia to working in Beverley? The hospital did service a wide surrounding area, whose circumference had gotten larger with the closing of so many hospitals in the smaller towns. Still, it was going to be a huge adjustment for Sean, who he knew had also grown up in Philly.

Storming out of the establishment came Ruth, a flurry of yellow dress and blonde hair, and she launched herself at him to envelop him in one of her signature hugs.

"Josh, I have been watching for you out the window. What took you so long? I thought the shop closed at five? How's your dad?" She continued with her litany of questions, and in true Ruth fashion, never waited for a response. She locked her arm in his, and they entered together. Josh saw Sean sitting in a booth in the center of the diner, smiling at them both.

"Ruth," Sean scolded, "let the man sit down. I'm sure he's been on his feet all day." And then Sean stood up, stuck out his hand for a brief handshake, but then pulled Josh close for a hug. Ruth and Sean were a very tactile couple, not afraid of public displays of affection. Even though Ruth had been Josh's first crush, he had never held on to those feelings, because it had become apparent rather quickly they were not, nor would they ever be, well-matched. He was man enough to admit that Ruth's life force was A LOT, and he, frankly, could never have been up for it. Few men could be.

"Josh, I ordered you a Diet Pepsi—that's still your drink, right? I was saying to Sean that I could remember the first time we ever met—do you remember? It was outside the high school, and you were getting out of your car, and trying to balance your backpack and—" she tilted her head to look at Josh, "—hell—what instrument did you play? Was it the tuba or trombone? Anyway," she continued, waving her hands in front of her, "you were trying to get the case out of your car, but you had your bottle of Diet Pepsi on top of your car, and just as I yelled to you to be careful—"

"The pop tipped over, got all over my backpack and tuba case," with a nod to Ruth, Josh continued, "and if you hadn't yelled at me, it would have gotten all over me." The three chuckled at the story, and Josh was ashamed he had ever considered canceling. He had always been too quick to duck his head in the sand when faced with something uncomfortable.

"God, Ruth, you've been saving people from worse fates for forever, huh? Must be how I lucked out with you," Sean told her, and pulled her to his side for a kiss on the cheek.

CHAPTER
Twenty-Six

Ruth

Looking at Josh, Ruth knew she had been justified sending him the warning text about canceling on dinner. As soon as she had seen him walking up to Betsy's Diner, he had the look of a hunted man. Josh had never been great with difficult situations, and she had guessed (correctly) that he would see having dinner with her and Sean as a difficult situation. She knew from experience that Josh preferred his life in careful little boxes, and now that he wasn't involved with her sister anymore, he would not know which box to put their own relationship in. Honestly, Ruth wasn't sure either, but she had known him for so long that she wanted to show Josh they could have their own box: one that didn't include Tess, for the first time since they had met. Since she and Sean were moving back here next month, it was especially important, and if Josh was still in Beverley, or would be in Beverley, she wanted to be in his life.

Rubbing her belly even though she was just in the beginning of her second trimester, Ruth slanted back against the booth, relishing still being able to squeeze in to the tight space—for now, at least. How in the hell had she managed to get knocked up when her firstborn was still a baby? She and Sean had wanted to have kids close in age, but she had not intended to have Irish twins (literally, since Sean's grandparents all hailed from Ireland). Last year she had been four months pregnant when she and her sister had taken the train to California for Tess's bachelorette party (for her failed wedding to Josh) and this year she was going to be five months pregnant when Tess married Sam on that same train, in a few weeks.

Ruth took a drink of Dr. Pepper, which she had found last year to be the cure for her morning sickness, happy that it was still working like a charm. "So, Josh, Tess told me that you reached out to Sam after I saw you." Ruth reached out to squeeze Josh's hand. "That was so generous of you—it meant the world to both of them."

Josh cleared his throat, and then admitted, "I won't lie; it took a lot, but I'm not going to keep any bitterness about it. I want the best for them, I really do, and it seems like they are the best for each other."

Sean reached over to his wife and pulled her hand away from Josh's and into his. "Okay, Babe, enough mothering. Are we here to eat or do more relationship counseling?"

Sometimes her husband's astuteness could be so confounding, but she was willing to admit one thing: she was, in fact, here to eat.

The group settled on their supper choices: patty melt for Ruth, taco salad for Sean, and the hot beef sandwich with extra mashed potatoes for Josh. "Every time I have come here for a meal with my dad since I've been back, I have wanted the hot beef, but they took it off the menu, for whatever illogical reason, and now it's only a special on certain days—none of which have coincided on the day I have actually eaten here, until now," Josh confessed, with seemingly great anticipation for his supper choice.

Ruth was aghast. "What? Oh, I see it here on the specials insert—I hadn't noticed that before. Who does that? Who takes the hot beef off the menu? Anyone on their worst day could come in here and think, 'Wow— you know what I would love? Two slices of white bread filled with thinly sliced roast beef and then smother the hell out of that bad boy with beef gravy'." Everyone laughed in agreement.

Ruth studied Josh and was relieved to see how at ease he appeared now, a complete transformation from when he had first arrived, she was sure, if her last meeting with him had been any indication. She had told her sister about meeting up with Josh tonight, and Tess had been thrilled. Even though she had moved on, she admitted to Ruth that she would always have a place in her heart for her first love.

Their teenage waitress, Sissy, sidled over to take their order, and once she walked away, Josh turned his head to Sean, asking, "I'm curious, Sean, how do you think you will handle living in Beverley? Big town here in South Dakota, but compared to Philadelphia, it must seem so tiny. The funny thing is I remember when my dad and I moved here after my mom was gone, and I was terrified of going to such a bigger high school. I went from having thirty kids in my grade to having like two hundred and fifty."

"And then you moved to New York City," Ruth exclaimed, "and never left. How weird is that?"

Josh nodded. "Yeah—it all seems like a lifetime ago, really. So, Sean, thoughts?" he prompted.

Sean laughed and shook his head, "I have always loved visiting here when we would come to see John and Ellen; even though we stayed with them out on the farm, we still came into town to go out to eat or see a movie or go to the park. Beverley is a beautiful little place, and I am looking forward to actually knowing who my patients are, you know? Life in Philly, hell—any large city, can be so anonymous so often. Here I might have the chance to see my patients as children grow up and then years later bring their kids to see me, and I like that notion."

"Yeah, I can see that aspect of it," Josh seemed to reluctantly agree. "But won't you miss the cheesesteaks, or going to a Phillies game, or seeing a concert?"

Ruth could see that to Josh, leaving an urban environment would mean giving up certain things, which was true, but Sean had been the first to assure her that they would be gaining just as much, if not more, by their rural move. "Good god, Josh, it's not another planet. His family is still in Philly, and we will be visiting there just as frequently as we came back here, probably more now that we have kids, and as far as concerts go, Sioux Falls actually books a lot of shows now, or we can go to Omaha or Minneapolis," she clarified. She knew his mental wheels were turning, trying to sort out how to properly box everything up.

The waitress brought their food to the table as only a local high schooler could: with complete disinterest, yet knowing her parents could possibly find out if she had been rude or performed dismally, she was also wearing a glowing smile on her face.

"I know, I know. Even though I have been here for several months, part of me can't wait to get back to New York, though. I'm not even sure how much longer I will be here as it is. I assume Ruth told you about my complete meltdown, Sean?" Ruth noted that even as he played it off as a joke, Josh's face had flushed, and his blue eyes had taken on a panicked look.

Sean reluctantly nodded. One of the things Ruth adored most about her husband was his even temper and complete inability to cause anyone unease. Okay, that was two things, but really, she could list his good qualities all day long, because he settled her in so many ways. She reached over and squeezed his knee to show him how much his kindness to Josh mattered.

Sean had a bite of taco salad, which he had drenched in ranch dressing, and once he swallowed, he told Josh, "I don't know if I ever mentioned it, but when I was doing my residency, I had gotten caught up in an emergency car accident that came in, and two children were involved. I stayed, worked much longer than I should have, and once the kids were stabilized, I managed to get *maybe* two hours of sleep. I then had to work the next morning. Well, I was so out of it, just groggy and bleary-eyed, and a simple case came in, and I just had to administer antibiotics, but I failed to read the nurse's note about the penicillin allergy. The kid's throat closed up. He went into anaphylaxis, and I had a panic attack. Mercifully, he was at the hospital already, but it shook me so hard. It was my first major mess up, so I know how easily something…heck anything…can happen. My god, Josh, you're a surgeon—the highest stress in the medical field. You need to take that scalpel of yours and cut yourself some slack. I think you have been working so hard for so many years, that this leave you're taking will end up being the refresher you need."

Josh nodded reluctantly in agreement while finishing his mashed potatoes. "I know, and I have gained remarkable perspective from everything that has happened in the past year. I just feel like the longer I stay here, the more momentum I am losing with everything."

"With everything? Like what else?" Ruth asked. As far as she knew, he didn't even have a place to live in Brooklyn anymore, unless he had renewed the lease on the apartment that he and Tess had shared. She recalled her sister saying that she had paid the rent for the last two months left on their lease, but that was months ago at this point. "Josh, is there someone you were seeing in New York?" She had always suspected it could happen, so she asked, "Maybe your office mate, Lana?"

Josh recoiled. "Absolutely not. Lana and I were only ever co-workers at best, and even friends would be stretching it these days," he hotly denied. "No, no one is waiting for me back in New York."

"Okay, so what do you have to go back for?" Ruth pressed. Ruth felt Sean's hand now squeezing her knee, likely trying to tell her to back off, but Ruth could be like a dog with a bone when it came to getting people to admit the truth to themselves, even if it didn't involve her. Well, make that *especially* when it didn't involve her. "Where will you live, Josh? Do you have a place to stay?"

"Ruth," Josh began, in a tone laced with steel that she had not heard him use in forever, "I don't need your input on my life. I know it's all coming because you care, but I will figure it all out, without your guidance. But I can't stay here forever." Josh looked at Sean, and said, "You guys moving here works for both of you on so many levels. It makes sense. But me moving back? It's like admitting I have failed, and I have done that already, with your sister. I do not need to add another failure to my life. I know I had a breakdown, if you want to call it that, but I love the rush, the fast pace of the city, the complicated surgeries that only I can make sense out of."

Sean and Ruth nodded in unison, with Sean adding, "I get it, and I apologize for my wife," and threw Ruth a look telling her that even he thought she had crossed a line. "If you sign up for something, you don't want to settle. Although as an aside, and maybe this is where Ruth was trying to go, the hospital here in Beverley is in desperate need of talented surgeons, which I made the mistake of telling Ruth just as we pulled up."

Ruth laughed, "You know me—I always think I know better than everyone else how to run their lives." She reached across the table to squeeze Josh's hand again. "I'm sorry, Josh, you just seemed so relaxed here. I only want the best for you."

"Don't worry about it," Josh assured her, and returned her squeeze. "Well, speaking of places to live, have you guys found a place in town? I happen to know of a house just around the block from my dad's place. Wraparound porch, two stories, plus a finished basement."

CHAPTER
Twenty-Seven

Effie

Effie grunted as she unloaded one of the last few boxes from her car and carried it up the stairs to her new home. Considering her good fortune, she surveyed her neighborhood from the wraparound porch. When she had come to Beverley on the day of her formal interviews, she had arrived almost an hour early, using that extra time to walk around town, and ended up strolling several blocks from Main Street. As a child, a trip to Beverley involved going shopping for school clothes and then enjoying lunch at Betsy's; teenage Beverley trips meant cruising Main Street and waving to the friends you had made from neighboring towns; now that Effie was an adult, she savored touring this part of town, populated with historical homes, all of them built between 1920-1940. Houses with porches, peaked windows, two or three stories, an occasional fourth story with a tiny window at the top of the house, and basement windows peeking out between the blades of grass on the side lawns. Two of the homes she encountered that day had "For Sale" signs in the front yards, and on a lark, Effie called about one of them: an attractive green house with white trim, which only had two stories, yet seemed plenty spacious for just her. The previous owners had removed two walls on the first floor, so the kitchen, dining room, and living room were almost one continuous room, yet maintained the independent feel of each room, thanks to the molding and large archways, so they still seemed separate. A master suite was upstairs, along with three other bedrooms and a separate bathroom. With the help of her parents (Effie suspected she had Burnside to thank primarily) she had secured a loan for the mortgage, despite the credit card debt caused by Damon. Though she had goaded her mom mercilessly over the years about Burnside's wealth and his standing in Beverley, he could be extremely generous with the people he loved, and he wanted to help the woman he truly considered his daughter to rebuild her life.

Now that almost all of the boxes had made it from her car to the porch, she took out her house key and unlocked the door to move them inside. The movers would come tomorrow with a second-hand sofa she had found online, a dining table with a set of chairs discovered by her brother at a garage sale last weekend, two sets of bookcases that had been hers since childhood, and an antique dressing mirror and bureau that had been in Diadema's family for several generations—her mother had insisted on Effie using them in her new home. Her new splurges had been a king-size bed with a gorgeously engraved headboard, two easy chairs for the living area, and a coffee table Effie envisioned holding her tea, book, and cookies on a snowy Sunday afternoon, all of which were set for delivery tomorrow as well. The house itself came fully loaded with appliances, so all Effie needed to concern herself with was touching up the rooms with fresh coats of paint, which she planned on picking up at the hardware store a few doors down from the library. Maybe yellow for the kitchen area, and a French-style blue for the dining/living areas?

Looking at her watch, she was shocked to see that it was almost seven o'clock, the grumble in her tummy scolding her for not noticing any earlier. Taking care of business, Effie called in an order to Betsy's Diner for a chicken sandwich with mushrooms, ranch dressing, and extra pickles, beer-battered onion rings, and a blueberry malt, then began toting in the boxes one by one as she waited for her food delivery. Bouncing down the steps, with her flip-flops slapping the soles of her feet, Effie retrieved her purse out of her car, dug into a side pocket and pulled out a twenty; as she straightened up, she noticed three people turning the corner from Third Street. A tall man with dark blond hair, a stocky red-headed man with glasses, and a small blonde woman with her hand resting on her belly. As the group drew half a block closer, she identified the tall figure as that of Josh, but who were his companions?

Since she had begun working in Beverley, it had been impossible to not catch frequent glimpses of Josh, especially since their places of work were only a couple of blocks apart. Whenever she walked over to pick up a coffee from Mr. Beans, she forced herself to not look over to the auto shop across the street, a demand she usually managed to obey, at least until her return trip to the library: then she was immediately powerless to stop her gaze from drifting over to see if Josh was within sight. Unsure of whatever she had done to cause him to leave her so abruptly that day she had visited him at the auto shop, she decided that playing it cool was her best course of action. He clearly was not interested in anything more than a casual friendship, totally fine, since she did not need to be starting anything resembling a relationship when she hadn't even finished her previous one, legally. She couldn't deny, however, that it had stung when he hadn't popped into the library to even say hello to her, as she had hoped he would, even as a friend.

Effie lifted her hand in a feeble wave to Josh, desperately going for a casual one-off, when suddenly the female in the group gave a boisterous squeal and trotted over to where Effie stood at the bottom of her driveway. Once she was at the bottom of the driveway, Effie recognized that the woman was Ruth! What was Ruth doing with Josh?

"Effie, how are you? Did you get the job at the library? Are you living here now?" Turning to look pointedly at Josh, Ruth laughingly told him, "Josh, I hope this isn't the house you wanted to show us, because it seems like it's already occupied!"

Not knowing which question to answer first, Effie chose the most obvious: "Yes, I live here. Or I will, once I get everything moved in tomorrow. And yes, I got the job at the library, and I have you to thank for it," she declared.

Ruth reached up and pulled Effie in for a hug. "You were first on my list of people to text once we moved back here. I am so excited for you!

Oh, let me introduce you to my husband, Sean," she said, pointing to the redhead, who was unconventionally handsome, with grinning blue eyes behind his glasses. Effie could see his appeal, no doubt. "And, this is my old friend, Josh," and as both women said his name in unison, Ruth shot Effie a look of amazement. "Wait—you know Josh? Tell me you don't know Josh!" And then Ruth gasped, "Oh-my-god—there is something here. Are you two dating? No, wait—don't tell me," and she held up a hand. "No, I got it wrong: you *want* to date," and her green eyes flicked back and forth between Josh and Effie.

Sure that color had flooded her face, Effie could not remember a time she had been more embarrassed. Was her attraction to Josh that easily noticed? And why was he just standing there, almost expressionless? Aware that her mouth was hanging open, she tried to form words, any words, to deny Ruth's assumptions.

Sean moved forward, saving Effie from desperately trying to melt into her driveway, which seemed like the quickest form of escape. Holding out his hand, he greeted her, "Nice to meet you, Effie. Ruth told me about you after she met you in the coffee shop that time. Sorry about my wife, by the way. I'd like to blame her pregnancy hormones, but the truth is that she is always like this," and he smiled at his wife in a way Effie could only describe as adoringly. Had a man ever looked at her like that? Maybe Damon, once he realized she had a spectacular credit history.

Josh cleared his throat, and then corrected Ruth. "We are absolutely not dating," he told her, as he flushed bright pink from his neck up to his hairline. "Effie and I actually know each other from way back—we lived in the same town before Dad and I moved here."

Ruth was taken aback. "What do you mean? Josh, are you saying you used to live in Clover Lake?" At his nod, Ruth continued, "I mean, I knew you had family there and in the surrounding area, but why am I just finding out that you used to actually live in Clover Lake?"

Josh shrugged. "It's a long story." And then he said no more, crossing his arms over his chest.

Effie, sensing unease from Josh, quickly added, "We've reconnected since I've been back in Clover Lake, and I guess now that I am living in Beverley, maybe we will see each other all the time," and she stared pointedly at Josh, hoping he would take the hint. Was that what she wanted? She was giving herself mixed signals every time she was around Josh. When she was alone, it was clear to her that she only wanted (or should only want) to be friends, but once he was within five feet of her, felt herself longing for a single glance from him. "So, how do you all know each other?" she asked the group.

Josh threw a look at Ruth, and explained, "We met in high school and have been friends ever since."

At Ruth's laugh, Effie caught a slight shake of Josh's head in Ruth's direction, but her new friend would not be deterred. "Really, Josh?" Then Ruth turned to Effie and said, "Remember me telling you that my sister blew up her life? Well, she also blew up Josh's, too."

"Oh, the wedding rehearsal…" Effie whispered, with all of the puzzle pieces fitting into place now. "You mean—you were engaged to Ruth's sister?" she asked Josh, open-mouthed with shock, who nodded reluctantly, remorsefully. She then whispered, "Wow—what a small world."

"Very much so, and even more so now that I know he used to live in Clover Lake." After she tossed a pointed glance in Josh's direction, Ruth looked up at the porch and said, "Did you carry all of those boxes up your steps yourself? That looks like a lot, Effie! How come no one is here to help you?"

Effie laughed, "Oh, it looks like more than it actually is—except for my boxes of books, which are still in my car. I'll have my brother get those out tomorrow—he loves a chance to display his physical strength. Boxes of books are surprisingly heavy, which I know from unloading books at the library, but I was so anxious to move out of my parents' house that I packed them too full, like an idiot."

Immediately, Josh went to the back of the CRV and opened it up, grabbed one of the boxes and started for the porch.

"Oh no, I wasn't looking for help—" Effie told him.

Sean was one step behind Josh. "Nonsense, Effie," he grunted as he lifted one of the boxes. "Okay, Josh made it look easier than it is," he grumbled as he carried the box up the steps, "but put us to work since we are here."

Ruth laughed, "This will do them good—they both had pie after supper, anyway. Well, truthfully, we all did, but I'm the only one eating for two!" Taking Effie's hand, Ruth demanded, "So let me see your house!"

Effie replied, "Well, there's not much to see yet, but follow me," and she led Ruth up the stairs, where Josh passed them on his way back to the car for another box, and his look to her made a shiver run down her spine. As she got to the porch, Effie lifted one of the boxes she had carried up earlier and entered her house as Ruth held open the door.

"God, I love these types of homes," Ruth remarked. "All of the wood trim everywhere. Real craftsman. Ooh, look at the molding," she marveled, pointing up at the ceiling in the living room. And your front windows, with the stained glass at the tops? And those window seats? God, if the house Josh is going to show us is half this beautiful, I will die!"

"Let's save any talk of dying until we are at least ninety," Sean advised his wife, depositing another box in the house, and came up behind her to enfold her into his arms.

"All done with the boxes from her car?" Ruth asked Sean, while Effie stepped back out onto the porch to grab another box.

Once outside, she picked up a lighter box from the porch, then watched breathlessly as she noticed Josh rolling up his sleeves before lifting the last two boxes from her car, and the sight of his forearms straining with the weight of the boxes left her flushed as she stood immobile while holding her box.

"Oh, yeah, Josh is playing hero and insisted on getting the last two," Effie heard Sean jokingly tell Ruth, who laughed in response.

"These really weren't that heavy," Josh grunted as he climbed the steps, seemingly gasping for air, his red face telling of his exertion, as he awkwardly stepped through the front door now being held open by Sean.

"Effie, are you coming in?" inquired Sean, who was still holding the screen door open. She entered her house, and her eyes tracked Josh's movements, as he carefully placed both boxes on the floor between the living room windows.

With a raised eyebrow, Ruth observed him appraisingly and then commented, "Well, Josh, you certainly have gotten much sturdier since the last time I saw you lift anything."

Then Josh suddenly appeared before Effie and took the box from her arms, giving her an embarrassed smile before turning with it and sat it on top of the heavy boxes he had just carried in.

Looking out one of the windows, she noticed a teenage boy speeding down the street on a bicycle, with a white grocery bag dangling somewhat precariously from the handlebars. "Effie Van Holland?" he called out, just as he skidded to a halt on the street in front of her house.

"That's me," she called through the window screen. "My food is here," she told her company, and walked out the screen door and began to descend the stairs, but Josh was right behind her.

"I'll grab that for you—why don't you go inside and sit with Ruth," he suggested.

Effie attempted to hand him the twenty from her pocket, but Josh was down by the delivery boy before she could blink. After he handed the teenager a couple of bills, informing him to keep the change, he then brought Effie her bag of food.

Effie tried again to give Josh her money. "Here, this is for my supper," but it was waved away.

"Consider it a house-warming present," he told her, as he followed her into the house.

"Well, thank you terribly, for everything," and she looked at Ruth and Sean and included them, "thanks to all of you. I'm sure you had better things to do than hump my heavy boxes into my house," Effie laughed, and put her dinner bag onto the empty remaining window seat. "You never did say what you were doing before I coerced you all into helping me."

Ruth smiled at Effie and said, "Oh! Sean and I are moving here next month, so we took a quick trip back to check out some homes; when we had dinner with Josh earlier, he told us there was a house in this neighborhood for sale."

"And on that note, we should leave Effie here to enjoy her dinner." Sean reached down for Ruth's hands and pulled her up from the window seat.

Effie looked to Josh, who was standing in her doorway staring intently at her, and had his arms raised over his head, holding onto the door frame, and looking sexier than she could have thought possible. Josh replied to Sean, "Yep, the house I wanted to show you guys is actually on the next block, down the street from my dad's house." Something seemed to come over him, then, because he lowered his arms as he nodded somewhat formally to Effie.

"Oh, okay, well good luck on your house hunting," Effie told Ruth and Sean, and she followed them to the door.

Ruth grabbed Effie in another hug and told her she would text her when they were back in Beverley. She watched the group amble down the block, with her eyes on Josh until they disappeared behind a row of bushes.

CHAPTER
Twenty-Eight

Josh

Having asked his dad for a *possible, slightly* longer lunch break, Josh was making a beeline for the library from Mr. Beans. He had decided to surprise Effie with lunch as a way to (hopefully) apologize for his increasingly odd behavior around her. After showing Sean and Ruth the house he had in mind for them, which they had loved, Ruth had read him the riot act for his stilted demeanor with Effie, despite the fact that he had carried most of her heavy boxes into her house *and* bought her dinner on that Saturday night.

"Damn, Josh, you could have acted like you not only knew her but also *maybe* enjoyed her company. I have not seen anyone act that stiff since three years ago when my grandpa died and Mom insisted on having a viewing with the casket open. Seriously, aren't we beyond that stage in evolution where we have to see our dead loved ones displayed?" Then she continued on her Ruth-tangent, and Josh tuned her out; instead of hearing Ruth berate him, his internal dialogue had taken over, and had done a bang-up job of it on his own.

Josh had tried to see Effie the following day, and in the early morning had put on a pair of shorts, ratty old t-shirt, and running shoes, doing his best to look like a casual jogger whose route happened to go right by Effie's new house. After running around the block three times in the hopes of catching her sitting out on her porch swing while sipping coffee, he had given up and gone home; his task had only proven one thing: he was terribly out of shape. In the afternoon, he made the decision to just be direct; thus, armed with a pan of freshly baked brownies in one hand (thanks to Tess for having taught him that simple recipe years ago) and a bottle of wine he had found in his dad's cabinet, he walked around the block to Effie's house. Once he turned the corner, however, he saw a moving van parked out front, flanked in front by the car she had brought into his shop those many weeks ago, and in back by an old truck he saw her brother exiting. Quickly, he turned around and headed for his dad's house. Hoping desperately that wasn't Effie he had seen coming down the steps of her house, and he had worried about it all last night. The last thing he wanted her to think was that he was a stalker, creeping by her new home multiple times a day.

Now here he was, with almost two weeks having passed, and no word to or from Effie. Wracking his brain while eating a grilled cheese for dinner last night and watching multiple *Seinfeld* episodes he had seen a million times, he made the decision to just make a move, already. Josh sent her a text asking if she was working tomorrow, and telling her that he needed to stop by the library anyway, so hoped to see her. She had remarked with a simple "yes". Hoping for more information, or maybe just more encouragement, he had held the phone in his hands for an hour, wishing for the little dots that would let him know Effie had more to say, but that was it. Well, he could hardly fault her for being distant with him, and he was determined to make it up to her, because he would enjoy having someone close to be friendly with for however long he had left in Beverley.

Josh had shed his coveralls before leaving the shop: he had chosen to wear his nicest pair of "work" jeans and a dark blue shirt in order to look somewhat presentable for Effie. Picking up two chicken salad sandwiches, served on Mr. Beans' special seven grain bread, and two orders of their homemade potato chips, he also carried iced teas for their drinks, after asking at the coffee shop if they knew what Effie's preferred lunchtime beverage was.

As he stood at the bottom of the library steps, the front doors seemed to loom as colossal portals in front of him, and he could not recall the last time that he had been quite this nervous before seeing a woman. Reminding himself that she was just a friend, his long legs took the stairs two at a time, and with a swagger he had never before possessed, but felt he needed fiercely in this situation, he strode into the library like a man on a mission.

Once the doors allowed him entry into Effie's world, Josh looked around for her. He hadn't been to the library here in Beverley since he was in high school. Much to Tess's chagrin (and probably would be Effie's also), he had never been much of a pleasure reader: there was too much he had had to learn about the human body to ever divert him from reading anything medical or biological. However, as he passed by the front desk, a table of new releases caught his eye, and the one author he *did* enjoy reading so many years ago was represented: Stephen King. After his mom had left, while his dad spent longer hours than usual at the shop to avoid the loneliness of an empty house, he would ride his bike over to the much smaller (but well-represented with books) library in Clover Lake. Once there, he ensconced himself in one of the massively comfortable reading chairs, picking a new Stephen King book every few days to begin reading. He could have checked them out, but then what? Go back to his house, still filled with his mother's perfume, and sit in the living room that contained the sofa she would sit on while they all watched television together at night? Or read in his bedroom, on the bed where Melanie used to read him bedtime stories? Sit at the dining table, where he could still taste the lasagna his mom cooked for him each year on his birthday, never having to ask him what he wanted, because she knew it was her son's favorite? So many moments since she had left would cause him to break down. Absolutely nothing was the same without her there, and although his dad had done his best, no one could take the place of his mom. He used to wonder what it was about him that wasn't enough for her to stay. When he was a small boy, she would sing him songs that seemed to drip with the love she had for him. So how could she just leave? What was so wrong with him that his love hadn't been enough for his mom to stay? When he had read the letter she had left, nothing in it had made it better for him, and every re-read only served to fill him with more despair. Over the years, he had learned to put his memories of his mom in a mental box, only taking them out in order to soothe him if something he deemed even more terrible than her abandonment had occurred. The DNA test he had found in his brief-case still remained unopened, for what purpose would it serve? He wasn't striving to find she had gone out and made another family—wasn't looking to find that perhaps he had some much-younger half siblings roaming the world.

"Sir? Excuse me, Sir?" Pulled out of his mother-musing, he focused on the older woman standing in front of him, pulling a cart of books from a back room. "I'm sorry, but food and drink aren't allowed inside the library," she told him, looking pointedly at the lunch he held in his hands.

Josh flushed as he apologized profusely, and then he asked, "Can you tell me if Effie is around?" He held up the bag in his left hand and added lamely, "I brought her lunch."

The older woman beamed. "Oh, you must be her friend Josh. Your dad owns that auto shop down the street, right?" At Josh's nod, she continued, "He is the only one I trust to work on my car. He is so reliable and explains everything so I understand it. The way he takes an extreme amount of care, making sure my car gets exactly what it needs." Josh wasn't sure how to reply to any of this, so waited as she recounted all of his dad's finer points. Then she finally told him, "We just adore Effie here—she's been the added boost we have needed for our younger readers." The woman must have sensed some impatience, or possible desperation, from Josh, because she then apologized. "Sorry, she just clocked out for lunch, and I believe she was heading over to the park across the street. I know she enjoys reading there in the gazebo on her lunch breaks," she added helpfully. "I'm Liza, by the way—Head Librarian," and she stuck out her hand to him.

Josh looked at her hand, wondering how he was going to juggle two drinks and a bag of food in order to shake her proffered hand, and then decided to put the drink in his right hand down on the cart in front of him. Wiping his hand free of the condensation from the cold drink, he shook her hand. "Pleased to meet you. I'm Josh," he said, although with her knowing nod he realized that had already been established.

"Oh, yes, we know. You have been such a comfort to Effie since she moved here," Liza informed him. "She told us how you moved all of her boxes into her house the other day. So gallant, I told her. You don't find that kind of chivalry every day," Liza proclaimed, with a hand over her heart for emphasis.

A comfort? Gallant? Chivalry? Well, that was news to him, because he had worried his strange behavior may have put Effie off of him entirely, although she had certainly looked surprised when he carried two boxes at a time that night, in a lame attempt to try and impress her. Must be a slow news day if she was talking about him to her new co-workers, he thought. Josh doubted that any news of him could have ever been deemed gossip-worthy: in all honesty, he was probably the most boring person he knew.

Josh crossed the street to the park, which was conveniently located directly across from the library. The weather was insanely perfect today: warm breeze (unusual in late-May for eastern South Dakota) and the sky was the bright blue he knew from the Impressionist paintings that Tess loved. He spotted Effie immediately, and as predicted, she was in the gazebo with her head tucked down. Probably reading a book, he guessed. So intent was she, that she did not appear to hear him climb the stairs of the gazebo. He took a moment to study her before announcing his presence: she had slipped off her shoes, and had her legs up on the bench, fully stretched out so Josh admired the pink of polish on her toes. She was wearing a longer skirt that drifted over her slim calves, the hem dancing with the breeze that came up. Her peach-colored top was open at the collar, and he had a glimpse of delicate collarbones peeking through. Clearing his throat before watching her became weird, Effie startled at the sound, and dropped her book in the process, a clearly loved, well-read copy of a romance novel, judging by the sight of the bare-chested man and bosom-heaving woman on the cover.

"Sorry if I am disturbing you, Effie," he began, hoping to see a look more welcoming than confused on her face. "I wanted to surprise you with lunch, but you probably already ate. I'm sorry," he awkwardly apologized again. "This was not my best idea—I'll let you read in peace," and he turned to go, because he knew from Tess how avid readers *hated* being interrupted while engrossed in their book. "I'll just leave this for you," and he put the drink he had brought for her on the ground next to her bench. "It's iced tea. The barista at Mr. Beans said you get one every day for lunch. Except I guess today," he rambled. Time to go, because he was veering into a decidedly uncomfortable zone. "Have a good day," he told her, and then started to go back down the stairs.

"Wait," Effie called out to him. "You were talking so fast I haven't had a chance to say anything," she said with a laugh. "I love iced tea—thank you very much for bringing me one. And did you say you brought me lunch? I was just going to walk over to the coffeeshop and get something but wanted to read a couple of chapters first." She looked up at Josh, clearly taken by surprise. "No one has ever surprised me with lunch before," she confessed, with a touch of wonder in her voice.

And with her blush and beaming smile of encouragement, Josh took a seat on the bench that was now free from her legs. He put the bag between the two of them and began their impromptu date by asking her how she was enjoying working at the library. Watching her face light up, he congratulated himself on a job well done. Finally.

CHAPTER
Twenty-Nine

Effie

Effie studied Josh as she sipped her iced tea. Astonished could not begin to describe her reaction upon seeing him standing under the gazebo. Since starting at the library, she had been coming to have her lunch here, and it really was a perfect spot, no matter the weather. Plus, its location was far enough away from the playground equipment to provide the solitude she craved for reading, yet close enough she could hear the tinkling laughter carried over by any breeze. Today she had just wanted to finish her novel before strolling over to get her lunch from Mr. Beans. Some days she brought her lunch, but she always got a large iced tea from the coffee shop, regardless. Once she had her kitchen in working order, she imagined she might bring her lunch every day; on second thought, she thoroughly enjoyed the activity of walking over to the coffee shop, waving to people she was beginning to recognize on the busy Main Street and socializing with other customers while waiting for her food. Although she was essentially an introvert, building a community was becoming more important to her, and being introverted did not have to mean being isolated.

She had been honest when she had confessed to Josh that no one had ever brought her lunch before. Damon had been part of her life for so long, but he had rarely been in town long enough to do anything considerate or meaningful for her on an everyday basis, and it was always the little things people tended to remember and hold dear, or so she had always heard.

Ugh—Damon. The call from her friend Alice a few weeks ago had been a harbinger of doom: Damon had been trying to contact her almost every day since then, and she had avoided his calls, until last night. It had been two weeks since she had moved in, and as she sat in the silence of her house, enjoying the newly painted French-blue walls, she had thought about the morning of her moving day, as she was heading down to her truck, when she could have sworn she had seen Josh coming up the block— it had been difficult at first to make a firm identification, but his shape was right, as was the graceful cadence at which he walked. Just as she was raising her arm in a wave, he had turned around and gone in the direction from which he was coming originally. Strange, but it was turning out he had developed some quirks since she had known him years ago; maybe he had them all along and they were simply more pronounced. She'd like to spend more than ten minutes in his presence to find out the other ways in which he had changed. Ergo, she had been knee-deep in analyzing Josh as the evening breeze fluttered her curtains, when her phone rang beside her with a blocked number showing. For a moment her breath had caught in her throat, and she considered that perhaps Josh, in his peculiarity, was calling. Hoped, anyway, that it was Josh—finally using the number she had left at the auto shop before she had even known that the mechanic was her Josh Livingston. Then, like a slap in the face, reality had hit her hard as she heard Damon's voice on the line.

"Damon—what the hell? You're hiding your phone number now as a way to dupe me into answering your call?" She hit herself in the forehead with her phone, wondering why every single decision she made concerning him was the wrong one: even decisions she *didn't* know involved him sucked, because they ended up *involving* him!

Damon let out a furious breath. "What else did you expect me to do? You weren't picking up my calls, every text still reads as unread, and I'm sure you haven't bothered listening to the messages I have left for you. You always bitched that people don't leave messages anymore, yet here I am, pouring my heart out to you on the phone, and you can't even deign to do me the courtesy of listening, can you?" Wonderful, just what she needed: Damon on a tear. She resolved to simply let him ramble, let him say whatever he felt he needed to, so she could be done with him, and he would move on. He drew in a breath, and said carefully, "What I am trying to say, and what I said in those messages, is that I fucked up, Effie. I fucked up, and I own that. I never should have lied to you about getting fired, I never should have lied about where I was all of those times, and I'm sorry." Now she heard him with a bit of a wobble in his words, as if he was holding in tears. "I love you, and I didn't appreciate that. But I will do better, I promise. I just need one more chance, and that's it. Just please come home. I can't make it without you, and you know that. Please, Baby, I'm begging you. I have things settled with Kristy—she's letting me stay in our apartment with her. I just need you here."

Translation: Damon was now fucking Kristy, which came as no surprise. Kristy had always thought he was hot, and she enjoyed sex very pragmatically. A long-term commitment phobe, Kristy would use him as long as she had a use for him. They were actually perfect for each other. She let out an exasperated breath. "What I don't hear you apologizing for is cheating on me, breaking your wedding vows, and ruining my credit to support whatever lifestyle you call this. Just saying 'I fucked up' is not an apology: you were terribly misinformed by your mommy." Damon had huge issues involving his mother that ranged from weird to terrifying. "I have moved on. I am happy, moved into my new house, and have started a new life. Now you're begging me? Remember all of the times I begged you?" She shook her head and sternly told herself to snap out of it. "You know what? Never mind. I don't want to get into this with you. You're a narcissist, which I have actually known since our first date, but like all stupid women everywhere, I thought I could change you. But I can't. And, like all stupid women everywhere, I can do better. I am doing better. The only thing I want from you now is a divorce, and that should be finalized in less than two months. And what about your 'other' woman and the child you have on the way?"

Damon replied hotly, "She dumped me, Effie. Told me I was still hung up on you. And guess what? She said the baby isn't even mine—all that money I spent on her, all the time I wasted. I was an ass. Please, I am sorry," he sobbed into the phone. All the money he wasted—screw him. All HER money he wasted, not to mention all of her time wasted on his nonsense. God, he was disgusting.

"I do not care about your circumstances, Damon. We are done. Don't call me again." She hung up the phone and finally blocked his number. Then she texted Kristy, telling her she could do better than wasting her time with him.

Now here she was with Josh sitting beside her, finally; Josh bringing her lunch and her favorite beverage; Josh leaving her tingling all over from simply his proximity. She watched his long, graceful fingers deftly open the bag. How had she never noticed how strong his hands looked: like they could hold someone's life in them and make them better?

"Work is great," she said, finally answering the question he had asked her as he had taken a seat beside her. "I love this library; exceedingly smaller than the one I worked in before in Denver, but that means I get to see the same people coming in to see what new releases we have, or read a periodical, or talk to the students doing research. You know, when I was in high school, I would drive over on Saturdays and read books here at the Beverley Carnegie Library that the Clover Lake Library didn't carry. It's so strange that we never bumped into each other." She took a bite of her sandwich and smiled at Josh. "Delicious—thank you immensely for thinking of me. It was so thoughtful. Just like the night when you helped me by carrying in all of my boxes—that was such a massive relief to me. My brother was beyond thrilled he had to do less work!" She laughingly told him. Needless to say, Effie had not stopped fantasizing about Josh lifting those boxes, and her imagination had run wild when she attempted to sleep the two weeks since, with thoughts of those arms around her, of him taking care of her lusty needs. And now, watching his hands with those long fingers or seeing his tongue dart out to catch a crumb while he ate… she was going crazy.

"I was glad we were there in time to help you. I mean, Sean did a lot, too, and I'm sure your brother could have gotten the job done more quickly." Josh made a move to get up, having finished his lunch. "I can let you eat your lunch in peace—I don't want to keep interrupting you," he nodded to her book. "Probably your only chance to get some reading time in, I imagine, what with having to unpack from your big move." He bent down to grab his drink, but she reached out a hand to stop him and held on to his wrist, feeling his pulse pounding under her fingers.

"No, please, stay. I spend too many breaks alone with my thoughts, and I have never realized what a depressing person I am," she laughed, and Josh chuckled with her. "Besides, I don't know if you can tell, but I have read that book at least a hundred times." He sat back down, with her hand still on his wrist, which felt so strong but also delicate: not how she would have imagined a mechanic's wrist to feel. What else was there to this new Josh she had yet to discover? She wondered dreamily.

CHAPTER
Thirty

Effie's touch on his wrist was still making his skin feel as if he had been scorched by lightning, even though she was no longer touching him, having gone back to eating her sandwich. In the last year of their relationship, Josh had been so focused on finishing his residency and getting the fellowship, and Tess had been wrapped up in wedding planning and her baking, which left their hours rarely in sync. Physical intimacy was limited, to say the least, that a touch given freely by someone he was attracted to seemed a lifetime ago; until now, he thought.

With Josh now sitting closer to her, the heat from his thigh burned through her skirt, and she shivered. "Are you chilly?" he asked, and, like an idiot, she shook her head 'no'. She longed for him to move closer to her, not farther away, so she should have told him she was freezing.

He continued, "I never realized how shaded the gazebo is. It just occurred to me that I have never sat here—never really surveyed the town from this point of view." And he looked out onto Main Street, or as much as they could see from their vantage point: the street lights adorned with hanging baskets of brightly colored petunias, benches placed outside of businesses, where mothers with children stopped to take a break while answering a phone call, shop owners sweeping the sidewalk in front of buildings to ensure customers would feel tempted to stop in and buy something. Josh knew from his dad how some of the businesses had struggled over the years, worse after several chain big-box stores had opened up closer to the interstate. Truthfully, the interstate hadn't helped Main Street businesses; in fact, it encouraged travelers to keep on driving, with the focus being on making "good time" and beating other people to whatever destinations they had in mind. So many of these old buildings, built of brick with fine details and touches that weren't included in modern architecture, had sat empty, in varying states of crumbling decay for one or two decades—until a resurgence had surfaced twelve or so years ago. Townsfolk had realized the charm that downtown held for so many people, and how individualized stores could provide a more detailed shopping experience than the general one customers were getting on the outskirts of town. Now bars and restaurants had outdoor seating in the warmer months; the small lake on the south end of the park, which had been neglected for so many years, froze enough in the winter to allow ice skating, reinvigorating the activity that older generations had enjoyed when they were children, so now they brought their grandchildren. Josh felt wistful looking at everything, knowing he would not be here to see any ice skating in the winter.

Effie's voice broke into his reverie. "Can I ask you a question?" At his nod, she continued, "Why didn't you keep in touch with anyone from Clover Lake after you left? It was like we finished the school year, and you were there, but when September came around, poof: no Josh. And no one knew where you had gone. I guess your cousins knew, but they weren't telling anyone?" Josh stared at her, dumbfounded that he had even been missed. According to one of his other cousins, Daniel, no one had asked where he went. No one cared. "I missed you," Effie told him, and the sincerity in her voice stunned him.

Effie had been incredibly hurt when she returned to school that year and there was no Josh trying out for the one-act plays. No Josh marching with his trombone in the band, practicing for the homecoming parade. No Josh in physics, which he had informed her that he was taking a year ahead of the others in his junior class; he had even promised to be her study partner because she sucked at science, and he was so fucking smart. She had been desperate to know where Josh had gone, even considered asking his cousin Daniel, football star and one of the most popular kids in Clover Lake High School, where Josh had disappeared to. Though Clover Lake was a small town, smaller than Beverley by far, no way could she approach him.

"You were here, in Beverley, the whole time." Her gaze studied his face, imagining an alternate world in which she *had* encountered him somehow. "How did I miss running into you? Coming over here to see a movie or eat fast food? Or cruising Main Street?"

Josh hung his head, because the truth was that he had intentionally kept a low profile once he moved here. He wasn't out cruising because he didn't *want* to run into anyone. The crushing humiliation he had experienced when his mother had abandoned him and his father had been too much to bear, and instead of perhaps feeling any sadness upon leaving Clover Lake, the relief to be moving to a brand-new place, where no one was aware of his past, had overcome not only that but also any anxiety about making new friends and building a new community in Beverley.

As Josh shut his eyes, Effie at first feared he was also shutting her out, but it dawned on her that he was probably looking for an explanation, without having to get too emotional. Living with Diadema, she knew the signs well of someone wanting to repress what they were feeling, so they didn't have to let anyone in. She could not imagine how he felt—they both had lost a parent, but hers had at least left unwillingly. Too vivid was her memory of finding out that Josh's mom had disappeared, and for years all anyone could discuss in Clover Lake was "poor Henry, stuck being a single father to Josh". The town had watched as Henry visibly became more bereft every day, and even her own mother, who usually had no comment on other people's secrets and pain, noted how Henry had refused any help from anyone in town, even his own family. He had closed ranks around him and Josh, so when the day came when Henry no longer worked at the auto shop in Clover Lake with his father and brother, no one was really surprised. Except for Effie, who liked to sit near Josh and his cousins during swimming breaks at the pool. Both of her best friends went away for the summers: one to music camp, and the other to her grandparents, something Effie had been jealous of since she wasn't close to either sets of her own grandparents. Josh never made a comment about her body or her Native ancestry. She remembered how much he had loved to read Stephen King, and they talked about his books, or what movies they wanted to see. He had been so accepting and open, and she wondered when he had lost that, and if he would ever get it back?

"Sorry," she heard him say quietly. "Things were so different after my mom left, and it was weird how everyone knew about it, you know? Having so much family in town, I guess I just imagined everyone would have known we moved to Beverley. It was nice, though, to go somewhere and start over. Something that seems to be a repeating theme in my life."

What was he doing? He did not want to over share with Effie, regardless of how natural it felt. He knew his dad's friends and employees were aware that he was a surgeon in Manhattan, but it was not something he wanted spread all over town. In his experience, people from small towns tended to get kind of defensive with people from big cities, especially if they had originally lived in said small town. Just as urban dwellers could be fickle about rural dwellers, he knew, and Josh had found it challenging to straddle both sides of the line.

Effie, of course, was quite familiar with suddenly having to start over, so she looked to Josh and smiled, saying, "Well, for what it's worth, I am happy we are here now, together. Especially since you brought me lunch! So thoughtful, Josh—how did you know I was over here, anyway?"

Josh blushed, admitting, "I stopped in at the library looking for you; actually, I got scolded for trying to bring food on to the main floor. I can't remember the last time I got reprimanded in the library, so that was fun," and they both laughed at that.

"We have teenagers wanting to bring all sorts of snacks in after school, but I tell you, it's the moms with babies who are the worst, and the thing is, the food is always for them! All kinds of used candy bar wrappers or pop bottles left in the children's department. They're not even eating anything healthy!"

Effie looked down at her watch, not wanting this lovely lunch to end, but her shift started again in ten minutes, and she needed to freshen up before going back to work. "I'm sorry, Josh, I have to get back to the library." She stood up, but as she did so, the shoes she had kicked off had somehow gotten tangled up at her feet, and she tripped over them, ending up back on the bench, this time bringing her body flush against Josh's. The heat of his breath drifted across her cheek, and his hand slid across her back. She tipped her head back and saw those summer-blue eyes staring into hers. His pupils were dilated, and under her hand, his thigh clenched. Her mouth had dried up, and as she opened her lips, his mouth was suddenly on hers, and she was responding as if her life depended upon it—as if his kiss was a life jacket and she was sinking in the ocean. The hand not clenching Josh's thigh moved up, and under it she felt his broad chest, and ran her fingers over the muscles, and then up to his neck, where she sunk her nails into his skin. Over and over, their lips met, and Josh's arms pulled her body to his, completely encircling her. Never wanting this kiss to end, she pressed her chest into his until the two of them were almost reclined on the bench. Becoming aware of a hardness on her thigh, it wasn't until it began ringing that she realized it was his phone, and she pulled back in surprise. Josh and Effie were each dazed and confused, but his damn phone seemed to understand and kept ringing incessantly.

Josh reluctantly reached into his pocket, and seeing his dad was calling, he looked at the time. Hell, he had told his dad he'd be gone half an hour at the most, and over an hour had passed. Josh wanted nothing more than to stay on this bench, entwined with Effie, for the rest of the day. As Effie put her shoes back on, he ran a hand through his hair, and was shocked to find himself asking, "Maybe we could do this again? I mean, not *this*, but have lunch," he stammered. "Not that I wouldn't *like* to do *this* again." Shut up, Josh, he told himself.

Blushing because she knew exactly how he felt, Effie smiled and said, "How about we go to a movie? Tonight, if you're free? I haven't been in ages." She had never been one for beating around the bush, and she desperately wanted to spend more time with Josh, with or without the public make-out session. Something about him still seemed shuttered, and she was determined to get him to open up, preferably *with* a private make-out session...

CHAPTER
Thirty-One

Unsure of how to comport himself after that kiss, all Josh could do was stumble back to the shop, wondering how he would make it through the rest of the day without obsessing over his upcoming date with Effie. If he could, in fact, label it as a date. What else would it be? Try as he might, he could not recall a time he had become so overwhelmed by a simple kiss, although calling it "simple" was not doing their kiss any justice. As he shook his head in an attempt to clear it, his thoughts brought him back to middle school and then his first two years of high school, when he would have given anything to kiss Effie. Hell, he had done all he could to just be near her, but she had been so far out of his league. What would she do if she knew the truth about him now—that he was a surgeon living in New York City? His truth wasn't something he had meant to hide from her—it had just never come up. While they had spoken at length about what had brought her back to South Dakota, he had never confessed that he was newly back as well. Had that been intentional on his part, or at least subconscious? Opening up to others was something he always found extremely excruciating, and it had been one of the points of contention in his relationship with Tess. Since their break-up, upon reflection, he could see that his control issues most likely stemmed from an inability to communicate: if everything stayed in the proper place and on course, he would have no need to explain anything. Once his own mother had abandoned him, with only a brief letter left in her wake, his dad had not gone into any more detail, so Josh was left to follow in his father's footsteps: the less detail, the better.

He supposed at some point he would have to inform Effie that he was only here short-term, but honestly, he didn't see how this could do anything but hurt their friendship, relationship, or whatever it was that had begun between the two of them. As he stepped back into the shop, his dad's concentration was focused on the black Ford pickup that Henry had been servicing for the last two days. "How was lunch?" he asked, never taking his eyes off the truck engine.

Josh felt himself flushing from head to toe—the curse of being fair-skinned, as his dad glanced at him knowingly, raised eyebrow included. "It was…it was good," he managed to sputter out as a response, and began to redress in his coveralls.

"You know, I don't think I have ever seen you take off those coveralls before going out for lunch. When I came out of the office, and saw them on that chair, I was worried that maybe you had decided to take the afternoon off. But, no, I knew my son would never just take off without telling me, so I asked the guys, and Lenny said he saw you walk over to the coffee shop." Now his dad finally stood up, having finished with the Ford, and wiped his hands on a rag as he walked to the other side of the truck. "But then you were gone for over an hour, and that wasn't normal, either. For this reason, I made another comment to the guys, and Juan just happened to be coming back from his lunch break. He told me that he had gone to the library to return some books, and he saw you in the park." And with this detail added, Henry's eyes looked straight into Josh's. His dad had never been particularly interested in Josh's love life, and while he had shown affection to Tess, Josh had the feeling that his dad wasn't too bothered about who was making his son happy as long as he was, indeed, happy.

"Oh, yeah? Funny, I didn't even notice Juan over there," Josh attempted to be as vague and as breezy as possible in answering his dad.

"No, no, I don't suppose you would. You see, Juan said his wife called him when he was on his way out of the library, so he walked over to the park to talk to her. And since it was so sunny out, he thought maybe sitting in the gazebo would be cooler than standing out on the sidewalk. Turns out the gazebo was much hotter than being in the sun after all," and with true Henry style, his dad tossed his rag into the bin by the office door, poured himself a cup of coffee from the steaming pot just inside the office, and then sauntered to his chair behind the desk, where he studied Josh behind the large window from over the rim of his coffee cup.

From the several feet that separated them inside that garage, Josh heard the questions through the walls that his dad would never ask. Stunned that Henry had even broached the topic of his lunch date, Josh was at a loss for words. Not only because his dad was discussing his personal life but also due to humiliation that he had been seen behaving so uncouthly in such a public place. Public displays of affection were not in Josh's wheelhouse, and he certainly had never before condoned heavy make-out sessions in front of an entire town. Getting caught up in a moment was one thing, but forgetting himself so completely as to time and place was something else entirely, and Josh was not exactly comfortable in these circumstances. Maybe he should text Effie and ask for a rain check for tonight? She was sure to be mortified if she knew they had been spotted on that park bench.

Making a mental note to do just that later this afternoon, Josh went back to work, doing his damndest to avoid the questioning looks every man in the shop seemed to be shooting his way. Thankfully, he had two cars scheduled in this afternoon for an oil change, and while normally he preferred the more cerebral aspects of working in an auto shop as it pertained to car diagnostics, the task of changing the oil allowed his mind to wander, ignoring everyone else, giving him plenty of time to replay the events of his lunch break in his mind, and how Effie's touch had shaken him so. In the last year of his relationship with Tess, their physical moments had been growing more infrequent, and in the last six months leading up to their wedding, they had ceased altogether. Now he knew why, of course, but even at the time, he honestly wasn't sure if he had truly noticed.

There had been Lana, of course, in the office, who always seemed to be reaching for his hand, or brushing up against him as she walked by. How blind he had been not to have noticed her attraction to him, because, with hindsight, he saw it all so clearly. Lana had only ever been a friend, though, and as attractive as she was (with those dark-blue eyes and honey-colored hair, she was an absolute stunner), he had never desired her, despite his disgusting attempt to seduce her on his very darkest day. Josh felt another wave of mortification, but this time it concerned his treatment of his friend and co-worker. Last night he had taken the time to reread her email to him for the hundredth time, yet this time he had rallied his courage and composed a note back to her finally, after months; it was despicable he had left her unanswered for so long.

"Dear Lana," he had written back to her,

"Thank you for your email to me all those months ago. I am ashamed it has taken me so long to write back to you, but in all honesty, I have been embarrassed by so many things that occurred during that time that I needed space and months to process everything.

Have you ever had your life all planned out and then suddenly the rug is pulled out from under you? That is the only way I can sum it all up in my head. For so long, really as long as I can remember, all I have wanted to do was become a surgeon, but you have known me long enough to know that 'just' being a surgeon would never suffice—no I strove to be the best, and I'd like to think that for a while, maybe I was on the right path to that. It was a singular focus, and one that drove me to ignore almost all other aspects of my life, including my relationship with Tess. I can now admit that I admire her for her bravery and honesty in ending our engagement. I wish she had done it earlier. In all honesty, I would have been marrying her out of comfort, believing it to be love. I don't know why I am being so frank with you about my personal life, other than I know that these problems bled over into my working relationship with you, and with the friendship that developed. Perhaps it was never fair of me to discuss issues Tess and I were having, because that gave a more intimate atmosphere to *our* relationship, which left a disconnect between us being just friends or something more. While you are an amazing woman, I have only ever viewed you as my friend; however, saying that diminishes how important that friendship was to me.

For so long, you were the one I trusted to have my back, and that is why I was so shocked to find out that you had also applied for the fellowship. I felt betrayed and hurt that you would hold me in such low regard, but I can see now that you were probably afraid to be honest with me. You deserved that fellowship; I want you to know I firmly believe that. You were ready for it in ways that I now recognize I wasn't. Truthfully, I still don't think I am ready for it. I do still see myself as a surgeon, but am working on the other parts of myself to make me a better doctor, in general, and a better human, overall.

I plan to return to New York sometime in the near future and finish my residency, and I sincerely hope that we can meet up and maybe resume our friendship, only more as equals this time. I regret making you my emotional sounding board and putting you in an impossible situation. I am honored that you held me in such high regard, but I do believe that you are meant for a bigger love than you would have found with me. I don't know what, if anything, I have left to give someone else.

Please take care, Lana, and know I wish you the best in everything. I look forward to seeing you soon.

Best,

Josh".

CHAPTER
Thirty-Two

Effie

After locking the doors to the library, Effie walked around to the bike rack located on the side of the building and unlocked her bicycle. Once she had officially lived in Beverley, she had spent her first few days walking to work from her house; it was only around half of a mile, and so picturesque, since not only did she get to walk through the park, but the majority of her walking route was essentially residential, and the streets were lined with tall oak trees, cottonwood trees whose leaves shimmered in the sunlight, and plum trees, whose flowers Effie anticipated seeing in the spring next year; some yards had Japanese maples in the front, and all sorts of bushes dotted the landscapes, too: hydrangea, forsythia, and lilac. One day while she was walking home, she had altered her route a bit, wanting to get a few more steps, so she had used the eastern entrance to the park, and that had taken her into an area of Beverley with a mix of newer construction ranch-style homes and then a mobile home park. The day had been blisteringly hot, and unfortunately not as much foliage for protection from the sun—even though she possessed a darker complexion, she still tried to be mindful about getting too much solar exposure. She had just decided to head straight for home, when she had seen a sign for a rummage sale and impulsively followed the directions, which took her to the end of a street several blocks along the route. It had been years since she had been to a garage sale, yard sale, rummage sale—whatever you wanted to call it. As a teenager, she and her friend Claudia had loved to spend Saturday mornings driving to different towns in the area with Claudia's mother, in search of some unwanted or discarded family heirlooms that could be purchased for mere cents on the dollar. Truth be told, most of it was hideous, with items like crocheted tissue box covers, half-used cleaning products, and mismatched Tupperware, but Effie had often come home with an armful of books or perhaps a few items of vintage clothing, much to her own mother's chagrin. Diadema was of the notion that all the sale items were flea-ridden, therefore in desperate need of fumigation. This particular rummage sale had been about to close up shop on that Friday, and as Effie looked around at the remaining items still on tables in the driveway, a piece of shiny silver had caught her eye. Holding her hands to help shade her eyes from the flashing sun being reflected in the metal, Effie could see as she drew closer that it was a ten-speed bicycle perched against a tree.

"Is this bike for sale?" she questioned the woman, who was folding clothes up and placing them in a bin at her feet. A lit cigarette smoldered in the ashtray on the table in front of her, and a sweating can of Shasta root beer was seemingly attracting every single one of the neighborhood flies.

"So long as you are prepared to pay full price for it. My husband bought it for our ungrateful daughter before she left for college, and he had the decency to use my credit card to pay for it, the son of a bitch. Then he decided to leave me for an old 'classmate' of his who he 'reconnected' with at his 'class reunion'," the woman informed Effie, all the while using a generous amount of air quotes. Well, she had no trouble relating to this woman, so she asked her to hold the bike for her while she jogged over to the gas station that she had walked past the next block over to withdraw the amount from the ATM.

Upon returning, Effie handed the woman her money, and as she was getting on her new bike to ride to her house, the woman called out to her:

"If you see a black-haired bastard and a red-haired slut holding hands, be sure to run the sons-of-bitches over, please," and then she lit another cigarette and threw her head back, with her cackling echoing in the neighborhood, and it set Effie's mood for her trip to her house. Black-haired bastard or not, he had great taste in bikes, because it was beautiful, and outfitted with a bell, basket, and reflectors on all the wheels, and she rode it with a determined vengeance as she sliced through traffic cones and around opened car doors. Only twice did she fear for her life: once as a pack of teenagers rode her way on their bikes, parting their group only at the last second, and then as an unleashed dog ran out directly in front of her with its owner a few-too-many paces behind.

Today, Effie now relished the feel of the wind catching her hair as she rode around the river, taking the long way home to her house from the library, which involved utilizing the street behind the library, and connecting to a bike path where the river ran parallel. From there, she followed the path where she then turned south until hitting the rodeo grounds, and biked home on a less-used street. There was nothing quite like getting the wind at your back while balanced on two wheels. She had owned a bike in Colorado, but Damon had borrowed it one night while he was high as a kite and crashed it into a police cruiser. The bike had been totaled, and he had been arrested for reckless driving and public intoxication.

Pushing Damon out of her mind, Effie instead brought Josh front and center. No one had ever made her feel as sexy as Josh had on that bench today. His skin under her fingers had been hot enough to burn, and his lips had devoured hers. She had texted him before leaving work, asking him what movie he wanted to see, and then sent a second text about just meeting up at the theatre, but had not received a reply yet. Maybe it had been a mistake to ask about meeting up at the theatre? What was wrong with her? Of course it was! The Josh she had known—the Josh he still seemed to be—was a gentleman, and she had probably affronted him with her suggestion of meeting there. When would she learn to let someone else take the reins? Impulsivity was one of her downfalls, and had only led to destruction for her, and one only needed to look so far as her string of exes for proof.

Speaking of exes, Effie mused as she slowed down to glide into her driveway, her lawyer had messaged her a couple of days ago, informing her that she was mailing some documents for her to have notarized concerning her divorce. Eagerly, Effie sprang off her bike and parked it in her garage before trotting back to her mailbox located on the curb. As she pulled open the box, a green pickup drove by, and with the windows rolled down, she could see that it was Henry Livingston; judging by his raised voice, he was arguing quite heatedly with whomever was on the other end of the phone he was holding. Shocked, Effie blindly removed her mail from the box and watched as Josh's dad drove down her street and turned the corner to his house. Effie had seen Henry a few times standing outside his garage, warmly greeting his customers or calling 'hello' to passersby on Main Street. All of those times he had stopped briefly at whatever he was doing to send her a wave, and she never witnessed any displeasure at all from him, but whatever was going on now seemed to be unusually disturbing.

Effie turned and approached her house, and as she climbed the few steps up to her porch, she rifled through her stack of mail. Most of it was junk, with no notice of missing a certified letter from her lawyer; however, one piece of forwarded mail did pique her interest, and it was from a name she had only ever heard in passing since she was five years old: Abigail LeBeau. Why would her cousin, who she had not spoken to in almost thirty years, be writing to her? Abigail was the oldest daughter of her uncle, Simon, and a few months older than Effie, if she recalled correctly.

After Effie tossed her junk mail in the recycling bin that sat under a small hall table at the front door, she took the letter over by the kitchen. After pouring a large tumbler of iced tea, Effie sat down with a box of Triscuits, shook a few out, and proceeded to open the letter.

"Dear Euphemie," the letter began,

"I can't believe how much time has passed since we last spoke, as children. So many times, I have wanted to reach out to you and reconnect with the cousin I loved and the friend I adored as a child. I don't know what has held me back, but there was too much bad blood between our grandparents and your mom's family, and it trickled down into the entire family. I know my dad regrets it deeply—he lost both his best friend and his little brother the day your dad died. I know our grandparents also have great remorse for the way they reacted to the loss of their son. They knew at the time that they reacted horribly, but were so immersed in their own grief that the only thing they saw was their own pain. I don't think it helped that in the time prior to his accident, your dad was planning to leave the reservation, and that was seen as a betrayal to his own parents. I am not defending their stance, just trying (hoping) to explain. The LeBeau family has strong ties to Grass Valley, and despite it being a place where white men sent Indians to die, our Dakota ancestors made it into something beautiful; it was seen as a rejection, then, when Nathaniel announced he had married a non-native, and then another blow came when your parents made plans to move away. None of these things excuse any bad behavior, most of which was simply extreme reactions—not true feelings.

Growing up, I, too, felt rejected by you, since you never came to visit our grandparents or me. How could you turn your back on the family that loved you? I asked myself repeatedly. As I got older, I realized that it was not your decision, and in truth, children often have no voice concerning what happens to them. Then, I blamed your mother, which was incredibly easy, for she was the one to keep you from us. I imagined that she was erasing your heritage to fit into her world and to make it easier for her to move on, which we all had learned she had done rather quickly. Our grandparents did try to contact you over the years, but having received no word from you in return, they gave up eventually. Now that I have my own children and husband, I can more fully understand and appreciate the kind of pain your mom must have been facing after your dad, her husband, died. My husband is also white, and we moved to Grass Valley after our first son was born, and I could see how my beloved husband struggled at times—honestly, still continues to do so, but he never gives up, bless him. It made me see that your mom made the choices she thought were right for herself and for you, in trying to rebuild her life, and it had been your parents' choice *together* to begin their journey forward, off the reservation.

Should our grandparents have tried harder to keep in contact with you? Absolutely no question about it. But anger and remorse combined can be a difficult duo to overcome. My reason for writing is that I hope you are a stronger and more forgiving person than one in previous generations. Our grandparents are celebrating their 60th wedding anniversary, and I know their biggest gift would be your presence. The loss of you, the only daughter to their youngest son, has been one of the biggest losses of their lives, and I am fervently hoping you can begin to help them heal—I have witnessed the pain of that loss and the regret in their faces whenever they speak of you, which is often. Please let me know you will be coming?

All my love,

Abigail LeBeau Connor".

Stunned, Effie found it difficult to catch her breath. Abby had included the details of the anniversary celebration, which was in a few weeks, and a photo of the couple from the local newspaper. How could she ever face these people—her people—alone? No way would her mother ever be convinced to join her. On the other hand, how could she even consider *not* going? To reconnect with the family that had been lost to her thirty years ago? This was what she had desired for so long, and now to know that everyone had been reeling in pain all of these years, not quite knowing how to move forward, beyond words said in the heat of a moment. Effie put the letter back on the small table by the door, because she had other things to think about tonight, and she launched herself up the stairs to select an outfit appropriate for a date with the man she got to second base with on her lunch break in broad daylight.

CHAPTER
Thirty-Three

Effie And Josh

Drawing in a nervous breath, Josh rounded the block to Effie's house, smoothing down the collar of his black and silver button-down shirt as he did so. He had composed a text to her in his head as soon as he had arrived home, intending to postpone their movie night, but just as clicked on her name in his text screen, a message appeared suddenly: "Since the theatre is only a few blocks away, want to meet me at my house and walk over?"

Feeling relieved at her new text, he couldn't help but wonder why the women in his life were always one step ahead of him, anticipating he was always on the cusp of canceling? He could hardly cancel *or* postpone after that, especially since he had never replied to her initial text asking about what movie they should see, or her second text asking him if he wanted to just meet at the theatre. How was he supposed to acknowledge that, then, especially since it would make it an official non-date? After he looked at the theatre's website, he saw a horror movie called *Mommy's Little Helper* was playing, and the premise sounded just disturbing enough to be intriguing. Josh had been obsessed with horror films from the '70s when he was a teenager, and if he recalled correctly, Effie had also been a fan. Thinking back to a warm summer night when he was fifteen, he recalled that he and his cousin, Liam, had been in the video store in Clover Lake trying to agree on what to rent that Friday night. For some reason, Liam had been obsessed with romantic comedies, while Josh had been trying to talk him into the classic *I Spit on Your Grave*. Just as Josh had reached for the DVD case, it had disappeared. Looking to his left, he had seen Effie holding it. She, too, was pleading the case of her choice to her friend, Claudia, and from the look on Claudia's face, she was more easily swayed than Liam. Who was Josh to deny them the privilege of a movie he had already seen at least ten times? Liam and Josh had left with *When Harry Met Sally* and just before leaving, he had caught a grateful smile thrown his way from Effie.

Effie had also remembered the moment from the video store as soon as Josh had sent her the suggestion for tonight's movie, but perhaps for a different reason. In truth, she had *not* been a horror fan but had been trying for months to spend time with Josh outside of school when they weren't working on a play. She had made offers to meet up with him at the roller skating rink, or the ice cream shop that had stood on top of the highest hill in Clover Lake for fifty years, but he was always busy with his family in some way. She had tried to get him to go to a few parties with her, though, but he rarely attended any social gatherings. Effie had overheard him that night in the video store explaining the finer points of the movie to his cousin, and she spontaneously grabbed the box, hoping to invite the boys over to Claudia's house to watch the video together. Josh, however, hadn't even looked her way until he and Liam were exiting the store, and Effie made one last attempt to say something, but he was gone before she could make any utterance.

The vanishing of Melanie Livingston had been one that Clover Lake had talked about for years—how could a mother leave her own child? People created all sorts of theories, with Diadema heavily weighing in on the mix. She and Henry had gone to high school together, much like their children, and Diadema always spoke in a wistful tone whenever she talked about him. Her mom loved to recount how everyone in town had been shocked when Henry had arrived in Clover Lake with the elegant Melanie in tow. Back from a summer working at the Grand Canyon, Henry had met Melanie when her car had broken down. Melanie was headed to California from Florida to become a movie star, she was purported to have told Henry. Three months later, they were married and living in Clover Lake, with Henry forgoing college to begin working full time at his family's garage. Of course, everyone had speculated at the time that Melanie *must* be pregnant, but when no baby came, the townsfolk had to silently apologize for their assumptions. Diadema had the feeling that Melanie would not last in the small town, and Effie knew from experience how vindicated her mother could be, if proven right. To this extent, while Melanie leaving had not been a surprise, her husband and son also fleeing years later, with barely a goodbye to anyone, and no word from extended family? That, Diadema was frequently heard announcing for several years after it happened, had been a shock. Of course, Effie had known none of this firsthand, but her mom had told the story often enough while she had been growing up, with the lore on heavy repeat after Melanie had left, that it seemed to be part of Effie's history as well.

As Josh hesitantly approached the porch stairs, Effie was bounding down them, and for a moment his throat constricted, his senses quickly becoming overwhelmed by nearly every aspect of her: her scent wafted to greet him, a subtle cinnamon and vanilla; the lilac-colored dress made her skin glow and brought out the golden tones in her eyes, and it took every ounce of restraint in him to not reach out to follow the curve of her cheek with his finger. Instead, he settled for waving at her as she tantalizingly stood within touching distance.

Effie held her breath, while closing her eyes briefly, certain that Josh was going to reach for her and pull her into an embrace, but when she remained untouched, she opened her eyes again and found Josh's eyes so very close to her own, looking down at her mouth. They were eye-level, as Effie was still standing on her bottom step, not quite sure if she was breathing or not, and parted her lips in expectation; since she had never been much of a wallflower, she began to sway into him, bracing her hands against his sturdy chest as she did so. Only then did a pack of young boys ride by her house, a bicycle gang of at least ten, yelling and whistling, failing to comprehend the charged moment they were interrupting.

Effie sighed with frustration, "Those boys are the same ones who almost made me crash my bike the other day. Plus, I am pretty sure I caught their ringleader in the library today doing his best to sneak a copy of *Our Bodies, Our Selves* into the bathroom."

Josh reluctantly laughed, slightly annoyed at having their intimate moment ruined, yet trying to take the disruption in stride. Offering Effie his arm as she descended the final stair, he replied in a shocked tone, "Wow—really? Are you okay? You didn't actually fall off your bike, did you?" After she assured him she had been spared such an indignity, he continued, "Wasn't that book considered more scandalous when our parents were teenagers? You'd think kids today would be after much more risque items."

"I know," Effie agreed, "little buggers. They appeared to be more into the thrill of the hunt than what the prey actually was. Oh, before I forget, someone stopped in the library today right before closing, said he works at your dad's shop—Juan, I think his name was? Said to tell you 'hi', but it was weird because he also said he had just come from work, so I wasn't sure why he would say that—you didn't leave early, did you?"

The couple turned onto State Street, and Josh was spared having to confess about Juan spotting them in the park, because Effie's attention turned to someone waving at her from across the street. Turning onto Dakota Avenue, he could feel the eyes of every person on them as they strolled, still arm-in-arm, and he was positive they all had the same question: what was Effie doing with him? Even if they knew he was a surgeon who lived in New York City, it would not carry the same weight here as it did back east. What seemed to matter the most here, in places like this, was how "hard" physically your work was for the day, and with the mechanic work he was currently doing, he was earning the respect of the same people who would potentially be disdainful of him if they knew the truth about his reality.

Effie smiled at several people along the way, including Ashley, owner of Beverley Bake Shoppe, the bakery two blocks away from the library, a single mom around her age who had a love for bodice-rippers from the eighties and nineties: Johanna Lindsey, Judith McNaught, Julie Garwood, Jill Barnett, and Jude Devereaux. Effie fully enjoyed when Ashley came in to check out books, because the two of them always ended up in deep conversation about how the character development in those books was still unparalleled compared to current romance novels. Turning the corner to the movie theatre, Steiner Cinema, she heard a voice from behind her call "Effie?", and turned to see Adam, the deputy sheriff and reader of William Faulkner and Walt Whitman, who also had a penchant for Japanese manga that Effie had found quite surprising, since outwardly he appeared slightly stiff and formal.

"Hi, Adam, nice to finally see you outside the library and out of uniform," and it was then she noticed the extremely attractive man who stood near him, but also ever so slightly behind, almost as if hiding in Adam's shadow. "Oh, hi, Paul," she said, having recognized him a moment later, "I didn't see you there at first. How are you enjoying the José Saramago you checked out the other day? One of my professors in college absolutely loved his stuff, but I could never quite get into it—too cerebral for me."

Both Adam and Paul smiled at her, seemingly relieved to be put at ease. Small towns like these could be difficult to navigate, but almost everyone Effie had met so far, both in the library and out of it, seemed open-minded and accepting of love in all of its forms.

Josh reached out his hand and shook Paul's hand in greeting. "How is the Bronco running now?" He had met Paul the week earlier when Adam had picked him up from the shop. As Paul answered, he also greeted Adam with a handshake. Adam had been a freshman when Josh had moved to Beverley as a junior; he had been in Tess's class but also in the high school band and had played the clarinet beautifully.

The two couples chatted a few moments before entering the theatre to buy tickets to separate movies. "Let me know how *Mommy's Little Helper* is, will you, Effie? I will be in next week to debrief," winked a more relaxed Paul, who was clearly more interested in Effie's date than in their movie selection, and then Effie and Josh were alone at the snack bar.

Josh carried the large popcorn and his soda, and Effie had her drink and the packet of Peanut M&M's, which they both agreed was the perfect movie snack. Entering the darkened theatre, he followed Effie to the row off the side, with only two seats.

"Is this okay?" she asked. "I don't want to end up surrounded by anyone else."

Josh nodded, but looked around at the near-empty room. Never in his life had he watched a movie from the side rows—he always chose a center seat whenever possible, or as near to it as he could get. "Don't you think we would have a better view from over there?" He pointed to the middle of the theatre. "Or even there?" And then he gestured to the first few rows.

"What? No way! Way too close, for one thing, and I love these side seats. Have you never sat over here?" As he shook his head, Effie could see that Josh was uncomfortable with sitting to the side, but she thought he could do with a bit of shaking up. "You are in for a serious treat here, Josh. The view is better because you don't have to take everything in at once like you do from the center. Also, just in case you get some talkies in here, they never sit to the side. Oh no, they want to be front and center, just so they can annoy everyone around them." Effie sat down and patted the seat next to hers. Josh, the Josh she knew years ago, had some quirky habits back then that over time seemed to have cemented into place. Effie was used to trying to fix bad boys—failing every time to get them to become a bit more strait-laced. Josh was the opposite of all of them, and she didn't want to *fix* him, per se, but loosen him up. She had never met a mechanic as tightly wound as Josh was, yet he also had a vulnerability she could see floating just below the surface, almost as if he wasn't quite sure where he fit in the world.

Josh sighed and reluctantly sat down in the seat next to Effie's, placing the popcorn between them, and took a sip of his soda before putting it in the drink holder on the back of the seat in front of him. The previews started up; Josh reached over to grab a handful of the salty, buttery popcorn, and it was so warm and crisp that he devoured it immediately and went for another handful. Instead of popcorn, he felt soft, feathery fingertips. Immediately he began to withdraw his hand so Effie could get her popcorn, but he felt her smaller hand grab onto his, and then her slender fingers laced between his. Suddenly popcorn was not what he was hungry for on this sultry summer evening, in this dark and cool room, where the two of them were tucked all alone to the side. His thumb stroked over the top of her hand, and he felt a shiver reverberate from her as the room darkened completely and the movie started.

CHAPTER
Thirty-Four

Henry

"I told you to quit calling me," Henry hissed into his cellphone. "When you called me earlier, I was barely out of the shop. Do you have any idea how reckless that was? Anyone could have heard me answer the phone."

"By anyone, I presume you mean our son? Why didn't you tell me that he was back there? Not to mention *working* in the *shop*?" No one's voice dripped with disdain the way his ex's did, Henry knew from up close and personal experience. He had met Melanie when she was at a particularly vulnerable time in her life, and he had fallen madly in love with her within minutes—maybe even seconds. Unfortunately, it was much more difficult to maintain that love when it was only surface-deep. She had desperately wanted more for her life than he could, or was even able to, give.

The summer they had met, he and his two best friends, believing they needed a grand adventure before college, had applied for jobs at the Grand Canyon. Only Henry had been hired, but he had much to prove to both himself and his extended family, so he had packed his backpack, filled the tank of his '69 Chevy Camaro, kissed his mom goodbye the day after his graduation ceremony, and had headed west. Until that time, Henry had never been further west than Rapid City, not to mention as far south as the Grand Canyon. That summer had been a time of self-exploration and freedom, away from the intensity of his large extended family that seemed to always be lurking not just in every corner of Clover Lake, but the surrounding towns as well; the population of the area was small enough, but when you add cousins, aunts, and uncles, there had been zero expectation of privacy.

Henry had also been nursing a broken heart, because although he and Diadema Sommer had attended prom together when he was a senior, she had rejected all other advances from him, admitting the morning after prom that she had only agreed to be his date after quarterback and general all-American hero Dirk Timmons had canceled on *her* two weeks before prom, taking head cheerleader Alicia Peterson to prom instead. Small town dating pools grew incredibly smaller as everyone got older. Henry usually referred to Dirk as Dick, but everyone had no choice but to be nice to him since his dad owned the only grocery store in town, which sponsored so many of the extra-curricular activities often in need of his funding.

Since he had been a small boy, Henry had one goal: to become a doctor, and he was enrolled to begin his pre-med courses at the university in Vermillion in the fall. Seeing his father come home every night with oil-stained hands had made him eager to have a career where his worth wouldn't be judged by how physically exhausted he was at the end of the day.

The Grand Canyon, breathtaking and immense, was so unlike anything that surrounded his hometown, and he had loved the desert atmosphere. Teenagers and young adults came from around the world to spend their summers working in gift shops, stocking camping supplies, or assisting tour guides, and Henry befriended anyone he came into contact with, never meeting a stranger, his mother often marveled about her son.

And then Melanie breezed into the canyon, more glamorous than any other girl Henry knew from Clover Lake. She had sleek blonde hair, crystal blue eyes, with a slight southern drawl from living on the Florida panhandle (it's technically still the South, she was fond of stating). Melanie, with her love of tight pants and even tighter shirts, had every male eating out of the palm of her hand. Not originally planning to work in the canyon, she was on her way to Hollywood, "I'm the new Marilyn Monroe," she breathily told Henry the night he met her, "my high school drama teacher told me he thinks I have what it takes to be a star." Henry was unable to do anything but believe her: everyone was inevitably drawn to Melanie. Unfortunately for her, she did not descend from a long line of car mechanics, and her Ford Pinto had not survived the drive west from Florida beyond Texas. Melanie had used the last of her money to catch a bus to Arizona, arriving two weeks after Henry.

Henry had hung on each word Melanie uttered, and she drank in his attention as if slaking her thirst in this dry, desert heat. Over the next two months, all others were forsaken as Melanie began working side-by-side with Henry at one of the gift shops, and the two spent all their free time together. Melanie regaled him with her plans to conquer California, and they daydreamed about plans for him to visit her during college breaks. She planned their future together with Henry working as a doctor in Los Angeles, and Melanie starring in blockbuster movies—Henry would accompany her on red carpet premieres and be her date for the Academy Awards, of course, because she swore he was the best-looking guy she had ever seen: "Imagine how much better you would look in a suit, Henry.".

August came then, and with it, plans for Henry to head back to South Dakota in a little over a week. Melanie had been under the weather for the past few days when she flew into his cabin, frantic over her missed period. A pregnancy test the next day at the nurse's office confirmed her worst nightmare. No Hollywood for Melanie, and no medical school for Henry; instead, he had sucked up all of his pride and asked his uncle for a job at the auto shop, something he had previously sworn he would never do, and now had no choice. Attitudes around town ranged from disbelief to dismissive, with almost no one being sympathetic to the loss of the combined dreams of the newly married couple.

Despite never intending to become a wife or mother, Melanie had settled into her roles as best as she could, having had no guidance from her own wrecked childhood: her parents divorced when she was three, with her father having deserted her and her younger sister not long after; her mother with her multiple marriages, and more children each time, never realizing babies can't fix broken marriages. Henry had been the love of Melanie's life—for a time, anyway. He never deluded himself into thinking he was anything more than a stopgap, and although she had never been unfaithful, she had also never been fully committed.

Unfortunately, one week and one rushed wedding after the couple settled in with Henry's parents in South Dakota, Melanie got her period. Joshua was not actually conceived until three years after his parents had been married; three long years in which Melanie told Henry daily how much she regretted not waiting to take a real test at a hospital, and Henry commiserated silently, yet also secretly pleased that the previous test had been faulty, because despite her inability to truly love him, he was in love with her.

It had not shocked Henry to find her gone the year Josh had been twelve—if he were brutally honest, he would admit she stayed longer than he had ever thought possible. He had, however, been stunned that she had left behind her son, and then with no word to him whatsoever. The letter that Josh had clung to and treasured all these years had never been written by Melanie at all; no, that was Henry's doing. Josh had never questioned why the letter was typed and then signed with such a flourish. Josh had asked repeatedly to read what his mom had written to his dad, and Henry would come up with vague answers, all intended to distract or redirect his attention elsewhere. What else was he to do? Could he have done? As hollow as Henry had felt at Melanie's leaving, he knew Josh's pain and disbelief had the potential to overwhelm both of them.

All that he had ever wanted for himself he had poured into his only son: his dreams of becoming a doctor, his hopes of Josh finding true love, as Henry had never found. Henry had been fond of Tess, but in truth, he had always felt that both were together due to proximity, a situation far too similar to the relationship he had shared with Melanie: different dreams and different sacrifices. Much more promising was Josh's developing relationship with Euphemie, who differed so greatly from her own mother, yet Henry could also see the same strength and drive that Diadema had. Effie was a woman of substance who could help Josh in finding his inner strength, someone capable of shining a light on his son and making him believe he was deserving of love.

All of Josh's burgeoning emotional growth could be stymied, though, with the reappearance of his mother. Melanie had, for some unknown reason, and after years of showing absolutely no interest in either one of them, begun calling Check Care Auto Shop in Beverley. At least, he had assumed her interest was sudden, until his brother let it slip that in actuality, she had been calling his dad for years at the family shop in Clover Lake, getting updates on Josh and occasionally Henry. When she discovered from one of his dad's employees that Josh was currently on a sabbatical back in Beverley, she began calling Henry directly, after the same employee gave Henry's cell number to her. Melanie was mothering Josh by annoying Henry now every week.

"How could you let him do this, Henry? You are standing aside, watching Joshua destroy everything he has earned, by allowing our son to come home and what? Wallow in self-pity? He's *working in your garage?* What's next? His name embroidered on a pair of overalls, with a wrench in the pocket, in place of his doctor's coat and scalpel?" Henry had let her say every single scathing thing because, in truth, he had been saying the same things to himself since his son had returned. "He was meant for bigger things—things that you and I were robbed of, ironically, because of him."

"Now you wait just a damn minute," Henry cut in, trying to keep an eye out on the streets as he drove home one-handed, with his cell phone clenched in his left hand. "Direct all of your crap to me—I can take it. But you *never* say anything to Josh like that. Do you think I *want* him to follow in my footsteps? I am supporting him the best I can, by myself, as I have done for over the last twenty years. How much loss is he supposed to handle, living all by himself in New York City? He's not like you, who pushes everyone away who tries to care too much. At least he isn't suffering in a love-less marriage, unlike us."

Her sharp intake of breath indicated she hadn't been expecting the personal shift to their relationship. "I don't need you to remind me what a failure I was as a wife. But I did love you. How do you think it felt for me? Living back there in that tiny little town, and seeing your reaction every time we ran into the girl you never got? The one you really wanted? Did you never realize I could see how much you loved her? How much you kept from me once we moved there?" Henry heard her voice break. "Your precious Diadema—god her name is burned into my brain, even after all of these years. Are you still pining for her, by the way?"

"Did it occur to you in all the years we were together that if I had received the smallest token of *your* withheld affection, I would not have needed to pine for a woman who never really noticed me? How pathetic I felt—to never be wanted by the only two women that I ever loved in my life? All of the women who wanted to comfort me after you left, and then when I moved here, telling everyone my precious wife had died. I was a popular widower, believe me. Only I could feel nothing for any of them." Henry pulled into his driveway, puzzled to see his son's truck there. Didn't he have plans tonight?

As usual, when the conversation turned toward them in any serious fashion, Melanie had little to say, so Henry continued, "Rehashing our history never gets us anywhere. Josh will be going back to New York in the next month or so. Don't worry—he is nothing like me. Do me a favor and stay well and truly out of our lives."

CHAPTER
Thirty-Five

Effie And Josh

Effie walked on clouds as she and Josh exited the theatre, and she could not recall the last time she had never wanted an evening to end. Typically, Effie supposed people were more inclined to hold hands during, say, a romantic comedy, perhaps a drama, if it were swoon-worthy enough. She and Josh, though, bucked that trend and had spent most of their movie (which turned out to be even more entertaining than the trailer had made it seem) holding hands. Something so erotic about their palms facing each other, being pressed into one another, and then Josh would move his thumb over the center of her palm just before disengaging his hand from hers to grab a handful of popcorn. Each time Effie ate some popcorn, she'd lick her fingers free of the butter and salt, imagining she could taste Josh as well. Never before had a bucket of popcorn been eaten with such care, such relish, or so slowly.

Josh was a tuning fork standing next to Effie outside the theatre, as if every chord in his body was responding to hers and pinging with desire.

The foreplay of their evening, all over a tub of popcorn, had driven him to distraction and if pressed, he would in no way be able to even summarize their movie—had he even seen anything on screen? Unable to stand it a minute longer, he tugged on her hand and drew her around the corner of the theatre—the corner not on Dakota Avenue. And in the dark, he pulled her to him, staring into her eyes as he held her face in his hands. Effie nodded up at him, and his mouth descended on hers. She tasted salty and sweet, more intoxicating than any liquor. Who was he right now? He wasn't normally a man who pulled women into dark shadows to make out with them, was he? For once in his life, Josh didn't want to reason. He didn't want to make sense out of anything—he only wanted to *feel*. And feel, he did, running his hand from her face down her back while pulling her even closer.

Effie in turn slid her arms up, circling them around his neck, desperately needing the feel of his body meshed with hers. She turned them so her back was against the cool brick of the theatre, and as his lips kissed their way down her neck, she dove her hands under the back of his shirt, relishing in the warmth of his smooth skin. Raking her nails over his back, she moaned as his mouth found hers again. It would be so easy to simply lose herself in this moment with him, but she wanted *more* from him than another public, hormone-fueled, loin-burning, make-out session. Effie knew the two of them could be building something real together here—finally—and for once she was determined to take things slowly (as much as she reasonably could) and listen to her heart *and* her head.

Summoning every ounce of strength in her tingling body, Effie gently broke off their kiss. "Do you know how long I have waited to kiss you like this?" she asked, stroking his smooth cheek—he must have shaved before picking her up at her house. "So long," she answered at the shake of his head. "Since we were in high school, maybe before."

Josh stared at her in a stunned silence. "What do you mean? You had half of the boys in school panting after you. I was such a nerd—still am. Completely uncool."

"And none of them had your grace…your kindness…your intelligence. You were so sweet, so unassuming, and I always felt absolutely at ease with you." She took his hand, and told him, "There is nothing more important to me, at this point in my life, than sincerity and the ability to feel like myself with someone, I'm realizing." Wanting the night to last, she glanced down the street and asked him, "Do you want to grab a coffee before we head back?" At his nod of affirmation, she took his hand in hers, led him to the sidewalk, and they walked hand-in-hand, with Effie steering up Second Street, where Mr. Beans stood at the end of the next block.

Josh was suddenly struck with a wave of defeat that was quickly overtaking his mood. "You know," Josh gave a small laugh, "you make me sound like a sofa or rocking chair. Meet Josh—he's just another piece of furniture," and try as he might, he could not keep his comment from becoming accented with the slightest dose of bitterness. When would someone find him daring? Sexy? Irresistible? He had done his best tonight, only to have Effie pull away and lead him over here, where it seemed half of Beverley was gathered on this Friday night. The last thing he wanted was a crowd of people; he just wanted to be alone with her. He hesitated at the opening coffee shop door, where music from the open mic night escaped onto the street. "I'm sorry, Effie, I just think I am beat after working all day and the movie, and it's too loud in there. Do you mind if I just walk you home?"

Feeling disappointed, she pasted a smile on her face and put more energy into answering than it probably deserved, replying perkily, "Sure." What else could she do? Beg him to spend more time with her? Maybe he wasn't vibing with her as much as she thought. Effie reminded herself that she was not looking to start a new relationship, anyway, so if he wanted casual friends, she could be a casual friend.

For whatever reason, Josh was putting off an annoyed vibe, and she had no idea what could have happened to get under his skin. As they walked back to Effie's house, under the light of the full moon and seemingly every star in the galaxy, she brought up the movie, thinking that at least it was a safe, friendly territory to tread. Trying not to read too much into it, she relaxed when all of his comments about the movie were generally positive, so he must have had a good time tonight?

Walking up the sidewalk to Effie's house, Josh said stiffly, "Well, thank you for the nice night. I guess I will see you later?" And as he gazed intently at her, his eyes dropped to her lips, moving of their own accord, and before he could further humiliate himself, he started to turn on his heel to leave. How had he done this before? How had he ever taken a chance with a woman, like when he had broken up with Tess after college? He had dated several women in those years until he eventually got back together with Tess—the difference was, he thought, they had not meant anything to him. Not like Effie did.

"Wait," cried Effie, as she reached out and grabbed his hand again, unwilling to let him go home in this funky state of mind. Not wanting to end their night with this sense of unease, she pulled him back to her, saying once more, "Wait." She drew in a breath. "I was hoping we could have a drink on the porch, talk a little more? Enjoy this glorious evening? It's just…" she hesitated, "it's like we see each other but never get a chance to *talk*." She nodded toward the porch, decked out with a swing and two Adirondack chairs. "I've got some wine in the fridge, in case you wanted to come up? I'm sorry if I said the wrong thing earlier, and I'm sorry about the coffee shop—I just wanted to spend more time with you; you were right, it was too noisy, but it's nice and quiet here." She tilted her head back to look at him. "Please…stay?

Josh stared into her tawny eyes, helpless to do anything but have a drink with Effie. "Of course," he whispered, and he followed her up the stairs, took a seat on the porch swing, and watched her enter the house to retrieve the wine and some glasses. Unsure of what was happening between them, Josh had vowed to himself on the way over that he was going to do his best to take it all in stride. Removing his phone from his pocket, he saw there was a text from Ruth, letting him know the exact date that she and Sean were moving to Beverley, having decided to rent a house near the hospital, and would be in touch when they got to town. She also told him that Tess and Sam had gotten married today, in a small, intimate wedding with only family members present. The wedding was not new information for him, though, as Sam had called him a few days prior to the wedding to tell him personally, which he had appreciated. He truly wished both of them the very best, he told Sam, and when he was back in New York, he promised to get together with them. Ugh—he definitely did not want to think about New York now. Not here, and not with Effie.

Inside the house, Effie put her stereo on, and started with The Judds' greatest hits—who could resist the smoky voice of Wynonna Judd serenading them on a steamy summer evening? She stepped back outside and observed a pensive look on Josh's face. "Josh? You seem a million miles away," Effie stated as she unloaded a small tray onto the table next to the swing. She had brought out the chilled wine, glasses, small plates, Triscuits, and slices of Colby-jack cheese and summer sausage. "I realized when I was in the kitchen that I was starving, and I can't be the only one!" As she handed him a plate filled with snacks, she prompted, "What was on your mind just now?"

"I just got a text from Ruth," he told her, and gave her what he knew of her family's plan to move, while he built little sandwiches with the crackers, meat and cheese, and then handed Effie a plate that held two of them.

Smiling her appreciation at Josh's thoughtfulness, she ate one of the treats in two bites, and then exclaimed, "Oh, how exciting! I will have to text her to let me know, as well. She is so funny—I can't wait to get to know her more. You guys go back a long way, huh?" Effie couldn't help but feel a bit jealous, knowing that after Josh left Clover Lake, he had made such good friends with Ruth and her sister, Tess. Almost like she was replaced by them—if Josh hadn't moved, it could have been her, and not Tess, who Josh had loved. Maybe the two of them—Josh and Effie—would have survived as a couple? Maybe even be married now? Living in this same home she had bought, close to his dad, and close enough to her mom, raising a family together. Stop, she warned herself. Do not go there.

"Yeah, you could say that. I mean, not as long as I've known you," and Josh's eyes found hers, putting as much meaning into his look as possible. "Both she and Tess were there for me, in this new, bigger school. I felt so alone, so out of place. I was this chubby kid who didn't quite fit in anywhere. Invisible, but also with everyone staring at me all the same."

Effie whispered, "I always thought you were so special, Josh. It must have been extremely difficult to have your mom leave like she did. Especially in Clover Lake, where everyone knows everyone's business. It must have been a bit easier here in Beverley, right?"

How could he tell her that everyone in Beverley thought his mom had died, and in reality, no one knew she had abandoned him? In his head, thinking about it now, it seemed crazy that his dad had even suggested the lie, but truthfully, it had made things easier. No one questioned a dead parent, as he had found out. No one wanted to upset him by asking any follow-up questions, but to admit this now, to Effie? She would never understand. He took a sip of wine, wanting profoundly to tell her the truth about everything—his past mistakes, and how he was terrified to go back to New York to face some of them.

Deciding to lead with some current truths, Josh admitted, "It is easier here—now, anyway. I had been away for years, until my break-up with Ruth's sister, Tess. I didn't handle it well; I never handled any of it well, honestly. I was too caught up in my career, which imploded when my relationship did." He tilted back in the swing, took another drink of wine, and then said, "I guess you're probably wondering what happened with me and Tess, huh? What I did to screw it all up?" he asked, hoping it came across as self-deprecating.

"I assure you, when it comes to relationships, I am not one to judge. If you want to talk about it, though, I'm a good listener," and she reached down with her toe and gave the swing a nudge to lightly glide under them.

"Well, first of all, it was probably all my fault—I worked too much, didn't listen to her about spending time together. Then, when she was on her way to her bachelorette weekend, riding the train across the country, she met, or I guess I should say, re-met, my friend Sam. Neither one recognized the other," and at her quizzical expression he laughed, "I know, I don't understand it, either. I guess you had to be there—which, according to them, even if I had been, it wouldn't have mattered: they fell in love. The thing is, she didn't tell me any of this, but for some reason, still kept planning our wedding. Until the day before, when she saw Sam at the rehearsal—then she left me standing in the church, at the altar, alone." Josh closed his eyes, awash in humiliation. "Part of Ruth's text also informed me that Sam and Tess got married today, which I already knew because Sam had the decency to call me and give me a heads up. So that's my love story."

Effie felt a burning anger at Tess, wondering how she could hurt someone like Josh in this way. Having been on the receiving end of numerous betrayals before, she knew the pain and disillusionment they brought. "God, Josh, I am so sorry—you did not deserve that, no matter what the reasoning was." Effie could tell he was trying to process, so she offered, "When I moved back to Clover Lake, I was in the throes of starting over, too. Living in Denver had been great, but it turns out I wasn't built for the big city, which is something my ex kept trying to convince me of over the years: turns out the bastard was right about one thing, at least."

"Your ex?" Josh questioned, recalling that Liam had mentioned an ex when they had been out for dinner.

Effie laughed, "Oh, yeah, soon-to-be ex-husband. It took me a long time to admit it wasn't working, but I hope I learned a life lesson from it all." At Josh's questioning look, she added, "Don't be involved with liars! All he did to me, probably from day one, was lie. That's it—I'm over it! No more lies, and that includes white lies, lies of omission, little lies, big lies: they're all the same."

Josh sunk slightly into the swing, kicking it back a bit too aggressively with his foot accidentally, which caused Effie's wine glass to lurch forward. In turn, she caught it just in time, but the arm that had been resting next to Josh's flew over his knees as she did so.

Laughing uncontrollably, Effie tipped the remains of her glass into her mouth and turned to put the glass on the table next to her. Listening to the chorus of "Why Not Me", she looked over at Josh, who was watching her with such on intensity, it caused a shiver down her spine.

"You are so beautiful," he remarked, "so graceful, so filled with light. All I can think of in this moment is how much I want to kiss you again, not the past or lies, or exes." And every bit of what he said was true. He dreaded thinking of how disappointed she was bound to be in him, for so many reasons. He could now almost imagine the agony Tess had been in on the train after meeting Sam: pledged to Josh, but desiring another man. For now, Josh was torn, only his angst was between this woman and all that he dared not admit to her.

Instead, he reached for her: the woman he had loved long before he met Tess, or even Ruth, never imagining any world in which she would want him back. "Can I kiss you?" he had to ask, in case there was any chance he was misreading any signs, and he listened as "Mama, He's Crazy" played in the background, and he was: crazy for this woman next to him on this porch swing, in this South Dakota town.

Effie nodded, desperately needing him at that moment, and rose up to put both her legs on the outsides of his, so she was straddling him on her swing. Forgetting they were, in all actuality, still in a public place, she settled onto his lap. As her mouth met his, she drove her hands into his hair, and his arms pulled her closer to him.

Josh felt himself reacting to Effie, and he held on to her hips as she ground them into him. They devoured each other underneath the summer stars, until Josh stood, with Effie's legs wrapped around his waist. She groaned into his ear, "Sofa," and he backed her up to the house, bracing himself against her. She managed to reach down and open the door with her free hand. Somehow the entwined couple made it through the doorway, and Josh took an unknown number of steps to the sofa, while never pulling apart from Effie. He bent down so she could lie back, and as she did, she clutched at his shoulders, intending to never let him go.

CHAPTER
Thirty-Six

Diadema

As she stared at the phone in her hand, Diadema wondered where her daughter could be. Should she call her? It wasn't like Euphemie to be late, but Diadema had been waiting in the diner for fifteen minutes already, with two texts still unanswered. The two of them had made plans earlier in the week to have breakfast this morning at Betsy's Diner, but Diadema also had some errands to run in Aberdeen this afternoon, so she could not wait forever for her eggs Benedict. Now, if Hamilton was involved, tardiness could and should be expected. Something didn't feel right to her, so she followed her mother's intuition and left the diner to go check on her daughter.

Driving back through town, Diadema surveyed what was becoming her daughter's new world, and she felt a new peace knowing she was remarkably closer to home. Diadema had loathed visiting her in Denver, even more so when Damon had been around (which thankfully wasn't often). To the outside world, Diadema had praised her daughter's husband, focusing solely on his looks, because he was only skin deep. How her beautiful and brilliant child could have such terrible taste in men was probably what shocked Diadema the most. The first time around with Nathaniel, she had chosen love, and then with Burnside, love had followed after wanting the stability she knew he could provide. Nathaniels's death had ravaged her, and she had somehow fallen under the thumb of her parents, both financially and emotionally. Getting sent to her aunt's house in Ohio had been a blessing, and meeting Burnside a godsend. His parents had been friends of her aunt's, and the two had been set up a few months after her arrival. Burnside had lost his wife the year earlier, as well, so he had understood her overwhelming grief, and did not rush her in her process. Over the time that followed, they had begun to heal together; when she was ready to return to South Dakota, Burnside had suggested they marry, and to provide her daughter with the father she had lost, Diadema had readily agreed. Perhaps Euphemie had rebelled against their idea of romance, which was steeped more in comfort and ease, less in desire and passion.

After pulling into Effie's (why must she insist on using such a ridiculous name?) and parking her car, Diadema peeked through one of the windows at the top of the garage door and saw her daughter's car inside the garage. Okay, maybe she had overslept, but it was so out of character. It was possible, she supposed, that Euphemie took her bike to the diner, and they just missed each other. She was always going on about that new bike, and how she loved riding it around town, romanticizing the wind in her hair and the sun on her skin, when in reality Diadema knew full well how bad the mosquitos got around here during the summer, and how stifling with humidity the air could feel.

Once she was on the porch, she saw the bottle of wine on the small table, along with two glasses that looked as if they had been tossed onto the swing. What in the world? she thought. After noticing the overturned plate, that looked as if at one point it may have held cheese, and the box of crackers strewn over the wooden porch floor, Diadema felt a queasiness in her stomach, dreading that something terrible had happened here last night to her daughter. Giving the door a quick knock, she waited, but heard nothing. When another knock failed to bring her daughter to the door, she hesitantly turned the doorknob on the front door, both relieved and concerned when it opened with ease. Euphemie should know better than this, after living in Denver; even in a town as small as Clover Lake, they had always locked their doors.

As she pushed open the door, Diadema called, "Euphemia? Hello? Is everything okay?" and she stopped in her tracks, noting the discarded clothing on the floor next to the sofa. Was that a pair of men's shoes lying there, with her daughter's bra on top of one of the shoes? Diadema gaped at the dress and Oxford shirt on the back of the sofa, and decided her mortification would be worse if she stayed in this house a minute longer. She turned toward the door, but on her way out, something caught her eye on the table to the right of the doorway: a letter addressed to her daughter. Was this the letter she's been waiting for from her divorce lawyer? She wondered. On impulse she picked it up, hoping to see that the marriage Euphemie had impulsively entered into way too many years ago was soon to be over. Instead, she could see it was a different letter entirely, and one that must have taken Euphemie by as much surprise as she herself felt reading it.

Back at Betsy's, not feeling much better than she had before she left to check up on Euphemie, Diadema requested a table for two, and sent her daughter another text telling her she had a table at the diner and would be here for another half an hour. Just as she was stirring cream into her coffee, a voice above her asked, "DD?" Startled, she spilled some coffee onto the table as she wondered who would be using a nickname she had not allowed anyone to call her since her beloved husband had died.

The voice turned out to be that of another lost man in her life, Henry Livingston, and despite the gray at his temples and the lines of a life lived evidenced across his face, he looked almost exactly as he had in high school. Her avoidance of Henry was the reason she had Euphemie take her car into his shop. Burnside trusted Henry's shop in Beverley over that of his father's shop in Clover Lake, and he had surprised her a couple of months ago by asking her to do it instead. Thank god her daughter and son had been there to have them do it for her. Hamilton, she thought, finally getting his act together—she'd been secretly terrified that he would live with them until he was thirty. She regretted being so lenient with him as a child, and she knew Euphemie thought they had been too tough on her, in comparison. How did one parent two children born so many years apart, with two completely different fathers? Diadema had done the best with both of her children, and she was beginning to see the fruits of her labor rewarded with both of them finding fulfilling lives for themselves. Hopefully.

"Henry Livingston," she breathed out. "Fancy meeting you here." Okay, calm down, she advised herself, but she had always found it difficult to *not* feel somewhat fluttery whenever she was near Henry. One of her biggest regrets from her early life had been how she had treated him all of those years ago: using him to make another boy jealous. Someone who had been completely unworthy of her, as a matter of fact, and in turn she found herself completely unworthy of Henry: someone who was so kind and gracious, so sincere, and in return she had been cruel and callous. His unwavering interest in her, even after she had rejected his repeated attempts to date her after that prom, had been what had made her ready to receive love from Nathaniel later in college.

"Hi, DD. It has been a spell since I've seen you. I thought I would get the chance after the time your husband told me he could not bring in your car himself. Not surprising, though, when you sent your kids instead." He looked at her meaningfully, and she blushed in response. "Are you eating alone?" he asked hopefully. Too hopefully, and that was why she always insisted Burnside take her car to the shop. Whenever she ran into Henry, she was reminded of the path not taken, of how things could have been different if she had not thwarted his interest in her back in high school. They had never been on the same timeline.

"I hope not—I am waiting for my daughter to meet me here, actually," and she softened enough to smile at him, and motioned for him to sit down.

Henry nodded, "Of course. I see her quite a bit these days, since she started at the library. As a matter of fact, she and my son went to a movie last night."

Diadema choked on her coffee, instantly aware of whose shirt and shoes those must have been scattered around her house. "Oh, really?" she asked, as innocently as possible.

"Trust me, it was a complete shock to me as well—I mean, who would have thought that our children would end up dating? Well, I guess maybe I am jumping things a bit to call it dating, especially considering the fact that he will be leaving soon." He shook his head as the waitress asked if he needed a menu, and then informed her that he was waiting for his takeout order.

"What do you mean 'leaving'?" Another surprise for the day. Euphemie had told her about befriending Josh again after all of these years, and how both of them were freshly out of long-term relationships; however, she had not mentioned it being a short-term reunion.

Henry appeared taken aback by her emphatic tone. "Oh, I just meant that he will be headed back to New York City soon. Effie must have mentioned that Josh is a surgeon there—technically a surgical resident, but he only has a few months left and then he's done."

Diadema was stunned, as she remembered it had been Henry's dream to be a doctor, all those years ago, and how people had been a little too fond of pointing out what a shame it had been when he had come back to Clover Lake to be a mechanic instead. Diadema knew the high price to be paid to live up to the expectations of others.

She shook her head, "I have to be honest, she has been so busy with moving and then getting this new job at the library that she probably meant to tell me but forgot." Oh Euphemie, she thought, what have you gotten yourself into? Getting involved with an unavailable man, when your divorce isn't even final? Her daughter had always been tight-lipped where her private life was concerned, but she had hoped that they had turned a corner with their own relationship recently. Now, however, with this news of her love life, and then the letter she had read back at her house, Diadema realized such was not the case.

The waitress came over with a carrier bag and handed it to Henry. "Well, this is me. I will leave you to your mother-daughter breakfast," and he nodded to the entrance, where she saw Euphemie heading toward the table. "Nice seeing you, DD."

"You, too, Henry," and she gave him a small wave as he turned and walked away, nodding at her daughter as they passed near the hostess stand.

"Sorry I'm so late, Mom. My alarm didn't go off, and then I had to take a quick shower. Why was Henry Livingston sitting at your table?" And Effie poured herself a cup of coffee from the carafe sitting in front of her, dousing it with a liberal amount of cream and sugar.

"Perhaps more interesting, Dear, is what Josh Livingston was doing at your house this morning, and why you were *really* late?"

CHAPTER
Thirty-Seven

Josh

"I hope I'm not calling too early…I actually just intended to leave a voicemail," Josh said hesitantly. Back at his dad's house and still reeling from his night with Effie, Josh made a phone call to Sam, wanting to extend well wishes to him and Tess, while also hoping that the man who had been his closest friend since college could offer some life and love advice in return.

"No, not at all; actually, I was up early to write a bit before Tess wakes up," Sam said hesitantly, and then cleared his throat, so Josh rushed in to put him at ease.

"I just wanted to say congratulations and to wish you both the very best. I know I texted both of you yesterday, but I felt bad about not calling directly. Then, of course, I didn't want to wait too long to call, which would make it awkward, or call too soon, which would make it weird. But here I am now, calling the morning after your wedding." Why must he start everything semi-normally, and then have it spiral down, leading to his humiliation? Incidentally, it was also what concerned him about whatever he had going on with Effie. Last night had been better than any dream he had ever had, or could even imagine; too often, though, his judgement led him astray, so he didn't know if he could trust in his feelings. When he had come back to South Dakota, he had only one mission: to get his life together so he could return to New York. And he had, in a way. At least, he was getting there, and lately it felt like he could be almost there, and the yearning had been building inside of him to return to his true love—surgery. Every time he picked up a wrench, or any other small tool at the shop, the weight of it represented all of his mistakes he had made when he was last in the operating room; he was ready to put his dad's tools back where they belonged and pick his own up again. Upon returning to his dad's house this morning, after enjoying a lengthy and quite steamy shower with Effie, he had gingerly taken his lab coat out of his suitcase. When he had initially unpacked his clothes upon arrival, the coat had been left in the case, wadded up into a ball of frustration. The rush of satisfaction he had felt as he slipped his arms into the sleeves almost paralleled how he had felt kissing Effie goodbye this morning. Almost. Now here he was wondering how the two pieces of his life puzzle were going to fit together, and it seemed overwhelmingly bleak. There was no Effie in New York, and likewise, no surgery in South Dakota.

All of these thoughts had brought him to gather his courage and swallow his pride to call Sam. How had he and Tess done it? How had they overcome their obstacles (and they had had a significant number of them) to forge ahead in order to be together?

Sam laughed, "We were just talking last night about how much we missed you." Josh responded with a laugh, certain that he had been the furthest thing from their minds. Sam continued, "You were the one person, aside from my family, that I would have wanted at my wedding. We owe you everything, Josh. You don't know how much your goodwill brought such an ease to us beginning our life together, despite how difficult it all was at first. Without you, Tess and I would never have happened. And I know how condescending that could sound, but I mean it."

"I know you do, Sam. What you may have lacked in integrity, you more than make up for with sincerity," Josh remarked, and after a pause, both men burst out laughing, because this was exactly the type of response he would have made years ago—before he was so caught up in his own head, terrified of messing up or making the wrong decision, yet equally afraid of doing everything right.

"Well played, Josh, and certainly well-deserved on my part. My next book is actually about a man who screws over one of his best friends in order to be with the love of his life," Sam joked.

"So sure to be a bestseller, then." How long had it been that he had felt so light? Was this the Effie-effect? One night with her and he was a new man; at least, more reminiscent of the old man he once had been. "Ruth also texted that they are moving here soon."

"Yeah, isn't that wild? They are heading back today, so they could start getting everything ready for the move. They are both looking forward to it; I know Tess is going to miss having her sister so close. But it gives us a reason to visit more often. At least we will be back from our honeymoon before they move."

"Are you going somewhere special for your honeymoon?" Josh thought about how upset Tess had been when he had suggested they postpone a honeymoon in order for him to concentrate on his career.

"We won't be going anywhere else for our honeymoon, actually, just staying on the train. It seemed appropriate to get married and then honeymoon in the place where we fell in love. Sorry—is this too much?"

"No, Sam, I don't want you to feel like you guys need to keep anything from me." He longed to be included in the lives of two people who had been so important to him for so many years. "But what about her bakery?" Josh wondered how she could take very much time off after just starting a business.

Sam let out another laugh: as long as Josh had known Sam, one of his best qualities was his ability to so fully embrace life and the changes that come with it. Sam didn't get caught up in his head the way he did, and maybe that came from being the eldest of five boys, but while Sam still had an intensity about him, it was overlaid with an ease Josh had never possessed.

"No worries in that department—she hired amazing staff, and one of them follows Tess's recipes to a 'T'," Sam informed Josh. "Tess has created something really special in that coffee shop. The bones were already there, and she built up on it. You should come over when you're back in New York."

An awkward pause hung over their conversation then, as Josh realized that Sam, and by extension Tess, must know about his forced sabbatical, and Sam seemed to instantly regret his words.

"Josh, I'm sorry. I didn't know if I should say anything the other day when I called you and maybe shouldn't have said anything now." Sam paused for a moment and then continued, "Or maybe I should have reached out to you when I did find out, but we were so focused on the wedding and the bakery." Sam took a breath and sighed heavily, "Anyway, I am sorry all around—it sucks that any of that happened. I know how driven you are, Josh, and how badly you have wanted to be a surgeon. Not to mention how you have worked your ass off all of these years, studying and training."

"Saying it 'sucks' pretty much sums it all up. Honestly, though, I am learning to own my mistakes, not just trying to bury them. I've definitely had an awakening on this leave of absence, though, in more ways than one," he admitted.

After a beat, Sam confessed, "We did hear about a certain woman who may have caught your eye—is she part of your awakening?"

Josh laughed heartily, knowing that no secrets ever remained when Ruth was involved. "What did Ruth tell you?"

"Just that you seemed really into this woman, and she was definitely into you. Effie, I believe her name was? Cute name, and by Ruth's account, and Sean's too, she sounds like quite a woman." Sam sounded impressed, so Ruth must have spoken only in glowing terms.

"Effie is quite a woman," Josh agreed, "no doubt about that. Why she would want to be with me is questionable, though." He was going for resigned, but it came out more like self-pity.

"What the hell, Josh—why wouldn't she want to be with you? You're wicked smart, hot as hell, and an incredible human. Plus, there's the little fact of you being a surgeon," Sam stated. "Seriously, though, how are you two navigating your move back to New York? I assume you will probably be returning sooner rather than later, according to what Ruth told us."

Josh's silence told Sam all he needed to know, and the groan was loud and clear in Josh's ear. "Ugh, Josh, which part doesn't she know? The surgeon Josh part or the New York City Josh part?"

How much worse was this going to get? Josh wondered. He saw himself so clearly at this moment through his friend's eyes, and he hated the image.

"Josh, no, don't do this," Sam implored. "You just told me about owning your mistakes. What happened? Why does this fantastic woman seemingly know nothing about you?"

"It's not like she doesn't know *anything*, more like it hasn't come up. We know each other from years ago, back before I even knew Tess or Ruth, and we happened to reconnect here, totally out of the blue." Did this sound as lame to Sam as it did in his own head? He was well aware he had no excuse for not bringing up his circumstances, but admitting why he was in Beverley, back in South Dakota, would be presenting the fact of his downfall to Effie, and the idea of her disappointment was unbearable.

"I just needed someone to see me as worthwhile," he whispered to Sam. "Someone who wasn't aware of just how badly I had destroyed my life. She already knows I had a fiancée who essentially ditched me at the altar. My first interaction with Effie was me as her mechanic, and we had a spark there—she was interested in me then—just thinking I was a mechanic. I tried to think of how to correct her assumption and tell her that in reality I was a loser who was so close to finishing my surgical residency but instead —" Josh dragged a hand over his face, and continued, "And then it was like once I didn't tell her about any of it, it became harder to find a way to do so. Plus, why would she want to start something with me if I were leaving eventually?"

"That was her choice to make, though." Sam gave a little laugh, "This situation is almost ironic, you know, considering Tess didn't tell me the truth about herself on the train."

"Okay, and how did you take it when you found out she hadn't been completely honest with you?" Josh asked, unable to keep any hope out of his voice.

"Relieved," Sam confessed, "because then I had her, you know. I was hurt at first when I found out, but I just loved her tremendously, and everything else had been so sincere, so true, between us, that I let love win."

"I'm not sure Effie and I are to that point yet, though. Probably easier for her to just move on once I am gone." The idea of it saddened him immensely.

"Don't shortchange yourself or her. People surprise you every time. The longer you wait, though, the more difficult it will be for both of you," Sam advised.

CHAPTER
Thirty-Eight

Effie

E ffie sat in stunned silence across from her mother, unsure of comeback. It wasn't that she was ashamed of her mother finding out about her and Josh, but that Diadema could be so judgmental. When Effie had come off a string of losing relationships intent on marrying Damon (who only ended up being another knot, albeit a very huge and annoying knot, in the same string) Diadema had done her best to convince Effie not to do so: "He's not smart enough for you", "I've seen the way his eyes look at other women", and "Why does he never pay for anything" had all seemed like attempts for her mom to dull the high she had been on in those early days of being madly in love with him. Yes, they had gotten engaged early on, but Damon was so charming, and extremely gorgeous, and yes, Effie did see the way he looked at other women—as if he wanted to devour them entirely, with his bedroom eyes and sexy lips; the problem was when he focused all of his sexual energy directly on her, everything else got erased. Plus, she was young, fresh out of grad school, and despite a fair amount of experience with the opposite sex, still extremely naïve in many ways. Even though she had been so young when her dad died, she had still been affected by the intense love that had burned between her parents and had made that her goal for life. Unfortunately, she had failed to find it every single time, but maybe now with Josh she could get it right. Things were already so different from anything she had experienced before—he was the complete opposite of any man she had ever been with, or even been interested in: honest, sincere, stable, smart, and no doubt he had quirks, but so did she, and she did not need her mother ruining things between them so early in their relationship.

"Maybe we should first talk about the letter I saw on your table," Diadema suggested, as she poured herself another cup of coffee from the carafe on the table, "and why you didn't tell me about it." Effie felt like a boomerang, so focused had she been on her mom bringing up Josh that the change of topic threw her—she was not expecting her mom to have seen the letter from Abigail.

Probably because you can't handle anything having to do with my dead father's family, she retaliated in her head, but instead went with, "First of all, thank you for sifting through my mail. It's nice to know that when you let yourself inside my house this morning, you took the time to rifle through my things. I hope you looked in my fridge to see if I needed any milk or eggs. Better yet, did you run your fingers over my furniture and check if I've dusted recently—I know how you love an immaculate house." Effie had learned early on that if she felt attacked by her mom, the best defense was offense, but now seeing her mom's mouth tense up and watching the way her eyes left Effie's to look away, her own response left her cold. What was she accomplishing by acting like this? Certainly not establishing a better bond between them. And Effie had been the one who had acted poorly, by being late to a breakfast date that *she herself* had invited her mom to. Trying to imagine Diadema's reaction when she had walked into the house and, instead of finding her daughter, saw clothes strewn all over, caused Effie to flush once again.

Drawing in a breath to calm herself, Effie then apologized, "Sorry, I'm sorry, that was uncalled for." She looked at her mom, asking, "Can we start again?" At Diadema's nod, Effie said, "I just got the letter in the mail yesterday, and then I had a date with Josh last night, and well…I guess you saw how things turned out with that. Honestly, I haven't even had time to process what my cousin wrote."

With a raised eyebrow, Diadema said, "Your cousin? Have you spoken to Abigail before yesterday?"

"What? No. Why?" This was taking a turn she hadn't seen coming.

"Calling her your 'cousin' seems a bit familiar, that's all. I mean, you haven't seen each other since you were young children," Diadema replied, with a defensive edge to her voice.

"Ooookay, Mom, what is up? That letter came from out of the blue, and did you see the envelope? It was originally mailed to my address in Denver, which Abby probably got online somehow, and then it was forwarded here. Why are you being so weird about this? I was going to tell you about it this morning, anyway."

Her mom sagged back against the booth and closed her eyes, and Effie noticed then a tear running down her cheek. "Mom?" She reached over to take her mother's hands in hers, which Diadema squeezed in response.

"Now it's my turn to apologize. I'm sorry. I overreacted. I was surprised to see that letter, and then when I ran into Henry here, he told me you and Josh had a date last night, which you never even mentioned to me. After seeing his clothes at your house, I realized it was more than a date." Diadema took a shaky breath following her stream of consciousness, and confessed, "I guess I was overwhelmed by everything happening in your life, but you hadn't told me any of it." Diadema reached for a napkin and wiped her eyes. "I wanted us to be closer when you moved back—not further apart."

Effie wiped the tears which had formed in her own eyes. "About Josh: the date happened quickly, spontaneously. We had lunch together yesterday, which he surprised me with, and then I asked him to the movies last night. Okay? We haven't been seeing each other, or anything like that." Her mother raised an eyebrow at that, and Effie chuckled and admitted, "Well, obviously, we've *seen* each other." God, this was awkward, she thought. "Now can we move on past my love life? As for the letter: I'll be honest, I don't even know what to do about the invitation to the party. How do I go where I don't know anyone? Be with family who already know each other?"

"But is that what you want to do? Are you considering going?" Maybe it was the hormones clogging her brain since last night, but she swore her mom almost sounded hopeful. Was it possible they were both feeling hormonal? After all, she and Henry Livingston had seemed rather cozy when Effie had arrived at the diner.

"I'm not sure—I have some time, anyway, to figure it out." The waitress had clearly been giving them their space due to their dramatics, but now was at their table and ready for their orders. Mother and daughter each ordered the eggs Benedict, along with a side of hash browns for Effie, who happened to be starving. "Did you read the letter, Mom?"

"I scanned it. I was on my way out of your house, and it caught my eye. Abby clearly takes after her mother, because that is how I remember her to be—generous and warm." Diadema looked at Effie, and amended her statement, "Actually, both of her parents were wonderful, and your grandparents could be, as well."

Stunned would be downplaying the feeling Effie had at hearing her mother refer to her paternal grandparents as "wonderful". Maybe her mom was flying high on caffeine—just how much coffee had she had before Effie arrived? "I'm scared, Mom," she admitted.

Diadema gave her a surprised look in return. "Effie, you are always so fearless—what are you scared of? They're your family."

"Exactly! Family who should have acted better—who should have reached out before now. I don't know how to handle cousins and aunts and uncles…grandparents!" Effie cried indignantly.

"You need to decide what you need in your life, from everyone, and if you think or hope they can improve it, make it better, more meaningful, then you take the chance." Effie had never heard her mother sound more sincere than she did right now. Or more emotional. "There comes a time when forgiveness is all that is needed in order to move on, and that was a lesson I failed to learn all of those years ago. People make mistakes; they make terrible choices, but usually from a place of love. People don't screw up because of hate—they screw up because they love too much and are afraid of losing it."

As her favorite meal of the day approached their table, Effie moved her coffee so the waitress could put her plate there in front of her. Now was the time for honesty on her part, and Effie whispered, "But what if they don't like me, or they think my dad wouldn't be proud of me?" And this was what she was most terrified of.

Diadema shook her head. "No way: you, my gorgeous girl, were his greatest accomplishment and the love of his life. I see so much of him in you, and they will, too." Her mom picked up her fork to finally begin eating, and then said casually, "How about I go with you?"

Effie gasped, certain she must have misheard. "What? Go with me? Are you serious?"

"Now that I think about it, it makes perfect sense," Diadema nodded. "I already know everyone, and you would have me there as an excuse if you are feeling overwhelmed and want to leave. Plus, if the LeBeaus are going to be in your life again, that means they will be in my life as well, and I need to make amends as much as they do. Maybe more, since I've had you in my life all of these years."

Effie felt tears welling in her eyes again. "Wow, Mom. That means everything to me." She took a shaky breath and, feeling particularly brave and unstoppable, said, "Okay—let's do it!"

Diadema smiled and stole a forkful of hash browns from Effie's plate. "Perfect. Now that we have finished that discussion, why don't you tell me why I am the last to know about you and Josh Livingston. Effie, you know I have always adored that boy."

CHAPTER
Thirty-Nine

Josh

Once he and Sam ended their call, Josh was suddenly overcome with the need to tell Effie the complete truth about himself, but first he wanted to set in motion the plan for the near future, and that meant returning to New York to finish his residency. Figuring he still had an hour or so until she was finished with brunch with her mother, he opened his computer and began to compose an email to Dr. Gilmore, his attending surgeon, and Dr. Scanlon, the head of surgery, where he spoke from the heart. He wrote of what he had learned about himself, after all of these months away from his residency, and how much practicing medicine meant to him. He told them how he now realized that he didn't need surgery to fulfill his life, but to complement it, and that he was ready to finish his residency and move on to be not the best surgeon he could be, but the better surgeon he *wanted* to be. "Through this darkest time of my life, I was given the chance to mature as a human, and the light that I have found as a result has shown me that I not only need to do better, but will be better," he wrote. "I have gone back to my roots here in my small town, finding the community of support I never knew I needed or realized I had. Having my dad beside me during this time, having him believe in me, and having him entrust his life's work with me, means I know I have what it takes to forge relationships with other doctors, so they can also put their trust in me." His email was not just a mea culpa, but a sincere acknowledgement of the growth he had needed to do.

After sending that email, he then wrote the landlord of the apartment he and Tess had shared for so many years, inquiring if he knew of any short-term leases available for rent immediately. Next, he emailed his friend Cal, who had so generously let Josh stay with him after his break-up with Tess, and apologized for any lack of respect he may have shown to him, his daughter, and his ex-wife. Finally, he wrote to Lana, and hers was the most difficult to write; he had never heard back from her after he had sent her the reply to her email. To her, he apologized for any harshness that may have come across in his communication with her. He told her how much he valued their friendship and how he respected her as a surgeon.

At the sound of the screen door slamming at the back of the house, Josh looked up to see his dad coming through the kitchen door with a bag of takeout containers, the enticing scent of breakfast foods wafting his way. "Hey, Dad," he said. "I hope something in there is for me—I'm starving."

"Haha, well, it seems to be your lucky day. I took the liberty of ordering all of our favorites for breakfast; I wasn't sure if you were going to be around or not, even though your car has not moved since yesterday." Henry threw Josh a pointed look. "Oh, and you will never guess who I ran into there: your Effie and her mom. Man, it has been a long time since I have seen Diadema. Too long."

Wondering if he should ignore the comment about his car, Josh was also attempting to block the fact that it weirdly sounded as if his dad were thirsting for Effie's mom. He knew they had gone to school together, but not that they had even been friends. He chose the less psychologically damaging of the two topics to address: "his Effie". "As I'm sure you know, not that I want this to get strange or anything, but I did spend the night over at Effie's. Don't be obvious about it, though, if you see her later."

Henry raised an eyebrow as he got plates out of the cabinet for their breakfast. "And will I? Or, more importantly, will *you* be seeing her later?"

Josh nodded his head. "Most definitely. Oh, I have some other news, Dad: I reached out to Dr. Gilmore about restarting my residency, and I am trying to find a place to rent back in New York, too."

As they sat down to eat at the walnut table that had been his great-grandmother's, Henry exclaimed, "That is worth celebrating with diner takeout—I am proud of you, Josh. It takes a lot of courage to be able to do as much self-reflection as you've done. I have seen you change in these past months, and you are a better man for it all." As he loaded up his plate with hash browns and sausage, he asked, "So, how will everything fit into your new romance?" He paused for a moment, and then continued, "I don't want you to get overwhelmed; this is a lot to manage right now: starting back up with your residency and then dealing with a long-distance romance?" His dad ceased talking while he put one of the diner's signature homemade butter-swim biscuits on his plate and then immediately added a second one. Looking pointedly at Josh, he asked, "Or does Effie not know that she will be in a long-distance relationship? I had a chance to talk a bit to DD before Effie got there, and to me, she seemed surprised to hear that you had been living in New York." Henry ate a slice of bacon, and then said, "It also seemed to be news to her that you are a surgeon, but maybe Effie didn't tell her mom about that, either?"

Josh choked on a bite of biscuit he had just been swallowing. Hearing the disbelief in his dad's voice made Josh flush with shame, and he braced himself for what was to come next from him. His morning was not going to be complete without the most important person in his life giving him a well-deserved lecture, he thought. Although his dad had rarely raised his voice to him in anger, his ire came through in waves of disappointment. "Look, I already heard it from Sam, but you should know that I messed up with Effie about all of this from the beginning. I intend to be honest as soon as I see her, though."

"By everything, I assume you mean who you are, what you do, and where you live?" Henry put his fork down next to his eggs. "Son, you have essentially been dishonest with her about anything that concerns you. How is she going to handle the truth?"

Josh ran his hands through his hair, and admitted, "I have no idea, and that is what I am terrified of: I have everything to lose by telling her the truth, but I also have everything to gain."

"I don't need to tell you, but word around town is that she has gone through a lot, and it would be terrible to add anymore to that. Just like you, she has experienced too much loss in her life already."

Josh was desperate for at least his father to understand. "I never meant to hurt her—hell, I never intended to become involved with anyone when I came back. Everything that has happened with her has come as a complete surprise to me." Josh looked at his dad. "You know, I would have given everything to have had something like this with her in high school, before we moved away; truthfully, I still can't believe it is all happening, and I don't want to mess it up. I don't know how to begin telling her the truth, especially when I know how much it will hurt her."

"All you can do is give her the information, Josh. Speaking of honesty, though, there is something I need to tell you. Something that has been going on for a while." For a fleeting moment, Josh swore he saw a look of panic cross his dad's usually calm features.

"What is it, Dad?" The moment was interrupted when Josh heard his phone ding, and upon checking it, he saw that he had a new email. "Sorry, Dad, I just got a message."

Since it was the weekend, he had not expected any replies to the messages he had sent earlier, but in his inbox sat two emails, and the first was from Dr. Gilmore, who declared that he had been waiting for this moment of awareness from Josh, and he was thrilled to tell him that he could come back at any time—just say the date, Dr. Gilmore had written. The second email he read was from his former landlord; unfortunately, he did not have any rentals available, but he would make some inquiries. As he was composing a response to Dr. Gilmore, an email from Cal had come in, and Cal had assured him that there were no hard feelings. In fact, he and his ex-wife were going to try again to be a family again and had just moved into a larger apartment. Cal said if not for Josh staying with him in the first place, forcing him and his ex to communicate more frequently, they never would have reconciled, so Josh was more than welcome to stay if he needed.

Josh shared his good news with his dad, and then sat for a moment in stunned silence, unable to believe all of the good fortune happening to him in twenty-four hours: first Effie, then his surgical residency news, and now potentially a place to stay until he can sort himself out when he goes back. It seemed now was the time to bring his past, present, and future together. And hope desperately that Effie will not only understand but also forgive him.

CHAPTER
Forty

Effie And Josh

Effie and Josh were lying on a blanket on the riverbank, with their shoes kicked off and legs scissored together. Currently, Effie's favorite thing was stroking her hands across Josh's chest, which she had abundant access to after she had unbuttoned the top three buttons of his shirt. God, she found him unbelievably sexy, with his slightly formal button-down shirts he always seemed to wear when he was away from work, and the solid strength he exuded. She tilted her head up to kiss him and savored the taste of him on her lips. She felt his hand slide over her hip and under the back of her sleeveless top, where his touch sent shivers down her spine. She had known last night as soon as she straddled him on her front porch swing that one night with him would never be enough, not after waiting for him for so many years. Josh was the complete opposite of any man she had ever known, and part of her wondered if maybe she had selected so many inappropriate men for that simple reason: they were not Josh. Just as things were getting interesting, a group of teens rode past them on their bikes and rang their bells, almost as if to applaud them as they passed. Damn teenagers, she thought, wondering if the same group had also been responsible for interrupting them before their date yesterday. Well, Effie *thought* she had picked a secluded spot near the tree line, but clearly not. Immediately after that, she noticed two older women walking along the path, and one of them pointed at her and Josh. Effie began laughing and then sat up to grab the bottle of wine out of the bag she had carried with her in her bike basket. "I have a surprise," she announced, as she also procured two cups from the basket, along with a bag of honey mustard pretzels.

"Mmm," Josh murmured appreciatively, as he bent forward and kissed the small of her back exposed to him as she stretched, feeling more relaxed than he had in months, if not years. After her breakfast with her mom, Effie had called Josh and suggested they take a bike ride around the river, and he had exuberantly agreed to that idea. As he was dusting off his old bike in the garage at his dad's place, he saw that the tires could use some air in them. Not finding the air pump in its usual place by his dad's workbench, Josh approached the door that connected the garage to the house so he could just shout in to his dad to ask him. While opening the door, he heard his dad whispering angrily, "I told you I would take care of it, and it is all handled. He is going back to New York." There was a pause and then Josh heard his dad say, "I want this to stop now. Your communication with me ends now." Who in the world could his dad be speaking to? As far as he knew, his dad primarily talked to the guys at the shop and then whatever assorted relatives passed by the house or called on the phone; he peered around the door and saw that he was, indeed, on the phone.

"Dad?" At the sound of Josh's voice, Henry spun around, tipping over a glass of water that had been sitting on the counter.

"Damn it!" Henry cursed, and in Josh's moderately long life, he could probably count on one hand the number of times he had heard his dad swear.

"Okay, something is clearly bothering you. What's wrong, Dad?" he asked as he took the towel from his father's hands and began wiping up the liquid.

Henry sighed, "Nothing that should concern you. You have a lot to look forward to, Josh, and I want you to keep your eye on the future. All of this," Henry said, pointing to the phone, "is in the past."

"Umm, okay, but that didn't sound like anything that is in the past." Josh worriedly studied his dad, who was normally so unflappable. "Please, Dad, if something is wrong, I want to help you. You were all I had when Mom left, and sometimes when I think back on everything, it kills me to think about how you must have felt having to carry on raising me all alone. All I have ever wanted was to be a small percentage of the man you are," Josh admitted to his dad.

"God, Josh, if only you knew the truth about what a complete fraud I felt like most of the time," Henry confessed. "You are not the only one who has made mistakes and regretted them for years."

Having never witnessed anything but quiet confidence from his father, Josh had a hard time coalescing the fraud Henry purported to be with the dad Josh had experienced him as. He poured his dad another glass of water and placed it on the counter, where his dad had sat down on a barstool there. "What do you mean when you said you made mistakes? Do you mean moving us from Clover Lake to Beverley?"

Henry shook his head. "No, that was the right thing to do. Clover Lake was smothering both of us. One of my regrets was ever moving *back* to Clover Lake all of those years ago, after your mom and I were married. We should have maybe stayed away: I should have gone to college like I planned, and we could have lived on-campus. Instead, I settled back to life there as if I had never left. And your poor mom: she was left to fit in with *my* life, and *my* family."

Josh had known growing up that there had been friction between his mom and her in-laws, but wasn't that always the case, to some extent? His parents had never let any of it come between them, and Josh had never been in doubt about his mother's love. Until she had suddenly left.

"We had different dreams, your mom and I, and only recently—I guess with you being here—have I been able to see things more from her perspective. I can't help feeling that if I had been more supportive, more understanding, maybe she would never have needed to leave," Henry confessed, with more regret in his voice than Josh could bear.

Putting a hand on his dad's shoulder, Josh told him, "I know first-hand how impossible it is to pull yourself out of a pit that seems bottomless. Dad, you did all that you could, and I have a feeling Mom would not have been happy anywhere." Josh decided to prod his dad into full disclosure so the two of them could be free from any misguided half-truths. "I know that you were the one who wrote me her goodbye letter."

"No, no, that was your mom—" Henry protested.

"Dad, please, I'm thirty-five years old; you don't need to protect me anymore. I hadn't read that letter in years, but after I came back, I took it out and couldn't believe how blind I had been. It was so obvious, reading it as an adult, that it was you who cared enough to make me think she gave me a second thought when she left, not her." Josh reached down and pulled his father in for a hug. "Thank you. That letter more than likely saved me from any more trauma that could have occurred from her abandoning us, but I don't need to be protected anymore." He pulled back and squeezed his dad's shoulders, hoping that possibly they wouldn't have to carry the weight of this responsibility any longer. "Now, I need to get my bike tires filled so I can pick up Effie."

"Wait, Josh, there's one more thing you should know," and Henry proceeded to tell Josh about the phone calls he had been receiving from his absent mother.

And now here he was, with Effie by the river, part of him wishing his mom were here to see that some people thought he was worthy of affection, time, and attention.

"Josh? Josh?" He broke out of his thoughts and saw that Effie was kneeling over him, holding out a cup of wine.

He gratefully accepted the drink with a small smile. "Thanks. I love that you thought of all of this."

"It's such a beautiful day, and I had, like, a pretty surprising brunch with my mom. She actually shocked me," Effie said, and then took a sip of her wine.

"You weren't the only one to get a parental surprise this morning, then." Wondering if he should tell Effie about the phone calls his dad had been receiving, he ruled against it, not wanting to cast a cloud over their lovely picnic. Instead, Josh held up his glass of wine and said, "Let's toast: to our parents."

Effie laughed and toasted with him. "First time I've ever done that," she admitted after taking a large drink of wine. "I actually saw your dad this morning at Betsy's."

"Yeah, he said." Josh put his cup on the soft grass and reached a finger out to stroke Effie's knee. "Did you know that our parents almost dated in high school?" Josh watched as Effie's jaw dropped in shock.

"What? Tell me you're joking!" She squealed.

"Haha, no, it's true…it seems as though my dad had a thing for your mom when they were in school. Maybe he still does to this day," he said, shrugging. "In fact, he says one of the reasons his marriage to my mom failed is because she was always comparing herself to your mom. He was always having to convince my mom that he loved her more." Josh laughed, and Effie groaned.

"Ugh—can you imagine if they had gotten together? No way, and please remove the image from my brain!" Effie laughed again. "Wow—this actually kind of explains this vibe I got from them when I got to the diner. Almost like I was interrupting something. Not that Mom would ever be unfaithful or disloyal to Burnside." She defended her mom, knowing that however unconventional she considered her mom's marriage, it was strong and loving.

Unable to hold in the truth he had learned just a couple of hours earlier, Josh told Effie, "Interestingly, my dad confessed today that a note my mom supposedly wrote to me when she left us was not from her at all." Now he was the one who took a large drink of wine.

Effie's eyes widened in suspense. "Well, who was it from?"

"My dad—he wrote it so I would feel less crappy about her leaving. Can you believe that? All these years, I consoled myself with the fact that her letter was proof of how much she loved me, even if she had to leave. In actuality, her letter only proved how much my dad loved me, even if it was a lie, all this time." Picking up his cup, he drained the contents into his mouth.

"Oh, Josh," and Effie gingerly sat her glass of wine in the grass, then took Josh's and placed it next to hers. She reached to him, enfolding his body into hers in a hug. "I'm so sorry. You must be devastated, knowing your dad has lied to you for all of these years. He should just have told you the truth from the beginning," she whispered.

His arms tightened around her, intent on absorbing her goodness and positivity. "This is the best part, though: after abandoning me without any word, it seems that she has been in contact again with my dad. Calling him, wanting updates, thinking she can help."

"Help? Help how?" And with this, Josh knew how ironic it was, speaking to Effie about lies and misdirections, when he should be taking control and confessing *this minute* about his own, but her body was too warm, too soft, and he was so relaxed. He had already said too much that was interrupting their idyllic picnic, and now not only Josh's mistruths were casting clouds over them, but so was his dad's letter, that no matter how well-intentioned, had in reality still been just a lie.

Josh kissed Effie partly to distract her but also because being able to smell her and hear her, so close to him, was distracting him. She was vanilla and sunshine, and he drew a line down her throat with his mouth, and gently pushed her back onto the blanket. Her hands sunk into his hair, and she moaned as his mouth moved down to the tops of her breasts, over her shirt.

"You drive me crazy," Effie said huskily into his ear, as her legs came up to encircle his hips.

Another group of amblers came around the bend in the river, and Effie began laughing when she heard one of the septuagenarians comment about the view of the river, and her friend cheekily answered "What river?", which was followed by whisperings that could only be alluding to Effie and Josh. Effie giggled and playfully nudged Josh off of her so she could sit up, straightening her tank top as she did so.

One of the reasons Effie had wanted to come out here was the lack of distractions they would face, as opposed to them staying at her house, all alone on a sweltering afternoon, with the bed still unmade. "Anyway, you were saying that your dad has been in touch with your mom?" She wanted to connect with Josh, and getting him to open up about his parents, especially his mom, was integral to their budding romance. Both of their childhoods, steeped in trauma, could potentially bond them if they healed together.

Josh nodded his head. "Yes, and he's not happy about it. Neither am I, obviously." He gave a frustrated laugh. "After all this time, *now* she wants to be in our lives, or mine, at least, vicariously through my dad."

"No matter how much time passes, though, she is still your mom. I understand how you feel," and Effie nervously told him about the letter from her cousin, and the invitation to meet, or re-meet, her extended family.

"My god—that's incredible! I thought I had a story to share, but your news is way more interesting. So, are you going?" Josh gazed at Effie in amazement, in awe of the courage she showed by even considering attending her family reunion.

"I think so," Effie said hesitantly. "My mom told me that she would go with me, and that was out of nowhere. I never thought she would have any interest in seeing any of my dad's family, but she wants to make things better, too."

"You should be proud of her, Effie. It takes a lot to admit that you got it wrong making a decision years ago; sometimes, regretfully, a bad choice seems like the only one possible to make." And just as he was on the brink of confessing everything to her, Effie tossed him a passionate look.

"Speaking of bad choices…" and Effie pulled Josh back down to her as she laid back on the blanket, "let's make some together."

CHAPTER
Forty-One

Effie And Josh

Following their ten-mile round-trip bike ride along the James River on Saturday, the couple stopped for a mushroom and Canadian bacon pizza from Gino's, a fantastic Italian restaurant in Carlisle, a smaller town a few miles from Beverley, and then on the last leg of their ride home, they stopped and ordered malts at The Dairy Barn, just outside of Beverley. Effie had sipped her hot fudge malt on the way back to her house, while Josh had consumed his peanut butter malt, it seemed, in just a few swallows. By the time they had stepped through Effie's front door, both were in need of a shower, and by the time they were finished, so was the hot water. The next day, both claimed exhaustion from the previous day, giving them the perfect excuse to not leave Effie's house. Instead, they spent the morning in bed, where Josh learned just how sensitive the backs of Effie's knees were, and he savored how she melted into him when he did nothing but kiss her. Once out of bed, Josh biked to Beverley Bake Shoppe and picked up fresh, buttery croissants while Effie fried up bacon and made perfectly runny-yolked over-medium eggs. In the afternoon, over tall glasses of iced tea, the couple sat on the front porch swing reading: Effie, with her legs on Josh's lap, finished reading her romance novel, and Josh downloaded a book from the New York Public Library: the Stephen King he had thumbed at the Beverley Carnegie Library. That evening, over hot charcoals in the backyard, Josh grilled to perfection steaks that Effie thawed from her freezer, while Effie made garlic bread and fresh corn on the cob for their supper that night.

Never before in her life had time flown so quickly, and Effie marveled when a week had passed, and she could not remember when she had been so comfortable or felt so loved; to her delight, she had also discovered that the wonderful Josh she had known as a teenager grew up to be an incredible man. Though both Effie and Josh had worked during the week, they met every day for lunch, which Josh always picked up from Mr. Beans on his way to meet her, sitting under "their" gazebo in the town square. Every day after lunch was consumed, Josh would read from his novel, while Effie scribbled away in a notebook she had begun to carry with her. "What are you working on over there?" he asked her one lunch date, curious to see her writing and not reading for the second day in a row.

Effie blushed, knowing she would have to tell someone at some point about her secret pursuit. Hesitantly, she confessed, "I've been jotting down ideas I've been having for a young adult novel." As Josh's jaw dropped, she quickly continued, "It's only in the early stages, and I'm sure it will be nothing, but I just like putting pen to paper for now." Because he could tell how much courage it had taken for her to tell him as much as she had, he gathered up his strength to finally tell her his truth. Just as he drew a breath in, she turned her head, gave him a look of sheer happiness, and he was powerless to do anything but kiss her in reaction. A little too conveniently, then, the moment for honesty disappeared.

Each evening after work during the week that followed, the couple would meet at the garage; from there, they would ride their bikes to the grocery store and together choose something for them to make for dinner together. After dinner, the two of them would sit on her front porch, eating ice cream bars or popsicles as the lightning bugs danced around them, helping to illuminate the night. Three nights in a row the sky was so clear that they laid on beach blankets in her backyard and quizzed each other on the constellations, holding hands with nary a space between them otherwise. Finally, she got it right, she congratulated herself silently, proud to be in a mature relationship.

Meanwhile, Josh had been avoiding his dad's house, where Henry's questions concerning Effie were starting to be more annoying than helpful. Josh told him every day at the shop that he just needed one more day to figure out how to tell her; once he was with her at night, though, he was preoccupied by her, and the last thing he wanted to do was upset their fragile happiness.

On this particular Sunday, Effie was making them blueberry buttermilk pancakes (Josh's favorite), maple sausages, and eggs, and while she cooked Josh had gone out to pick up a copy of the Beverley Digest, the local newspaper, after lamenting how he missed getting The New York Times delivered. "You could come to the library to read it—the only person in town I see come in to read it is the director of nursing from the hospital."

"Oh," Josh had explained casually, "it's just that I miss doing the Sunday crossword. I had a subscription to the weekend editions for years."

As she was flipping the pancakes, Effie was genuinely surprised to hear about his subscription, never having met anyone else who'd had one. She looked at him doing the crossword in the local newspaper. "Why did you stop getting it delivered? It's always sad to me when people stop doing the things they love."

"I moved, and I guess it slipped my mind to change the address," he said absentmindedly, since he was filling in sixteen-down.

"You know, you never did say why you were living with your dad. How long have you been staying with him?" questioned Effie, as she put the breakfast on the table. She waited to hear his answer, and in that time, he put butter on his pancakes, poured some maple syrup over the stack, and drank at least half a cup of coffee. She wondered what could be taking him so long to answer the question.

Finally, unable to put off answering her question any longer, he told her, "I have been living at my dad's house since February." Now was the time to confess everything, he prodded himself. After their incredible week together, in which the only time they had spent apart was when they were at work, she would have to understand why he had withheld the truth from her. More than that, though, he hoped she was beginning to fall as much for him as he had already fallen for her.

Effie was surprised to hear it had been so long, and laughed. "February? Wow! You lasted a lot longer than I did when I moved back home. I could not *wait* to get out of that house. Although getting my job at the library spurred my move, my sleeping accommodations would eventually have been a significant instigation for finding my own place," she said with a shudder, remembering the bar of the sofa bed she had endured every night. A light bulb moment occurred in her head just then, and she rushed out, "Oh, I'm sorry, maybe this is too much to talk about? I should have realized that you probably moved in with your dad after you and Tess broke up, right? That makes sense." And she reached over and stroked his arm, silently berating herself for her lack of sensitivity.

He was an absolutely terrible, he told himself, as he watched her flush with embarrassment, knowing she believed her question had stirred up hurtful memories for him. Unwilling to remain untruthful any longer, he said, "To be honest, yes, I did move in after the break-up, but there's more to it than that. In fact, there's something I need to tell you."

Effie got a sinking sensation in her stomach, both at his words and the somber look on his face, and she watched Josh with dread, afraid of what he was going to tell her. How was she going to handle bad news when she was filled with so much hope, so much love, already?

At that moment, a knock shook her front door, followed by a voice calling through the screen door, "Is anyone home?" To the astonishment of both Josh and Effie, Liam busted through the door. "Do I smell sausage?" He sniffed the air, walking into the dining area. He leaned down, kissing Effie on the cheek, taking her by complete surprise. "Looking gorgeous as usual, Effie. Somebody pinch me—are those blueberry pancakes?" And then he yelped loudly. "Ow—what the hell?"

"You did ask someone to pinch you, cousin. Now, do you mind explaining what you are doing here?" Josh questioned, annoyed not only that Liam had interrupted his breakfast with Effie, but also because he had been so close to *finally* coming clean about going back to New York.

Liam rubbed his arm, answering, "I stopped by your dad's house, and he told me you were over here. Good thing he had the address handy. Now, Effie, where can I find a plate?" he asked, rifling through her cabinets.

"Never mind," he told her, and brought a plate to the table, along with a knife and fork he had finally procured from a drawer, after opening and loudly closing at least five others. "I don't know what you two have been up to all weekend, but thank god you two are decent."

"Liam," Josh began, with measured patience, "no offense, but what are you doing here?"

"Well, I had a bachelor party in Sioux Falls last night, so I am on my way home from that and thought I would swing by Beverley to see my favorite cousin first." Liam looked at Josh and flashed a devilish grin. "You would not believe the woman I met," he sighed as he closed his eyes and reclined back in his chair. "She is unbelievable…exceptional…superb… nothing next to you, obviously, Effie, but she was pretty phenomenal."

"Are you talking about the stripper you met while she was working?" Josh asked dryly. "You do know that is frowned upon, right? Didn't you get into trouble the last time you were in Sioux Falls for a bachelor party?"

Liam looked offended. "Absolutely not. No strip clubs involved last night. We went to a concert and then out for dinner at some fancy sushi place. Anyway, she was at the concert with her friends, and they ended up going with us to the restaurant. Pretty sure I am in love." Josh was definitely certain his cousin was not, in fact, in love. Liam had not been in a relationship longer than three months since he started "dating" at the age of thirteen. He had too much money, was too good looking and far too cocky.

"Well, Liam, we are honored you had time in your busy schedule to stop here and have breakfast with us," Effie joked. She had never really gotten to know Liam, even though they were almost the same age; he had lived in Saint Charles, a neighboring town only eight miles from Clover Lake, but would often spend summers with Josh, hanging out at the city pool in Clover Lake. Their paths also crossed during track season in high school, and he had excelled in the mile run. Liam had always been way too smooth for her, seeming to have at least three girls at a time hanging on his every word. Now, as she studied the cousins side-by-side, she found Josh's earnest sincerity much more appealing than Liam's brand of trouble.

Taking a bite of his stack of pancakes, he grinned and gave Effie a thumbs up with his mouth full. After taking a drink of his coffee, he turned to Josh. "Why didn't you tell me your big news, cousin?"

Josh stopped breathing as dread creeped up his spine, making it impossible to even move. Suddenly everything was as if he were watching it from afar, and he heard Effie ask him about his big news. But what could he say? He didn't even have a story prepared to divert this conversation away from the truth. Yet he still wasn't ready to ruin the unexpected happiness he had found with Effie, nor was he looking forward to facing the disappointment he knew she would feel. And then there was the matter of Liam in the room, always with his quick wit and breezy life. Liam, who had followed Josh to college in New York City, even though he had no clear plan for his future, but he did have unlimited resources, thanks to his mother's family money. Liam, who had been like a brother to him since he was born, but who had never had any of Josh's awkwardness or experienced any of his losses.

Effie watched Josh sit completely still at her table, and she looked back and forth from Josh to Liam, willing an answer out of one of them. What was Liam talking about—what big news could Josh have that he hadn't told her yet? Liam had asked the question so excitedly, yet Josh looked as if he was close to being ill.

"Josh? What big news do you have?" Effie hated the tremor in her voice, knowing it told of her vulnerability.

Liam looked confused. "Dude, why aren't you saying anything? It's amazing—you get to be a surgeon again! You have been so stressed out about having to take that leave of absence, but now maybe you can chill out."

"Surgeon?" Effie questioned, begging Josh with her eyes to correct Liam, tell him that he was wrong, tell Effie that Liam was joking. When he said nothing, Effie prodded him. "Josh? What's he talking about?", desperate now for an answer.

Josh closed his eyes, trying to get Liam to leave with the power of his mind, but it was not working. "Effie, there's something I need to tell you," he said softly.

"Although I do have to say that I am a bit pissed that you didn't tell me first that you were going back to New York so soon. Instead, I have to hear about it from Uncle Henry? That's cold," Liam admonished his cousin, as he carried his plate to the sink. "Well, I need to head out, but I was thinking that maybe I will go back east with you. I have some time off from work coming up, and I need a change of scenery. It has been too long since I've been to the Big Apple. Anyway, hate to eat and run, but I'll catch you guys later. Josh, I'll call you, and Effie, the breakfast was perfect," and off he went, flashing them a peace sign, after giving Effie another kiss on her cheek.

CHAPTER
Forty-Two

Effie

As she sat by the lake waiting for Ruth to arrive, Effie could not understand how almost a week had passed since Liam had interrupted her bliss with Josh…since harsh reality had crashed down on both of them…since Effie had spoken to Josh. No calls, no texts, nothing at all, but perhaps it was for the best. She couldn't blame him, really, for not being upfront with her, because in truth, she would probably have just remained in the "friend zone" with him if she had known he was going back to New York. Strangely, it wasn't his deception of living in South Dakota that hurt the most, but his misrepresentation of his career that had hit her harder. How could he have kept something so vital to his entire being from her—hidden that integral part of him? Being a surgeon was his identity—that was abundantly clear when he had finally confessed, and she witnessed just how much it meant to him, and to *lie* about something so crucially important—how was she to process any of it? She had not been able to stop rerunning their conversation in her head over the past four days.

"Is it true?" she had whispered, agony lacing her words. "I'm not interested in any excuses about why I am the last person in all of Beverley to find out that you are a *surgeon,* or that you evidently live in *New York City.* I just want to hear, from your lips, that it is true." At his pause, she had said quietly, "A simple verification is all that I need right now, and then you can be on your way back to your real life." And she had implored him with her eyes, willing him to deny everything his cousin had just revealed, but all he did was nod his head lamely.

"Effie, please," he had started, as she unsteadily rose to her feet, clutching the table for support. Josh stood up, reaching for her hand, which she denied him.

She had held up her hand, then, to ward off his pleading, and to keep him at a distance. "No. Just no. You don't get to beg for my understanding now, if that's where this is leading." She closed her eyes, because the mere sight of Josh had caused her too much pain. "God, how do I get it wrong every time?" Her voice was so low, partially due to the fact that her throat was not cooperating with her need to speak, but also part of her wanted to make him come closer to her so he could hear her better, still in desperate need was she of the heat from his body, the scent of his aftershave. More audibly, then, she said, "Every fucking time. I mean, my divorce isn't even final yet, from a man who did *nothing* but lie to me probably every day since I met him. I finally—*finally!*—get a fucking clue and leave him. And who do I meet? My boss who acts like he wants to be my friend, but in reality wants to screw me, and then my high school crush, who I thought was my friend but *lied* to me. I mean, don't get me wrong: you screwed me, Josh, but in more ways than Boyd probably would have. Definitely in more ways than Damon did." Effie swiped at the tears falling relentlessly down her face, and she saw how Josh was helpless to do anything but feel the blade of her words slicing into him, and she reveled in it, wanting to hurt him as much as she was hurting.

"I cared for you—I trusted you. More than any other man, ever. You were Josh: honest, sweet, unassuming Josh. I thought you were a small-town mechanic, but instead you're a surgeon from New York City? Do you know how stupid I feel? How gullible?" she sobbed.

Josh rushed in then, as if finally able to speak, "And I am sorry for all of it—have been sorry every day since we met up again—for lying to you, deceiving you, not being honest. But I was scared, Effie. I was afraid to believe in anything: my career, myself…you." He took a breath, clearly desperate to explain. "I had just been dumped by my fiancée, don't forget that. She hated that I worked terribly long hours, and that I was so dedicated to being a surgeon. Now I can see that no matter who I am, it is never enough for anyone."

"STOP," Effie had yelled. "Stop putting yourself down. *You* were enough for me. You working in that *garage* was enough for me. You living in *Beverley* was enough for me. But none of that was real, was it?"

Josh appeared to be crushed, asking, "What are you more upset about—me not actually living in Beverley or the fact that I am not a mechanic?" Effie shook her head in disappointment at him, that he thought these details mattered to her, and not the overall deception behind their truths. Josh shot her a look of anguish and then he had said, "All of these months at my dad's shop, I did the best I could to piece my life back together, trying to find my place in the world, back in New York but also here. Do you know how difficult that was for me? Feeling like a fraud no matter where I was or what I was doing? Eventually I found a rhythm working in the shop, yet at the same time, everything I had worked so hard for—for so long—was just going unnoticed, unacknowledged; nobody at dad's shop cared that I was a surgeon, but I did. All this time I have still been me. I wanted so badly to tell you—was going to tell you soon—probably today. I have tried to tell you this whole week, but I didn't know where to start; I was terrified how it would change us and your feelings for me." Josh reached out and pulled her into his embrace, and Effie allowed it, since she had been yearning to make the physical connection, wanting to forgive him, to push aside her pain.

Effie was unsure how to react to any of this. "I still don't understand why you are even here, though—why did you leave New York? Or stop being a surgeon?"

His hand had taken hers—his graceful hand, with the long, deft fingers she had always thought too beautiful to belong to a mechanic—and as he began rubbing his thumb over her delicate knuckles, he did his best to explain, "The truth is that I made some mistakes at the hospital…mistakes that could have cost me my residency. I hadn't slept; I drank too much the night before, after I found out how I had been betrayed by my best friend and my ex-fiancée. To top it all off, the morning before the surgery, I was informed that I didn't receive this huge fellowship—something I had spent months preparing for, sacrificing my personal life, changing our wedding plans because of the pressure. To have that *also* blow up in my face? I should not have been in that operating room in my state, but my ego was too big." Josh gave a laugh filled with derision, "My ego was too big, but ironically, it was also completely busted. I had something to prove, and it ended up almost costing someone her life." Taking his hand from Effie, he rubbed his eyes, and she could see the emotion he was holding back, yet he continued, "Anyway, I was advised to take a leave from my residency to get my act together. Being back here, working in the shop, and meeting you, they have all helped. And then last week I found out that I can go back now," he had announced, almost with pride.

Effie had been stunned. "So all week long, while I have been falling for you more every day, you have been planning on leaving me to go back to New York?" How could he just abandon them like this? What had the week meant to him? Anything at all? His whispered words, about how much he cared for her, how happy she made him, what had any of it meant? She felt helpless, because the joy he had expressed about their newly developed relationship paled in comparison, she could see now, to how he felt about his career. She had to give him points for that, she thought. Unlike her ex-husband, Josh had a career and would not ruin her financially—only emotionally, it seemed. And after his confession, she had turned away from him to begin clearing the table from their breakfast, their lovely and love-filled morning a distant memory at that point.

"Effie, can we please just talk about this? Ask me anything. Anything!" Josh had seemed to beseech her. "I deeply regret not being honest with you from the beginning, but please try to understand. I didn't know how to tell you, or when? When should I have said something? At the shop that very first day? I didn't even know who you were, remember? Or that night at the bar, when we ran into each other? You were on a date. I didn't know where we were going with us, and granted, everyone from my dad down to my old friend Sam told me to tell you, but…"

"Oh my god, everyone really did know except me." Effie had closed her eyes then, picturing her mom's expression when she walked into the diner and saw Diadema with Henry, and recalled thinking that at the time something had seemed off about her then—she wondered if maybe Henry had told her mom. But why wouldn't her mom have told her? "Please go, Josh. I need time…space…I don't know. I just want to be alone."

Josh had reached for her again, but she had evaded his embrace. "Effie, please, you haven't asked me anything. I want to talk! Let's talk! I can tell you about my residency program, or the other surgeons I work with—" and he had stopped, as Effie had brushed by him on the way to the kitchen, refusing to even look at him.

Effie had stood with her back to him, while she had loaded the dishwasher, until finally she braced her arms against the sink. "Josh, please leave," she sobbed. "I can't do this now."

Josh had stood immobile at the table, still in the place she had left him when she had carried the dishes to the kitchen. "Effie, I am terrified if I walk out that door, I may never see you again. Please, please, let me stay."

But Effie had not been able to take any more, and she had turned, exiting the kitchen, and had started a slow ascent up the stairs, leaving Josh behind, while also facing the grief that had been threatening to overtake her.

That was four days ago, and now she waited for Ruth in the park. Ruth, another link to Josh. Ruth, who could potentially have answers to some of her questions.

"Effie? Effie?" Pulled out of her misery, which lately always included staring at her phone, in the hope that Josh would be reaching out to her either by text or phone call, Effie took notice of Ruth approaching her from the sidewalk facing Main Street. Ruth had texted her that morning, in fact, telling her that she and her family had gotten to Beverley the previous day, and she would love to see her whenever she was free. Unable to face another lunch break alone without the company of Josh, she had sent a reply asking if noon would work for her, and Ruth had promptly sent back a "thumbs up". No way could she handle being near the gazebo, or the park for that matter, so Effie had suggested Lake Shelley, located two blocks away from the library, on the other side of the park.

Grateful to no longer be alone, and thankful she finally had a friend to talk to, she smiled a wobbly smile at Ruth. Effie had pondered calling her friends in Denver, but that life now seemed so far removed from where she was now. Would they understand? Chances were, they would understand only far too well at how incredibly stupid she was when it came to men.

"Oh, Effie, what's wrong?" Ruth asked with concern, as she sat down on the bench next to her and put an arm around her shoulders. Effie collapsed, sobbing, relieved that here was someone who *knew* Josh, and could possibly help her comprehend, so she could move forward, past all of the hurt and sense of betrayal. "Okay, what's he done? Only Josh can cause this kind of chaos in women who otherwise would never put up with any bullshit."

Effie laughed, and as she sipped on the iced caramel mocha Ruth had considerately brought for her, she wondered how much Ruth already knew, but she proceeded to fill her in anyway…

CHAPTER
Forty-Three

Ruth

Ruth listened as Effie pretty much confirmed all that she would have guessed could have gone wrong with this relationship. As long as she had known Josh, he had hated confrontation, and it was only last year that he had begun to push back more with Tess when he was challenged; Ruth suspected it was because he could feel Tess pulling away from him long before she had even met Sam.

"If it's any consolation, Josh has never been a great communicator. Not that I'm excusing him, by any means," she quickly added, as she saw Effie's expression of disbelief. "When Sean and I had dinner with him last month, he was still processing everything that had happened to him these last few months, and it would be a lot for anyone to handle. The hardest part for Josh, I am sure, was to have to come back here defeated. Josh has always wanted to prove to everybody that he was bigger than this place."

"What do you mean?" questioned Effie.

"Well, when Josh decided he wanted to be a surgeon, the only person from his family who supported him was his dad. Everybody else, they thought he should just stay and run the shop, like his dad did, and his grandfather before that, not to mention his uncles who work still in Clover Lake. But Josh has always had plans—big plans. And none of them ever included staying around here. To this extent, for Josh, to even *consider* not going back to New York is a sign that he has failed. Plus, the deal with his mom and her memory…that all factors into it."

Effie nodded, "I can see that—he would have the most to prove to her as a kind of retribution since she left him."

"Yeah, when we first met him, Josh refused to talk about her at all, only ever talked about his dad. Of course, rumors ran rampant around town about the single dad and his son, but it wasn't until Christmas that year that he told us that she had even died." Ruth can still recall the look of devastation on his face; after that, he never brought her up again, and neither had she nor Tess.

"Died? What are you talking about? Josh's mom didn't die—you must have misunderstood him," Effie told her. "Josh's mom left him—and his dad—when he was twelve."

Ruth felt her jaw hit the floor, "What…the…hell? Are you serious? No way. I can't believe this!" Ruth exclaimed, and then scooted back against the park bench and rubbed her pregnant belly, processing what Effie had just said. "Hot damn, this is the missing piece of the puzzle that really profoundly explains Joshua Livingston. Holy hell." Completely stunned and almost speechless, all Ruth could do was to consider how it all made a kind of sense, in a warped Josh-way. "Effie, when Josh and his dad moved to Beverley, they told everyone that she died—there's no misunderstanding that. But now to find out that he was abandoned by his own *mother*." Ruth's eyes tickled with tears, "I can't imagine just leaving Eloisa or this little peanut," she said forlornly, as she rubbed her belly again, "and to finally understand the level of abandonment he must have felt—no, fuck that— that he STILL feels." Ruth paused, closed her eyes, rubbed them, and then sighed, "and then to have Tess leave him for his friend? Oh, poor Josh."

"Do you think it excuses him not being upfront with me, though? Am I in the wrong to be as upset as I am about his secrets?" Effie sounded defeated and unsure.

"Absolutely NOT—you are entitled to however you're feeling. Honestly, I'd feel pissed as hell if Sean kept half as much from me." Ruth sighed then, admitting, "That being said, I have, upon occasion, been known to withhold information if I deem it to be for the greater good."

Effie mournfully laughed, "I doubt Josh's motives were as clear-cut as yours have been." She heaved a great sigh before continuing, "I guess what I am most upset about is what this means for the future. I am astounded that the Josh I knew so many years ago grew up to be a surgeon—that is beyond impressive. But he is in New York City," and then she pointed to the library across the street, "and I'm not. Ruth, I just bought a house. I have a new job here that I love. And I am close to reconnecting with family I haven't seen in *years*. I can't leave, and it sounds like he won't stay." Just then, an alarm went off on Effie's phone, and she looked at it before adding, "Plus there's the fact that I haven't even heard from him since the truth came out—what am I supposed to do? Go to him, and what—? Beg him to talk to me honestly for once? Frankly, I am tired of begging men to talk to me. I did too much of that with my ex, and nothing ever changed. This whole thing is impossible," she sighed again and held up her phone. "Anyway, that was my alarm—I need to get back to work. Thanks for everything, Ruth."

The women both stood up, and Ruth squeezed Effie's hand. "Listen: for now, why don't you try to just enjoy your time with Josh? If you guys want to be together, you will figure out a way—it happens all the time. I hope I don't sound too cliché? But as my mom always says, 'Don't put the cart before the horse'." Ruth glanced down at her watch, knowing she needed to be heading back to her mother's to pick up Eloisa. As she hugged Effie, she added, "Oh, and I definitely want to hear more about this family drama of yours."

Ruth watched as Effie scuttled back to the library, and then texted her mom telling her she would be there soon, but later than originally planned. Then she left her car parked on the street near the entrance to the park and scurried over to the auto shop, or as fast as one could scurry while also being many months pregnant. As she stepped inside one of the open bays, her eyes scouted for Josh. Not seeing him, she noticed his dad in the office and waddled her way over to him. Knocking on the door, she said, "Hey,

Mr. Livingston, how are you?" As she entered the room, the scent of cinnamon and coffee greeted her.

Henry Livingston looked up, and a grin took over his face. "Ruth Lefferts! Oh, sorry, I always forget you are married and a mother now," he chuckled. "Soon to be a mother of two, from what Josh told me. Congratulations! None of that Mr. Livingston business, either—you know you only need to call me Henry."

Ruth had always had an affection for Josh's dad—always so earnest and serious, but also warm and loving. Much like Josh, actually, and now she couldn't help but feel a new empathy for him, knowing he had been left alone by Josh's mom to raise his son. How had that affected both of them? How would it have changed Josh if his mother had never left? Who was he before it happened?

"Sorry, sorry, I should know better, but old habits die hard," she apologized. "Yes, *Henry*, my husband and I clearly need new hobbies," she laughed and rubbed her belly. "I don't want to interrupt your workday, but is Josh around?"

"He should be back any minute now—he took a car out on a test drive. Would you like a cup of my special coffee blend? It's cinnamon sugar cookie."

Ruth declined, "No, thank you, although it does smell delicious. I've had my allotted cup already for the day." She did, however, accept his offer of the seat in front of his desk.

"How is Tess?" Henry asked hesitantly. "I'm glad those two figured everything out in the end," he admitted, and then took a sip of the steaming cup of coffee on his desk.

Ruth nodded, "Me, too. You know she got married?" At his nod of affirmation, she added, "Tess and Sam are ridiculously happy, and hopefully will be back here for a visit soon." Ruth paused a spell before asking, "How is Josh doing?"

Henry never had been one to get too personal, so Ruth was surprised when he told her, "He is pretty conflicted, I guess you could say. All he wanted from the time he got here was the green light to go back, and I can see his head is in a spin, because he has been seeing someone."

Ruth nodded, "Yes, I just came from seeing his 'someone'. Effie is wonderful. I happened to meet her the first time Sean and I were here, back in May."

"He does care for her, and I want him to be happy," Henry paused briefly, "but I also don't want him to give up everything he has worked so hard for. All I have ever wanted is for him to take the opportunities I missed out on."

Suddenly Ruth heard from the garage, "Dad? I'm back. No problem with that Mustang anymore—" and Josh stopped as soon as he saw Ruth in his dad's office.

Ruth smiled warmly at Josh, not wanting to cause him any more stress. "Hey, Josh, surprise! I tried calling you to tell you that Sean and I would be here this week, but for some reason, I never reached you." Now she looked at him pointedly. "Can we talk for a minute?"

Henry cleared his throat, and said, "Take as much time as you need, Son. I need to step out anyway for an afternoon cinnamon roll—goes so well with this coffee. Ruth, always a pleasure," he said, and bent down and gave her a one-armed hug her on his way out of the office, discreetly shutting the door upon leaving.

Josh immediately began straightening random papers left on his dad's desk, and knowing him as she did, she knew damn well he was only trying to avoid looking at her. Because she was feeling generous, she let the game continue for a minute or so, and then unable to stand the silence any longer, she blurted out: "Josh? What the hell is going on? What are you going to do? Are you really going to turn your back on Effie…and what you have started here?"

Josh finally turned to her and looked her directly in the eyes, and she was completely taken aback by how lost he looked, how confused. He perched on the edge of the desk and admitted, "I don't know what I want to do, but I am positive about what I *need* to do."

"I understand, Josh. No, I do," Ruth assured him at his anguished look. "You feel pulled in two directions—one is your duty and the other is desire. Oldest split in the world, I imagine. But why can't you have both?"

Josh raked a hand through his hair, which had grown longer than Ruth had ever seen it—surely a sign that he was able to change course? "It's not that easy, Ruth. And how could you understand? You have always known what you wanted and have never faced any obstacles in getting it. Case in point: your career. Your husband. Now two babies."

Ruth gave him an open-mouthed look of exasperation. "You think that was all easy? Never in a million years did I dream of leaving South Dakota as I was growing up. I thought I'd get a job probably in Sioux Falls or Rapid City as a speech therapist. Then I met Sean online, having no idea where he lived, on a complete fluke. Do you know how hard it was to move to Philadelphia? By myself? No friends, no family, just taking a chance on love—on Sean. How miserable I was, even though I had found the love of my life, in those first couple of years without my parents. Without my sister, my best friend, who I missed every single day, until Tess moved to Brooklyn to be with you. And now I have left her again to come back home."

Josh asked skeptically, "Okay, and now you are back, and you have your family. How does that help me?"

"Ugh, Josh, sometimes you are so thickheaded," she slapped him on his leg. "You do realize there is a hospital in this very town, don't you? One that is desperately searching for more doctors, specifically surgeons. Sean told me that you would not have a problem finishing your residency there if you wanted. Plus, you may even be able to finish sooner in a smaller hospital. Josh, you could be a big fish in a little pond here!"

"Are you crazy? And perform what kinds of surgeries here? Knee replacements and appendectomies? Hardly the kind of cutting-edge procedures I have spent the last few years training for. And then I what? Prove everyone right in my family—everyone who never believed in me. Told me I wasn't cut out for New York?" He vehemently shook his head. "I have to do this as much for me as for my dad!"

"You don't think your dad would be thrilled to have you here, in the same town as him? You would still be a surgeon!" Ruth breathed in deeply, hoping Josh couldn't tell he was on her last nerve, but Ruth never did take kindly to anyone who didn't instantly see that she was right. "You are his only child, and he is not getting any younger, I hate to point out. The big question is: do you want to be right, or do you want to be happy?"

CHAPTER

Forty-Four

Josh

He had waited long enough, having spent the last few days beating himself up for hiding everything from Effie. The time had come to admit what an idiot he had been, at the very least, and then see what their relationship status was after he had a chance to do what he had never done before: grovel. Countless times he drafted texts that went unsent or pulled up her name on his phone, but never pressed it to call her. What could he say? Anything he came up with never felt like enough.

Ruth's visit helped to counteract his inertia, and she had assured him that simply taking the plunge was his best course of action, and since she seemed to believe that Effie was feeling as miserable as he was, his humiliation would not be for long. Per Ruth's parting question, he desired to be both right and happy, but he supposed if he could only choose one, then happy would suit him best. Especially if Effie was here, happy alongside him, as she had been during their times together last week. It had been so long since anything in his life had felt as effortless as the joy and satisfaction he found in Effie's company. Part of their ease together was in no doubt due to the prior friendship they had all of those years ago; knowing that she had a crush on him in high school, just as he had on her, had sent his head spinning and ego soaring.

Josh had plans to have dinner that evening with Liam—they were supposed to be finalizing their trip to New York. Josh still intended to go, but he had no idea how long he would actually be there, so he was grateful that his cousin was traveling with him. Liam had an embarrassing amount of time and money, and his cousin had generously offered to book them a hotel suite that Josh could stay in while he figured out his future plans. Liam had been fortunate enough to have a mother who came from a family that owned a string of successful car dealerships in central South Dakota. Never having been the most serious student, this lineage benefitted him when he attended NYU, because his party-boy persona had almost failed him when it came time to actually graduate with the business degree he had sought. Luckily for Liam, the smallest dealership became his to manage when he had come home from New York five years later, after finally graduating by the skin of his teeth; it was evident now that his personality, while not conducive to classroom-learning, was welcome in the world of car sales, and he was thriving. His fun-loving cousin would be a welcome relief to the tension Josh would likely be overwhelmed with as soon as he left Beverley. And Effie.

Before seeing Liam, though, Josh needed to run home and take a quick shower. As he had done every day since leaving Effie's house four days ago, Josh was walking home from work to his dad's place. The time spent walking the blocks to the shop in the morning and then home in the afternoon was giving Josh well-needed reflection; it also meant that he could (hopefully) discreetly walk past Effie's house in the chance of running into her either leaving for or returning home from her work. Needless to say, he had not been lucky enough to even glimpse her near her house, but maybe now that a better plan was beginning to form in his imagination, she would be there—perhaps in her front yard, watering the hydrangeas the two of them had planted together last week. One humid morning a week ago, while they were each getting ready to go to work, Effie had mentioned the vision she had of planting her favorite flower bush along the perimeter of her house. Josh had borrowed his dad's truck, left work an hour early that day, and had driven over to the library to surprise Effie with a trip to the garden shop on the eastern edge of town. Unbeknownst to her, Josh had called ahead to the shop to ensure they had some of the bushes in stock, and he paid for them over the phone; all they had to do was pick them up. Effie had let out a small squeal when Josh loaded them onto the cart, and then she had thrown her arms around him and whispered into his ear every single way she would thank him later that night. Needless to say, the planting had taken place much later than originally intended.

As he turned on to Effie's block, he saw a car with Colorado license plates parked on the street near her bright green mailbox. Effie had not mentioned that she was expecting visitors this week, but it was at least a day's drive to Beverley from anywhere in Colorado, so this could not just be some random pop-in. Looking past the Corvette, Josh noted the Mustang in the driveway, which belonged to Effie's mother. Now that was even stranger, he thought to himself, observing that Effie's front door was still shut, which meant she was not yet home from the library. Effie loved to let in all the natural light possible, and never kept her heavy wooden door closed during the day if she was home. She was particularly fond of the way sunlight filtered through the stained glass that adorned the transom windows above the front door. She considered herself lucky that she had found this Craftsman-style house and was making every effort to respect and enhance all of the original features that were still intact.

Still not seeing anyone outside the house, he surmised that Diadema must have let herself in with her spare key, something Effie was growing increasingly uncomfortable with, as her mom had done it several times already. Diadema seemed intent on finding fault with the smallest details that Effie had either missed or not yet gotten around to taking care of and would then text Effie a list of matters she felt needed to be seen to immediately. "Like I'm made of money," Effie had complained to him. "I don't want to live in a museum—I had enough of that after I moved back home. She is so overbearing! And now that she is going with me to this LeBeau family reunion, she is even worse, believe it or not," Effie had complained to him one night last week. "She is insisting on me getting a haircut again, and now wants us to go clothes shopping in Sioux Falls for a new dress for me to wear to it, even after I showed her some new stuff I already picked up from Threadz." Threadz, located diagonally across Main Street from Check Care Auto, was the clothing boutique in town, and he had no problem envisioning Effie in any of the outfits he had seen on display in their windows. "Josh," she had laughed, "please tell me I've done the right thing by agreeing to take her along!" He had known Effie was just venting, and she was actually touched that her mother had volunteered to go. The thought of meeting her dad's family had her stomach in knots all last week, and now he wondered if she was more relaxed about it. Of course, he had been hoping to be the one to keep her calm, but all he had succeeded in doing was stressing her out even more.

Missing Effie intensely, Josh slowly walked from her house to his dad's, where he showered and changed. Finishing his Stephen King novel allowed him to pass the time while waiting for Liam to meet him at La Hacienda, Beverley's premium Mexican restaurant. Almost immediately after he placed an order for two margaritas, Liam sailed into the booth across from him. "Hey, Cuz, I love this place! Ooh, I see you've helped yourself to the chips and salsa already. Did you order me a margarita?" At Josh's nod, Liam continued, "I hope you got me a frozen one—it's so hot outside." Josh nodded again and waited to get a word in edgewise. "Now, let's talk New York. Mom is good with me being gone for a week or so and get this—Cait is going to cover for me while I'm away." Cait was Liam's younger sister and had recently moved back home from Mobile, Alabama. The fact that she had graduated from Tulane University was a sore point between the two siblings, as was the fact that she had stayed in the Gulf area after graduating with her law degree. It had been assumed by the family that she would promptly return home and work as the head legal counsel for the family business, but that did not transpire; at least, not until almost a decade later.

"How is Cait doing? I can't believe I haven't seen her since she moved back. She always was my favorite cousin," Josh said, entirely to annoy Liam. Since he had not grown up with any siblings, he did get a sick thrill out of pitting his cousins against each other, which he fully understood was such unJosh-like behavior.

Liam was saved from having to discuss his sister by the arrival of their margaritas. "You are the love of my life," he announced to the waitress, as he raised his glass and toasted, "to New York." Josh clinked his glass to

Liam's, the action reminding him of the picnic he and Effie had shared, which seemed a lifetime ago already.

"So…exactly how long are you planning on staying in New York?" Josh questioned Liam. "It's just…I've been thinking that *maybe* I might not be there as long as I originally thought."

Liam shot him a confused look. "What do you mean?"

Watching his cousin stuff his face with salty tortilla chips and spicy salsa, Josh replied hesitantly, "It's just that I have been reconsidering my game plan—you know, exploring alternatives."

"Okay, Dude, what the hell are you talking about? As long as I can re-member, you have had one focus in the world—become a big-shot surgeon in one of the biggest cities in the world. In fact, you were actually quite an-noying about it in college. You know, after we graduated from high school, I spent the summer believing that since both of us were going to college in New York, we would spend our weekends partying, but once you joined that fraternity, you were super serious and had no time for me. No wonder it took me longer to graduate," Liam pouted, which was truly as hideous as it was when he had done it as a child. Josh thought so, anyway, but the waitress evidently found it attractive and gave his cousin a wink as she deposited another basket of chips on the table before taking their order.

"So now you're blaming *me* for you ditching classes and almost never opening a book?" Josh asked incredulously. "Besides, the fact is you *did* eventually graduate, just with an extra year tacked on," Josh pointed out to his cousin.

"God, I was glorious, wasn't I?" And all Josh could do was laugh along with Liam, because the truth was that he was glorious, in a completely over-the-top way, and thus the perfect person to be traveling with soon. "I assume this career reflection has to do with a certain goddess named Eu-phemie?" He looked at Josh for verification, and at Josh's nod, continued, "Well, you know my policy has always been to never turn down a good time." Liam stopped and cleared his throat, "I also know that Effie is more than a good time to you, so if you are rethinking your future, you must be pretty serious about her."

Josh looked at his cousin, nodding earnestly. "I am, but I can't stop myself from thinking that the only person who has never failed me in my life is my dad…and I can't fail him now. Or myself. The whole time I've been back home, I've just had on repeat in my head that I need to go back to New York and finish what I started. Rebuild my life there. But now, meeting Effie has recalibrated what the future could be for me."

Their waitress came to their table and delivered their food, sliding a piece of paper with her name and phone number on it to Liam, which he slid into his pocket after tossing Josh a cheeky grin. "So, tell me more about this Lana you used to work with—any chance of me getting an introduction to her while I am in the city?"

CHAPTER
Forty-Five

Meeting with Ruth had given Effie much needed clarity, and she was eager to get home and somehow convince Josh to talk to her. Enough with him avoiding her—although could she truly refer to it as avoiding? Every day since his big reveal, she waited with bated breath, standing in her doorway, as she watched him pass by her house. Please come, she would silently hope to herself, willing him to walk up her driveway and then be standing at her door, ready for her to launch herself into his arms. She was ready to move on and figure out a way forward for the two of them, and now she was to the point of giddy, filled exceedingly with anticipation. She had the strength for a long-distance relationship, after all; he had said his residency was close to being finished, so what? A year, maybe more? Having no idea how much of his residency had already completed, and absolutely no clue how long a surgical residency takes, she was only guessing, after having searched the internet. She would have to ask Ruth how long Sean's residency had taken. But a year of them living apart, with visits every couple of months—that seemed possible. Besides, she wasn't even divorced yet, so this could help slow the speed at which she and Josh had been moving in their relationship. At the rate they were going, they would have been living together by the end of the week and married next month; she wasn't necessarily striving for a second marriage on top of her failed first.

Filled with a new sense of hope, Effie stopped on the way home and picked up a bouquet of brightly colored dahlias and zinnias, and the purple, yellow and orange flowers sitting in her basket brought her immense joy on the bike ride to her house. Jamming out to "Rumour Has It", she sang along with Adele as she turned the corner to her house, where any joy or optimism she had been feeling was smashed by the sight of the black Chevy Camaro sitting in her driveway. "What the fuck?" she muttered to herself. Was she hallucinating? Never before in her life had she wished for some kind of sick disease to explain away the fact that she was, for some reason, seeing Damon's car parked in her driveway. As she pulled up to her house, "Turning Tables" started up on her phone, and she knew she had underestimated her soon-to-be ex, because he had clearly enlisted the aid of her mother, whose Mustang was also parked in her driveway, and who for some reason always seemed to side with Effie's partners during any arguments Diadema was privy to. Turning tables, indeed, Mom, she thought to herself.

After hopping off her bike, she wheeled it into her garage, leaving the flowers in the basket; she would wait to celebrate once Damon was gone. Never before could she recall dreading the walk up a set of stairs as she did now, knowing what she would find once she opened her front door. At least her mom had the foresight to let herself in, instead of waiting for Effie to arrive home—this way, she was given the chance to compose herself before facing Damon. Like why the hell was he even here? There was absolutely nothing left that she needed to say to him; they had barely spoken when they had been living together, but now he needed to see her face to face?

Steeling herself, Effie reached a hand out to open her front door, and was stunned to find it opening of its own accord, by her traitor mother. "Mother, what a surprise," she started, when Diadema stepped out of the house and came so close to Effie, forcing her to back up to the railing. "What the hell, Mom?"

"I know what you're thinking, but I in NO WAY brought him here. He showed up at the house this afternoon, demanding to know where you were, where you lived. I didn't know what else to do but bring him here—he assured me that he needs closure. Your brother is in the house, too, because I figured at the very least, he could help me with back-up." Diadema took her daughter's face in her hands and said, "He has been *very* charming since I agreed to bring him here, but do NOT for one minute forget all of the pain he has caused you. Get him out of here so you can live your life." And then she kissed her daughter's cheek, opened the door back up, and called Hamilton outside.

Ham enveloped his sister in a bear hug, telling her, "One word from you, one yell, and I am through that door to beat the shit out of that low-life. Got it?" Effie kissed her brother's gorgeous face, and on trembling legs she walked into her house.

"Finally—do you know how hard it has been for me to track you down? The least you could have done was leave an actual address with me. Luckily, during one of the times you were rambling about growing up in Clover Lake, I was paying attention." Damon laughed at his lame joke and attempted to pull her into his arms.

"Umm, excuse me, but what the hell is going on, Damon? Why are you here? I thought I made myself clear to you when you called me months ago that we are done," and then Effie pulled her door open and pointed at it in an attempt to get him to leave.

Holding his hands up in a show of defeat, Damon said, "Okay, okay, sorry. Look, I owed it to us to give it one more shot to beg you to have sympathy on me. I have realized how full you make my life—how complete I am when I'm with you."

Effie laughed, unbelieving, "You have *got* to be joking. What you really mean, I think, is how empty your bank account is without me there, or how dark the apartment is without me paying the electric bill."

Damon brought his hands to his heart, "No. No. I swear to you I am sincere—I miss you." Damon took a breath, and then confessed, "I never appreciated you the way you deserve, Effie, and I apologize for that. I always took for granted that you would be there for me, waiting until I got home from whatever tour I was on, always ready to pick up where we had left off. The truth is, I could see how strong you were, constantly. How smart—so fucking smart. You didn't need me: I could have been gone for a year, and everything was always taken care of, paid for, looked after. And I guess that feeling of not being needed wore on me." Damon paused, and Effie stayed silent, needing to hear what great revelations he had to tell. "You've met my parents—you know how fragile my mom is and how much stock my dad puts into being 'A MAN'. Growing up, I watched how he treated my mom…how little he thought of her, and I *swore* I would never do that. Yet there I was, every day, acting like an asshole…acting like *him*." Damon looked at her as he had not done during the years they had been together, as though he was just now noticing her for being *Effie*.

As her eyes filled with tears, she remembered how horrified she'd been at the way both of his parents treated each other, as though they were some sort of caricature to the other. As much as she may have teased her own mother about her marriage to Burnside, she knew they loved each other completely and saw each other as equals. She sighed heavily, then asked him, "Oh, Damon, if only we had this discussion years ago—why didn't you ever say anything?"

"And admit what an imposter I felt like? I can barely even say it now." He pulled her hands into his and pressed them against his chest. "I am telling you sincerely that I have changed, Effie. Please—PLEASE—give me, give us, another chance. I will admit that I brought the divorce papers with me, but I'm hoping that we can just tear them up, or burn them—who gives a shit what we do with them? But then we can move on from this and try again."

What the hell was happening? Effie thought. If only Damon had said *any* of this to her a year ago: hell, even six months ago, before she left. Yet even that would probably have made no difference—in the end, he would still be the same damaged man he had always been. She had yearned so badly for them to get it right, every single time. "Oh Damon," she started, and withdrew her hands from his, "we can't. I have moved on: emotionally, physically, mentally." She looked up at her front door and saw her brother peeking in while opening it ever so slowly. She waved at him, hoping to signal to him that he and their mom could leave. He winked at her and smiled, catching her hint, and then discreetly shut the door again. Effie took Damon's hand and led him to sit down on the sofa. Once they were both sitting, she scooted a couple of inches away, not wanting to give him the wrong impression. "I have already let us go, and you need to do the same. The reality is that we were probably never truly right for one another. Yes, I took care of everything while you were away, but frankly, I was never all that bothered by you being gone, and *that* bothered me more than you actually not being there."

He stared at her with regret shining in his eyes. "I guess you're probably right—I was always walking away from you, but you let me go every time." Damon slumped down on the sofa and told her, "I knew this was a lost cause, but I had to see you one last time, I guess. Sorry for all of the bluster, because you definitely deserved better, in all ways."

She rose to walk over to the cabinet above her refrigerator and pulled out a bottle of bourbon her brother had given her the day she had moved in. Bringing the bottle and two small glasses back with her, she poured the alcohol liberally into each glass and handed him one of the shots. "Here's to finally figuring things out," she toasted, which made her think of the wine she had shared with Josh on their beautiful picnic. After tossing back her shot, she poured them each another round, and then asked, "Now where the hell are those papers? I want to sign them before I get too drunk."

CHAPTER
Forty-Six

Josh

"**W**ould you quit doing that? Seriously!" Josh admonished Liam, as he felt his cousin glancing over at him again. He had reservations about how he was going to endure their road trip to New York with Liam's constant mother-henning; it was going to be a *loooong* two days. "And can you please explain to me why we are driving a pickup to New York City? Do you have any idea how much this is going to stick out in Manhattan? Why couldn't we just take your Corvette?"

Liam threw him an indignant look from the driver's seat of the Ford truck he had "borrowed" from his dealership. "Well, excuse me, but maybe if you had given me more of a heads up than just texting me yesterday morning, telling me to get ready to hit the road. With a little more than a day's notice, I could have gotten us a convertible or something sexy like that." Liam sped up to pass a semi he had been following for the last thirteen miles through road construction.

"Take my Corvette," Josh heard his cousin mutter, "as if I want to put that many miles on my baby?" The two of them had left Beverley that morning before the sun had even risen, with Josh eager to put some distance between himself and the world he had left behind there. "You know, you're just lucky I travel so light, since you gave me zero heads-up."

Josh would have liked a heads-up also, he thought sullenly. Yesterday now seemed like it had happened a decade ago, yet it also kept repeating over and over in his head, taking up space rent-free there for the last twenty-four hours. He had woken up so full of promise and optimism the day before, but then an hour later, his dreams were crushed like the glass ornaments that had fallen off of the Christmas tree the year his mom had left. After having supper with Liam two nights ago, Josh had gone back to his dad's house and begun to make arrangements for his return to the hospital the next week. That night he could barely sleep, filled with promises of what his future would look like—a future that included Effie. On his way to work the following morning, he had headed to the shop on foot again, hoping that his timing would finally coincide with Effie leaving for the library; just as he rounded the block to her house, Josh was rewarded with seeing Effie step out onto her porch. Strangely, the Colorado car was still in the driveway, but he supposed that made sense that her friend (what was her name again?) would stay with her for the night. Claudia! The name popped into his head when he was just two houses down from Effie. As he got closer, Effie took a few steps from her door and a figure with light brown hair rose from the porch swing. Recognizing now it was a man on her porch, and definitely not her friend Claudia, Josh watched with dread as the man pulled Effie into a hug. The embrace then turned into a kiss, and Josh could not watch anymore. Turning on his heel, he reversed course and ran back to his dad's house to get his car so he could instead drive to the shop.

"Josh," Liam cautiously began, "are you ready to talk about why we had to leave so suddenly? I assume something happened with Effie? Or did nothing happen with her, and that was what had us being chased out of South Dakota like the devil was at our backs?"

Josh, unable to answer anything about Effie yet, kept his eyes on the road ahead of them, but he could feel every time Liam's questioning glance slid his way. Upon leaving Beverley, the two of them had driven a state highway until they hooked up with the interstate and were currently in Iowa, heading south, about ten miles away from their interstate change for the rest of the drive east.

"It's just that—the other morning at breakfast you two seemed so lovey-dovey, throwing off your happy-couple vibes. I don't understand what happened between then and last night, when you were hell-bent on going back to New York." Liam threw a side glance toward Josh in the passenger seat, and Josh was suddenly compelled to roll down the car window, possibly trying to let out either the overwhelming new-truck smell or the ringing sound of his cousin's question. And then he cranked up the radio, hoping to quell Liam's curiosity.

As "Take It on the Run" blasted out of the speakers, Liam reached over to turn down the volume. "That's it, isn't it?" Josh continued to remain stubbornly silent, but Liam was undeterred. "When I busted in on your breakfast, everything I said was news to her...am I right? No, you don't even have to confirm it. I know you better than anyone else in the entire world, and as I sit here, driving your sorry ass across the country, fleeing from the woman I know you love, maybe even more than you loved Tess, I am in complete awe of your ability to fuck up something that good. I'm not going to say anything more, because I know that you know what an idiot you are right now."

Josh rolled his window back up, because he knew his cousin was absolutely correct: he was an ass, just as everyone had been telling him for the past month. Now he was terrified that his silence concerning the truth had pushed Effie back into the arms of her ex and out of his life forever.

"Look, it's going to be a long fifteen hundred miles if you remain silent the whole trip. We can talk about absolutely nothing, but I need some conversation in between this music mix you are DJing. And what is with all of the REO Speedwagon? Dude, we weren't even *alive* when this was popular. I feel like I'm riding with my dad. I'm telling you right now, I won't be able to fight the feeling any longer if we don't stop to get some food in the next ten minutes."

"Fine," Josh muttered, "anything to shut you up for longer than five seconds."

"What was that, Josh?" Liam cupped a hand to his ear to try to amplify his cousin's voice.

"I was just telling you that the next exit has a bunch of places we can get something to eat." Josh rubbed his chin, feeling the scruff on his face that he hadn't bothered to shave off since he had left Effie's house. Shaving seemed pointless without having someone to rub her hands on his cheeks.

Liam took the exit, and upon spotting a café called "Molly's Place", which claimed to be "home of the biggest pork tenderloin sandwich in Iowa", he swung into the parking lot and parked their truck. "You know how much I love a good p-loin sandwich," Liam declared, patting his stomach. Josh merely grunted in response.

The cousins walked into the restaurant and chose a booth near the far corner of the restaurant. A waitress in her fifties brought them two glasses filled with ice water and two menus and said, "Be right back for your order. Any drinks right now?"

Liam ordered a Pepsi while Josh shook his head. "What, is this the phase of your life that you become one of those people who only drink the free water in a restaurant? I mean, this is not a good look for you—first the Speedwagon and now the water? You are essentially giving up on life with these life choices. Please tell me you are getting actual food and not a salad?"

"What's wrong with a salad? Look at this southwestern salad on the menu. That sounds good!" Josh pointed to the salad on the menu. "Black beans, avocado, shredded chicken, chili lime vinaigrette."

"Yeah—if you're a soccer mom out to lunch with all of her shitty friends who are too afraid to have what they really want, which is the turkey club sandwich."

"Turkey club? You think turkey club is manlier than the southwestern salad?" Josh scoffed.

Liam hissed back, "At least it doesn't have a direction in its name!"

The waitress reappeared at their table, asking for their order. Liam ordered his pork tenderloin sandwich with extra pickles and mayo, and Josh, not necessarily swayed by Liam's argument, but also not wanting his cousin to tease him about it all afternoon, was having the same.

"Don't think my order had anything to do with yours," Josh warned Liam.

"Never—after all, I'm getting the cheese curds and you're having curly fries," Liam remarked with a grin. "So now do you care to tell me why we left like a couple of outlaws? I was looking forward to spending a few more delicious nights with Paulina."

"Paulina? Who the hell is P—never mind: the waitress from the other night, right? Not that you will remember her in a week, anyway."

"Exactly! And that is why, my dear cousin, I am so concerned about your current state of affairs." Liam took a sip of his drink, and then gave Josh such an unexpected earnest look that he immediately became suspicious: Liam did not do earnest: Liam did fun, carefree, no worries at all. "Look, I know I have my persona I put out there in the world, but I have always admired your ability to be so serious and dedicated. I just don't understand why you left so quickly without sorting things out with Effie. At least, I'm assuming that you didn't work things out with her, considering you have not mentioned her name once since we left. The other night you were non-stop about how you two could have a long-distance relationship while you finished up your residency, but as far as I know, you didn't even see her yesterday, did you?"

Josh waited as the waitress put their food down in front of them, sighed heavily, and then answered, "Technically, I did see her."

Liam looked up from his sandwich, asking, "What? Why haven't you said so? Wait—what do you mean *technically?*"

Josh put his face in his hands. "She spent the night with her ex—although I guess maybe he isn't her ex anymore? I was walking to work and when I got to her house, I saw them together on her porch—kissing."

"What do you mean 'her ex'? Like her husband?" At Josh's nod, Liam continued, "Are you sure, though? You've never even met the guy, have you?"

"It was either her ex or some random guy she was kissing in front of her house, for all the world to see. Anyway, there was a car with Colorado plates in her driveway the night I met you for supper, and that car was still there yesterday morning, so you tell me who else it could be! Plus, her mom was also there when I first saw the car: they were clearly having some sort of family reunion. Effie seemed to have forgotten all about me, so if she was going to live her life, I figured why was I wasting time not living mine?"

Liam stared at him, open-mouthed, with such a look of astonishment. "Wow. So, you just left? That's it—no confrontation, no explanation?"

"What was there to say? I don't need to be dumped by two women in one year, Liam. I think I have had enough heartbreak for now." In actuality, though, Josh had not left town with absolutely no word to Effie: he had written her a letter and left it for her in her mailbox, but so far she had not let him know that she had read it. Now he felt he had further humiliated himself, not having the guts to speak to her personally. And no way could he admit to Liam what he had done.

"See, this is why I keep things on the casual side! No hurt feelings, no sense of betrayal—" he stopped suddenly and shook his head. "But that is me: No Expectations Liam. Not you, though. So now I will ask: what the hell are you playing at? This isn't some Hallmark movie, where a small misunderstanding leads to someone being butt-hurt, and they leave town licking their wounds without so much as a word to their romantic interest. This is fucking real life, Josh! Your life," Liam pronounced, as he grabbed a fist full of Josh's fries. "I am going to tell you something I have never in my life said: I am extremely disappointed in you. You haven't been fair to Effie and, more importantly, you haven't been fair to yourself."

"A Hallmark movie? Really?" Josh was flabbergasted. "What should I have done? Marched up onto her porch and demanded an answer as to why she was kissing her ex?"

"Yes, you idiot. Damn, you sound so stupid. You have no idea what was even happening! Wasn't this guy like a total douche? Effie is fucking smart, Dude. No way would she get back together with him," Liam said, frowning at Josh. "And Hallmark is not my choice—too much time with my mom on the weekends," he said defensively.

"Okay, so why was he there?" Josh demanded.

"I don't know, and now neither do you! Who knows? Look, maybe he was trying one more shot with her, but no way would she give it to him!" Liam finished his lunch, and then told Josh, "You owe her more than this, Josh. You can't run away with your tail between your legs because you're what—afraid to care again? Think about it. Which you will have plenty of time to do, because I am still driving this next leg, and you will sit in that passenger seat and figure a way out of this holy shit of a mess you have created."

CHAPTER
Forty-Seven

Effie

The insane relief she felt when she finally had Damon officially out of her life paled in comparison to the intense sorrow she was currently experiencing with the loss of Josh. It had been a few days since she had seen him walk or drive past her house, and she had not spotted him going in or coming out of the shop, either. She had thought about asking Ruth if she had spoken with him, but the one time Effie had texted her, she had gotten the impression that Ruth was busy enough with the move, pregnancy, and little Eloise without her Josh-drama. Something was up, though, because she had never *not* seen him for this long of a stretch since they had reconnected, or at least it felt like it.

After dealing with Damon and his rather sad attempt at reconciliation, Josh and his depth of caring were even more appealing. Effie could empathize with why he kept the truth hidden from her, and understood his actions were from a place of care, for himself and for her, and even more so that it would never have been his intention to hurt her: he was protecting himself. Effie had been waiting for him to make a move and come to her: it didn't matter for what reason or motivation—she didn't even expect him to apologize; what she wanted was to know she mattered, and that he was going to fight for them. But now she simply could not wait any longer.

Sucking up her dignity and drawing in her courage, she decided to head over to Henry's house on her way home from work and force Josh to talk to her. Who knew how long he would continue to hide away from her? Enough with any feelings of guilt or shame he had—if they were going to move forward with each other, they had to talk. She was beyond ready to figure out a plan for a long-distance relationship; she had been to New York City a couple of times, enamored with its electric vibe and eclectic look. With a sudden energy, she bounced off her bike, stood it up in the driveway, and then sprinted up the steps to Henry's front door. Knocking softly, she noticed only Henry's truck in the garage. The car Josh had been using was not there, but sometimes if the weather was nice, he would walk home from the shop, leaving his vehicle parked overnight, hitching a ride with his dad the next morning.

The bright blue door swung open, revealing Henry on the other side. "Effie," he said hesitantly, "how are you?" He seemed concerned, but maybe because he thought she was there to upset his son?

"I'm fine," she answered, smiling at Josh's dad. "Is Josh around? It's just…I've been wanting to talk to him all week, but we keep missing each other, I guess. I'd call him, but things like this are better done in person. You're probably wondering if I'm still upset, but I'm not. Completely over it, actually." Shut up, Effie, why are you rambling? And why was Henry just standing there with his door open, not inviting her in or anything?

"Didn't you hear? I guess I assumed that Josh talked to you before he left…" Henry, for some reason, seemed reluctant to tell her something. What did he mean "left"? She stood there, immobile, waiting for him to explain, and then he said, "I'm sorry, Effie, but Josh isn't here."

"Ooookay, do you know when he will be back? You know what? Never mind—I'll just text him. Which I should have done days ago, but then my ex-husband showed up with divorce papers…although I guess at that time he wasn't my ex yet, since I hadn't signed them…but he is now…" Kill me now, she thought, before I make an even bigger idiot out of myself. "Anyway, sorry, TMI."

"Effie," Henry looked at her, seemingly imploring with his eyes for her understanding, "Josh is gone. He left for New York three days ago. He went to your house the day before he left, and he said you…ahem…" he cleared his throat, "he said you had a visitor leaving from your house that morning."

"Yeah, that was my ex, like I said," Effie began to explain again, and all of a sudden it occurred to her what Henry was referring to—that fucking kiss goodbye the next morning. After the two had drunk what was left of the bourbon, Damon had passed out on her sofa, drunk and exhausted from his ten-hour drive from Denver to Beverley that day. She had taken pity on him and thrown an Afghan across his body, then proceeded to eat the entire Tupperware bowl of cookie salad her mom must have brought with her when she had escorted Damon to her house earlier. When she was a kid, her mom always made cookie salad at least once a week during the summer, and both mother and daughter preferred it over ice cream as their cold, creamy treat on a hot summer day. Diadema must have been keeping up her tradition and, knowing Effie would be in need of the comfort once Damon showed up, brought some of the dessert with her. Effie had then gone to her bedroom and watched four hours of *Gilmore Girls* before sleeping an entirely dreamless night. Upon waking the next morning, she had discovered Damon in the exact location she had left him; accordingly, she had roused him and informed him he needed to leave so she could get ready for work. They had hugged at the door, and then Damon, being Damon, kissed her before she had any chance to react; he still walked away alive because as quickly as he had kissed her, he had also ended it as swiftly. "Damon, my ex, drove up from Denver and brought me our divorce papers. I had to sign them…but I didn't…I mean, nothing happened. I just let him sleep on the couch that night…" and Effie closed her eyes, imagining the pain and betrayal Josh would have felt—MUST HAVE felt—seeing it. "But why didn't he say anything? I didn't even see him that morning."

Henry sighed, "You know Josh, Effie. He's not good with confrontation or arguing or anything like that. He was confused, and I don't know… what can I say? I'm not exactly a master at relationships…you know when his mom left, I did not handle anything the right way—I can see that now. Hell, if I'm being completely honest, I didn't do anything right when it came to Melanie. Her leaving was as much my fault as hers, and it has taken me all of these years to admit that. Instead of staying in Clover Lake and dealing with the fallout of her leaving, I just up and moved us here because I naively thought that a new town could mean a fresh start." Henry motioned for her to follow him into his house and quickly arranged the cushions on the sofa so she could sit unfettered. He then walked into the kitchen and returned with a glass of water for Effie. "Sorry, I should have invited you in immediately," he apologized.

She shook her head, waving his apology away with her hands. "I remember when you guys left. It was like he was there at the end of the school year, and then I never saw him all summer, which wasn't that unusual because I knew from summers past you would take trips with your family to Lake Tahoe. But then when he wasn't there to try out for the one-act plays that fall, and no one knew where he went, I was so confused. And hurt, I guess, which was silly because we hadn't been particularly close, but I thought we were friends…theatre nerds together." She took a long drink of water, hoping to clear whatever was closing up her throat.

"Imagine being Josh—I told him not to tell anyone. I mean, obviously our family knew where we had gone, and my mom tried to warn me that I was making a mistake, but who listens to their parents, at any age? I knew best, though, or so I had a bad habit of thinking, and I told him to pretend that his mom had died, rather than face any questions here about why she just up and left us. And then in his senior year, all that pressure I put on him to go to a fancy college and become a surgeon. I just pushed him and pushed him. He had incredible promise, Effie—he still does! He's the best of me and his mom. Despite all of the pain she caused, sometimes I wish she was here to see it."

As Effie let a few tears fall, she reached out to put her hand on Henry's arm. "You're a good dad, Henry. I imagine my dad would have been like you in so many ways. Thanks for talking to me. Ugh—I hate that he saw Damon kiss me, that I may have hurt him. But I also hate that he just left, without telling me why, or without at least telling me he was leaving! That's twice now that I was under the assumption I meant something to him, but it didn't seem to matter when it was time for him to go."

Henry handed her a tissue out of the box sitting on the coffee table in front of them. Effie took it, blew her nose, and then stood up. Henry rose alongside her, and she turned to him and gave him a hug. "You know, you were probably too good for my mom, right?" As Henry's face blushed bright pink, she laughed and left the house.

Her brain was in overdrive after her talk with Josh's dad, and part of her just wanted to put everything aside for a bit. Tomorrow was the day of her reunion with the LeBeaus, and she wanted to be fully present for it. She planned to pick her mom up around eight in the morning so they could get to the Grass Valley reservation by ten. She pulled her bike into her garage and then walked back to the curb to check her mail. Opening the mailbox, she pulled out her mail and rifled through it as she walked up to her house and climbed the porch steps: a catalog for running shoes, her cable bill, this week's edition of the Beverley Digest, and a letter, with no postmark. What in the world? She thought. Was this also a piece of junk mail? She almost threw it into her paper recycling bin, but a whim of curiosity caught hold of her, and she opened it, still not recognizing the handwriting, but it was addressed to her. "Dear Effie," it began. She turned over the page and saw Josh's name signed at the bottom. Collapsing onto the porch swing, she read:

"Dear Effie,

For so long, I had one focus in my life: becoming a surgeon. It was, I can see now, more than likely, what led to the demise of my relationship with Tess. I didn't know how to be a good partner, and that was proven when she left me. I never thought, out of all the things in my life, that surgery would fail me, and then it did, or at least I thought it did. Being back home in South Dakota, though, I finally understand that *I* was the one who failed surgery. I have had so many losses, Effie; some you don't even realize.

Going back to when Dad and I moved to Beverley, and lying about what happened to my mom didn't help to make me a better person or trust in my decisions. My entire childhood, thinking my mom loved me, started to feel like a lie. How could I admit the painful truth years later, to tell Tess the truth about my mom—tell her what, exactly? That her fiancé was a loser whose own mom wanted nothing to do with him? Then when I found out that my mom has been keeping tabs on me all these years through my grandpa, but *still* doesn't care enough about me to come back? Another blow, and another example of not being enough for the women I love.

I remember when the high school guidance counselor told my dad that my ACT scores were the highest he had ever seen in his career, and that I should be looking at Ivy League schools if I seriously wanted to be a surgeon, so he suggested I also take the SATs. Dad immediately began looking at ways to pay for everything, which included refinancing both his house and his auto shop. There were still school loans and grants, but I have no loans in my name, and to this day, my dad refuses to let me know what any of it cost him financially.

Now here I am: having to choose to either resume my career in New York, and take a chance that you would be interested in a long-distance relationship, or take a chance on us and give up New York and maybe start from scratch in a smaller place somewhere, with the possibility I might not be fulfilled professionally. Having failed personally so miserably this last year, I have no confidence in my ability to be the loving, competent partner you deserve, or that you had even asked me to be. The day before I left, I saw you at your house with your ex, and I get it. I don't know if you guys got back together or what the situation is, but that is when I knew I needed to go back and finish the one thing that has meant everything to me over the past ten years. And it was you who gave me the confidence to do it, and so I thank you. I also want you to know that I love you.

Effie, you inspired me. You made me believe I was capable of finding joy in love again. And I'm sorry I didn't get to tell you in person that I love you. I love you, and I regret being too rattled to talk to you before I left—you deserved that, and I am sorry. This letter pales in comparison to having a real conversation, but I hope you can forgive me for that. Just know that I am always talking to you, always loving you, wherever I am.

All my love,

Joshua Livingston".

CHAPTER
Forty-Eight

In the months that Josh had been away, their office had been so lonely. He had been the first friend she had made at the hospital at the start of her residency, and once he was gone, she had realized that maybe he had been her only friend. Every television show she had ever seen about doctors had them all having lunch together, comparing medical procedures, and discussing their sex lives, but Lana's reality differed harshly from that fiction. For one thing: she always brought her own lunch, never being able to reckon the cost of eating out, even if it was only in the hospital cafeteria, which incidentally happened to be the home of the best banana bread in upper Manhattan, and a splurge she allowed herself once a week. Money was always a sore subject with Lana, and when you had grown up as poor as she had but were raised around people whose money flowed much more freely, you learned how to downplay your poverty. For instance, when Josh happened to buy her a coffee that first time from the upscale coffee shop down the block, she had to keep up her moneyed façade

293

and return the favor. After that, every morning they worked together, they alternated treating each other to coffee. Now, about comparing medical procedures? Once she earned (not won, like some fellow residents were wont to claim) the fellowship, all misguided beliefs about swapping surgical stories flew out the window, like her mother's paycheck (due to having to raise four kids on her own); or flew out the window, like her deadbeat dad, who had left when Lana was eight. And lastly: discussing her sex life? What sex life? Lana had not been laid since she lost her virginity at the age of sixteen, to the (get this—this was going to be really good!) quarterback at her high school, also the only son of the family that employed her mom to clean their house once a week. Awkward, right?

All reasons why she had treasured her friendship with Josh, and missed him terribly when he left, no matter how difficult their last day together had been. She had at long last felt seen with Josh, and now he was finally back, although seemingly almost as miserable as he had been when he left. Dr. Gilmore, their attending surgeon, had brought her into his office last week and told her that Josh would be returning. Two days ago, there he was, sitting in his old chair. They hadn't spent much time together, however, as he and Dr. Gilmore had spent hours enclosed in Gilmore's office the first day. The following day, they had some seemingly important business in Dr. Scanlon's office yesterday, and that was the real mystery—why would he be meeting with the head of surgery again? And so far, Josh had not been scheduled for any surgeries; maybe he was being eased back into the program?

Lana looked up from her desk as Josh entered their office with two coffees and a shy grin on his face. "Good morning, Lana," he greeted her, placing one of the coffees on her desk. Pulling up a chair to sit across from her, he then said, "I was hoping I could have a moment to talk to you?"

She shrank into herself, awash in humiliation once again at that damn email she had written him. Why she had ever confessed feelings of love to him confounded her even now—she spent most of her life going slow and steady, and then on the rare occasion she allowed herself to get swept up in some sort of impetuous act, it always ended with remorseful regret at best, and stinging embarrassment at worst.

"That's okay, Josh. We don't need to talk. In fact, I am due for surgery," she rushed on, even while knowing he could have already checked the board and seen she in fact *did not* have a procedure scheduled until that afternoon. "Anything that was said by me, or by you, can we not let that be just water under the bridge? I've changed; I presume you have as well?" How much can she blather on while shuffling random papers around on her desk, hoping it all at least looked somewhat necessary? She did her best to not look directly at him, hoping it wasn't obvious that she was avoiding his gaze.

Josh put out a hand on the stack of papers she was clutching. "Please, Lana, I owe you a massive apology." She looked up at him then, into those summer-blue eyes that had always held such kindness and support. And that was why she had fallen for him. She had always known that he never returned her affection, and probably never would, but she had to take a chance after he left. Part of her still had feelings for him, but she was used to living a solitary life by now, comforted by it, actually, after having grown up in chaos.

"It's really not necessary, Josh. I was a fool—" she whispered, before he cut her off.

"No, I was the idiot. I'm sorry if any of my actions led to you misconstruing my friendship for you. I have no other way to say this except honestly. You were a true friend to me when I needed it—all last year when my relationship with Tess was unraveling, you were there. It was probably wrong of me to even have discussed my personal life with you, and I can see how that muddied the waters. But you were steadfast and loyal, and always my friend, and it has been an honor to share this office with you for two years—I guess it's more like three at this point. I want you to know that you are a brilliant surgeon—that fellowship was well-deserved." Overwhelmed by his sincerity, she lifted her coffee to her mouth for a drink, hoping she didn't spill any due to her shaking hands.

"I appreciate that, Josh; there could be no higher praise from anyone. I was just hoping we could forget all of that and start over?" she suggested, with a hopeful lilt at the end of her question.

He shook his head, "No, not start over—move forward. I'm tired of trying to bury things in the past," he said, and she smiled at him, with relief coursing through her. "Okay, well, now that all of that is solved, I have a huge request from you: my cousin came with me from South Dakota, and he has been hounding me to meet some of my doctor friends. Would you meet us for a drink tonight? I think Dr. Gilmore is coming out, too, and maybe Cal and his wife."

Lana's fellowship often kept her in the office for an hour after almost everybody went home for the day, so she replied, "I don't know, Josh. It would probably be too late by the time I get there."

"I have to go to Brooklyn first, anyway—I am going over to see Tess and Sam and check out her bakery, so I won't get there too early. Come on," he cajoled her. "My cousin is nuts, but usually entertaining. Plus, I have big news I want to celebrate!"

Reluctantly, she found herself agreeing, "Okay, fine, I'll do my best to try to make it, but only one drink." She enjoyed Dr. Gilmore but had never socialized with him out of the hospital, and she had met Cal a couple of times when he had stopped by to see Josh and found him to be incredibly down-to-earth and always had an amusing story to tell about Josh from their med school days.

"Fantastic, Lana! I would really appreciate it if you could be there tonight. I will text you the place—it's only a couple of blocks from the hospital, which is pretty convenient, since we're staying at a hotel near here." Josh pulled the door open, and with a wave at her, he breezed back out.

She called to him, "Wait—what's your cousin's name?" But he was gone, with the door shut behind him before her question finished.

She continued on with her day, deliberating what Josh's big announcement could be, never knowing him to be quite so dramatic. Her scheduled procedure was a kidney transplant for a former cancer patient, and it consumed the rest of her day, so by the time she was showered and redressed, exhaustion was creeping in. She really did have paperwork that needed to be done before tomorrow, and took out her phone and texted Josh her apologies for not making it to the pub for drinks; upon rereading his excited text to her from earlier, that included the name of the pub, she changed her mind again, and mustered up her energy to go to the pub after all: one drink, then she could just swing back here and finish up her paperwork.

Whistling Dixie, the bar Josh had chosen, was only two blocks from the hospital, and how it had ever escaped her notice was mystifying: a country-themed bar in upper Manhattan? Nearly every head in the place was crowned with a cowboy hat, even the women. She flushed, feeling entirely out of place as she looked down at her wardrobe: she had worn a sundress this morning to work, and it was a little lower cut than she normally preferred, so she had also worn a camisole underneath. However, during her surgery, she had become so hot that she had sweat stains on the cami after taking off her scrubs. So here she was in her bodice-hugging dress, adorned with daisies, and the length stopping right above her knees.

Lana scanned the crowd, looking for Josh's dark blond head, certain that he, at least, would not be wearing a Stetson. Coming up empty, she made her way through the mass of patrons singing "Friends in Low Places", a country staple that took her back to her childhood, because her older brother had loved that song, and still did, as a matter of fact. When she finally reached the bar, she ordered a Coors Light, thankful she could drink what she wanted before Josh got here. Lana always felt the need to pretend to be much more posh than she could ever hope to be, so around other people she maybe wanted to put on airs for, she would order a martini or cosmopolitan—something that was deemed more sophisticated.

A baritone voice spoke at her ear, "I'll have what she's having," and as she glanced to her right, a hand shot out holding a twenty-dollar bill for the bartender. "My treat," the voice said again, sending shivers down her spine, and her gaze traveled up and up, to a face that stole her breath, and she felt all common sense go with it. He was absolutely beautiful, in an overwhelmingly masculine way, she thought, with the most intense gray eyes she had ever seen—so light, and with a touch of blue (or was that green?) dotting them, and an entrancing dark ring around the iris. Something about them was familiar to her, but not the rest of him: chestnut-colored hair, shoulders that she was convinced could carry the world, and tall—probably an inch or so over six-feet. Though she had always had a thing for tall men, she usually found them intimidating, considering she, herself, was only an inch above five-feet tall. Intimidated was definitely not the word she would use to describe her feelings toward this man beside her.

He grinned at her, "Hello, Darlin'. You are just what I have been hoping would walk into this place tonight." Her new friend picked up the bottle of Coors Light that had been placed in front of him by the burly bartender.

"Really? How long have you been waiting?" Flirting had never come easy for her, so whatever was taking over her body right now was extra-terrestrial. Maybe it was him—he was her flirting muse. Well, she may as well have fun until Josh got here, and she watched appreciatively as he tilted his head back and drank from the bottle, the muscles in his neck working while he did so.

"For you, I'd wait forever," and he pointed at the bartender, and suddenly two shots of clear liquid appeared before them, along with slices of lime and a salt shaker. "I've been hoping a woman as sexy as you would walk in here and do a shot of tequila with me," and he licked his wrist, sprinkled salt on it; then she felt his hand reach for her fingers and, bringing her arm closer to him, up to his mouth, he slowly gave her wrist the same treatment. Electricity coursed through her body at the feel of his tongue on the delicate skin of her wrist, and when the salt fell, she couldn't breathe. He handed her the shot glass, clinked it with his, and tossed back his shot. The muscles in his neck worked the liquid down, and quickly she did the same, before she passed out in front of him. Maybe waiting fourteen years to have sex again had been the biggest mistake of her life, because one drink with a sexy stranger was doing her head in. He placed the lime in her mouth, leaned over and whispered, "Suck it in, baby." This was wrong, this was wrong, so wrong, on so many levels. Women like her DID NOT attract the attention of guys like him. She was too smart, too serious, too prone to frown. Yet here she was, smiling up at him, more turned on than she had ever been. Was it wrong to want to have a good time? She did not see one person from the hospital here, and the anonymity of the place was cloaking her in a way that made her feel adventurous and tingly, maybe even a bit dangerous.

Lana drank from her beer, her eyes never leaving his. "Not to be cliché, but are you from around here?"

He threw his head back and said, "Baby, you can be whatever you want to be. But no, I am not 'from around here'," and then he put his lips next to her ear, whispering, "I do, however, have a hotel room across the street, whenever you are interested." And he brought his head up and winked at her. Obviously, she would NEVER even CONSIDER following a complete stranger to his hotel room, no matter how attracted she was to him.

Lana was the one then to throw her head back and laugh, and informed him, "As appealing as that sounds, I am actually meeting someone here." Maybe thinking of meeting up with Josh would be enough to bring the temperature down inside of her.

He lifted a sexy eyebrow at her, and replied, "Well, what a coincidence, I am too," and he drank another great swig of beer, and then over the speakers, a slow song began to play, and her new friend grinned down at her, and grabbed her hand in his. "Dance with me," he insisted, and she looked around the bar.

Shaking her head, she told him, "No one else is dancing, though. I don't see a dance floor, either." Her resistance was futile, and as he pulled her into his embrace, she ran her left hand up his arm until it stopped at his bicep, while he threaded the fingers of his free hand with that of hers.

Almost in a trance-like state, she stared up at him as he hummed along with the song being played: "Neon Moon." Lana swayed with this handsome stranger, unable to believe that she was dancing to a country song in this bar. Growing up, her mom had been obsessed with music from the '50s and '60s, but her older brother had loved country music and would let Lana sit with him in his room as he played song after song from his collection of CDs he had managed to procure somehow, despite no one having extra spending money in their home.

She cleared her throat as she looked away from the intensity of his gaze. "You do know that this song is about an alcoholic, don't you?"

Then her breath caught in her throat as he grinned at her. "Darlin', I had a feeling as soon as I saw you that you would be the smartest woman in this place," and he spun her around in a twirl, catching her in both arms as she was propelled back to him.

The song ended, and "Rocky Mountain Way" serenaded them as she followed his lead and sat back down at her barstool, while he signaled the bartender again. "So while you and I are waiting for our friends to arrive, why don't we have a little fun?" This time after the bartender sat the shots and limes next to her shoulder, he grabbed her arm first, gave the tender skin of her wrist a long, slow lick   with those gray eyes never leaving hers—and again sprinkled salt on her skin left glistening by his tongue. In a move that surprised her more than him, she grabbed his arm, and returned the sensual favor, relishing the feel of his skin under her tongue, tasting the salt that still remained there from before. He threw a dash of salt on his wrist and handed her a shot, motioning for her to drink it. When she slammed the shot glass down, he handed her a lime. After both had completed the ritual, Lana removed her slice of lime from her mouth, and after putting it on the counter, she licked her fingers, watching as his eyes dilated, making the gray disappear into complete black.

This sexy stranger pulled her off her barstool into his arms again, and this time both of his arms remained holding her close, and Lana felt his breath in her ear as the music serenaded them. Powerless to stop the moan from escaping her mouth, she put her face to the buttons of his shirt, breathing in his scent of body wash and desire.

He cupped her face in his hands and she rose up on her toes to reach his mouth first, with his hands in her hair. She heard his Apple Watch buzz with an alert, interrupting their kiss, and he glanced down. "Well, it must be my lucky night—it seems I am being stood up." He reached a fingertip out and traced a path across her shoulder blades and up the side of her neck, and from out of thin air, he tossed a bundle of twenties on the bar.

Looking around once more for Josh, Dr. Gilmore, or *anyone* she even remotely recognized, she gave up and let her wilder impulses take over. Lana took his hand and proceeded to the front of the bar; once outside, she pressed her back against the building, bringing his body up to hers. Kissing him until she was breathless, she moaned, "Lead the way." Had she bothered to look at her phone, she would have seen the message that came in almost simultaneously as his Apple Watch alert, with a text from Josh telling her that he would not be able to meet her for drinks after all.

CHAPTER

Forty-Nine

Josh

"Could you please refrain from making that screeching noise?" Liam complained for the hundredth time in five minutes.

"It's called eating breakfast. This is a fork," Josh proceeded to wave his cutlery in front of Liam's face, "and this is a knife—both of which are required when eating chicken and waffles. Which, by the way, I would definitely recommend." After studying his cousin's pale complexion, he amended his breakfast suggestion. "Although you may want to just stick with toast and scrambled eggs, considering your, uh, delicate disposition this morning. What in the hell happened to you last night, anyway? You were out cold when I got back to our room."

"Thank god," Liam announced at the appearance of the waiter, "coffee: black, and lots of it." He stared at Josh with red-rimmed eyes and asked, "Why didn't you wait for me before coming down for breakfast? And what is the big news you texted me about last night?"

"Oh, yeah, sorry about last night. Once I got to Tess and Sam's, it was hard to leave. What she has made out of the coffee shop is amazing! And even though it has nothing to do with me, I am so incredibly proud of her. Of both of them, actually." Josh had come away from his evening with the couple with a new perspective on almost every aspect of his life. Tess's business was thriving, and she had recently successfully converted it from a coffee shop that happened to sell baked goods to a bakery that now happened to sell coffee. Tess and Sam had plans to add on a room at the back for a small bookstore, which would make it a dream fulfilled for both Tess and Sam. Work was beginning soon on the upper floors of the three-story building, also, to make it into a true home for them, with bedrooms and an office for Sam on the top floor, and living space and large kitchen on the floor above the bakery. Josh had been surprisingly touched by how content Tess was, but he also felt a tad guilty, or perhaps a bit sorry for himself, that she had never looked as glowingly content in any of their years together.

"Oh, really? No more bitter feelings or lingering resentment that you were betrayed by your fiancée or best friend?" Liam poured spoon after spoon of sugar into his coffee.

"Might want to take it easy on that sugar, buddy. Don't want diabetes, you know?" As Liam scowled again at him, Josh continued, "Anyway, I am seeing their relationship in a new light and thinking of myself as kind of their matchmaker. So again, sorry for canceling on you. Oh, that reminds me, I should make sure Lana didn't turn up at the bar looking for me—she seemed pretty sure she wasn't coming out, but I need to reach out to her to apologize if I stood her up, too, since she didn't respond to my text last night." He picked up his phone and shot off a text to Lana, positive that if she had tried to meet him at the bar, she would have at least acknowledged his text, or he would have heard from her even before that, once she got there and he was a no-show. Before he had left the hospital yesterday, everyone else he had spoken with about meeting up for a drink had to cancel, for one reason or another: the life of a doctor. Of which he was well aware. Lana had been the only one he *hadn't* heard from, but she had been very iffy about meeting up, anyway, so it had slipped his mind to contact her sooner when he ended up being in Brooklyn longer than he had intended to be.

"Despite my head feeling like it is about to explode, you canceling on me was the best thing to happen to me in a long time—you did me a favor," Liam admitted, finally looking more alive than like the walking dead.

"Does that explain the two glasses on your nightstand I saw this morning?" At Liam's smug nod, Josh continued, "You must have worked some fast magic, since I was back in the room just after midnight last night, and no trace of Cinderella to be found."

After having his coffee cup refilled for the third time, Liam was looking even perkier—he had also ordered a Belgian waffle and a side of bacon, so he was making progress. "Josh, I think…I think I may have found the one."

"Found the one where, exactly? And when?" Here we go, Josh thought, typical Liam. He never had a problem "falling in love"; no, his problem was "staying in love". No, make that just general "commitment".

"Last night, at that bar by the hospital. God, Josh, she is amazing. So sexy. And smart." Liam closed his eyes, slumped back in the booth, and sighed.

Josh raised an eyebrow at his cousin, not that he could see with his eyes shut, and said, "Smart, huh? You deduced this when, exactly? Before or after the shots of tequila?"

Suddenly, Liam opened his eyes. "How did you know about the tequila?"

Josh laughed, "Hello? This is your standard operating procedure. You buy the shots, you do the little thing with the wrist and the salt—you can't tell me that still works?"

With indignation, Liam replied, "It may have been a ploy other times, but last night, it meant something."

"Okay, so what's her name? Where does she live? What does she do?" As Liam avoided Josh's gaze, he confirmed what Josh had suspected: he knew absolutely nothing about the new love of his life. "So, no personal information, then," he answered for his cousin. "I hope you at least got her number, so if you are ever in the city again you can see her."

"Maybe we should focus more on your love life, Cuz," Liam refuted snidely. Evidently Josh's words had hit their mark, if his cousin was lashing out, and he sort of felt sorry. Sort of. Then: "I'm sorry, I'm sorry," Liam rushed on before Josh had a chance to argue. "As a matter of fact, I didn't get her number, *but* I gave her mine."

"Oh, perfect, then. Once the hangover clears and the morning-after doubts recede, I'm sure she will give you a call." Josh took a deep breath, knowing he has being too hard on Liam—he was the epitome of a good time, and if that was all he wanted out of the world, why should Josh make it his job to get him to be serious? "Look, Liam, I'm the one who should apologize, once again, it seems. Honestly, I am always in awe of how un-seriously you take life. Maybe if I had more of your attitude or outlook, I wouldn't be in my head all the time, overthinking absolutely everything." Josh drank some of his newly refilled coffee and ruminated on his recent decisions. "Being back in New York and seeing how happy Tess and Sam are has made me realize how I need to choose that—I want to choose happiness. I want Effie in my life, in any way I can, and I see now that leaving before I had a chance to speak to her about our future, or clarify things about her ex, that was a huge error on my part."

Liam nodded vociferously. "Yep—huge fuck up on your part, actually." His breakfast arrived, with a grateful sigh from Liam, and he slathered butter on his waffle, saturated it with maple syrup, and then ate two slices of bacon at once.

Josh was wounded, and informed his cousin, "You don't have to be so happy about it. Anyway, how can you be sure?"

"Well, if you bothered to answer your dad's phone calls yesterday, you would know what I know," Liam told him.

"What do you mean—phone calls?" Josh took out his phone and saw that his dad had tried to reach him several times yesterday. "He must have called when I was meeting with Dr. Gilmore. Why didn't he leave a message? Or text me?"

Liam waved his hand, "You know that generation—they never text when they can have a one-minute phone conversation. And they never leave a message because they know our generation doesn't listen to voicemail, anyway."

"Point taken—okay, so what...he called you?" Josh watched as his cousin flagged down the waiter to order another side of bacon.

"Yeppers, and confirmed what I knew all along: Effie did not get back together with that scuzzball ex. In fact, it sounds like he is officially an ex now. The kiss was a non-starter in her life, and it seems she is pining for you," Liam announced with a broad grin on his face, as he added more syrup to his already soaked waffle.

Josh stared at Liam, mouth agape, "Pining for me? My dad told you that?"

"Well, not in those exact words, but you know Uncle Henry—not much of a 'word man'. But she did go to his house, wanting to see you." Liam ate the rest of his Belgian waffle and finished Josh's breakfast potatoes.

Josh felt his stomach drop, and his whole body became enflamed with a feeling of anxiousness. He had thought what he was doing was right, and this news had only confirmed it. He cast his mind back to that near-perfect week he and Effie had spent together, when every pleasure had seemed endless, and each moment magnificent. Was that how his life could be with Effie in it? Was this the only chance he could have knowing true contentment? To have what Tess and Sam have, or what Ruth and Sean have? He didn't want to be alone, like his dad, spending every meal getting only one plate out of the cabinet, washing dishes by hand because it took too long for one person to fill a dishwasher with used kitchen items.

"That doesn't change any of my plans," he told Liam. "I met with Dr. Gilmore yesterday, and discussed my future with him, and that's the news I wanted to tell you." How would he balance career and love? Could he be satisfied with having less?

CHAPTER
Fifty

Effie

Effie had been home for half an hour when Ruth called her, asking her if she was coming to the street dance later that evening. "I don't think so. I just got home and am exhausted. Besides, how do you have any motivation to go to a street dance? It's a million degrees outside, and you're pregnant."

Ruth laughed on the other end of the phone, "That's why I want to go! My parents have Eloisa for the night, and a couple of Sean's sisters are in town and since they have never experienced a street dance, I want to show them one—come on, Effie, it'll be fun! I heard the band warming up this afternoon, and they were soooo good! Pretty soon I won't have the desire to go anywhere, and then I won't be *able* to go anywhere when the baby is here."

"I don't know, Ruth—I still need to find the right way to reach out to Josh so we can clear the air; I hate that I haven't reached out to him about the letter he left for me." Ruth had been the only person, aside from Henry,

307

who knew Josh had left her a letter, and during an emotional afternoon coffee meet up a couple of days ago, Effie had let Ruth read it.

"This is so Josh," Ruth stated during their coffee date, "but at the same time, I can see how much he has changed deeply. You know, with everything that went down with him and my sister, Josh never acknowledged his responsibility for any of it as it was happening. But this," Ruth said, holding up the letter, "this is a Josh I have never seen before."

"He loves me, Ruth," Effie whispered painfully to her friend, to Josh's friend, seeking any guidance she could provide. And Ruth somberly nodded, a simple confirmation that gave her everything she needed.

Now she sat in her house, listening to her friend on the phone. "Well, come out tonight," Ruth advised, "and maybe we can come up with a plan for you and Josh. Nothing will happen to you if you're just sitting at home."

Ruth had eventually convinced Effie to meet her downtown in an hour. Plenty of time for a nap, then. Effie went up to her room, where the central air conditioning had made it particularly frigid, and laid down underneath the star quilt that she had brought home with her today: a gift from her grandmother.

She had picked up her mom early this morning from Clover Lake, and together, armed with iced coffees and breakfast burritos, they had driven to Grass Valley Reservation to meet up with her family. Her stomach had been in knots, but for once she could focus on something other than Josh, so her nerves had been a welcome reprieve to the confusion and worry over her ambiguous relationship. She had no idea what to expect going to the reservation: what would it look like? How would they be treated? She had been to a few other reservations when she was younger, usually for track meets or basketball games, and conditions varied depending on which reservation it was. She had always despised the shortened "rez" they were often referred to: derogatory and demeaning, meant to belittle everyone who either currently lived there or came from there. Grass Valley, though, exceeded anything she imagined—it was stunning, with gently rolling hills, so green and lush with wildflowers. A private Catholic grade school sat on the edge of town as they pulled in, and the intricate brickwork was a testament to the care that had gone into building it over a century ago; yet Effie could also feel the pain it had caused when non-Natives invaded this land, forcing the indigenous population to conform to their white ways, compelling the Dakota people to forget their culture, cutting off their connections to their heritage and ancestry.

"That's where your father went to school, Effie. When he first brought me home, everything seemed like another world. There was so much I did not know about. He told me that the families had been pressured to make their kids go to the school. They were prohibited from speaking their native language, and only allowed to speak English. It broke my heart to hear that his parents, his grandparents, they all had to cut off their long hair, for centuries a symbol of their strength, and keep it short. It devastated generations."

Effie had learned about some of this over the years, but was horrified to think about it so closely connected to her own heritage. Diadema had pulled over to park on the side of the road, but now drove away from the property and as she did so, she continued, "The school had turned their policies around by the time your dad started school, and actual certified teachers, not nuns, taught classes. Half of the teachers hired by the school were originally either from Grass Valley or another reservation, and they helped encourage so many children to want to learn, to get good grades, and then go to college so they could become something great." Her mom got quiet for a moment and then added, "In fact, I was teaching there before the accident happened..." and Effie filled in the blanks. She had reached over and squeezed her mom's hand, fully appreciating what it was taking for her mom to be with her today. "I want you to know that even though we were moving away from here, it was only going to be until your dad got his law degree—we always planned on coming back; that's the part that got lost in the aftermath of his death," her mom said sadly.

"Mom, I hope you know how thankful I am that you came with me—I don't know that I could have done it without you," Effie told her.

"Of course. If you want the whole truth, I am nervous, but actually looking forward to it. I got along with everyone in the family, except for his parents, but I can see now, especially after spending time with Damon the other day, how difficult it must have been for them to see their son be with someone so different from them. I was taking him away, and I'm not sure either one of us understood what that meant. You'll see today, at the powwow, how proud the LeBeaus are of their heritage; Nathaniel was also, but he had different dreams, ambitions. I can see now that his family would have been scared that we would be gone forever after he finished his law degree."

Effie looked around, trying to imagine growing up here, and she could almost see it. They drove past businesses that had protective gates over their windows, left in place from more troubled times on the reservation, yet then they passed the city park, with a huge swimming pool, bordered by massive oak trees, whose leaves danced with the light breeze in the air. Effie and her mom saw mobile homes with flowers planted in little window boxes, and they passed two-story farmhouses, with fresh coats of paint on them, and paved driveways lined with bushes, but also tiny homes so small they could only have held a single bedroom, that had several cars parked in front of them. Like every other town, the neighborhoods held a mix of middle income and lower income, with some clearly below the poverty line. According to the faces of the children she glimpsed playing in yards and on sidewalks, though they were happy.

Once they had driven about half a mile through town, her mom indicated that Effie should take the next right, so she turned the corner. Now she needed no further directions, because the street was lined with cars on both sides, and a steady stream of people were all headed to one house. She parked the car at the far end of the street and took the last sip of coffee, which at this point was more melted ice than coffee. "I'm nervous, too, Mom. What if they don't like me?" she whispered.

Diadema reached across the front seat for a very welcome, if somewhat unwieldy, hug for her daughter. She then took Effie's face in her hands and looked deeply into her eyes. "These eyes are the eyes of your father—your face has his shape. Your loving nature and forgiving heart? Do you think there is any way you would have gotten that from me?" Her mom laughed then, and Effie felt comforted. "They will love you because you are of him, yes, but once they get to know you, they will love you for the person you are: a blessing and a gift. Now, let's go introduce you to everyone."

They exited the car, each of them wearing very colorful dresses, thanks to her mom's guidance. At college, Effie had been to a couple of powwows, but she had a feeling they would be nothing compared to what she would experience today. She heard the drumming as soon as they got out onto the street, and then the voices reached them, people singing in their native Dakota tongue. As they neared the house, small children ran past them in their fancy dresses, adorned with beads and fringe, all in bright, cheerful colors. Her mom pointed her to walk around the perimeter of the house, and as they did, Effie saw how the backyard stretched as far as her eye could see, with people spilling over onto the banks of a large pond at the far end of the property. A small stage had been erected, and on it sat a circle of singers who were drumming, some wearing headdresses and others beaded headbands. The smell of barbecued meat wafted to her, and her stomach grumbled at the tantalizing scent. To her right, she saw a fryer with fry bread cooking and next to it a card table that held all the makings for tacos. A voice behind her laughingly said, "Those aren't technically Native, but everyone does love them some Indian tacos." Effie turned and saw a young woman standing at her shoulder, several inches taller than Effie, with a broad smile and shining eyes that could have mirrored her own, "Hi, Euphemie."

Her mom gasped from her other side, "Abigail?" At the woman's nod, Effie's mom continued, "My word, you are breathtaking. It's been so long since—" and she stopped talking, as years-held tears fell unchecked down her face. "How are your parents?"

Abigail said, "Please—call me Abby. Every time someone calls me 'Abigail', I feel guilty for something." Abby drew Diadema in first for a hug, which visibly brought a great relief to her mom, and then reached for Effie, and Abby said "Effie—it is Effie, right?" Effie nodded and Abby continued, "I am so thrilled that you are here. What can I get you guys? Drinks? Food? Ear plugs?"

The three women laughed, and suddenly a toddler raced up to Abby with arms lifted, "Mama…mama…up."

"And this is little Nate—named after your dad, Effie," she shyly informed them, lifting the adorable boy into her arms. "My first two were girls, but when we had a boy, I just had to honor my uncle Nathaniel. I remember him so clearly in some of my memories as a child."

Diadema nodded. "That's right—he was teaching both of you girls to ride a horse that summer."

"Well, he tried to anyway; I'm still scared to ride, I'll be honest. I'm a disgrace to my Dakota ancestors, or so my dad always tells me," Abby said with a laugh.

Effie whispered, "I remember now," and then she repeated more loudly, "I remember—we rode horses back there," she pointed at the open field behind the pond, now covered in alfalfa, but in her memory, it was yellowed grass, dead because of the drought they had that summer. She remembered her mom talking about how dry it was that year, but after they had held a ceremonial Sun Dance, it had rained for the next week that followed. That had to have been the last time her dad had dressed in his regalia.

"Come," Abby beckoned, "want to see grandma and grandpa?"

Effie nodded nervously and clutched her mother's hand, and Abby led them to the other side of the yard, where her grandparents sat under what looked like an ornate arbor, decorated much like one of the fancy dancers.

Abby put down the squirming Nate, and as he ran to his great-grandmother, she looked up and gasped, "Diadema? Euphemie?" Then she nudged her husband of sixty-five years, and both of them slowly rose from their chairs, opening their arms for them.

"Chaske," her mom greeted her grandfather, whose name, her mom explained to her in the car, meant "eldest son".

"Diadema, it has been too long. Effie, my heart has always been with you," he said gruffly.

Now her mom embraced her grandmother, "Aurora, I am so sorry for everything—"

"Shh, let us speak no more of old regrets and time that has passed." Her grandma rubbed Effie's knuckles with hands that Effie could tell just by touching had known the world and all of its losses; Effie could also tell by looking into her grandma's eyes, though, that she had also experienced many of the world's joys. "You both are here now, and that is what matters."

And with that, Effie and Diadema had joined her grandparents under the arbor, where they were surrounded for the rest of the day by varying family members: aunts, uncles, cousins, adults, children, babies. Too many names to keep track of, but her mom took pictures of Effie with all of them. Old friends of her father's came to meet her, also frequently embracing her mom, occasionally shedding tears. And all of the food—so delicious, with most of it being pre-colonial foods that were making a comeback on reservations and restaurants around the Midwest. She savored bison burgers, smoked trout, duck sausage, wild rice salad with dandelion greens, sweet potato chips with a maple ketchup, blue-corn cakes, and yet there was an extraordinary amount of food she didn't get to try. When Effie commented on the elaborate headdresses, her grandfather gently corrected her, telling her they were actually called roaches, not headdresses.

She and her mom had spent hours in Grass Valley, at the home where Effie herself had lived for the first five years of her life; being back there had felt like coming home, more than anywhere else she had ever experienced. When it was time for them to leave, hugging seemed inadequate, yet necessary. Plans were made for Effie to return soon, maybe even next month, and that was when her grandma gifted her an absolutely gorgeous star quilt that truly belonged in a museum.

"I made this for you when Abby said you were coming. Well, I may have had some help," and she winked at the women holding up the quilt.

Enfolding her grandma's tiny form into her arms, Effie whispered, "I love you," and did the same with her grandpa. As she and her mom drove away, Effie held onto her mom's hand for the first few miles, more thankful than she had ever been to her mom for her support, love, and encouragement. Such a feeling of contentment washed over her, and she began to open up to her mom about Josh. Shyly, cautiously, Effie confessed all the misgivings she had, but also the hope and promise a relationship with Josh offered.

Now, back at home underneath her beloved quilt, Effie felt a resurgence of energy, and texted Ruth that she would definitely meet her outside the coffeeshop in an hour for the street dance. If she was going to party tonight, she wanted to look her best, so she jumped in the shower, determined to set the night on fire.

Chapter

Fifty-One

Josh

Had the letter been a mistake? Although he had poured his heart and every ounce of sincerity he possessed into it, Effie had to be wondering why he had just left South Dakota and not spoken to her in person. He had thought that writing to her would not only be more meaningful, but also an easier way to save face if she had not felt the same depth as he did. While he had not expected to hear from her immediately, he couldn't help but feel concerned that she had not reached out, even though his dad had inferred she was pining for him. Maybe the way he had delivered the letter had been the mistake—leaving it to chance that she would find it in her mailbox? Did people even get mail anymore? All of his bills had been paperless for several years, so other than junk mail, there was rarely anything else delivered. After days went by with no word, he had begun to doubt she had even received the letter, but then he would rethink that maybe she *had* found it, read it, and completely disregarded it, wanting nothing more to do with him. Then the thought crossed his mind that maybe something happened, like with Tess and Sam: last year, when they were on that train ride, Sam had to leave suddenly and had left a letter for Tess, but the letter had never actually reached Tess because of a mixup with Tess's room number. Maybe her postman accidentally took it, mistaking it for outgoing mail? No matter what (if she had the letter or didn't have the letter, or if she loved the letter or hated the letter), he knew he had needed to make a decision about his life…his future…so he took a chance—something he had not done in years—when he met with Dr. Gilmore. He had inquired about finishing his surgical residency in South Dakota, and just as Sean had told him when they had dinner together a couple of months ago, Beverley General, and its affiliated hospital an hour away in Sioux Falls, were in almost desperate need of surgeons and doctors, especially ones who came from South Dakota: people who wanted to come back to their home state to practice medicine, with ties to the area, be a part of their communities again. Dr. Gilmore told him that between the two hospitals, there would be enough cases for him to finish his residency by the new year. However, he had warned Josh that it might mean the surgeries could be a bit more run-of-the-mill than what he had been used to in New York; however, with his reputation and residency pedigree, he would almost surely be sought after, especially with Sioux Falls growing in population; patients didn't want to have to go to Minneapolis or Denver for difficult surgeries.

Once his career had been sorted, he had to tie up the remains of his life in New York City, and that included cleaning out the storage space that Tess had moved all of his belongings into when they split up. While they had been having breakfast the morning after Liam's night out, Josh had filled his cousin in on his major life update once he had appeared sober enough to handle the news. Liam had then generously offered to stay and help empty it out. "Cuz, aren't you glad now that I *did* bring the truck to New York? Now we can just rent a U-Haul, load it up, and take everything back with us."

"I have never been more in awe of your genius, Liam, and I am saying that with as much sincerity as I am sarcasm. I just hate that it will take at least a day to load it up and then two days to drive back to Effie," Josh despaired, wanting to get back to South Dakota and sort everything out with Effie as quickly as possible.

Liam had clasped Josh's shoulder, "Never fear—Sam and I have been texting…ooh, there he is now," and Josh had looked up to see Sam crossing the dining room of the hotel restaurant, stopping briefly to ask a waitress for coffee.

"Yes, here I am, and Tess is thrilled with this idea," Sam had announced once he got to their table.

"Idea? What idea?" Josh was confused. He had already told both Tess and Sam about his life development the night before, which was why he had stayed so long at their place and failed to meet up with Liam.

Sam questioned Liam, "Oh, you haven't told him? Or were you too busy talking about the love of your life to fill him in on how we were going to help him with the love of *his* life?" Sam teased Liam.

Liam looked affronted. "Just because there is some benefit to me staying in New York City an extra day or two—"

Josh had interrupted, "Could someone *please* tell me what you two are talking about?"

"I am here to help your cousin save the day," announced Sam. "You know I have always loved a romantic gesture, so in order to rush you back to Effie, I am going to help Liam empty out your storage, load up the truck, and then drive back to South Dakota with him," Sam informed Josh, as he took the chair next to Liam. "I texted your cousin this morning asking how you were doing, and Sleeping Beauty here hadn't heard your big news yet. After I told him, and then he told me about meeting the 'woman of his dreams' last night," Sam was heavy on the air quotes here, "so we devised this master plan. Have pity on me, because how I will have the patience to put up with this knucklehead for three days will probably be a miracle."

"So you already knew my big news?" Josh asked Liam. "Why didn't you say anything?"

"Well, honestly, I wanted to hear it from you personally. I have to admit, my feelings are slightly hurt that I seem to be the last one to know…" Liam couldn't hold back the grin on his face, and he told Josh, "I'm proud of you, Cuz."

"I can't believe you two have been conspiring behind my back this morning," Josh laughed, filled with gratitude, and he rose from the table, hugging Sam, who had been his closest friend since college, and who had always tried to encourage Josh to think with his heart and not his head: it had taken a while, but he finally caught on. Then he turned to hug Liam, who had always had his back ever since they were young. Josh exclaimed, "I need to get to the airport, I guess!"

"Is this where the moving party is?" asked a voice from behind Josh, and he looked over to see Sam's brother Eric and another young man standing there. Eric was an actor/dancer/singer who had recently soaked up the bright lights of Broadway in the Tony-winning *The Big Lebowski.*

"Eric," Josh had cried, "wow—the last time I saw you, you were just a kid. What are you doing here?" Hugs all around, then, as he bestowed one upon Sam's brother.

"Well, when my big brother takes action, I know something huge is afoot, and you know us Charles brothers—we love a romantic gesture," and everyone at the table laughed, "so I brought Hudson down here and we are here to help." Josh smiled at Hudson, who, from the way he looked at Eric, was under the spell of a romantic Charles brother.

Now, as he stood in the park in Beverley, having arrived late last night, he heard the band playing "If Not for You", and he was filled with anticipation, having always loved that song. With the help of Ruth, he had engineered a surprise for Effie at the gazebo: "their" gazebo. Butterflies in his stomach had been doing their damndest to make sure he could not eat all day. Ruth, with the help of two of Sean's sisters, had made up some food for him and Effie to have for a picnic, because once he had Effie back in his arms, he knew he'd be starving. With the champagne chilling in a cooler, all he needed was Effie, which was turning out to be the case in every aspect of his life. No matter that he had never heard from her about his letter, because he loved her, and if he had to convince her with a romantic gesture, he would.

CHAPTER
Fifty-Two

Effie could not see through the crowd to find Ruth. She had been away for too many summers—missed too many street dances—and had evidently not noticed the stream of cars that had to have been entering Beverley when she had gotten home two hours ago. Walking up Second Street from her house on Plum, she turned onto Dakota, and noticed a gigantic sign that stood on the corner, announcing the street dance would follow the rodeo tonight. Okay, so she may have been so distracted that she had forgotten about the rodeo happening this weekend. Despite that, Effie was dressed appropriately for a post-rodeo street dance, wearing a purple paisley-print dress that fell just above her knees, and boots, pure cowgirl attire: a pair of brown and purple Justin Boots that she had bought years ago in college, and hadn't worn in probably ten years—they still fit like a glove. No tight Wrangler jeans for her, though, which was what many women were wearing. Not that she was against the formal wardrobe of the rodeo and its street dance; it was just too hot to even consider wearing denim.

As she neared the entrance to the street dance on the corner of First Street and Main, her eyes followed the length of First Street, and she could see a stream of trucks and cars making their way from the rodeo grounds, six blocks away. She had no sooner been a block from her house when the music began to reach her ears. Reba, Garth, and Trisha covers serenaded her on the journey, and then "Sweet Home Alabama" started up, sure to be a crowd-pleaser. Fond memories of being a teenager, traveling with friends every weekend to the various small towns in the area so they could go to the street dances. Meeting up with kids from the other towns, dancing the jitterbug with a boy who had been taught by either his mom or older sister, stealing kisses in a dark corner with the same boy later in the evening. Occasionally she would be stuck dancing with one of her female friends if there weren't enough boys to go around who knew the steps, but the girls were often better dancers than the boys, anyway, so it didn't matter. Not very often had she made it all the way to Beverley for their legendary rodeo street dances: forty miles away on country or state roads had seemed too far to travel, especially when so many towns were less than ten or fifteen miles from Clover Lake.

Effie was anxious to go through the gates and join the throngs of dancers, so she took out her phone to text Ruth: "I'm here. Where R U?"

Ruth promptly replied, "On my way. Go in and wait for us by Flower Power."

Okay, that was kind of weird, Effie thought. Why wouldn't she just wait for them at the coffee shop? It was inside the perimeter, but only just, and she wouldn't have to actually be in the crowd until Ruth and her entourage got there. Effie shrugged and approached an older gentleman who was taking money and handing out wristbands at the gate. She smiled at him and took a twenty-dollar bill out of her cross-body bag to give to him. He flashed a toothy grin at her and asked, "You're Effie Van Holland, right?" Stunned at how he could know her, he laughed at her expression and added, "My wife works at the library in the periodical section."

"Oh, Velma, right? You must be George, then. Nice to meet you."

"You too, and you put that money away—it's no good here. Someone has paid for your entrance already," George informed her.

"What? Are you sure?" At his nod, she asked, "Who was it?"

He shrugged. "Don't know, but I was told that Effie was to be taken care of. You have a nice night now." And with that, George secured a blue wristband around her wrist to signify she was older than twenty-one, and then he attended to the next person on the line.

The band began to play "Summer of '69" when she caught a flash of shining blonde hair across the street that looked like Ruth's, so she crossed over, but it turned out to be a case of mistaken identity, so she continued to walk towards the flower shop, which was the next block down.

"Effie! Sis!" Effie turned her attention back to where she had walked from and saw her brother weaving in and out of people on the street until he reached her. "I followed you across the street—I was trying to get your attention," he laughed.

"I didn't know you were going to be here tonight, Ham," and she gave her brother a hug, and he passed her an icy-cold bottle of Bud Light.

"Well, I came with a few buddies," and he nodded to two young men standing near the beer tent closest to the entrance. "I saw you come in and thought maybe you'd need one of these."

Effie took a long swallow, then told Hamilton with a whistle, "You are looking sharp tonight," indicating his light blue Western shirt, neatly tucked into a pair of tight-fitting jeans; he even had on a cowboy hat, clearly on the market for a date.

"Yeah, I clean up pretty well. I talked to Mom, and she said you guys had a nice day with your family," he remarked, as they continued walking down the block.

"God, Ham, Mom was amazing…everyone was. Let's go out for dinner next week and I can tell you all about it. Right now, I want to know how your classes are going," she said, knowing her brother was taking summer classes to finish up his associate's degree. "And why do you never stop and see me?" The college where he was taking the classes was also in Beverley, and she had expected to have him show up on her doorstep at least a couple of times to mooch a meal or need a place to crash if he was out enjoying the nightlife.

"Classes are great, and I am done next week!" He had to almost shout to be heard over the cacophony of music and voices. "Now, let's have some fun and see if I remember everything you taught me," and Hamilton grabbed her beer and put hers next to his on a table by the curb at the edge of the "dance floor" that was the street, spun her around, and began to two-step with her to her favorite Clint Black song.

Effie enjoyed dancing with her brother, who was so light on his feet, and knew she was the envy of so many young women right now. "Look at all of your admirers, Hammy," she teased, and as the song ended, her phone rang. "Oh, it's Ruth," she told Hamilton. "I have to meet her over by the flower shop." Hamilton waved her off as she answered her phone.

"Hey, Ruth," she said, holding a finger in one ear so she could hear more clearly, and she watched her brother amble over to a lone woman on the edge of the crowd, tipping his hat at her as he approached.

"Hey, Effie, we haven't made it in yet—we're just to the park. Do you want to come meet us here? Sean's sisters are so slow," she whispered to Effie over the phone.

Effie laughed, "Sure, no problem. It's packed over here, anyway. I'll have a better chance to find you guys over there."

CHAPTER
Fifty-Three

As Effie crossed the street over to the park, she once again passed through the street dance fencing. Her attention was caught by the fairy lights that had been strung up outlining the gazebo and surrounding oak trees, so they twinkled as if in tune with the music: "If Not for You" and once again, she was taken back to that magical week she had spent with Josh, and one particular evening under the stars. Josh had taken her hand in the kitchen and led her out the back door, enfolding her fingers with his as they walked outside. A fire was flickering in her fire pit, and he had placed two chaise lounges there, along with a small table that contained the makings for s'mores, one of her favorite treats. Josh had his phone serenading them while they toasted their marshmallows to crispy, gooey perfection, then assembled their s'mores and devoured the messy, delicious confections while trying to prevent an abundance of melting chocolate or dripping marshmallows from coating their hands.

When they were finished, and on a sugar high, they laid side-by-side, reclined in their chairs, to gaze up at the sky; "If Not for You" had come on, and Josh had begun humming along to the song. "I love this song," Effie had confessed, as she reached over and stroked his chest, "and now even more listening to you sing it." She loved the feel of his warm skin under her fingers as they slid under his shirt, his heartbeat fluttering with her touch.

Josh had laughed, protesting, "I wouldn't call what I was doing sing-ing," and he had taken her hand once again, entwining his fingers with hers, bringing her hand up to his mouth, and kissing every finger. She joined him on his chair, as his hands roamed her body and his mouth fused with hers, and contemplated at that moment that her life could be lived perfectly, having that evening on repeat.

And now here that song was playing again, and Effie felt a pang of longing course through her, and she missed Josh so greatly, more than she had ever experienced with anyone. She cursed herself for not replying to his letter, but she had been hoping so desperately that he would have personally reached out to her about it by now. She knew she was kind of being an idiot, and it felt as if she were playing games with him, but for once she wanted to be enough for someone to make a big move—not the kind of move Damon had made with his pathetic, last ditch effort bringing the divorce papers to her—but a move made for them to begin something beautiful, forge a future together.

Entering the park then, she looked around for Ruth or Sean, and saw no one, so she took the path that led up to the gazebo, and once she round-ed the corner to the front of it, her breathing stopped for a second, maybe two: hell, it could have been minutes, or hours, for all she reckoned, be-cause everything ceased the moment she saw him.

Josh had been waiting for her for what seemed like forever now, and when finally Effie came around that corner, his vision tunneled for her only. Somehow, he made the few steps over to her, surprising himself when he did not trip to fall at her feet, which was, ironically, where he belonged. "Effie, I'm sorry…I was so caught up in my own head all the time. No," he shook his head to get his words out the way they needed to be—the way she deserved to hear them, damning himself for not being more eloquent, wishing for once in his life he had excelled at words rather than science, and took her stunned face in his hands.

"No?" she asked him, completely bewildered as to how he was standing before her or what he was trying to tell her. "Josh what are you doing here? You're supposed to be in New York," she stated with disbelief.

"Let me start again, and I promise, from this moment on, I will try to get it right the first time: I love you, Effie, have loved you from the time you brought your mom's car into the shop. Well, actually, probably from all the way back when I was fourteen, and we had our first play practice together. I fell for you in secret, never imagining a day where you could ever possibly feel anything for me other than friendship. And then I left you, not my fault, but I did leave, with no explanation or goodbye or anything. And to know that I did that very same thing again to you? Effie, I should be begging you to even look at me, let alone give me another chance. From the moment I left Beverley…left you…all I could think of was how to get back. I can't choose between my career and you, because from the second I was heading away from you, the way my heart was breaking, that made the choice for me. All that has been getting me through these last few days was knowing I was coming back to you." Josh stopped to take a breath; he wasn't used to speaking for that length of time: usually someone interrupted him, or he just ran out of things to say, but he wasn't done yet, not with so much left unsaid to Effie. And then she started talking.

"But I don't understand…you came back to tell me that you missed me? I don't…you were in New York?" Her mind could not catch up to what was happening at this moment in her life—why was Josh here? Too scared to hope for anything, she began to back up, but Josh pulled her to him and kissed her, passionately, desperately, until she was hanging on to his shoulders for dear life. "You love me?" she whispered hopefully.

Josh nodded, reluctantly easing his arms around her to lift his head from hers. "Okay, I clearly need some lessons in explaining myself better," he softly chuckled. "What I am trying to say…what I meant to say, is that I am back. I am staying here in Beverley. I'm not going back to New York— well, I mean, except to visit, because I do love that city, but only with you… if you will come with me. If you will have me now."

"But what about your residency? You need to finish that," and she searched his face for answers, and what she saw told her all she needed to know: his earnest expression, his tender gaze spoke volumes about his devotion to her. Instantly, any remaining confusion left her mind, because whatever it was, together they would figure it out. She flung her arms around his neck, and the feel and fit of his body pressed tightly to hers was all she desired to understand currently, so with her lips pressed to his ear, she told him what she had been yearning to tell him since their first date at the movies, where they shared a bucket of popcorn: "I love you, Joshua Livingston."

And finally, they kissed, melting into each other, then his mouth was on her neck, her hands up his chest, until a voice from across the park yelled, "You two might want to keep things PG," and raucous laughter rang out. Reluctantly, Effie and Josh broke apart, and under the ivory glow of the city park lights, as the fairy lights twinkled their own applause, stood Ruth, Sean, and two young women who must be Sean's sisters, but also Henry, Hamilton, Diadema, and Burnside.

"What in the…what is everyone doing here?" Effie asked Josh.

"Well, it turns out even though I may be able to work my magic in the operating room, I always need the support of nursing staff; today, I needed a village to make something like this happen. Your mom has been updating me periodically during the day, and by the sounds of it, your newly reunited family sounds amazing," Josh told her as he kissed her forehead.

"And then I harassed you into coming to the dance," Ruth bragged, coming up to Effie and Josh and grabbing them both in a group hug.

Her brother piped in, "And I had my eye on you from the moment you came through the gate tonight. Our impromptu dance? That was Josh needing extra time for some finishing touches." Hamilton quickly revised, "Not that I'm not an excellent dancer," and he took the hand of one of Sean's sisters and swung her out onto one of the paths, and Hamilton began teaching her the finer points of country dancing, to the beat of "Boot Scootin' Boogie".

"The big news," Sean added, "is that I *finally* get to work with the renowned surgeon, Joshua Livingston. At least, I can finally work in the same hospital as his grace," and Sean popped the champagne he procured from the cooler next to the gazebo, while Diadema handed out plastic cups to everyone there.

"I'd like to make a toast," Henry said after the champagne had been distributed, "to Josh, for bringing everyone here tonight. Son, it takes a lot of courage to change your life suddenly and begin a new journey, and I am so proud of you."

"And to Effie," Burnside quickly jumped in, before anyone had a chance to drink yet, "Effie, who made me a dad for the first time: I may not always have known what to do or how to be a father at first, maybe even still I struggle, but you were always the only daughter I ever needed."

Then, while everyone wiped their eyes and enjoyed their bubbly, Josh took Effie up into the gazebo. "I'm here, Effie, and I am staying here. I am going to finish my residency at the hospital here in Beverley, and there may be days I will go to Sioux Falls, but I will be done in a few months, and then the hospital has already offered me a position on staff to begin a new program for surgical residents. The state needs more hospitals that can teach residents in all practices, it turns out," Josh told her excitedly.

"But what about New York? All of your time there? Beverley is not New York…it's just…I don't want you to decide in a year that your work isn't challenging enough." Effie sat down on a bench and pulled him down next to her, and looked into his blue eyes, knowing she would never be able to bear it if this wasn't enough for him—if she wasn't enough. "I love you immensely and completely, but I am scared."

"Effie, I am more excited by any of this than I have been in a long time. Not just that, though: I don't feel overwhelmed by it all. I have real opportunities to consult on cases in Sioux Falls—cases that normally would go to the Mayo Clinic instead. More than my career, though, is you." Josh stopped to cradle her face in his hands and let his eyes convey the depth of his sincerity. "I could have stayed in New York, but my life there, outside the excitement of my cases, left me empty inside. You, Euphemie Van Holland, have filled my life with everything it was lacking before. You have helped make me a better man and a better doctor. " Unable to resist a moment longer, they embraced again, with mouths whispering promises between kisses.

Over the pounding of his beating heart, Josh heard the band begin playing "Harvest Moon". He swept Effie up to dance under the fairy lights of the gazebo, singing into her ear, "Come a little bit closer, hear what I have to say." Everyone had drifted away, leaving Effie and Josh alone to celebrate their homecoming.

EPILOGUE

His stomach was filled with knots as he watched her walk up the stairs to reach him under the gazebo. Today was the culmination of all of their dreams and plans, and he and Effie would formally begin the life they had been building for two years. As soon as he had arrived in the gazebo a few minutes ago, Josh had looked out at his friends and family, who were gathered here today. Their gazebo, as he and Effie always referred to it, for it was a place that held the memories of so many events that marked the timeline of their relationship: their first make-out session, Josh's reappearance in Beverley after choosing Effie and their future together, and then last year when he had proposed here, during a rainstorm that had marked the first day of summer. A startlingly sunny day had greeted them, so they had walked over to the park for the Arts in the Park Festival. Josh, while carrying the engagement ring around in his pocket for weeks at that point, had been waiting for the perfect moment to propose—a moment that would be enough to equal the exquisiteness that was Effie. The ring had been given to him by Effie's mom, and it was the same ring that Effie's dad had placed on Diadema's finger when Nathaniel had proposed; after searching every jeweler's case in the area, and even some in New York, Josh had encountered difficulty finding an emotional attachment to any of the engagement rings presented to him. Then, with much hesitation, Diadema had taken him aside at a family dinner and shown him the ring with much hesitation, informing him that he could alter it in any way he saw fit for Effie. Knowing how much it would mean to tie their future together with the past, Josh had worked with a jeweler to have the solitaire diamond reset in the middle, surrounded by rubies, which were Effie's birthstone. Truly, it hadn't needed much embellishment, but he had also wanted to make it personal to both of them. When the skies had opened up unexpectedly last year on the day of the arts festival, Josh had hurried them into the gazebo, and the two of them had huddled together with what seemed like the entire town, waiting for the rain to end. Finally, it had tapered off, along with the crowd, and Josh had taken Effie's laughing face in his hands, kissing her before kneeling down on one leg. He had only managed to pull the ring box out of his pocket before Effie had pulled him up by his shoulders, crying "Yes, Yes, Yes,", and once he had finally asked her to marry him, she had answered by raining kisses all over his face.

In attendance today were: Ruth (matron of honor, once again, and unable to deny the matron title any longer) and Sean, and their three daughters, all under the age of three; Liam (best man, even though Josh was convinced that some of his possessions from the moving truck had made their way to Liam's house two years ago) and his wedding date (whose name Josh had yet to find out, since the couple had met just last week); Diadema and Burnside, a couple now married for over thirty years, yet seemed to be in the throes of a second-honeymoon period; his previous fiancée, Tess, and still-best-friend Sam, who announced last night at the rehearsal that they were expecting twins; Henry and his date, Charlotte, a woman his dad had been courting (his dad's words, not Josh's) the past few months; Hamilton, whose date was his long-distance girlfriend of the past two years, Margaret (who, incidentally, was also Sean's sister); his friend Cal and his wife, who had gotten remarried last year in a small ceremony both he and Effie had attended; Effie's grandparents, Chaska and Aurora LeBeau, her cousin Abigail and her family, her friend Claudia from Denver, her boss Liza, and finally so many extended relatives and friends on both the groom's and bride's sides that they had to get a special permit from the city to bring in enough chairs to the park for seating. And then Josh noticed Lana sliding into a chair in the last row, which was a relief. She had texted him that morning saying her flight had been delayed by an hour, and then he had heard nothing more, but he knew how much she wanted to be there. Interestingly enough, she was not alone, which was a shock, as she had not mentioned bringing a date. He and Effie had been back to New York three times since he had left, and each time they had made it a point to see Lana, who by now was almost more Effie's friend than Josh's. Finally, his cousin Cait had insisted on getting ordained on the internet so she could officiate their nuptials.

Josh had been the chief surgical resident when he had transferred to Beverley General, and now he was helping recruit candidates to the hospital from colleges around the country. Twice a week he drove to Sioux Falls for surgeries, and he found his job challenging and rewarding, but it was not his entire life. No, his entire life was currently making her way down the aisle to him, and both of them were excitedly anxious to ***finally*** be married in front of everyone they loved.

From Effie's perspective, they had waited an excruciatingly long two years to get married, but she had not wanted to rush from her failed marriage into one that she knew would last her a lifetime—she had wanted enough distance between these marriages that there was no confusion, which she was well aware might seem completely ridiculous, considering she and Josh had moved in with each other the night of the street dance two long years ago. Liam and Sam had arrived the following morning with the truck and trailer filled with Josh's belongings, and Effie had treated everyone to hot dogs on the grill and juicy watermelon slices for lunch that moving day. With encouragement from Sam, Effie had written and was currently editing her first novel for young adults, which she planned on making into a series. The protagonist was a young Sioux female who slays at the hundred-meter dash but also loves performing in school plays, with a plot twist: she has also fallen in love with the sweet but shy boy just before he suddenly moves away…

Now Effie, adorned in a simple blush-colored dress she had delightfully discovered in Threadz on Main Street, ascended the stairs of the gazebo on the arm of Burnside to the song "Can't Fight This Feeling Anymore", chosen by Effie after Liam had relentlessly teased Josh about how many times they had listened to it on the way to New York City two years ago, and turned out to be the perfect accompaniment to their relationship.

Effie treasured the path they had taken back to each other, which included both of them cutting losses from their individual and collective pasts. Effie and Josh had learned that cutting the losses in their lives did not always mean severing ties; for them, it was also the way to rebuild something from their shared history. A history that had begun too many years ago to enumerate.

What Josh and Effie were truly looking forward to was their honeymoon: three weeks in Scotland, with Josh having planned every detail of it on his own, from Glasgow to Edinburgh to the Shetland Islands. With the rustling of autumn leaves serenading them, Josh and Effie were finally pronounced man and wife. Later on, as they danced the first song at their reception, Effie sang along with Adele, "I promise I'm worthy to hold in your arms," in a full-circle moment, thinking of how both she and Josh had to let their doubts go, forgetting their pasts, to be together.

Josh smiled lovingly and so tenderly at Effie and answered back in song, "Nobody's perfect, trust me I've earned it." She knew he was wrong, of course, for they were perfect—for each other.

SERIES NOTE

Cutting Losses is Book Two in the series "Love, South Dakota Style". If you loved this book, be sure to read the other titles: *Excess Baggage* (Book One), *Mixed Messages* (Book Three), and *Second Chances* (Book Four). You will get to read in full how Tess and Sam fell in love, how Liam and Lana fall in love after their one-night stand, and revel in Henry finally getting his happy ever after with Charlotte.

The love never ends, so scan the QR code below to go to my website JodiCulliney.com to enter my world of books. Stay tuned for announcements concerning my book currently in progress.

ACKNOWLEDGMENTS

Special thanks to my first readers: my friend Claire, my sister Kris, and my husband Pete.

A very special thank you to my friend and college roommate Shilo, who provided insight and guidance with Effie and her Dakota heritage.

When I first began writing, at the insistence of my husband, I had no idea how important the role of music would be in visualizing my characters or certain plot points. With my first novel, **Excess Baggage**, Van Morrison's album *Moondance* was a beautiful soundtrack to the love story of Sam and Tess. With **Cutting Losses**, Adele's album *21* was a perfect accompaniment to the loss and devastation both Effie and Josh are feeling at the beginning of the book. As with the album, though, the characters also begin to feel hope, joy, and love again, so it was fitting to end with one of my favorite songs from that album.

Writing, for me, began as a way to tell a story that I would want to read, and much like Ashley, the owner of the flower shop, I spent my formative years devouring the romance novels of Judith McNaught and Julie Garwood, whose characters were multi-dimensional and had back stories and complicated reasons for their actions, and I missed that, so I tried to fill the void myself. I want someone to root for, someone to overcome whatever it is that is holding them back in order to find love.

I hope you enjoyed reading about the town of Beverley, which will be making future appearances in whatever I write. Purely fictional, Beverley is a blend of several bigger towns in South Dakota. All business created are also fictional, but people may find elements to them familiar.

I appreciate hearing from anyone who reads my books, and am grateful that out of all of the books available, you chose to read mine.

We'd like to thank the wonderful artists we found on fiverr.com for their talent and assistance in helping to bring to life my novels..

- Amazing cover art and design by Katarina @nskvsky
- Page layout, interior design and art by Brady Moller. @bradymoller
- Map of Beverly, cartography and design by Boris @briefaeon

Read about how it all began in Excess Baggage; eBook and paperback available from all your favorite booksellers here:
https://books2read.com/ExcessBaggage

ABOUT THE AUTHOR

Jodi Culliney, former bookstore clerk and lifelong lover of books, grew up in South Dakota, where she lived a peaceful existence until she met the love of her life and made the move to Brooklyn, NY. She has a Bachelor's degree in English from Black Hills State University and is working on her next novel.

Scan this QR code for a link to my Substack, https://jodiculliney.substack.com/ - It's called Reader Becomes Writer and it is where I write about how I started my journey and talk about my books!

Thanks for reading.

www.ingramcontent.com/pod-product-compliance
Lightning Source LLC
Chambersburg PA
CBHW070506310726
48976CB00002BA/367